Above the Human Landscape

Above the Human Landscape
A Social Science Fiction Anthology

Edited by
Willis E. McNelly
California State College, Fullerton

and
Leon E. Stover
Illinois Institute of Technology

Goodyear Publishing Company, Inc., Pacific Palisades, California

Library of Congress Catalog Card Number: 75-184131

ISBN: 0-87620-003-X (Cloth)
      0-87620-002-1 (Paper)

Y003X-5 (Cloth)
Y0021-9 (Paper)

Current Printing (Last Number):
10 9 8 7 6 5 4 3 2 1

Printed in the United States of America

CONTENTS

part three

Technology is for People

part four

People Create Realities

part five

Tomorrow will be B($^{e}_{i}$)tter

Afterword

Appendix

INTRODUCTION

Observe mankind and his social foibles from *Above the Human Landscape.* Peer at his personal and social habits. Project them to their ultimate, often illogically logical extremes.

These are some of the things that science fiction does well. Science fiction views man from the second balcony; it gazes at the social landscape from above, rather than becoming intimately involved with individual protagonists.

This view of man is not that of the cold, cynical intelligence of the Man from Mars who looks, perhaps with bored detachment, upon the petty comings and goings of miniscule humanity on this burnt out cinder, Earth. Rather, Science Fiction takes the viewpoint of passionate detachment or involved noninvolvement. Social science fiction is written in the mood of *Rasselas,* Samuel Johnson's prophetic vision of the then unknown social sciences.

> You, sir, whose curiosity is so extensive, will easily conceive with what pleasure a philosopher, furnished with wings, and hovering in the sky, would see the earth, and all its inhabitants, rolling beneath him, and presented to him successively, by its diurnal motion, all the countries within the same parallel. How it must amuse the pendent spectator to see the moving scene of land and ocean, cities and deserts!

The pendent spectator, hovering above the human landscape—with what *pleasure* he looks down! How it must *amuse* him!

Social science fiction, then, is sociology with a speculative heart—detachment with involvement. A watching "both in and out of the game," as Walt Whitman says.

The works collected here are the most significant examples of social science fiction that the editors could find. We present them for your entertainment and instruction: entertainment because they are good stories; instruction because they take the reflective position of the pendent spectator.

If you wish to know why we think these are good stories and why they carry a pleasurable load of significant ideas, read our afterword "Science Fiction as Culture Criticism." In the meantime—read, enjoy reflect.

To the onlie begetter . . .
Mr. H. H. all happinesse

Stephen Shames / Photon W∈t

one

Communities Are for People...

Grist of bees. Pride of lions. Flock of sheep. Pod of whales. Troop of monkeys.

What is *man's* unit of assemblage? A *tribe* of humans? A *nation* of humans?

But always the nostalgia for something *less* than a nation. Always the memory of Eden. Nations come and go, but the good earth abides. Ray Bradbury takes us back to primeval times in "The Highway." Things may fall apart for complex civilization, the center may not hold, but the simple life endures. Better to be ignorant of the modern world than to have lived and lost it.

Only a high output of energy, measured in mega-megawatts, can sustain industrial civilization. Take away electricity and the complexity of our social order would collapse; so might the population level. Life would be reduced to the scale of horse and buggy days, a reduction devoutly desired in "The Waveries" by Fredric Brown.

Nostalgia for the small community is not everybody's dream. Often the problem becomes how to combine rural peace and quiet on a human scale with urban novelty and big time excitement. Chad Oliver, an anthropologist, designs the ideal society in "Mother of Necessity."

The longing for a sense of community conflicts with a sense of incompleteness whenever it is realized. Whether it be a community of blacks, in "Black is Beautiful" by Robert Silverberg, or a community of oldsters in "Golden Acres" by Kit Reed, there is something partial about it—something unrealized. The retreat from national identity in the little community, the spatial separation of blacks from whites, or of the old from the young—how much fellow feeling can a person take before he longs to get *out* of Eden and into the big wide world of clashing differences?

THE HIGHWAY
Ray Bradbury

The cooling afternoon rain had come over the valley, touching the corn in the tilled mountain fields, tapping on the dry grass roof of the hut. In the rainy darkness the woman ground corn between cakes of lava rock, working steadily. In the wet lightlessness, somewhere, a baby cried.

Hernando stood waiting for the rain to cease so he might take the wooden plow into the field again. Below, the river boiled brown and thickened in its course. The concrete highway, another river, did not flow at all; it lay shining, empty. A car had not come along it in an hour. This was, in itself, of unusual interest. Over the years there had not been an hour when a car had not pulled up, someone shouting, "Hey there, can we take your picture?" Someone with a box that clicked, and a coin in his hand. If he walked slowly across the field without his hat, sometimes they called, "Oh, we want you with your hat on!" And they waved their hands, rich with gold things that told time, or identified them, or did nothing at all but winked like spider's eyes in the sun. So he would turn and go back to get his hat.

His wife spoke. "Something is wrong, Hernando?"

"Si. The road. Something big has happened. Something big to make the road so empty this way."

He walked from the hut slowly and easily, the rain washing over the twined shoes of grass and thick tire rubber he wore. He remembered very well the incident of this pair of shoes. The tire had come into the hut with violence one night, exploding the chickens and the pots apart! It had come alone, rolling swiftly. The car, off which it had come had rushed on, as far as the curve, and hung a moment, headlights reflected, before plunging into the river. The car was still there. One might see it on a good day, when the river ran slow and the muc cleared. Deep under, shining its metal, long and low and very rich, lay the car. But then the mud came in again and you saw nothing.

The following day he had carved the shoe soles from the tire rubber.

He reached the highway now, and stood upon it, listening to the small sounds it made in the rain.

Then, suddenly, as if at a signal, the cars came. Hundreds of them miles of them, rushing and rushing as he stood, by and by him. The big long black cars heading north toward the United States, roaring, taking the curves at too great a speed. With a ceaseless blowing and honking. And there was something about the faces of the people packed into the cars, something which dropped him into a deep silence. He stood back to let the cars roar on. He counted them until he tired. Five hundred, a thousand cars passed, and there was something in the faces of all of them. But they moved too swiftly for him to tell what this thing was.

Finally the silence and emptiness returned. The swift long low convertible cars were gone. He heard the last horn fade.

The road was empty again.

It had been like a funeral cortege. But a wild one, racing, hair out screaming to some ceremony ever northward. Why? He could only shake his head and rub his fingers softly, at his sides.

Now, all alone, a final car. There was something very, very final about it. Down the mountain road in the thin cool rain, fuming up great clouds of steam, came an old Ford. It was traveling as swiftly as it might. He expected it to break apart any instant. When this ancient Ford saw Hernando it pulled up, caked with mud and rusted, the radiator bubbling angrily.

"May we have some water, please, senor!"

A young man, perhaps 21, was driving. He wore a yellow sweater an open-collared white shirt and gray pants. In the topless car the rain fell upon him and five young women packed so they could not move in the interior. They were all very pretty and they were keeping the rain from themselves and the driver with old newspapers. But the rain got through to them, soaking their bright dresses, soaking the young man His hair was plastered with rain. But they did not seem to care. None complained, and this was unusual. Always before they complained: of rain, of heat, of time, of cold, of distance.

Hernando nodded. "I'll bring you water."

"Oh, please hurry!" one of the girls cried. She sounded very high and afraid. There was no impatience in her, only an asking out of fear. For the first time Hernando ran when a tourist asked; always before he had walked slower at such requests.

He returned with a hub lid full of water. This, too, had been a gift from the highway. One afternoon it had sailed like a flung coin into his field, round and glittering. The car to which it belonged had slid on, oblivious to the fact that it had lost a silver eye. Until now, he and his wife had used it for washing and cooking; it made a fine bowl.

As he poured the water into the boiling radiator, Hernando looked up at their stricken faces. "Oh, thank you, thank you," said one of the girls. "You don't know what this means."

Hernando smiled. "So much traffic in this hour. It all goes one way. North."

He did not mean to say anything to hurt them. But when he looked up again there all of them sat, in the rain, and they were crying. They were crying very hard. And the young man was trying to stop them by laying his hands on their shoulders and shaking them gently, one at a time, but they held their papers over their heads and their mouths moved and their eyes were shut and their faces changed color and they cried, some loud, some soft.

Hernando stood with the half-empty lid in his fingers. "I did not mean to say anything, senor," he apologized.

"That's all right," said the driver.

"What is wrong, senor?"

"Haven't you heard?" replied the young man, turning, holding tightly to the wheel with one hand, leaning forward. "It's happened."

This was bad. The others, at this, cried still harder, holding onto each other, forgetting the newspapers, letting the rain fall and mingle with their tears.

Hernando stiffened. He put the rest of the water into the radiator. He looked at the sky, which was black with storm. He looked at the river rushing. He felt the asphalt under his shoes.

He came to the side of the car. The young man took his hand and gave him a peso. "No." Hernando gave it back. "It is my pleasure."

"Thank you, you're so kind," said one of the girls, still sobbing. "Oh, Mama, Papa. Oh, I want to be home, I want to be home. Oh, Mama, Dad." And others held her.

"I did not hear, senor," said Hernando quietly.

"The war!" shouted the young man as if no one could hear. "It's come, the atom war, the end of the world!"

"Senor, senor," said Hernando.

"Thank you, thank you for your help. Good-by," said the young man.

"Good-by," they all said in the rain, not seeing him.

He stood while the car engaged its gears and rattled off down, fading away, through the valley. Finally it was gone, with the young women in it, the last car, the newspapers held and fluttered over thei⁻ heads.

Hernando did not move for a long time. The rain ran very cold down his cheeks and along his fingers and into the woven garment on his legs. He held his breath, waiting, tight and tensed.

He watched the highway, but it did not move again. He doubted that it would move much for a very long time.

The rain stopped. The sky broke through the clouds. In ter minutes the storm was gone, like a bad breath. A sweet wind blew the smell of the jungle up to him. He could hear the river moving gently and easily on its way. The jungle was very green; everything was fresh He walked down through the field to his house and picked up his plow With his hands on it he looked at the sky beginning to burn hot with the sun.

His wife called out from her work. "What happened, Hernando?"

"It is nothing," he replied.

He set the plow in the furrow, he called sharply to his burro "Burrrrrrr-O!" And they walked together through the rich field, under the clearing sky, on their tilled land by the deep river.

"What do they mean, 'the world'?" he said.

THE WAVERIES

Fredric Brown

Definitions from the school-abridged Webster-Hamlin Dictionary, 1998 edition:

> wavery (WA-vĕr-i) n. a vader—*slang* vader (VA-dĕr) n. inorgan of the class Radio
> inorgan (in-ÔR-gǎn) n. noncorporeal ens, a vader
> radio (RA-di-ō) n. n. class of inorgans 2. etheric frequency between light and electricity 3. (obsolete) method of communication used up to 1957

The opening guns of invasion were not at all loud, although they were heard by millions of people. George Bailey was one of the millions. I choose George Bailey because he was the only one who came within a googol of light-years of guessing what they were.

George Bailey was drunk and under the circumstances one can't blame him for being so. He was listening to radio advertisements of the most nauseous kind. Not because he wanted to listen to them, I need hardly say, but because he'd been told to listen to them by his boss, J. R. McGee of the MID network.

George Bailey wrote advertising for the radio. The only thing he hated worse than advertising was radio. And here on his own time he was listening to fulsome and disgusting commercials on a rival network.

Reprinted by permission of the author and the author's agents, Scott Meredith Literary Agency, Inc., 580 Fifth Avenue, New York, New York 10036.

"Bailey," J. R. McGee had said, "you should be more familiar with what others are doing. Particularly, you should be informed about those of our own accounts who use several networks. I strongly suggest. ..."

One doesn't quarrel with an employer's strong suggestions and keep a $200 a week job.

But one can drink whisky sours while listening. George Bailey did.

Also, between commercials, he was playing gin rummy with Maisie Hetterman, a cute little redheaded typist from the studio. It was Maisie's apartment and Maisie's radio (George himself, on principle, owned neither a radio or TV set) but George had brought the liquor.

"—only the very finest tobaccos," said the radio, "*go dit-dit-dit* nation's favorite cigarette—"

George glanced at the radio. "Marconi," he said.

He meant Morse, naturally, but the whisky sours had muddled him a bit so his first guess was more nearly right than anyone else's. It *was* Marconi, in a way. In a very peculiar way.

"Marconi?" asked Maisie.

George, who hated to talk against a radio, leaned over and switched it off.

"I meant Morse," he said. "Morse, as in Boy Scouts or the Signal Corps. I used to be a Boy Scout once."

"You've sure changed," Maisie said.

George sighed. "Somebody's going to catch hell, broadcasting code on that wave length."

"What did it mean?"

"Mean? Oh, you mean what did it mean. Uh—S, the letter S. *Dit-dit-dit* is S. SOS is *dit-dit-dit dah-dah-dah dit-dit-dit.*"

"O is *dah-dah-dah?*"

George grinned. "Say that again Maisie. I like it. And I think you are *dah-dah-dah* too."

"George, maybe it's really an SOS message. Turn it back on."

George turned it back on. The tobacco ad was still going. "—gentlemen of the most *dit-dit-dit* -ing taste prefer the finer taste of *dit-dit-dit* -arettes. In the new package that keeps them *dit-dit-dit* and ultra fresh —"

"It's not SOS. It's just S's."

"Like a tea-kettle or—say, George, maybe it's just some advertising gag."

George shook his head. "Not when it can blank out the name of the product. Just a minute till I—"

He reached over and turned the dial of the radio a bit to the right and then a bit to the left, and an incredulous look came into his face. He turned the dial to the extreme left, as far as it would go. There wasn't any station there, not even the hum of a carrier wave. But:

"Dit-dit-dit," said the radio, *"dit-dit-dit."*

He turned the dial to the extreme right. *"Dit-dit-dit."*

George switched it off and stared at Maisie without seeing her, which was hard to do.

"Something wrong, George?"

"I hope so," said George Bailey. "I certainly hope so."

He started to reach for another drink and changed his mind. He had a sudden hunch that something big was happening and he wanted to sober up to appreciate it.

He didn't have the faintest idea *how* big it was.

"George, what do you mean?"

"I don't know what I mean. But Maisie, let's take a run down to the studio, huh? There ought to be some excitement."

5 April, 1957; that was the night the waveries came.

It had started like an ordinary evening. It wasn't one, now.

George and Maisie waited for a cab but none came so they took the subway instead. Oh yes, the subways were still running in those days. It took them within a block of the MID Network Building.

The building was a madhouse. George, grinning, strolled through the lobby with Maisie on his arm, took the elevator to the fifth floor and for no reason at all gave the elevator boy a dollar. He'd never before in his life tipped an elevator operator.

The boy thanked him. "Better stay away from the big shots, Mr. Bailey," he said. "They're ready to chew the ears off anybody who even looks at 'em."

"Wonderful," said George.

From the elevator he headed straight for the office of J. R. McGee himself.

There were strident voices behind the glass door. George reached for the knob and Maisie tried to stop him. "But George," she whispered, "you'll be fired!"

"There comes a time," said George. "Stand back away from the door, honey."

Gently but firmly he moved her to a safe position.

"But George, what are you—"

"Watch," he said.

The frantic voices stopped as he opened the door a foot. All eyes turned towards him as he stuck his head around the corner of the doorway into the room.

"Dit-dit-dit," he said. *"Dit-dit-dit."*

He ducked back and to the side just in time to escape the flying glass as a paperweight and an inkwell came through the pane of the door.

He grabbed Maisie and ran for the stairs.

"Now we get a drink," he told her.

The bar across the street from the network building was crowded but it was a strangely silent crowd. In deference to the fact that most of its customers were radio people it didn't have a TV set but there was a big cabinet radio and most of the people were bunched around it

"*Dit,*" said the radio. "*Dit-dah-d'dah-dit-dahditdah dit—*"

"Isn't it beautiful?" George whispered to Maisie.

Somebody fiddled with the dial. Somebody asked, "What band is that?" and somebody said, "Police." Somebody said, "Try the foreign band," and somebody did. "This ought to be Buenos Aires," somebody said. "*Dit-d'dah-dit—*" said the radio.

Somebody ran fingers through his hair and said, "Shut that damn thing off." Somebody else turned it back on.

George grinned and led the way to a back booth where he'd spotted Pete Mulvaney sitting alone with a bottle in front of him. He and Maisie sat across from Pete.

"Hello," he said gravely.

"Hell," said Pete, who was head of the technical research staff of MID.

"A beautiful night, Mulvaney," George said. "Did you see the moon riding the fleecy clouds like a golden galleon tossed upon silver-crested whitecaps in a stormy—"

"Shut up," said Pete. "I'm thinking."

"Whisky sours," George told the waiter. He turned back to the man across the table. "Think out loud, so we can hear. But first, how did you escape the booby hatch across the street?"

"I'm bounced, fired, discharged."

"Shake hands. And then explain. Did you say *dit-dit-dit* to them?"

Pete looked at him with sudden admiration. "Did you?"

"I've a witness. What *did* you do?"

"Told 'em what I thought it was and they think I'm crazy."

"Are you?"

"Yes."

"Good," said George. "Then we want to hear—" He snapped his fingers. "What about TV?"

"Same thing. Same sound on audio and the pictures flicker and dim with every dot or dash. Just a blur by now."

"Wonderful. And now tell me what's wrong. I don't care what it is, as long as it's nothing trivial, but I want to know."

"I think it's space. Space is warped."

"Good old space," George Bailey said.

"George," said Maisie, "please shut up. I want to hear this."

"Space," said Pete, "is also finite." He poured himself another drink. "You go far enough in any direction and get back where you started. Like an ant crawling around an apple."

"Make it an orange," George said.

"All right, an orange. Now suppose the first radio waves ever sent out have just made the round trip. In 56 years."

"Fifty-six years? But I thought radio waves travelled at the same speed as light. If that's right, then in 56 years they could go only 56 light-years, and *that* can't be around the universe because there are galaxies known to be millions or maybe billions of light-years away. I don't remember the figures, Pete, but our own galaxy alone is a hell of a lot bigger than 56 light-years."

Pete Mulvaney sighed. "That's why I say space must be warped. There's a short cut somewhere."

"*That* short a short cut? Couldn't be."

"But George, listen to that stuff that's coming in. Can you read code?"

"Not any more. Not that fast, anyway."

"Well, I can," Pete said. "That's early American ham. Lingo and all. That's the kind of stuff the air was full of before regular broadcasting. It's the lingo, the abbreviations, the barnyard to attic chitchat of amateurs with keys, with Marconi coherers or Fessenden barreters— and you can listen for a violin solo pretty soon now. I'll tell you what it'll be."

"What?"

"Handel's *Largo.* The first phonograph record ever broadcast. Sent out by Fessenden from Brant Rock in 1906. You'll hear his CQ-CQ any minute now. Bet you a drink."

"Okay, but what was the *dit-dit-dit* that started this?"

Mulvaney grinned. "Marconi, George. What was the most powerful signal ever broadcast and by whom and when?"

"Marconi? *Dit-dit-dit?* Fifty-six years ago?"

"Head of the class. The first transatlantic signal of 12 December 1901. For three hours Marconi's big station at Poldhu, with 200-foot masts, sent out an intermittent S, *dit-dit-dit,* while Marconi and two assistants at St. Johns in Newfoundland got a kite-born aerial 400 feet in the air and finally got the signal. Across the Atlantic, George, with sparks jumping from the big Leyden jars at Poldhu and 20,000-volt juice jumping off the tremendous aerials—"

"Wait a minute, Pete, you're off the beam. If that was in 1901 and the first broadcast was about 1906 it'll be five years before the Fessenden stuff gets here on the same route. Even if there's a 56 light-year short cut across space and even if those signals didn't get so weak *en route* that we couldn't hear them—it's crazy."

"I told you it was," Pete said gloomily. "Why, those signals after travelling that far would be so infinitesimal that for practical purposes they wouldn't exist. Furthermore they're all over the band on everything from microwave on up and equally strong on each. And, as you point out, we've already come almost five years in two hours, which isn't possible. I told you it was crazy."

"But—"

"Ssshh. Listen," said Pete.

A blurred, but unmistakably human voice was coming from the radio, mingling with the cracklings of code. And then music, faint and scratchy, but unmistakably a violin. Playing Handel's *Largo.*

Only suddenly it climbed in pitch as though modulating from key to key until it became so horribly shrill that it hurt the ear. And kept on going past the high limit of audibility until they could hear it no more.

Somebody said, "Shut that God damn thing off." Somebody did, and this time nobody turned it back on.

Pete said, "I didn't really believe it myself. And there's another thing against it, George. Those signals affect TV too, and radio waves are the wrong length to do that."

He shook his head slowly. "There must be some other explanation, George. The more I think about it now the more I think I'm wrong."

He was right: he was wrong.

"Preposterous," said Mr. Ogilvie. He took off his glasses, frowned fiercely, and put them back on again. He looked through them at the several sheets of copy paper in his hand and tossed them contemptuously to the top of his desk. They slid to rest against the triangular name plate that read:

B. R. OGILVIE
Editor-in-Chief

"Preposterous," he said again.

Casey Blair, his best reporter, blew a smoke ring and poked his index finger through it. "Why?" he asked.

"Because—why, it's *utterly* preposterous."

Casey Blair said, "It is now three o'clock in the morning. The interference has gone on for five hours and not a single program is getting through on either TV or radio. Every major broadcasting and telecasting station in the world has gone off the air.

"For two reasons. One, they were just wasting current. Two the communications bureaus of their respective governments requested them to get off to aid their campaigns with the direction finders. For five hours now, since the start of the interference, they've been working with everything they've got. And what have they found out?"

"It's preposterous!" said the editor.

"Perfectly, but it's true. Greenwich at 11 P.M. New York time; I'm translating all these times into New York time—got a bearing in about the direction of Miami. It shifted northward until at two o'clock the direction was approximately that of Richmond, Virginia. San Francisco at eleven got a bearing in about the direction of Denver; three hours later it shifted southward towards Tucson. Southern hemisphere: bearings from Cape Town, South Africa, shifted from direction of Buenos Aires to that of Montevideo, a thousand miles north.

"New York at eleven had weak indications towards Madrid; but by two o'clock they could get no bearings at all." He blew another smoke ring. "Maybe because the loop antennas they use turn only on a horizontal plane?"

"Absurd."

Casey said, "I like 'preposterous' better, Mr. Ogilvie. Preposterous it is, but it's not absurd. I'm scared stiff. Those lines—and all other bearings I've heard about—run in the *same direction* if you take them as straight lines running as tangents off the Earth instead of curving them around the surface. I did it with a little globe and a star map. They converge on the constellation Leo."

He leaned forward and tapped a forefinger on the top page of the story he'd just turned in. "Stations that are directly under Leo in the sky get no bearings at all. Stations on what would be the perimeter of Earth relative to that point get the strongest bearings. Listen, have an astronomer check those figures if you want before you run the story, but get it done damn quick—unless you want to read about it in the other newspapers first."

"But the Heaviside layer, Casey—isn't that supposed to stop all radio waves and bounce them back."

"Sure, it does. But maybe it leaks. Or maybe signals can get through it from the outside even though they can't get out from the inside. It isn't a solid wall."

"But—"

"I know, it's preposterous. But there it is. And there's only an hour before press time. You'd better send this story through fast and have it being set up while you're having somebody check my facts and directions. Besides, there's something else you'll want to check."

"What?"

"I didn't have the data for checking the positions of the planets. Leo's on the ecliptic; a planet could be in line between here and there. Mars, maybe."

Mr. Ogilvie's eyes brightened, then clouded again. He said, "We'll be the laughing-stock of the world, Blair, if you're wrong."

"And if I'm right?"

The editor picked up the phone and snapped an order.

6 April headline of the New York *Morning Messenger,* final (6 A.M.) edition:

RADIO INTERFERENCE
COMES FROM SPACE,
ORIGINATES IN LEO

May Be Attempt at Commu-
nication by Beings
Outside Solar
System

All television and radio broadcasting was suspended.

Radio and telev᠎ ᠎n stocks opened several points off the previous day and then dropp᠎ sharply until noon when a moderate buying rally brought them a fe᠎ points back.

Public reaction was mixed; people who had no radios rushed out to buy them and there was a boom, especially in portable and table-top receivers. On the other hand, no TV sets were sold at all. With telecasting suspended there were no pictures on their screens, even blurred ones. Their audio circuits, when turned on, brought in the same jumble as radio receivers. Which, as Pete Mulvaney had pointed out to George Bailey, was impossible; radio waves cannot activate the audio circuits of TV sets. But these did, if they *were* radio waves.

In radio sets they seemed to be radio waves, but horribly hashed. No one could listen to them very long. Oh, there were flashes—times when, for several consecutive seconds, one could recognize the voice of Will Rogers or Geraldine Farrar or catch flashes of the Dempsey-Carpentier fight or the Pearl Harbor excitement. (Remember Pearl Harbor?) But things even remotely worth hearing were rare. Mostly it was a meaningless mixture of soap opera, advertising, and off-key snatches of what had once been music. It was utterly indiscriminate, and utterly unbearable for any length of time.

But curiosity is a powerful motive. There *was* a brief boom in radio sets for a few days.

There were other booms, less explicable, less capable of analysis. Reminiscent of the Wells-Welles Martian scare of 1938 was a sudden upswing in the sale of shotguns and sidearms. Bibles sold as fast as books on astronomy—and books on astronomy sold like hot cakes. One section of the country showed a sudden interest in lightning rods; builders were flooded with orders for immediate installation.

For some reason which has never been clearly ascertained there was a run on fish-hooks in Mobile, Alabama; every hardware and sporing goods store sold out of them within hours.

The public libraries and bookstores had a run on books on astrology and books on Mars. Yes, on Mars—despite the fact that Mars was at that moment on the other side of the sun and that every newspaper article on the subject stressed the fact that *no* planet was between Earth and the constellation Leo.

Something strange was happening—and no news of developments available except through the newspapers. People waited in mobs outside newspaper buildings for each new edition to appear. Circulation managers went quietly mad.

People also gathered in curious little knots around the silent broadcasting studios and stations, talking in hushed voices as though at a wake. MID network doors were locked, although there was a doorman on duty to admit technicians who were trying to find an answer to the problem. Some of the technicians who had been on duty the previous day had now spent over 24 hours without sleep.

George Bailey woke at noon, with only a slight headache. He shaved and showered, went out and drank a light breakfast and was himself again. He bought early editions of the afternoon papers, read them, grinned. His hunch had been right; whatever was wrong, it was nothing trivial.

But *what* was wrong?

The later editions of the afternoon papers had it.

EARTH INVADED, SAYS SCIENTIST

Thirty-six line type was the biggest they had; they used it. Not a home-edition copy of a newspaper was delivered that evening. Newsboys starting on their routes were practically mobbed. They sold papers instead of delivering them; the smart ones got a dollar apiece for them. The foolish and honest ones who didn't want to sell because they thought the papers should go to the regular customers on their routes lost them anyway. People grabbed them.

The final editions changed the heading only slightly—only slightly, that is, from a typographical viewpoint. Nevertheless, it was a tremendous change in meaning. It read:

EARTH INVADED, SAY SCIENTISTS

Funny what moving an S from the ending of a verb to the ending of a noun can do.

Carnegie Hall shattered precedent that evening with a lecture given at midnight. An unscheduled and unadvertised lecture. Professor Helmetz had stepped off the train at 11:30 and a mob of reporters had been waiting for him. Helmetz, of Harvard, had been the scientist, singular, who had made that first headline.

Harvey Ambers, director of the board of Carnegie Hall, had pushed his way through the mob. He arrived minus glasses, hat, and breath,

but got hold of Helmetz's arm and hung on until he could talk again.
"We want you to talk at Carnegie, Professor," he shouted into Helmetz's ear. "Five thousand dollars for a lecture on the 'vaders'."

"Certainly. Tomorrow afternoon."

"Now! I've a cab waiting. Come on."

"But—"

"We'll get you an audience. Hurry!" He turned to the mob. "Let us through. All of you can't hear the professor here. Come to Carnegie Hall and he'll talk to you. And spread the word on your way there."

The word spread so well that Carnegie Hall was jammed by the time the professor began to speak. Shortly after, they'd rigged a loudspeaker system so the people outside could hear. By one o'clock in the morning the streets were jammed for blocks around.

There wasn't a sponsor on Earth with a million dollars to his name who wouldn't have given a million dollars gladly for the privilege of sponsoring that lecture on TV or radio, but it was not telecast or broadcast. Both lines were busy.

"Questions?" asked Professor Helmetz.

A reporter in the front row made it first. "Professor," he asked, "have *all* direction-finding stations on Earth confirmed what you told us about the change this afternoon?"

"Yes, absolutely. At about noon all directional indications began to grow weaker. At 2:45 o'clock, Eastern Standard Time, they ceased completely. Until then the radio waves emanated from the sky, constantly changing direction with reference to the Earth's surface, but *constant* with reference to a point in the constellation Leo."

"What star in Leo?"

"No star visible on our charts. Either they came from a point in space or from a star too faint for our telescopes.

"But at 2:45 P.M. today—yesterday rather, since it is now past midnight—all direction finders went dead. But the signals persisted, now coming from all sides equally. The invaders had all arrived.

"There is no other conclusion to be drawn. Earth is now surrounded, completely blanketed, by radio-type waves which have *no point of origin,* which travel ceaselessly around the Earth in all directions, changing shape at their will—which currently is still in imitation of the Earth-origin radio signals which attracted their attention and brought them here."

"Do you think it was from a star we can't see, or could it have really been just a point in space?"

"Probably from a point in space. And why not? They are not creatures of matter. If they came here from a star, it must be a very dark star for it to be invisible to us, since it would be relatively near to us —only 28 light-years away, which is quite close as stellar distances go."

"How can you know the distance?"

"By assuming—and it is a quite reasonable assumption—that they started our way when they first discovered our radio signals—Marconi's S-S-S code broadcast of 56 years ago. Since that was the form taken by the first arrivals, we assume they started towards us when they encountered those signals. Marconi's signals, travelling at the speed of light, would have reached a point 28 light-years away 28 years ago; the invaders, also travelling at light-speed would require an equal time to reach us.

"As might be expected only the first arrivals took Morse code form. Later arrivals were in the form of other waves that they met and passed on—or perhaps absorbed—on their way to Earth. There are now wandering around the Earth, as it were, fragments of programs broadcast as recently as a few days ago. Undoubtedly there are fragments of the very last programs to be broadcast, but they have not yet been identified."

"Professor, can you *describe* one of these invaders?"

"As well as and no better than I can describe a radio wave. In effect, they *are* radio waves, although they emanate from no broadcasting station. They are a form of life dependent on wave motion, as our form of life is dependent on the vibration of matter."

"They are different sizes?"

"Yes, in two senses of the word size. Radio waves are measured from crest to crest, which measurement is known as the wave length. Since the invaders cover the entire dials of our radio sets and television sets it is obvious that either one of two things is true: either they come in all crest-to-crest sizes or each one can change his crest-to-crest measurement to adapt himself to the tuning of any receiver.

"But that is only the crest-to-crest length. In a sense it may be said that a radio wave has an over-all length determined by its duration. If a broadcasting station sends out a program that has a second's duration, a wave carrying that program is one light-second long, roughly 187,000 miles. A continuous half-hour program is, as it were, on a continuous wave one-half light-hour long, and so on.

"Taking that form of length, the individual invaders vary in length from a few thousand miles—a duration of only a small fraction of a second—to well over half a million miles long—a duration of several seconds. The longest continuous excerpt from any one program that has been observed has been about seven seconds."

"But, Professor Helmetz, why do you assume that these waves are *living* things, a life form. Why not just waves?"

"Because 'just waves' as you call them would follow certain laws, just as inanimate *matter* follows certain laws. An animal can climb uphill, for instance; a stone cannot unless impelled by some outside force. These invaders are life-forms because they show volition, because they can change their direction of travel, and most especially because they retain their identity; two signals never conflict on the same radio receiver. They follow one another but do not come simultaneously. They do not mix as signals on the same wave length would ordinarily do. They are not 'just waves'."

"Would you say they are intelligent?"

Professor Helmetz took off his glasses and polished them thoughtfully. He said, "I doubt if we shall ever know. The intelligence of such beings, if any, would be on such a completely different plane from ours that there would be no common point from which we could start intercourse. We are material; they are immaterial. There is no common ground between us."

"But if they are intelligent at all—"

"Ants are intelligent, after a fashion. Call it instinct if you will, but instinct is a form of intelligence; at least it enables them to accomplish some of the same things intelligence would enable them to accomplish. Yet we cannot establish communication with ants and it is far less likely that we shall be able to establish communication with these invaders. The difference in type between ant-intelligence and our own would be nothing to the difference in type between the intelligence, if any, of the invaders and our own. No, I doubt if we shall ever communicate."

The professor had something there. Communication with the vaders—a clipped form, of course, of *invaders*—was never established.

Radio stocks stabilized on the exchange the next day. But the day following that someone asked Dr. Helmetz a $64 question and the newspapers published his answer:

"Resume broadcasting? I don't know if we ever shall. Certainly we cannot until the invaders go away, and why should they? Unless radio communication is perfected on some other planet far away and they're attracted there.

"But at least some of them would be right back the moment we started to broadcast again."

Radio and TV stocks dropped to practically zero in an hour. There weren't, however, any frenzied scenes on the stock exchanges; there was no frenzied selling because there was no buying, frenzied or otherwise. No radio stocks changed hands.

Radio and television employees and entertainers began to look for other jobs. The entertainers had no trouble finding them. Every other form of entertainment suddenly boomed like mad.

"Two down," said George Bailey. The bartender asked what he meant.

"I dunno, Hank. It's just a hunch I've got."

"What kind of hunch?"

"I don't even know that. Shake me up one more of those and then I'll go home."

The electric shaker wouldn't work and Hank had to shake the drink by hand.

"Good exercise; that's just what you need," George said. "It'll take some of that fat off you."

Hank grunted, and the ice tinkled merrily as he tilted the shaker to pour out the drink.

George Bailey took his time drinking it and then strolled out into an April thunder-shower. He stood under the awning and watched for a taxi. An old man was standing there too.

"Some weather," George said.

The old man grinned at him. "You noticed it, eh?"

"Huh? Noticed what?"

"Just watch a while, mister. Just watch a while."

The old man moved on. No empty cab came by and George stood there quite a while before he got it. His jaw dropped a little and then he closed his mouth and went back into the tavern. He went into a phone booth and called Pete Mulvaney.

He got three wrong numbers before he got Pete. Pete's voice said, "Yeah?"

"George Bailey, Pete. Listen, have you noticed the weather?"

"Damn right. *No lightning,* and there should be with a thunder-storm like this."

"What's it mean, Pete? The vaders?"

"Sure. And that's just going to be the start if—" A crackling sound on the wire blurred his voice out.

"Hey, Pete, you still there?"

The sound of a violin. Pete Mulvaney didn't play violin.

"Hey, Pete, what the hell—?"

Pete's voice again. "Come on over, George. Phone won't last long. Bring—" There was a buzzing noise and then a voice said, "—come to Carnegie Hall. The best tunes of all come—"

George slammed down the receiver.

He walked through the rain to Pete's place. On the way he bought a bottle of Scotch. Pete had started to tell him to bring something and maybe that's what he'd started to say.

It was.

They made a drink apiece and lifted them. The lights flickered briefly, went out, and then came on again but dimly.

"No lightning," said George. "No lightning and pretty soon no lighting. They're taking over the telephone. What do they do with the lightning?"

"Eat it, I guess. They must eat electricity."

"No lightning," said George. "Damn. I can get by without a tele-phone, and candles and oil lamps aren't bad for lights—but I'm going to miss lightning. I *like* lightning. Damn."

The lights went out completely.

Pete Mulvaney sipped his drink in the dark. He said, "Electric lights, refrigerators, electric toasters, vacuum cleaners—"

"Juke boxes," George said. "Think of it, no more goddam juke boxes. No public address systems, no—hey, how about movies?"

"No movies, not even silent ones. You can't work a projector with an oil lamp. But listen, George, no automobiles—no gasoline engine can work without electricity."

"Why not, if you crank it by hand instead of using a starter?"

"The spark, George. What do you think makes the spark."

"Right. No aeroplanes either, then. Or how about jet planes?'

"Well—I guess some types of jets could be rigged not to need elec-tricity, but you couldn't do much with them. Jet plane's got more instruments than motor, and all those instruments are electrical. And you can't fly or land a jet by the seat of your pants."

"No radar. But what would we need it for? There won't be any more wars, not for a long time."

"A damned long time."

George sat up straight suddenly. "Hey, Pete, what about atomic fission? Atomic energy? Will it still work?"

"I doubt it. Subatomic phenomena are basically electrical. Bet you a dime they eat loose neutrons too." (He'd have won his bet; the govern-ment had not announced that an A-bomb tested that day in Nevada had fizzled like a wet firecracker and that atomic piles were ceasing to function.)

George shook his head slowly, in wonder. He said, "Streetcars and buses, ocean liners—Pete, this means we're going back to the original source of horse-power. Horses. If you want to invest, buy horses. Particularly mares. A brood mare is going to be worth a thousand times her weight in platinum."

"Right. But don't forget steam. We'll still have steam engines, stationary and locomotive."

"Sure, that's right. The iron horse again, for the long hauls. But Dobbin for the short ones. Can you ride, Pete?"

"Used to, but I think I'm getting too old. I'll settle for a bicycle. Say, better buy a bike first thing tomorrow before the run on them starts. I know *I'm* going to."

"Good tip. And I used to be a good bike rider. It'll be swell with no autos around to louse you up. And say—"

"What?"

"I'm going to get a cornet too. Used to play one when I was a kid and I can pick it up again. And then maybe I'll hole in somewhere and write that nov—Say, what about printing?"

"They printed books long before electricity, George. It'll take a while to readjust the printing industry, but there'll be books all right. Thank God for that."

George Bailey grinned and got up. He walked over to the window and looked out into the night. The rain had stopped and the sky was clear.

A street-car was stalled, without lights, in the middle of the block outside. An automobile stopped, then started more slowly, stopped again; its headlights were dimming rapidly.

George looked up at the sky and took a sip of his drink.

"No lightning," he said sadly. "I'm going to *miss* the lightning."

The changeover went more smoothly than anyone would have thought possible.

The government, in emergency session, made the wise decision of creating one board with absolutely unlimited authority and under it only three subsidiary boards. The main board, called the Economic Readjustment Bureau, had only seven members and its job was to coordinate the efforts of the three subsidiary boards and to decide, quickly and without appeal, any jurisdictional disputes among them.

First of the three subsidiary boards was the Transportation Bureau. It immediately took over, temporarily, the railroads. It ordered Diesel engines run on sidings and left there, organized use of the steam locomotives, and solved the problems of railroading *sans* telegraphy and electric signals. It dictated, then, what should be transported; food coming first, coal and fuel oil second, and essential manufactured articles in the order of their relative importance. Car-load after car-load of new radios, electric stoves, refrigerators, and such useless articles were dumped unceremoniously alongside the tracks, to be salvaged for scrap metal later.

All horses were declared wards of the government, graded according to capabilities, and put to work or to stud. Draught horses were used for only the most essential kinds of hauling. The breeding program was given the fullest possible emphasis; the bureau estimated that the equine population would double in two years, quadruple in three, and that within six or seven years there would be a horse in every garage in the country.

Farmers, deprived temporarily of their horses, and with their tractors rusting in the fields, were instructed how to use cattle for ploughing and other work about the farm, including light hauling.

The second board, the Manpower Relocation Bureau, functioned just as one would deduce from its title. It handled unemployment benefits for the millions thrown temporarily out of work and helped relocate them—not too difficult a task considering the tremendously increased demand for hand labor in many fields.

In May of 1957 thirty-five million employables were out of work; in October, fifteen million; by May of 1958, five million. By 1959 the situation was completely in hand and competitive demand was already beginning to raise wages.

The third board had the most difficult job of the three. It was called the Factory Readjustment Bureau. It coped with the stupendous task of converting factories filled with electrically operated machinery and, for the most part, tooled for the production of other electrically operated machinery, over for the production, without electricity, of essential non-electrical articles.

The few available stationary steam engines worked 24 hour shifts in those early days, and the first thing they were given to do was the running of lathes and stampers and planers and millers working on turning out more stationary steam engines, of all sizes. These, in turn, were first put to work making still more steam engines. The number of steam engines grew by squares and cubes, as did the number of horses put to stud. The principle was the same. One might, and many did, refer to those early steam engines as stud horses. At any rate, there was no lack of metal for them. The factories were filled with non-convertible machinery waiting to be melted down.

Only when steam engines—the basis of the new factory economy —were in full production, were they assigned to running machinery for the manufacture of other articles. Oil lamps, clothing, coal stoves, oil stoves, bath-tubs, and bedsteads.

Not quite all of the big factories were converted. For while the conversion period went on, individual handicrafts sprang up in thousands of places. Little one- and two-man shops making and repairing furniture, shoes, candles, all sorts of things that *could* be made without complex machinery. At first these small shops made small fortunes because they had no competition from heavy industry. Later, they bought small steam engines to run small machines and held their own, growing with the boom that came with a return to normal employment and buying power, increasing gradually in size until many of them rivalled the bigger factories in output and beat them in quality.

There *was* suffering, during the period of economic readjustment, but less than there had been during the great depression of the early 30s. And the recovery was quicker.

The reason was obvious: in combating the depression, the legislators were working in the dark. They didn't know its cause—rather, they knew a thousand conflicting theories of its cause—and they didn't know the cure. They were hampered by the idea that the thing was temporary and would cure itself if left alone. Briefly and frankly, they didn't know what it was all about and while they experimented, it snowballed.

But the situation that faced the country—and all other countries —in 1957 was clear-cut and obvious. No more electricity. Readjust for steam and horsepower.

As simple and clear as that, and no ifs or ands or buts. And the whole people—except for the usual scattering of cranks—back of them.

By 1961—

It was a rainy day in April and George Bailey was waiting under the sheltering roof of the little railroad station at Blakestown, Connecticut, to see who might come in on the 3:14.

It chugged in at 3:25 and came to a panting stop, three coaches and a baggage car. The baggage car door opened and a sack of mail was handed out and the door closed again. No luggage, so probably no passengers would—

Then at the sight of a tall dark man swinging down from the platform of the rear coach, George Bailey let out a yip of delight. "Pete! Pete Mulvaney! What the devil—"

"Bailey, by all that's holy! What are you doing here?"

George wrung Pete's hand. "Me? I live here. Two years now. I bought the *Blakestown Weekly* in '59, for a song, and I run it—editor, reporter, and janitor. Got one printer to help me out with that end, and Maisie does the social items. She's—"

"Maisie? Maisie Hetterman?"

"Maisie Bailey now. We got married same time I bought the paper and moved here. What are you doing here, Pete?"

"Business. Just here overnight. See a man named Wilcox."

"Oh, Wilcox. Our local screwball—but don't get me wrong; he's a smart guy all right. Well, you can see him tomorrow. You're coming home with me now, for dinner and to stay overnight. Maisie'll be glad to see you. Come on, my buggy's over here."

"Sure. Finished whatever you were here for?"

"Yep, just to pick up the news on who came in on the train. And *you* came in, so here we go."

They got in the buggy, and George picked up the reins and said, "Giddup, Bessie," to the mare. Then, "What are you doing now, Pete?"

"Research. For a gas-supply company. Been working on a more efficient mantle, one that'll give more light and be less destructible. This fellow Wilcox wrote us he had something along that line; the company sent me up to look it over. If it's what he claims, I'll take him back to New York with me, and let the company lawyers dicker with him."

"How's business, otherwise?"

"Great, George. *Gas;* that's the coming thing. Every *new* homes being piped for it, and plenty of the old ones. How about you?"

"We got it. Luckily we had one of the old Linotypes that ran the metal pot off a gas burner, so it was already piped in. And our home is right over the office and print shop, so all we had to do was pipe t up a flight. Great stuff, gas. How's New York?"

"Fine, George. Down to its last million people, and stabilizing there. No crowding and plenty of room for everybody. The *air*—why, it's better than Atlantic City, without gasoline fumes."

"Enough horses to go around yet?"

"Almost. But bicycling's the craze; the factories can't turn out enough to meet the demand. There's a cycling club in almost every block and all the able-bodied cycle to and from work. Doing 'em good, too; a few more years and the doctors will go on short rations."

"You got a bike?"

"Sure, a pre-vader one. Average five miles a day on it, and I eat like a horse."

George Bailey chuckled. "I'll have Maisie include some hay in the dinner. Well, here we are. Whoa, Bessie."

An upstairs window went up, and Maisie looked out and down. She called out, "Hi, Pete!"

"Extra plate, Maisie," George called. "We'll be up soon as I put the horse away and show Pete around downstairs."

He led Pete from the barn into the back door of the newspaper shop. "Our Linotype!" he announced proudly, pointing.

"How's it work? Where's your steam engine?"

George grinned. "Doesn't work yet; we still hand set the type. I could get only one steamer and had to use that on the press. But I've got one on order for the Lino, and coming up in a month or so. When we get it, Pop Jenkins, my printer, is going to put himself out of a job teaching me to run it. With the Linotype going, I can handle the whole thing myself."

"Kind of rough on Pop?"

George shook his head. "Pop eagerly awaits the day. He's 69 and wants to retire. He's just staying on until I can do without him. Here's the press—a honey of a little Miehle; we do some job work on it, too. And this is the office, in front. Messy, but efficient."

Mulvaney looked around him and grinned. "George, I believe you've found your niche. You were cut out for a smalltown editor."

"Cut out for it? I'm crazy about it. I have more fun than everybody. Believe it or not, I work like a dog, and like it. Come on upstairs."

On the stairs, Pete asked, "And the novel you were going to write?"

"Half done, and it isn't bad. But it isn't the novel I was going to write; I was a cynic then. Now—"

"George, I think the waveries were your best friends."

"Waveries?"

"Lord, how long does it take slang to get from New York out to the sticks? The vaders, of course. Some professor who specializes in studying them described one as a wavery place in the ether, and 'wavery' stuck—Hello there, Maisie, my girl. You look like a million."

They ate leisurely. Almost apologetically, George brought out beer, in cold bottles. "Sorry, Pete, haven't anything stronger to offer you. But I haven't been drinking lately. Guess—"

"*You* on the wagon, George?"

"Not on the wagon, exactly. Didn't swear off or anything, but haven't had a drink of strong liquor in almost a year. I don't know why, but—"

"I do," said Pete Mulvaney. "I know exactly why you don't—because I don't drink much either, for the same reason. We don't drink because we don't *have* to—say, isn't that a *radio* over there?"

George chuckled. "A souvenir. Wouldn't sell it for a fortune. Once in a while I like to look at it and think of the awful guff I used to sweat out for it. And then I go over and click the switch and nothing happens. Just silence. Silence is the most wonderful thing in the world, sometimes, Pete. Of course I couldn't do that if there was any juice, because I'd get vaders then. I suppose they're still doing business at the same old stand?"

"Yep, the Research Bureau checks daily. Try to get up current with a little generator run by a steam turbine. But no dice: the vaders suck it up as fast as it's generated."

"Suppose they'll ever go away?"

Mulvaney shrugged. "Helmetz thinks not. He thinks they propagate in proportion to the available electricity. Even if the development of radio broadcasting somewhere else in the Universe would attract them there, some would stay here—and multiply like flies the minute we tried to use electricity again. And meanwhile, they'll live on the static electricity in the air. What do you do evenings up here?"

"Do? Read, write, visit with one another, go to the amateur groups —Maisie's chairman of the Blakestown Players, and I play bit parts in it. With the movies out everybody goes in for theatricals and we've found some real talent. And there's the chess-and-checker club, and cycle trips and picnics—there isn't time enough. Not to mention music. Everybody plays an instrument, or is trying to."

"You?"

"Sure, cornet. First cornet in the Silver Concert Band, with solo parts. And—Good Heavens! Tonight's rehearsal, and we're giving a concert Sunday afternoon. I hate to desert you, but—"

"Can't I come around and sit in? I've got my flute in the brief case here, and—"

"*Flute?* We're short on flutes. Bring that around and Si Perkins, our director, will practically shanghai you into staying over for the concert Sunday—and it's only three days, so why not? And get it out now; we'll play a few old timers to warm up. Hey, Maisie, skip those dishes and come on in to the piano!"

While Pete Mulvaney went to the guest room to get his flute from the brief case, George Bailey picked up his cornet from the top of the piano and blew a soft, plaintive little minor run on it. Clear as a bell; his lip was in good shape tonight.

And with the shining silver thing in his hand he wandered over to the window and stood looking out into the night. It was dusk out and the rain had stopped.

A high-stepping horse *clop-clopped* by and the bell of a bicycle jangled. Somebody across the street was strumming a guitar and singing. He took a deep breath and let it out slowly.

The scent of spring was soft and sweet in the moist air.

Peace and dusk.

Distant rolling thunder.

God damn it, he thought, *if only there was a bit of lightning.*

He missed the lightning.

THE MOTHER OF NECESSITY

Chad Oliver

It isn't the easiest stunt in the world (the fairly young man said to the historian over a glass of beer) to be the son of a really famous man.

Now, Dad and I always got along okay; he was good to me and I like the old boy fine. But you can maybe imagine how it was after they kicked George Washington upstairs to Grandfather, and stuck my dad in his exalted shoes.

George Sage, Father of His Country!

People are always tracking me down and asking about George. You'd think he was some kind of a saint or something. Don't get me wrong—I think Dad is swell. But what can I say to all these weirdies who want to know about their hero? If I give them the real scoop, they think I'm insulting my own father just because I make him human, like you or me.

I've pretty well given up trying to tell the truth; nowadays I usually just mumble something about a dedicated life and let it go at that.

But you're interested in history. You want the facts.

Okay. I'm with you.

But remember: my dad was just like a lot of other guys. He didn't go for all this saint stuff, and neither do I. I'll give him to you just the way he was; take him or leave him.

They call it Peace Monday now, that day when it all started. I was just a kid, but I remember like it was yesterday. It was a wet year, 2002 was, and that Monday was typical. It was gray and rainy outside, and you could hear the wind blowing, and you were glad you were in the apartment, where it was warm. . . .

George Sage was stumped.

His ample body—not fat, but with a detectable paunch—was absolutely motionless in the hammock. His graying hair hadn't been combed all day. Distantly, he listened to the wind. His slightly glazed eyes examined nothing.

A slogan on the wall read: IT'S ALWAYS TIME FOR A CHANGE.

Lois, his wife, knew the signs. She was his only wife; she had to be sensitive to nuances. She tiptoed around the apartment as if the floor were liberally sprinkled with eggshells. She was glad that Bobby was staying in his room.

The silence thickened.

"Zero," George muttered cryptically, shifting in the hammock.

"What, dear?"

"There's nothing new under the sun," George amplified.

"Now, George," Lois said, trying to make a neutral noise.

"Don't nag, dammit! I'm plotting."

"I know you are, George."

"Sure," George said.

The silence flowed in again and congealed.

George breathed irritably.

Lois worked on her nails.

"Do you *have* to do that?" George asked finally.

Lois looked up innocently.

"Your nails," George explained. "You're scraping them."

"Oh." She put her equipment down, and tried to sit very still.

Outside, the rain was getting heavier; she hoped that it would let up soon so Bobby could go out and play. She was a little worried about George; he wasn't a young man any more, and he hadn't been as successful as Lloyd or Brigham. He was losing his confidence in himself, and of course that made it hard for him to come up with anything really *sharp*.

They had always hoped that Bobby might grow up and live in one of George's systems; that would have been nice. But there was only Westville left now, and even George found Westville a bit on the stale side.

She crossed over to his hammock and gently ruffled his uncombed hair. It was curious, she thought, how his hair had turned; about one strand in three was white as snow, and all the rest as brown as it had been 20 years before when they had met in college.

"Troubles?" she asked gently.

"You might put it that way, as the man said when he walked the plank."

"Try not to worry about it, dear."

George muttered something impolite, and then looked at her frankly. "We've tried everything, Lo," he said, his eyes very tired. "You know that. The people out there have seen it all now, and you can't impress them these days just by tossing in a clan instead of a bilateral descent system. It all seemed kind of new and exciting once, but now —hell, I sometimes think there's nothing as dull as constant, everlasting change."

"Maybe that's the answer," she said, trying to help. "Maybe if you drew up one that was long on tradition—play on the let's-put-our-roots-in-the-soil routine—"

"Please. I may be an old man, but I've still got *some* pride. Anyhow, Lloyd tried a back-to-the-good-old-days gimmick in Miami just last year, and even he couldn't put it through. The devil of it is, there's just plain nothing new under the sun, to coin an inspired phrase."

"There never was, George."

"What?"

"You *always* used to say that, way back even before we were married. You said it was a little like writing—only ten and three-quarters basic plots, or whatever it was, but the trick was to string 'em together differently."

"Well," George admitted, "it's a long damned way from Homer to Joyce, but I guess the old boy's still Ulysses, no matter how you stick him together."

Lois waited patiently.

"Ummmmm," George said, and sat up in his hammock. "Maybe if we just filched an item here and there from different systems—even made a random assortment—and functioned them—"

Lois smiled, and resumed work on her nails.

George walked over to the library line, dialed a stack of books, and proceeded to his desk. He sat down and began making rapid notes on his scratch-pad.

Bobby stuck his blond head into the room, and yawned. "Mom," he asked, "can I play in here?"

"Not now, Bobby," Lois said. "Your father's working."

Bobby eyed the ample figure of George at the desk, shrugged, and went back to his room, monumentally unimpressed.

Three weeks later, it was another Monday and the rain had showed up on schedule. It was a weary drizzle this time, and it exactly suited George Sage's mood.

Will Nolan, his promotions officer, slouched back behind his big

desk, extracted the lenses from his eyes, and studied the ceiling without
interest.

"It's great, George," he said flatly. "A great, great pattern."

George began to sweat. That was the mildest comment he had ever
got from Nolan in fifteen years—ever since his nomadic-reindeer-
herder program. It wouldn't have been so bad, but George had his own
misgivings, even more so than usual.

"Really swell," Nolan continued. "Of course, there may be some
small difficulty with the Patent Office."

"In other words, you don't think it's original enough to get a patent
on. And if we can't get a patent, we can't put it on the market. That
right?"

"Well, George," Nolan said shifting uncomfortably. There was a
pause of singular length. "Well, George," he repeated.

"Will, you've got to push this through. I don't care how you do it,
but it's got to be done."

"Nothing to worry about," Nolan said insincerely.

George eyed his promotions officer, more in sympathy than in
anger. George had few illusions about himself; he knew that his career
as an inventor had been on the mediocre side. Naturally since he
wasn't one of the big boys, he couldn't expect the top agencies to handle
his promotions. He and Will Nolan were in the same boat, and it was
not the sturdiest craft ever built.

"Let's look on the bright side," George said, trying to sell himself
as much as Nolan. "It's not subversive, is it? It doesn't violate any of
the American Ways of Life, does it?"

"It's clean, George. Real clean."

"Okay. It's got good things in it, right? It's got a small town deal
with country stores and neighborliness and a slow pace; that gives
tradition. Security. You know. It's got a cosmopolitan nucleus, right in
the center, that only operates on market days and holidays. When the
people Go To the City, they know they're supposed to act like an urban
population; that takes the tedium out of it, get me? It's a kind of
alternating social organization, and it requires enough service personnel in the urban nucleus to handle anyone who doesn't go for rural life
no matter how he's brought up. The big city gives 'em direction, expan-
sion. Now look, Will, the sex angle is good, you've got to admit that. The
teen clubs give the kids a healthy outlet, and the merit badges give
them status while they're adolescents. Not only that, but the chaperons
give the older adults something to do with their time—their valuable
experience isn't wasted at all. When the kids get ready to settle down
and get married, they'll go into it with their eyes open."

"Sex is always good," Nolan admitted.

"That isn't all," George went on, warming to his topic. "Look at the
way I've got the small businesses distributed: kids start right in, manu-

facturing and selling equipment for the high school and the football team. Farm children supply the lunch wagons, city kids handle accounts at the banks."

"Free enterprise.is always good," Nolan agreed.

"Sure, and I haven't neglected the spiritual side, either. Look at all the Sunday Schools, and how about that Pilgrim Society? I tell you, Will, this system has got *everything*."

"Has it got a name?"

"Not yet, no."

"Got to have a name, George. You know that. Can't sell a system without a name. We'll need some slogans, too."

"Okay, okay. What are your writers for?"

Will Nolan inserted the lenses in his eyes and made a few notations. "It's great George," he said. "If we can just get it by the boys in Patents."

"They *can't* turn it down. It'd be against the Constitution. What grounds would they have?"

"They wouldn't have a leg to stand on, of course, not with a great, great idea like this one. It's just that there isn't anything in it that's —well—*new*. You know."

George waved his hand with a confidence he was far from feeling. "Hell, there's nothing new about pyramids, the Roman circus, the Empire State Building, wigwams—not all by their lonesomes. But all in one society, that's different, different in *kind*."

"I'll push it, George," Nolan said. "Try not to worry."

George Sage was getting decidedly tired of having people tell him not to worry, but he realized that this was no time to blow up about it. He took a cue from Lois and made a neutral noise.

"I'll call you," Nolan said.

George left the promotions building and wandered aimlessly down past the Washington Monument. It was still raining: a bored, gray drizzle with all the character of a clam.

He walked on, hands in his pockets, beginning the long wait that always had emptiness at the end of it, emptiness that was neither success nor failure, but only existence.

"Damn the rain," he said. "Damn it anyway."

Election Day.

Perhaps it was of some significance—it had *better* be of some significance, George thought—that the weather could not have been more pleasant. A balmy sun coated the fields outside Natchezville with melted gold, and summer breezes whispered lazily through the sweet gum trees.

"Sit still, Bobby," Lois said. "Your father has to be careful not to fly our copter inside the city limits while voting is going on."

"Aaaaahh," Bobby commented, and continued to twitch around

Not without some disgust at himself, George noticed that the fingers on his left hand were firmly crossed. Well, the election was important to him; if Natchezville didn't give it a tumble, he might as well turn himself out to pasture. Nolan had just barely snaked i through the Patent Office, and Mr. George Sage was not precisely the fair-haired boy around Washington these days.

More like a bald-headed mummy, in fact.

The copter loafed along in the sunshine, and George swerved a few degrees to make certain he did not get too close to an ancient blimp tha Nolan had dredged up somewhere. The blimp hovered over Natchezville, trailing a long airsign: LET'S GIVE OUR KIDS A BETTER SOCIAL ORGANIZATION THAN WE HAD—FULL CIRCLE MEANS A FULLER LIFE!

Not bad, George thought. Not bad at all.

Natchezville spread out like a toy town below them and to their left was a pretty little village, with its white houses gleaming in the sun It was surrounded by large cotton plantations, for Natchezville was currently patterned after the Old South. If you looked closely, you could see belles in crinoline sipping tall drinks on pillared porches, and gray robots dancing in the slave quarters.

The Court House was a hive of activity as the voting picked up in tempo.

George switched on the TV. Yes, it was still there on Channel 7 a white circle flashing on and off, alternating with a bass voice tha kept chanting: *Full Circle—a design for living designed for living— Full Circle—a design for living—"*

George noticed that his hands were sweating, and wiped them on his handkerchief.

"We're lucky," he said for the tenth time, "that the competition isn't too hot this time around. Neither Lloyd nor Brigham has a system in the race—Natchezville would be pretty small potatoes for them Really, we've got only three challengers going down there. Krause's Urbania routine is all right—but we've got that *plus* the rural appeal Old Gingerton's Greenwich Village deal is strictly from senility, and the Mammoth Cave entry is just a dark horse."

Lois laughed dutifully.

George took the copter down almost to road level, where wagon and horses were plodding along toward Natchezville. He smiled and waved, but he was primarily intent on checking his roadsigns. Yes there was one now, starting just ahead:

WHEN YOU MAKE YOUR TURN
ON YOUR ROAD AND MINE
DON'T BE SCARED

TO BE PREPARED
TO GO TO THE END OF THE LINE
FULL CIRCLE

"I like that, Dad," Bobby said. "That's good."

There was a conventional billboard not far ahead, but it was too close to the city limits for him to risk a close look at it. Basically, it seemed to show two stupendously healthy and starry-eyed children gazing worshipfully in a future filled with circles.

George waved again, and took the copter up.

"Damn this waiting," he said.

"Try not to worry, dear," Lois advised.

George thought of a cutting retort, but had been married long enough not to make it.

The copter hummed through the air like an insect, as the sunlight faded and night shadows darkened the land below. A cool breeze sprang up in the north, and Bobby was getting emphatic about his hunger.

It was close to midnight when the copter's private-line TV blinked into life.

It was Will Nolan, and George knew the result by the glow on his face.

"We're in!" Nolan said. "Not a landslide, George boy, but a great, great victory. Congratulations!"

George grinned his thanks, put his arm around Lois, and headed the copter for home. Bobby made gentle boy-snores behind them. Stars sprinkled the sky and the moon was close and warm.

"I'm so proud of you, dear," Lois said.

"It wasn't really anything," George said. "But wait until the Concordburg elections next year! I've got an idea cooking that'll set them on their ears."

The copter hummed on through the friendly night.

Of course, as you might suppose (the historian said to young Robert Sage over a second glass of beer), what happened to your father and to Fullcircle is hardly understandable except in terms of the social and historical context of the phenomena. If I may interrupt you for a moment, I think I can show you what I mean.

Looking at the whole thing now, it all takes on a sort of spurious inevitability, as though it couldn't have happened any other way. That's the crudest sort of teleological thinking, to be sure, and we must be careful of it.

Still, if we consider certain tendencies in American culture during the last 75 years of the century just past—say from 1925 until the year 2000—it helps us to explain your father and what happened to him.

Take two key ideas: individualism and progress. You are doubtless

familiar enough with the notion of individuation, and the value American culture placed on the individual. You may not have realized tha-
the idea of progress is a relatively recent one in history. A great man-
peoples failed to see that constant change necessarily meant improvement—how do you know that what you're getting is better than wha:
you had, and what do you mean by *better?* But Americans believed i*
progress; it was part of their value system. If you weren't "making
progress" you were as good as dead, in an individual as well as a
national sense.

It was possible to demonstrate progress in some areas, such as
technology. If by progress you mean efficiency, it could be shown tha:
some tools were more efficient than other tools. Progress in terms cf
other spheres of culture was harder to define, but Americans believe-
in that kind of progress too. If you should ever go back and read some
of the historical documents of that period, Robert, I'm sure you will be
struck by the constant references to spiritual growth and social betterment.

Now, cultures are funny things. All of them change, but all of them
are inherently conservative; they have to be. You can't have a culture
—which is an integrated system—charging off in ten different directions at once. In America, the slogan might well have been this: the
same, with a difference. In other words, you must preserve the tradi-
tions of your forefathers, but be more up-to-date than they were.

You probably know that our industry was not always robotized and
controlled by cybernetic systems, but it is hard to imagine today that
it was ever anything else. This was a fundamental change in our way
of life. As long ago as the middle of the last century, a man named
Riesman was already pointing out that our culture was becoming ori-
ented toward the *consumers;* he called it "other-direction," I believe,
and he noticed the increasing dominance of peer groups and the growing discriminations of taste. People were becoming sophisticated in
what they consumed, you might say.

Atomic power, as you have read in your elementary history books,
meant the end of old-style warfare. War was no longer an efficient
instrument of national policy. It became necessary to win men's minds.
At the same time, the physical sciences went into a bit of a decline.
Most of the work went into the making of bigger and better super
weapons, which were never employed in warfare but were simply set
off first in isolated areas, and later on the Moon—in order to keep the
other side too scared to fight. The social sciences, meanwhile, had got
far enough along to know what made sociocultural systems tick.

It was rather neat, really. Americans had always loved gadgets,
and as they became more sophisticated they turned to really fundamental gadgets: social systems. It was all phrased in terms of healthy
variety and showing the world what we could do with free enterprise

and respect for the individual; but what it was, in fact, was social gadgeteering.

Inventors had always been highly regarded in America, but now the focus of their inventions changed. It was all very well for Edison to have thought up an electric light, of course, but how much more rewarding it was to invent a way of life for a whole generation!

What came out of it all was a series of flexible, delimited social groups—about the size of the old counties—with variant social systems competing for prestige. Every village and town had always thought of itself as different from and better than its neighbor down the road—perhaps you have heard of Boston or of some cities in Texas—and now they could really put on the dog. Of course, they weren't *completely* different; that would have been chaos. They were all American, but with the parts put together differently. And there was a national service culture—a government—that was centered in Washington and had colonies in each area.

I hope you'll excuse me for talking so long, Robert, but I think all this has a bearing on what your father did. The defects—if that is the right word—of this way of running things were not apparent until after the Natchezville elections, where Fullcircle began. That's why I'm particularly anxious to hear about the next decade or so, when you were growing up. I recall that George lost the Concordburg elections the next year, but after that I'm a little hazy.

I have always wondered just how long it was before your father knew what had happened to him. . . .

"Look," George Sage said, with a moderately successful imitation of long-suffering patience, "do you have to shoot marbles right under my hammock?"

"It's raining outside, Pop," Bob answered, laconically chalking another circle on the living-room carpet.

"It's always raining," George muttered, half to himself. "It's been raining for a million years."

"Don't be depressed, dear," Lois said.

"Now *you're* turning on me! How the hell am I supposed to get any work done?"

"Don't swear in front of Bobby, George."

"Aaaahh." George stared grimly at his son. "You know plenty of worse words than that, don't you, Bobby?"

"Sure," the boy said solemnly. "And my name is *Bob*, not Bobby."

"Hell," George said again.

"Come on, Bob," Lois said. "You run get in the copter and go to the store with Mother."

"Can I pilot?"

"Of course," Lois said, hiding a shiver of anticipation.

They hurried up to the roof.

George was alone.

It was ten years since he had won the Natchezville elections with his Full Circle. Not one of his ideas had panned out since. To make matters worse, he was in competition with himself.

And losing.

He swung out of his hammock, made some half-hearted notes on the pad on his desk, and called Will Nolan. The promotions officer faded into the screen like a reluctant spirit.

"Great to see you, George boy," he said with an appalling lack of sincerity. "What's new?"

"That's what *I* want to know. Any new figures on that Frankenstein of ours?"

"It wasn't Frankenstein," Nolan corrected, removing the lenses from his eyes. "It was Frankenstein's monster."

"Monster, shmonster. What's the box-score?"

Nolan sighed, fixing his gaze on the ceiling. "Your little creation —it's written as one word now, 'Fullcircle,' you know—has spread to six more communities in the last two weeks. It's winning every blasted election. A great, great system!"

"Great," George agreed, in utter despair. "Still the same routine?"

"Yeah. Nobody put it on the ballot, since nobody can get any royalties on it after the first time around; but the thing keeps winning as a *write-in* candidate. No advertising, no promotion, no nothing!"

"The best advertisement," George repeated wearily, "is a satisfied customer."

"Great." Nolan paused, at a loss for words. "Great."

"Will, what have I done? I'm just an average kind of guy, just trying to make a living; I'm no revolutionary, dammit!"

"Well, George—"

"That monstrosity—that Full Circle—I mean Fullcircle—is too good, that's what's wrong. It's got *everything!* All the joys of rural living, all the joys of the city—how can you beat it? *I* can't beat it, and I thought it up! Where will the damned thing end, Will? *Where will it end?*"

"I strongly suspect," Will Nolan said in complete seriousness, "that it's going to take over the world."

"Oh my God."

"Too late to invoke the Deity, my friend. We're headed for technological unemployment. A great, great situation."

"Maybe I'll get a pension," George said.

"I'll work on that angle. I should get one too; I sold it in the first place. Don't call me, I'll call you."

"So long, Will."

George cut the screen off and walked unsteadily back to his hammock. He closed his eyes but he could not relax.

"Survival of the fittest," he remarked to the wall.

He was no fool. He saw what was happening, saw it with hideous clarity. There was a fight for survival among social systems as well as in the animal kingdom; there were no primitive hunters left in London. The set-up in the United States, with its emphasis on local variations, would work fine, until a social organization came along that was markedly superior to all the rest. And then—

And then it spread.

Everybody wanted one.

It was the end of an era.

"I am Achilles' heel," George said.

The empty rooms began to get on his nerves. He slipped into his rainsuit and went down and out the little-used street entrance. The rain was a gray drizzle in the air, and Washington was hushed and colorless.

George walked, aimlessly.

His feet squished wetly on the old cement.

He didn't even feel like smoking.

It was two hours before he saw another human being. At first, the figure was just a dark shadow, coming toward him. Then, as it walked nearer, it took on substance and features.

It was Henry Lloyd. A few short years ago, he had been the most successful social inventor in the country.

Lloyd was looking very old.

"Hank!" George called out. "It's good to see you."

Lloyd stared at him icily.

"Monopolist," he said, and made a small detour to get around him. He said nothing more, and vanished up the wet street.

George Sage put his head down.

He walked slowly through the gray rain-haze, walked until night had come to the city. Then he headed back toward home, because he knew that Lois would be worried.

That wasn't the only reason, he supposed.

There just wasn't anywhere else for him to go.

So you see (Robert Sage said to the historian as they finished their third glass of beer) that it wasn't all milk and honey after Dad invented our way of life. There was a tough transition time, when Fullcircle was just catching on and a lot of people hated Dad's guts.

I'll tell you, getting that pension wasn't the easiest stunt in the

world; there was a time when I thought we were all going to starve to
death. People get sore when I mention that; they figure I'm just some
spoiled brat who likes to tell lies, but it's the truth.

All that Father of His Country stuff came later—much later.

Well, that's the way it was. I could tell you wanted the facts, so I've
given 'em to you straight. It's been a pleasure talking to you.

What's that? Sure, if you insist. I'll get 'em next time—that a deal?

Tell you what. Old George doesn't live far from here. Mother's
dead, you know, so Dad is all alone. He still won't admit to himself that
it's all over; that's the way artists are, I guess. Like as not, he'll be
sitting at that old desk of his, making notes and cussing the weather
He'll look busy, Dad will, but don't let that fool you.

He's lonesome, and likes to be able to talk to people.

I'm going over there now. Won't you come along?

BLACK IS BEAUTIFUL

Robert Silverberg

my nose is flat my lips are thick my hair is frizzy my skin is black
    is beautiful
    is black is beautiful
    I am James Shabazz age seventeen born august 13 1983 I am black
I am afro I am beautiful this machine writes my words as I speak them
and the machine is black
    is beautiful

Elijah Muhammad's *The Supreme Wisdom* says:

> Separation of the so-called Negroes from their slave masters' chil-
> dren is a MUST. It is the only SOLUTION to our problem. It was the
> only solution, according to the Bible, for Israel and the Egyptians,
> and it will prove to be the only solution for America and her slaves,
> whom she mockingly calls her citizens, without granting her citizen-
> ship. We must keep this in our minds at all times that we are actually
> being mocked.

Catlike, moving as a black panther would, James Shabazz stalked
through the city. It was late summer, and the pumps were working
hard, sucking the hot air out from under the Manhattan domes and

From *The Year 2000,* Doubleday, 1970. Reprinted by permission of the author and
his agents, Scott Meredith Literary Agency, Inc., 580 Fifth Avenue, New York, New York
10036.

squirting it into the suburbs. There had been a lot of grinding about that lately. Whitey out there complained that all that hot air was wilting his lawns and making his own pumps work too hard. Screw Whitey, thought James Shabazz pleasantly. Let his lawns wilt. Let him complain. Let him get black in the face with complaining. Do the mother some good.

Silently, pantherlike, down Fifth Avenue to Fifty-third, across to Park, down Park to Forty-eighth. Just looking around. A big boy, sweat-shiny, black but not black enough to suit him. He wore a gaucy five-colored dashiki, beads from Mali, flowing white belled trousers, a neat goatee, a golden earring. In his left rear pocket: a beat-up copy of the new novel about Malcolm. In his right rear pocket: a cute little sonic blade.

Saturday afternoon and the air was quiet. None of the hopterbuses coming through the domes and dumping Whitey onto the rooftops. They stayed home today, the commuters, the palefaces. Saturday and Sunday, the city was black. Likewise all the other days of the week after 4 P.M. Run, Whitey, run! See Whitey run! Why does Whitey run? Because he don't belong here no more.

Sorry, teach. I shouldn't talk like that no more, huh?

James Shabazz smiled. The identity card in his pocket called him James Lincoln, but when he walked alone through the city he spurned that name. The slave master name. His parents stuck with it, proud of it, telling him that no black should reject a name like Lincoln. The dumb geeps! What did they think, that great-great-grandpappy was owned by Honest Abe? Lincoln was a tag some belching hillbilly stuck on the family 150 years ago. If anyone asks me today, I'm James Shabazz. Black. Proud of it.

Black faces mirrored him on every street. Toward him came ten diplomats in tribal robes, not Afros but Africans, a bunch of Yorubas, Ibos, Baules, Mandingos, Ashantis, Senufos, Bakongos, Balubas, who knew what, the real thing, anyway, black as night, so black they looked purple. No slave master blood in them! James Shabazz smiled, nodded. Good afternoon, brothers. Nice day! They took no notice of him, but swept right on, their conversation unbroken. They were not speaking Swahili, which he would have recognized, but some other foreign language, maybe French. He wasn't sure. He scowled after them. Who they think they are, walking around a black man's city, upnosing people like that?

He studied his reflection for a while in the burnished window of a jewelry shop. Ground floor, Martin Luther King Building. Eighty stories of polished black marble. Black. Black man's money built that tower! Black man's sweat!

Overhead came the buzz of a hopter after all. No commuters today, so they had to be tourists. James Shabazz stared up at the beetle of a hopter crossing the dull translucent background of the distant dome.

It landed on the penthouse hopter stage of the King Building. He crossed the street and tried to see the palefaces stepping out, but the angle was too steep. Even so, he bowed ceremoniously. Welcome, massa! Welcome to the black man's metropolis! Soul food for lunch? Real hot jazz on 125th? Dancing jigaboo girls stripping at the Apollo? Sightseeing tour of Bedford-Stuyvesant and Harlem?

Can't tell where Bedford-Stuyvesant ends and Harlem begins, can you? But you'll come looking anyway.

Like to cut your guts up, you honkie mothers.

Martin Luther King said in Montgomery, Alabama, instructing the bus desegregators:

> If cursed, do not curse back. If pushed, do not push back. If struck,
> do not strike back, but evidence love and good will at all times.

He sat down for a while in Lumumba Park, back of the Forty-second Street Library, to watch the girls go by. The new summer styles were something pretty special: Congo Revival, plenty of beads and metal coils, but not much clothing except a sprayon sarong around the middle. There was a lot of grumbling by the old people. But how could you tell a handsome Afro girl that she shouldn't show her beautiful black breasts in public? Did they cover the boobies in the Motherland? Not until the missionaries came. Christ can't stand a pair of bares. The white girls cover up because they don't got much up there. Or maybe to keep from getting sunburned.

He admired the parade of proud jiggling black globes. The girls smiled to themselves as they cut through the park. They all wore their hair puffed out tribal style, and some of them even with little bone doodads thrust through it. There was no reason to be afraid of looking too primitive any more. James Shabazz winked, and some of them winked back. A few of the girls kept eyes fixed rigidly ahead; plainly it was an ordeal for them to strip down this way. Most of them enjoyed it as much as the men did. The park was full of men enjoying the show. James Shabazz wished they'd bring those honkie tourists here. He'd love a chance to operate on a few of them.

Gradually he became aware of a huge, fleshy, exceedingly black man with grizzled white hair, sitting across the way pretending to be reading his paper, but really stealing peeks at the cuties going by. James Shabazz recognized him: Powell 43X Nissim, Coordinating Chairman of the Afro-Muslim Popular Democratic Party of Greater New York. He was one of the biggest men in the city, politically— maybe even more important than Mayor Abdulrahman himself. He was also a good friend of the father of James Shabazz, who handled some of Powell 43X's legal work. Four or five times a year he came around to discuss some delicate point, and stayed far into the night, drinking pot after pot of black coffee and telling jokes in an uproarious bellow. Most of his jokes were anti-black; he could tell them like any Kluxer. James Shabazz looked on him as coarse, vulgar, seamy, out of date, an old-line pol. But yet you had to respect a man with that much power.

Powell 43X Nissim peered over the top of his *Amsterdam News,* saw him, let out a whoop, and yelled, "Hey, Jimmy Lincoln! What you doin' here?"

James Shabazz stood up and walked stiffly over. "Getting me some fresh air, sir."

"Been working at the library, huh? Studying hard? Gonna be the first nigger president, maybe?"

"No, sir. Just walkin' around on a Saturday."

"Ought to be in the library," Powell 43X said. "Read. Learn. That's how we got where we are. You think we took over this city because we a bunch of dumb niggers?" He let out a colossal laugh. "We *smart,* man!"

James Shabazz wanted to say, "We took over the city because Whitey ran out. He dumped it on us, is all. Didn't take no brains, just staying power."

Instead he said, "I got a little time to take it easy yet, sir. I don't go to college for another year."

"Columbia, huh?"

"You bet. Class of '05, that's me."

"You gonna fool with football when you get to college?"

"Thought I would."

"You listen to me," said Powell 43X. "Football's okay for high school. You get yourself into politics instead up there. Debating team. Malcolm X Society. Afro League. Smart boy like you, you got a career in government ahead of you if you play it right." He jerked his head to one side and indicated a girl striding by. "You get to be somebody, maybe you'll have a few of those to play with." He laughed. The girl was almost six feet tall, majestic, deep black, with great heavy swinging breasts and magnificent buttocks switching saucily from side to side beneath her sprayon wrap. Conscious that all eyes were on her, she crossed the park on the diagonal, heading for the Sixth Avenue side. Suddenly three whites appeared at the park entrance: weekend visitors, edgy, conspicuous. As the black girl went past them, one turned, gaping, his eyes following the trajectory of her outthrust nipples. He was a wiry redhead, maybe twenty years old, in town for a good time in boogieville, and you could see the hunger popping out all over him.

"Honkie mother," James Shabazz muttered. "Could use a black you know where."

Powell 43X clucked his tongue. "Easy, there. Let him look! What it hurt you if he thinks she's worth lookin' at?"

"Don't belong here. No right to look. Why can't they stay where they belong?"

"Jimmy—"

"Honkies right in Times Square! Don't they know this here's our city?"

Marcus Garvey said:

The Negro needs a Nation and a country of his own, where he can best show evidence of his own ability in the art of human progress. Scattered as an unmixed and unrecognized part of alien nations and civilizations is but to demonstrate his imbecility, and point him out as an unworthy derelict, fit neither for the society of Greek, Jew, or Gentile.

While he talked with Powell 43X, James Shabazz kept one eye on the honkie from the suburbs. The redhead and his two pals cut out in the direction of Forty-first Street. James Shabazz excused himself finally and drifted away, toward that side of the park. Old windbag, he thought. Nothing but a Tom underneath. Tolerance for the honkies! When did they tolerate *us*?

Easy, easy, like a panther. Walk slow and quiet.

Follow the stinking mother. Show him how it really is.

Malcolm X said:

Always bear in mind that our being in the Western hemisphere differs from anyone else, because everyone else came here voluntarily. Everyone that you see in this part of the world got on a boat and came here voluntarily; whether they were immigrants or what have you, they came here voluntarily. So they don't have any real squawk, because they got what they were looking for. But you and I can squawk because we didn't come here voluntarily. We didn't ask to be brought here. We were brought here forcibly, against our will, and in chains. And at no time since we have been here, have they even acted like they wanted us here. At no time. At no time have they ever tried to pretend that we were brought here to be citizens. Why, they don't even *pretend*. So why should we pretend?

The cities had been theirs for 15 or 20 years. It had been a peaceful enough conquest. Each year there were fewer whites and more blacks, and the whites kept moving out, and the blacks kept getting born, and one day Harlem was as far south as Seventy-second Street, and Bedford-Stuyvesant had slopped over into Flatbush and Park Slope, and there was a black mayor and a black city council, and that was it. In New York the tipping point had come about 1986. There was a special problem there, because of the Puerto Ricans, who thought of them-

selves as a separate community; but they were outnumbered, and most
of them finally decided it was cooler to have a city of their own. They
took Yonkers, the way the Mexicans took San Diego. What it shuffled
down to, in the end, was a city about 85 percent black and 10 percent
Puerto, with some isolated pockets of whites who stuck around out of
stubbornness or old age or masochism or feelings of togetherness with
their black brothers. Outside the city were the black suburbs, like
Mount Vernon and Newark and New Rochelle, and beyond them, 50,
80, 100 miles out, were the towns of the whites. It was apartheid in
reverse.

The honkie commuters still came into the city, those who had to,
quick-in quick-out, do your work and scram. There weren't many of
them, really, a hundred thousand a day or so. The white ad agencies
were gone north. The white magazines had relocated editorial staffs in
the green suburbs. The white book publishers had followed the financial people out. Those who came in were corporate executives, presid-
ing over all-black staffs; trophy whites, kept around by liberal-minded
blacks for decoration; government employees, trapped by desegrega-
tion edicts; and odds and ends of other sorts, all out of place, all scared.

It was a black man's city. It was pretty much the same all across
the country. Adjustments had been made.

Stokely Carmichael said:

We are oppressed as a group because we are black, not because we
are lazy, not because we're apathetic, not because we're stupid, not
because we smell, not because we eat watermelon and have good
rhythm. We are oppressed because we are black, and in order to get
out of that oppression, one must feel the group power that one has.
. . . If there's going to be any integration it's going to be a two-way
thing. If you believe in integration, you can come live in Watts. You
can send your children to the ghetto schools. Let's talk about that. If
you believe in integration, then we're going to start adopting us some
white people to live in our neighborhood. . . .
    We are not gonna wait for white people to sanction black power.
We're tired of waiting.

South of Forty-second Street things were pretty quiet on a Saturday, or any other time. Big tracts of the city were still empty. Some of
the office buildings had been converted into apartment houses to catch
the overflow, but a lot of them were still awaiting development. It took
time for a black community to generate enough capital to run a big city,
and though it was happening fast, it wasn't happening fast enough to
make use of all the facilities the whites had abandoned. James Shabazz
walked silently through silence, keeping his eyes on the three white
boys who strolled, seemingly aimlessly, a block ahead of him.

He couldn't dig why more tourists didn't get cut up. Hardly any of them did, except those who got drunk and pawed some chick. The ones who minded their own business were left alone, because the top men had passed the word that the sightseers were okay, that they injected cash into the city and shouldn't be molested. It amazed James Shabazz that everybody listened. Up at the Audubon, somebody would get up and read from Stokely or Malcolm or one of the other black martyrs, and call for a holy war on Whitey, really socking it to 'em. Civil rights! Equality! Black power! Retribution for 400 years of slavery! Break down the ghetto walls! Keep the faith, baby! Tell it how it is! All about the exploitation of the black man, the exclusion of the Afros from the lily-white suburbs, the concentration of economic power in Whitey's hands. And the audience would shout amen and stomp its feet and sing hymns, but nobody would ever do anything. *Nobody would ever do anything.* He couldn't understand that. Were they satisfied to live in a city with an invisible wall around it? Did they really think they had it so good? They talked about owning New York, and maybe they did, but didn't they know that it was all a fraud, that Whitey had given them the damn city just so they'd stay out of *his* back yard?

Someday we gonna run things. Not the Powell 43X cats and the other Toms, but *us.* And we gonna keep the city, but we gonna take what's outside, too.

And none of this crap about honkie mothers coming in to look our women over.

James Shabazz noted with satisfaction that the three white boys were splitting up. Two of them were going into Penn Station to grab the tube home, looked like. The third was the redhead, and he was standing by himself on Seventh Avenue, looking up at Uhuru Stadium, which he probably called Madison Square Garden. Good boy. Dumb enough to leave yourself alone. Now I gonna teach you a thing or two.

He moved forward quickly.

Robert F. Williams said:

When an oppressed people show a willingness to defend themselves,
the enemy, who is a moral weakling and coward, is more willing to
grant concessions and work for a respectable compromise.

He walked up smiling and said, "Hi, man. I'm Jimmy Lincoln."
Whitey looked perplexed. "Hi, man."
"You lookin' for some fun, I bet."
"Just came in to see the city a little."
"To find some fun. Lots of great chicks around here." Jimmy Lincoln winked broadly. "You can't kid me none. I go for 'em too. Where you from, Red?"
"Nyack."

"That's upstate somewhere, huh?"

"Not so far. Just over the bridge. Rockland County."

"Yeah. Nice up there, I bet. I never seen it."

"Not so different from down here. Buildings are smaller, that's all. Just as crowded."

"I bet they got a different looking skin in Nyack," said Jimmy Lincoln. He laughed. "I bet I right, huh?"

The red-haired boy laughed too. "Well, I guess you are."

"Come on with me. I find you some fun. You and me. What's your name?"

"Tom."

"Tom. That's a good one. Lookee, Tom, I know a place, lots of girls, something to drink, a pill to pop, real soul music, yeah? Eh, man? Couple blocks from here. You came here to see the city, let me show it to you. Right?"

"Well—" uneasily.

"Don't be so up tight, man. You don't trust your black brother? Look, we got no feud with you. All that stuff's ancient history! You got to realize this is the year 2000, we all free men, we got what we after. Nobody gonna hurt you." Jimmy Lincoln moved closer and winked confidentially. "Lemme tell you something, too. That red hair of yours, the girls gonna orbit over that! They don't see that kind hair every day. Them freckles. Them blue eyes. Man, blue eyes, it turn them on! You in for the time of your life!"

Tom from Nyack grinned. He pointed toward Penn Station. "I came in with two pals. They went home, the geeps! Tomorrow they're going to feel awful dopey about that."

"You know they will," said Jimmy Lincoln.

They walked west, across Eighth Avenue, across Ninth, into the redevelopment area where the old warehouses had been ripped down. Signs sprouting from the acreage of rubble proclaimed that the Afro-American Cultural Center would shortly rise here. Just now the area looked bombed out. Tom from Nyack frowned as if he failed to see where a swinging night club was likely to be located in this district. Jimmy Lincoln led him up to Thirty-fifth Street and around the hollow shell of a not quite demolished building.

"Almost there?" Tom asked.

"We here right now, man."

"Where?"

"Up against that wall, that's where," said James Shabazz. The sonic blade glided into his hand. He studded it and it began to whir menacingly. In a quiet voice he said, "Honkie, I saw you look at a black girl a little while ago like you might just be thinking about what's between her legs. You shouldn't think thoughts like that about black girls. You got an itch, man, you scratch it on your own kind. I think I'm gonna fix you so you don't itch no more."

Minister James 3X said:

First, there is fear—first and foremost there is inborn fear, and hatred for the black man. There is a feeling on the part of the white man of inferiority. He thinks within himself that the black man is the best man.

The white man is justified in feeling that way because he has discovered that he is weaker than the black man. His mental power is less than that of the black man—he has only six ounces of brain and the Original Man has seven-and-a-half ounces. . . . The white man's physical power is one-third less than that of the black man.

He had never talked this long with a honkie before. You didn't see all that many of them about, when you spent your time in high school. But now he stared into those frightened blue eyes and watched the blood drain from the scruffy white skin and he felt power welling up inside himself. He was Chaka Zulu and Malcolm and Stokely and Nkrumah and Nat Turner and Lumumba all rolled into one. He, James Shabazz, was going to lead the new black revolution, and he was going to begin by sacrificing this cowering honkie. Through his mind rolled the magnificent phrases of his prophets. He heard them talking, yes, Adam and Ras Tafari and Floyd, heard them singing down the ages out of Africa, kings in chains, martyrs, the great ones, he heard Elijah Muhammad and Muhammad Ali, Marcus Garvey, Sojourner Truth, du Bois, Henry Garnet, Rap Brown, rattling the chains, shouting for freedom, and all of them telling him, go on, man, how long you want to be a nigger anyhow? Go on! You think you got it so good? You gonna go to college, get a job, live in a house, eat steak and potatoes, and that's enough, eh, nigger, even if you can't set foot in Nyack, Peekskill, Wantaugh, Suffern, Morristown? Be happy with what you got, darkie! You got more than we ever did, so why bitch about things? You got a city! You got power! You got freedom! It don't matter that they call you an ape. Don't matter that they don't let you near their daughters. Don't matter that you never seen Nyack. Be grateful for what you got, man, is that the idea?

He heard their cosmic laughter, the thunder of their derision.

And he moved toward Tom the honkie and said, "Here's where the revolution gets started again. Trash like you fooling with our women, you gonna get a blade in the balls. You go home to Nyack and give 'em that message, man."

Tom said lamely, "Look out behind you!"

James Shabazz laughed and began to thrust the blade home, but the anesthetic dart caught him in the middle of the back and his muscles surrendered, and the blade fell, and he turned as he folded up and saw the black policeman with the dart gun in his black fist, and he realized that he had known all along that this was how it would turn out, and he couldn't say he really cared.

Robert Moses of SNCC was questioned in May 1962 on the voter registration drive in Mississippi:

> Q. Mr. Moses, did you know a Herbert Lee?
> A. Yes, he was a Negro farmer who lived near Liberty.
> Q. Would you tell the Committee what Mr. Lee was doing and what happened?
> A. He was killed on September 25th. That morning I was in McComb. The Negro doctor came by the voter registration office to tell us he had just taken a bullet out of a Negro's head. We went over to see who it was because I thought it was somebody in the voting program, and were able to identify the man as Mr. Herbert Lee, who had attended our classes and driven us around the voting area, visiting other farmers.

Powell 43X Nissim said heavily, folding his hands across his paunch, "I got you off because you're your daddy's son. But you try a fool thing like that again, I gon' let them put you away."

James Shabazz said nothing.

"What you think you was doing, anyway, Jimmy? You know we watch all the tourists. We can't afford to let them get cut up. There was tracers on that kid all the time."

"I didn't know."

"You sit there mad as hell, thinking I should have let you cut him. You know who you really would have cut? Jimmy Lincoln, that's who. We still got jails. Black judges know the law too. You get ruined for life, a thing like that. And what for?"

"To show the honkie a thing or two."

"Jimmy, Jimmy, Jimmy! What's to show? We got the whole city."

"Why can't we live outside?"

"Because we don't *want* to. Those of us who can afford it, even, we stay here. They got laws against discrimination in this country. We stay here because we like it with our own kind. Even the black millionaires, and don't think there ain't plenty of 'em. We got a dozen men, they could *buy* Nyack. They stay."

"And why do you stay?"

"I'm in politics," said Powell 43X. "You know what a power base means? I got to stay where my people are. I don't care about living with the whites."

"You talk like you aren't even sore about it," James Shabazz said. "Don't you hate Whitey?"

"No. I don't hate no one."

"We all hate Whitey!"

"Only you hate Whitey," said Powell 43X. "And that's because you don't know nothin' yet. The time of hating's over, Jimmy. We got to be practical. You know, we got ourselves a good deal now, and we ain't gon' get more by burning nobody. Well, maybe the Stock Exchange moved to Connecticut, and a lot of banks and stuff like that, but *we run the city.* Black men. Black men hold the mortgages. We got a black upper crust here now. Fancy shops for black folk, fancy restaurants, black banks, gorgeous mosques. Nobody oppressing us now. When a mortgage gets foreclosed these days, it's a *black* man doin' the foreclosin'. Black men ownin' the sweatshops. Ownin' the hockshops. Good and bad, we got the city, Jimmy. And maybe this is the way it's meant to be: us in the cities, them outside."

"You talk like a Tom!"

"And you talk like a fool." Powell 43X chuckled. "Jimmy, wake up! We all Toms today. We don't do revolutions now."

"I go to the Audubon," James Shabazz said. "I listen to them speak. They talk revolution there. They don't sound like no Toms to me!"

"It's all politics, son. Talk big, yell for equality. It don't make sense to let a good revolution die. They do it for show. A man don't get anywhere politickin' in black New York by sayin' that everything's 100 percent all right in the world. And you took all that noise seriously? You didn't know that they just shoutin' because it's part of the routine? You went out to spear you a honkie? I figured you for smarter than that. Look, you all mixed up, boy. A smart man, black or white, he don't mess up a good deal for himself, even if he sometimes say he *want* to change everything all around. You full of hate, full of dreams. When you grow up, you'll understand. Our problem, it's not how to get out into the suburbs, it's how to keep Whitey from wanting to come back and live in here! We got to keep what we got. We got it pretty good. Who oppressing you, Jimmy? You a slave? Wake up! And now you understand the system a little better, clear your rear end outa my office. I got to phone up the mayor and have a little talk."

Jimmy Lincoln stumbled out, stunned, shaken. His eyes felt hot and his tongue was dry. The system? The *system?* How cynical could you get? The whole revolution phony? All done for show?

No. No. No. No.

He wanted to smash down the King Building with his fists. He wanted to see buildings ablaze, as in the old days when the black man was still fighting for what ought to be his.

I don't believe it, he thought. Not any of it. I'm not gonna stop fighting for my rights. I'm gonna live to see us overcome. I won't sell out like the others. Not me!

And then he thought maybe he was being a little dumb. Maybe Powell 43X was right: there wasn't anything left worth fighting for, and only a dopey kid would take the slogans at face value. He tried to brush that thought out of his head. If Powell 43X was right, everything he had read was a lot of crap. Stokely. Malcolm. All the great martyrs. Just so much ancient history?

He stepped out into the summer haze. Overhead, a hopterbus was heading for the suburbs. He shook his fist at it; and instantly he felt foolish for the gesture, and wondered why he felt foolish. And knew. And beneath his rebellious fury, began to suspect that one day he'd give into the system too. But not yet. Not yet!

time to do my homework now

machine, spell everything right today's essay is on black power as a revolutionary force I am James Lincoln, Class 804, Frederick Douglass High School put that heading on the page yeah

the concept of black power as a revolutionary force first was heard during the time of oppression 40 years ago, when

crap on that, machine we better hold it until I know what I going to say

I am James Shabazz age 17 born august 13 1983 I am black I am afro I am beautiful

black is beautiful

let's start over, machine

let's make an outline first

black power its origin its development the martyrdoms and lynchings the first black mayors the black congressmen and senators the black cities and then talk about black power as a continuing thing, the never ending revolution no matter what pols like 43X say, never give in never settle for what they give you never sell out

that's it, machine

black power

black

black is beautiful

GOLDEN ACRES

Kit Reed

"I can walk, dammit." After a scuffle Hamish threw off the bell-boy's hand and went into the elevator himself. It troubled him that Nelda rode serenely, submitting to the roller chair. The bellhops pushed him in the corner of the elevator, crowding him with the second chair; they had it full of the Scofields' luggage, and when the elevator let them out on Four they took off with a look of spite, rolling the chairs down corridors so fast that Hamish had to run to keep up. His frail lungs failed him finally and he lost them; he came round the last corner to find himself alone on a long cement porch. The pale stucco building seemed to go all the way around a court, or square, and when Hamish looked over the porch rail he saw a pool and a garden below. He would have waved or called out but they were both empty, except for the California sunlight and a few improbable flowers. He turned back to the porch and a series of identical doors, all louvered, all closed.

"Nelda? Nelda?" He hated his voice; it sounded old and thin.

He was breathing heavily, whirling in indecision, when a door opened down the way; one of the bellhops beckoned with a condescending grin.

They had arranged Nelda in the middle of the suitcases and hat-boxes, tableau: woman arriving at a resort. Her hand fluttered at the bosom of her best voile dress; in a minute her smile would fly apart. "Hamish," she said, "isn't it beautiful?"

From *Mister Da V and Other Stories,* Faber and Faber, 1967. Copyright © 1967 by Kit Reed. Reprinted by permission of Brandt & Brandt.

The bellboys were lingering. "That will be all," Hamish said, but they were waiting. He made a little rush at them and then, because Nelda was pale and tremulous, he went on, trying not to look around him, "Just beautiful," and when he looked up this time the bellboys were gone.

"Look, they've put the TV where you can see it from the bed.'

He was looking out the door; when he had watched the bellhops around the last corner he closed the door and turned to her, full of misgivings:

"Nelda, I don't know about this place, I just don't *know*."

"Honey, you're going to love it; it's all we ever dreamed." She had her hat off now and she was beginning to make a little tour of the room, touching the metal bedsteads, running her fingers over the glass on the dresser tops. "Look," she said, "you can see the TV from your bed, just like they said in the brochure."

"Those look like hospital beds."

"You can crank yourself up any way you want." She quoted from memory: "Everything for safety and comfort." But she was running her fingers along the walls now, they were Formica, and when she spoke again her voice was slightly off key. "My knickknack shelf—I don't see any place for my knickknack shelf."

"I don't see any place for *anything*."

"They said I could hang my knickknack shelf."

But Hamish wasn't listening; he was moving restlessly, taking in the no-color drapes and bedspreads, the oatmeally peach Formica on the walls. The furniture was institutional and sparse: two luggage racks, one for each of them; two beds, two dressers, two straight chairs bolted into place; at waist height all the way around, there was a rail. He snarled in sudden resentment: "I don't need any goddam rail."

". . . AND THE HOT PLATE. I don't see the hot plate."

"In here," Hamish said from the tiny bathroom. "On the toilet tank. Say, where in hell are all the mirrors?"

Nelda's voice rose in a tiny wail. "Where can I plug in my hair-drier? How can I do my hair?"

Hamish was out of the bathroom before she finished. He had his arm around her, saying, "Honey, are you sure this is what you want? I mean, it's not too late to change our minds. . . ."

She wavered. "Oh, Hamish."

"We could be back in Waukegan before you know it. We could be *home*."

But he had lost her. As he spoke her arms dropped and in the next second she was tugging at one of the suitcases, wrestling it onto the bed. She took out a sun hat and put it on. "Hamish, Hamish, *this* is home."

"It's a damn motel."

"We sold everything to buy in here." She had a printed beach dress by the shoulders; she was shaking it out. "We're going to love it here."

"Nelda. . . ."

But it was already too late. She had her sunshade on the bed and on top of that her sneakers and her aqua Capri pants. "It cost us ten thousand dollars. There are thousands on the waiting list. Do you think I'm going to back out now?"

He went on patiently. "I. Just. Don't. Like. What. I've. Seen."

She turned, brandishing a purple sweater. "What would we tell the neighbors when we got back? What would we tell Albert and Lorraine?"

He knew what he wanted to say, he wanted to say "To hell with the neighbors, to hell with Albert and Lorraine," but something put him off; it wasn't the neighbors, it wasn't anybody who had been at the farewell party; he wasn't afraid of any of the rest of them, just Albert and Lorraine.

"We're going to love it here," Nelda said firmly. "It says so in the brochure." She had the children's pictures now; she was setting them on her dresser. "Albert. Eddie. Lorraine. There, that's lovely. Isn't it lovely, Spike?"

He jumped at the sound of the old name.

She came closer and her face had dropped years. "You'll see, Spike. It's going to be just like a second honeymoon. . . ."

He would have kissed her then, he would have taken her old bones in his but there was a knock on the door and before either of them could answer a young man came in, leading a bearded old man who leaned heavily on a cane.

"Mr. and Mrs. Scofield?"

Hamish stepped in front of Nelda. "I'm Hamish Scofield, of Waukegan, Illinois, and I'd like you to meet. . . ."

The young man walked on past; he ran a quick finger around the carnation in his lapel and said, under his breath: "Clutter. We don't like our people to live in clutter."

Working quickly, he folded Nelda's family pictures and swept them into the dresser drawer. Albert. Eddie. Lorraine. Hamish knew he ought to protest and he would have, too, if it had been her silver dresser set, or her velvet lined vanity. . . .

"There. I'm Mister Richardson." He was neat as a scissors in his pinstriped suit. "I'm the manager here, and this is Cletus Ford, our Second Oldest Resident."

The Second Oldest Resident raised a hand from under his beard; he and Hamish touched fingers just before Richardson brushed him aside, saying. "I came to be sure you were settled happily here at Golden Acres. And if there's anything. . . ."

Hamish and Nelda both began:

"Mirror, need a damn shaving mirror."

"My knickknack shelf, I need a place for. . . ."

Richardson was still talking—". . . if there's anything we can do to make you happier, you have only to get in touch with any of our several attendants. You will know them because they wear white, the color of Hope. And now. . . ."

"I *would* like. . . ."

"If you could just. . . ."

". . . a few simple rules."

Hamish stiffened. *"Rules."*

"Rules. Then Cletus here. . . ."

Cletus said, hopelessly, *"Mis-*ter Ford."

"Cletus here will tell you about the golden opportunities waiting for you, but first. . . ."

"Well," said Cletus, "there's the Rotary and the Golden Agers and. . . ."

"Cletus. . . ."

". . . and the Close Shave Club, I'm a charter member, and the Amvets. . . ."

Richardson had him by the shoulders. *"Cletus. . . ."*

"Mis-ter Ford?"

"Cletus, I want you to go over to that chair and sit quietly with your knees together and try and remember your place." The manager went on, through his teeth, "And if you can't remember your place, you know what will happen, don't you?"

Hamish couldn't be sure, but he thought he heard a distant rumble, as if of a gigantic grocery cart. If he heard it, then Cletus heard it too; the old man shrank, diminishing before their eyes, folding himself into a chair and clasping his hands neatly under his beard.

"Y-yessir. Yes *sir.*"

Hamish had his mouth open. He was listening hard but the rumble, or whatever it was, was gone.

"First, a little about our many benefits. Of course many of them are obvious, the swimming, the sun, the happy companionship of people your own age, parties in the moonlight, dancing on the esplanade. . . ."

Nelda said, dreamily: ". . . dancing on the esplanade."

"But there is much, much more. Did you know, for instance, that there is a dispensary on every floor, or that the Tower of Hope. . . ." Richardson smiled over his carnation ". . . that's what we call our hospital . . . the Tower of Hope is only three minutes away? Did you know there is an attendant on duty on every terrace twenty-four hours a day?"

Hamish stiffened. "At*ten*dant."

"To answer the cry of distress. The fall in the night. The sudden seizure at dawn."

"The doctors," Nelda said. "Tell Spike about the doctors."

"Specialists in every ailment of the human flesh." Richardson smoothed plump hands over his dark suit. "You are safe in our hands."

"Safe. See, Spike, I told you it would be wonderful."

"Reveille at seven sharp, marches over the intercom. . . ." Richardson was growing lyric. "Breakfast at eight, after you clean your room."

Nelda frowned. "Clean?"

"Walks and therapy until noon, then lunch. Then naps. Then clubs. Dinner at five-thirty, bed by nine. Cooking on special days, with permission from the desk."

"Permission from the desk my ass." Hamish advanced on him. "Dinner at five-thirty. Bed by nine. . . ."

"Bed by nine," Richardson said firmly. "You are safe in our hands. Safe to live out your golden years in this California paradise. Now Cletus here. . . ." Cletus was asleep; Richardson kicked him sharply, perforating one ankle. *"Cletus, here. . . ."*

"Huh? Whuh. Osteotomy club, cribbage teams, the. . . ."

"Cletus here is a living testimony to the good life. When he first came in here he was a hollow wreck. Weren't you, Cletus?"

". . . Progress Study Club, Great Grandmothers' Club. . . ." Cletus became aware of an ugly silence. "Sir? Oh, yes. Yessir."

Richardson went on, gratified. "A few days in our hospital, a few months in the sun, and look at him now. He's our Second Oldest Resident, loved by everybody in the place."

Nelda's face was naked. "Loved."

Hamish wanted to push the others out and take her in his arms but they were too many and he was too old; he said, in an undertone, "You'll always be loved."

Richardson had put his hands on old Cletus, trundling him into the spotlight. "O.K., Cletus, you're on." Stifling a yawn, he bowed himself out, barely remembering to say: "Remember, you are safe in our hands."

Hamish counted to 60, and when Cletus still hadn't said anything he stood over the old man. "Well?"

Cletus was scratching his head. "Well . . . oh, the clubs. Well. Well, we have the biggest Sunshine Booster group in the whole United States and a Masonic Lodge second to none. And we have the largest Kiwanis membership in the world. . . ." He was still talking, but he was distracted, drifting away on a distant sound. "And the Lions . . . and. . . ."

Hamish said, sharply, "You were telling us about the clubs."

"The clubs." Cletus came to with a little jerk. He looked around furtively, whispering. "Do you have any idea how *big* this place is?"

"Tiny," Nelda said. "Exclusive. It says so in the brochure."

"It's a boneyard." His voice dropped even further. "It's *vast.*"

"Only a few well-chosen couples," Nelda said doggedly. "It says so in the brochure."

Hamish hushed her. "Let him talk."

"I tried to walk to the edge of this place one day. Maybe I wanted to see if the world was still there; maybe I just wanted to know there *was* an edge. I walked and walked. You want to know something?" he went on in awe. "I walked for miles."

Nelda said crossly, "It only seemed like miles."

Hamish was leaning forward. "And you finally made it to the edge."

Cletus shook his head sadly. "Walked until m'legs gave out. They come and got me in a rolling chair. Probably just as well, come to think of it. M'blood pressure was giving me hell."

Nelda said, anxiously, "The clubs. Please. You were telling us about the clubs."

"Hell with the clubs. I always hated clubs."

"But the companionship. All the Golden Agers, just like you. . . ."

"Fossils," Cletus snorted. "Bunch of bones."

"You don't really mean it." Nelda turned to Hamish. "He doesn't really mean it. If he did, he wouldn't stay."

"Hate the buildings, too. All smell of mildew and Argyrol."

"The pool, how about the pool?"

"I'm too damn *old* to swim."

Hamish squinted at him, puzzled. "But you stay. . . ."

"Damn right I stay." Cletus drew them to the window. "Look out there. See that white thing sticking up, taller than anything else? That's the Tower of Hope. Hospital round here."

Hamish said, "What's that tall *black* thing?"

"Hospital around here," Cletus repeated, not answering. "The facings are made of Corning Glass."

He drew the shutters and faced them belligerently. "Damn right I stay. Where else could I get round-the-clock medical care? B-one shot every morning, all the hormones I can take. Doctors, nurses, guys to catch me if I fall." He was squinting at Hamish now; something he saw seemed to anger him. "Don't knock it, buddy. This place is keeping me alive."

"If that's all you get, it isn't worth it," Hamish said angrily. "If that's all. . . ."

Nelda cut him off. "That can't be all."

"All? That's *plenty.*" Cletus paused, listening to something they could not make out.

Hamish was on him in a flash. "What's that noise?"

The old man was crafty, insolent. "There isn't any noise." But there was, it was coming closer, and Cletus leaped like a spider. "Archie, M'God, I bet it's for Archie." Hamish tried to hold him but he was too late. "See you," he said, and scuttled out, slamming the door.

It took Hamish a couple of minutes to get it open and when he did he saw only the cement porch receding, the regular march of the posts. He turned back to Nelda then, wondering how he could get her to come away with him, how he could begin. She was already busy with the suitcase, pulling out clothes and spreading them on the bed.

"Nelda."

She wouldn't look at him; instead she picked up a mimeographed paper from the bedside table. "Look, the newspaper. It's called the *Golden Blade.*"

"Nelda, please, we have to get out of here."

"It says here they're having a Shipwreck Party Friday; and there are shuffleboard lessons today at four. ..."

Outside someone was calling faintly, "Cletus, Cletus. ..."

"We don't belong here, Nelda, I thought we might but we don't."

She turned on him in sudden spite. "Then where *do* we belong?"

"Cletus ... I know you're in here, Cletus. Come on out." The old lady came skidding into the room in white Ground Grippers and a white lawn dress. "Excuse me," she said when she saw them. "Where's he hiding this time, in the shower?"

Nelda put on her best air. "Beg your pardon?"

"He loves to curl up on the seat ... come on," she said impatiently. "They're looking for him and I've got to let him know."

"Well, he *was* here, but he. ..."

"Just like him to run out, just when the pressure is so. ..."

Hamish took her elbow. "What pressure?"

She shook him off. "Oh, you know. Being the Oldest Living Resident. Sorry I bothered you. ..."

Nelda stepped forward, intercepting her with a smile so bright that Hamish was embarrassed for her. "Don't go. We were just hoping we'd get to meet some of the people here."

Look, I have to. ..."

"I'm Nelda Scofield and this is Hamish. ..." Nelda's voice went up, quavering. "Couldn't you sit down for a minute?"

"I really ought to. ..." The old lady seemed to see the need in Nelda's face because she said, "Oh hell, sure. Name's Lucy Fortmain," and plopped in one of the chairs.

The silence was ragged, embarrassing; Hamish saw Nelda going through her purse, mentally sizing up the larder, realizing she had nothing to offer her guest. He had come this far for her so he fished in his pockets. "Have a Life Saver?"

The old lady turned with a gracious smile. "Hell, sure."

"I'm sorry we don't have anything more exciting to offer," Nelda said. Hamish saw she was on the verge of tears.

Lucy patted her hand. "Lemon was always my favorite."

"That collar," Nelda said. "That's a lovely looking collar."

"Daughter made it. Tatting. I taught her when she was a kid."

"It's lovely," Nelda said.

"Margaret, m'oldest. Do you know, I have seven kids?"

Nelda touched her flat bosom. "We have two—a boy and a girl."

"Oh, how old are they?"

"Thirty-nine and forty-three. Lost our youngest when he was in his teens."

"Forty-three," Lucy said thoughtfully. "That's just about the cutest age."

"You should have seen ours when they found out we were leaving," Nelda said. "They were fit to be tied."

"Oh, so were mine," Lucy said. "You know how kids are."

"They begged us to stay with them in Waukegan, but when I showed them the brochure, how beautiful it was, well, they just had to give in gracefully; Mother, they said, we'll just have to give in gracefully."

Lucy said, "Well, *my* kids said, if it was any place but here they'd come and drag me out, but they know I'm in such good hands. . . ."

"I know." Nelda was gaining confidence. "I sensed that about the place as soon as we came in. All the attendants, the doctors. . . ."

". . . All the help," Lucy said. "It's as close as the buzzer by your bed." She lowered her head, brooding. After a while she said, with determined cheer: "And there are lots of parties and stuff, clubs and dances and all. My kids could never give me all that."

"It's all so friendly," Nelda said.

"Well. Uh. Yes. They have people to pick you up if you fall and people to come in the night if you have a bad dream, and people on the terrace, they're paid to talk to you, and people to bring you shots you don't even want. . . ." Lucy was beginning to sound depressed. "It's all just great. If only. . . ."

Nelda pressed her. "If only?"

Lucy shook herself. "Well. I'll say one thing. We all have a lot in common here. Same problems, same regrets. We've all come the same distance, and we're all going the same way." She snorted. "All in the same damn boat."

Hamish said, quietly, "What do you mean, going the same way?"

"I can't explain. It's just that for everything they give you in this place they take something away." She went on bleakly, "Some mornings I get up and don't know who I am. There isn't even any mirror, so I can check."

"You were telling us about the people," Nelda said with bright determination. "Interests, friends, all the things that keep you here."

"I'd leave in a minute if they'd let me." Lucy stood like a small ramrod. "Kids don't want me. *That's* why I'm here."

Nelda's voice rose. "No."

"Well, I'm off. Thanks for the Life Saver. If you see Cletus, tell him they're after him."

"Wait a minute. . . ."

She was in the doorway. "How many charms you got on your grandmother bracelet?"

Nelda said, defensively: "Five."

"You lose. I've got 24." The door closed on her.

"Damn jail," Hamish said, testing for a reaction; Nelda had her head turned so he couldn't see her face. "Just like a damn jail. Even the damn chairs are bolted down."

"Now, now, settle down."

"Damn jail," he said again. "Prison furniture. Prison rules."

She put down the nightie she was unpacking and turned. "I suppose there weren't any rules at Albert's house? Or when we were living with Lorraine? 'Don't use that chair, Daddy. . . .'" Her voice was ugly, but he recognized the inflections. "'We're going to have some people in for dinner, Mommy. I wonder if you and Daddy would mind. . . .'"

"Don't." He knew it was already too late to head her off.

"You used to have to smoke in the coal room at Albert's; Lucy made you stop tying flies. And how about all those mornings when you had to go down cellar at five or six, so you wouldn't wake up anybody when you coughed?"

"They're our *kids,* Nelda. You'll put up with a lot of things for kids. Nelda, we were born in Waukegan, and that's where we belong."

"So you want to go back and let them go on hurting us. They don't need us anymore, Spike, don't you see? They passed us one day when we weren't looking, they outgrew us, and every day since then they have been getting bigger and stronger, and the two of us. . . ." She took his hand. "We had to get out of there before we just faded away."

"Dammit, Nelda, they're our past. They're all the future we've got." Hamish freed himself without even noticing what he was doing. He was at the window now, tired and thoughtful. "I read somewhere about how they used to handle it in New Hampshire, or maybe it was Vermont. Put the old people out in the barn every winter, stacked 'em like cordwood, and left 'em to freeze until spring." He pressed his forehead against the shutters, dreaming. "Then one sunny day in spring all the children and grandchildren would come for them; they'd lay the old bodies out in the sun to thaw so they could help with the planting. There they were, out of the way until somebody needed them. And when they woke up they were home where they belonged, all warmed up, with plenty to do."

"Hamish, that's *terrible.*"

"They were *needed.* What's so terrible about that?" From where he stood he could see part of the porch and the fringes of the court below; he could not see but imagined a hundred thousand identical quadrangles stretching beyond, all quiet, all orderly, all crammed with bodies full of pills and injections. The old people were all in their places, hooked up to intravenous tubes, and around them the rooms were neat and tidy with no junk in sight; someone had swept out all the fragments of their past and there they were, laid out with their hair brushed smoothly and all the character laundered out of their clothes. He and Nelda would be just like them soon. They would be. . . . He turned to Nelda, breathing hard. "They were *needed.* Who needs us here?"

When Nelda spoke her voice was so low he hardly heard her. Straining, he made it out: "I need you, Hamish."

He couldn't help himself; his mouth filled with tears.

"Please, for me. Remember how it was. . . ." She didn't go on; she didn't have to, her tone struck echoes, and winter was in the room; he was at her bedside, nursing her after her fall and promising anything just to make her live; winter was in the room and he was keeping her alive on promises, feeding her on gaudy, color-shot brochures.

He sighed heavily. "I remember." Then, on a last hope. "You were sick, you *needed* to think. . . ."

"I still need. I need to be safe. I'm sick to death of being tired and sick and being afraid of being sick. Promise you'll stay, Hamish. For me?"

He wasn't ready to face her; he didn't have to because the door slapped wide and Cletus was in the room like a lightning bolt, with limbs flailing and electricity crackling in his beard. Before they could stop him he slammed the door and headed into the tiny bathroom; he was burrowing in the shower. When Hamish went in after him and tried to pull him out he turned and spat like a cat.

"Let go, you son of a bitch, they're after me."

Lucy was next, crowding into the tiny bathroom, and the three of them went round and round, Cletus flapping and blubbering, Lucy trying to pull him off the shower seat. "Come on, Clete, no use fighting. The cart's outside."

"Let go, dammit."

Hamish found himself crowded against the basin; he hunkered up on it, trying to stay out of the way. He was conscious of Nelda whimpering just outside the bathroom door.

"Come on, Clete," Lucy was wheedling. "Come on boy, come on. Tchum on."

He poked his head out. "Have they gone?"

"You know damn well they haven't gone." She grabbed quickly, before he could duck back into the shower; she nodded to Hamish and together they began maneuvering him back into the room.

He pulled back, saying sullenly, "Why did you have to come along and ruin everything?"

The old man couldn't see her face but Hamish could; it was lined with pain. She said, "God knows I didn't want to. I just thought it might make it a little easier."

He was whimpering. "I want my shot; it's past time for my shot."

"You've had so *many* shots, Clete, and angiograms, and vitamin pills, and X-rays, and IVs. Come on, baby, they'll take you along all neat and tidy, and maybe. . . ."

He snuffled hopefully. "Maybe?"

"Maybe they'll even give you a shot before you go."

He bounded away from her, howling. "I don't want to go."

Hamish stepped in front of the old man; he could feel his back hairs going stiff and he had to clear his throat twice before his voice would work properly. "Look here," he said to Lucy, "You have no right. If he doesn't want to go with you. . . ."

She looked at him without passion. "He has to go. It's time."

Cletus was blubbering. "But I've only been here for a *minute*. . . ."

"Fourteen years. Fourteen mortal years." She moved past Hamish, putting her arm around the old man's shoulder. "You smoothed the way for me when I came in, knew it was hard for me, being shoved in here. If I'd known then that I was going to have to come for you. . . ." She jammed her fist into her mouth, trying not to cry. When she was able she said to Hamish, "He wasn't always like this. Used to put up a hell of a fight. He got us napkins at dinner, and later lights. . . ."

"It can't be time, I haven't had my shot. I'll be good, I promise I will. . . ." Cletus was wiping his nose on his beard.

"Come on, Clete. Brace up. Take it like a man."

"I won't go. It's not my turn." He wrenched out of her grip, grinning slyly. "It's not my turn at all. It's your turn."

"Oh, Clete, you're a caution."

He giggled, falling into an old pattern of banter. "Or maybe you're so ugly they won't take you."

"You old goat. . . ." She brightened. "Hey, that sounds more like my old Clete. Now go on out there and show those guys you can take it like a man."

"Oh Lucy, I'm afraid."

Lucy looked over his head at the Scofields. "Would you believe he was the best linotypist in the East? *That's* what this place does to you."

He was weeping, wiping his eyes with her hand. "Please don't let them take me, please."

"Takes it right out of you."

"Lucy, Lucy, Ma. Mom. Mom. *Mommy.* . . ."

She still stood proudly but her old face was glazed with tears. "You see?" She patted Cletus on the shoulder. "There there, baby. You'll be all right. . . ."

Hamish said, quietly, "Maybe you'd better tell us about it."

But she wasn't listening. She was patting Cletus, saying, "You'll be all right, I'll take care of you. . . ." Hamish would have shaken an answer out of her but she was busy with her own thoughts, planning. "Well," she said abstractedly, "I'll show *them.*" Then she was busy with her buttons and in the next second her dress fell to the floor and she stood, straight and proud of her stiff white muslin underslip. "Here," she said to Cletus. "You just slip into my frock."

"Lucy. . . ." The old man should have been protesting. Hamish wanted to take him by the shoulders and shake him and scream into his face until he turned and went outside and *fought. . . .*

It was too late. Cletus took the dress and shimmied into it, stuffing his beard into the bodice, not caring that his hairy arms and black trouser legs stuck out incongruously. When he was ready Lucy held him off at arm's length, revolving him with one hand.

"Yes," she said finally, "you'll do. Now you go on out, and if they try and stop you duck into the Ladies Room. I don't think they'll follow you into the Ladies Room."

"Lucy, I. . . . I don't know what to say."

"Never mind. Let's just say you're not up to it, and I am." She gave him a shove. "You go wait in the Ladies Room until you hear them leave."

He danced on the doorsill for a minute, looking as if he would thank her, or apologize, or beg her to change her mind, but it was apparent to all of them that he didn't really want her to change her mind; in the end, he wasn't even able to thank her. Instead he said, dully, "It's time for my shot."

Lucy watched out the window, turning back to the Scofields with a grim smile. "He made it." She smoothed her slip and put a hand to her hair. "Well. . . ."

Hamish moved toward her. "You're not going out there. . . ."

She was cool and proud. "Why not?"

"You know what's out there."

"Hell yes. The dead cart. From the Tower of Sleep."

Nelda's voice went up and up. "It isn't even your *turn.* . . ."

"I'd rather go now, while I still have some choice. After all, I've still got my pride. Pride's all I have left." She looked past Nelda, talking directly to Hamish. "You understand. If I'd just held out, you know, when they tried to put me in this place. I could have sold flowers or something, to earn my keep."

Hamish said, "Or camped in the train station."

"Or gone on relief," Lucy said wistfully. "Anything but this. I gave up everything when I let myself be suckered into this. Well, it's been nice knowing you." She raised one hand in a gladiator's salute.

"Hang on, dammit. Hang *on*."

She turned to Hamish. "You're still your own man. Better get out before it's too late."

The door slammed behind her. There was a second of silence from outside, then the sound of a scuffle, the rattle of bodies against metal and the crash of heels on the cement. Hamish could hear the sounds of arms and heads in desperate friction and over it, Lucy's voice rising: "Let go of me, you bastards. I'll climb on by my*self*."

There was a long pause and then the rattle, or rumble, receding as the cart took her away.

Before the sound faded Hamish was at the suitcase, stuffing Nelda's resort clothes in willy-nilly, putting sneakers in on top of her Capri pants and finishing off with the sunshade, not minding that clothes stuck out of all the cracks when he sat on top and tried to close the thing. "Come on," he said, assuming she was with him. "If you want those damn kids' pictures, you'd better get their pictures. I'll sneak the suitcases out the back and wait in the bushes by the gate. . . ."

"No."

". . . You can tell them you're going out for a little walk. . . ." He climbed off the suitcase slowly, seeing that she had taken the family pictures to her bosom. She was sitting quietly in one of the two straight chairs. "Give me those damn things. Don't you want to take them home?"

"I'm not going."

"The dead cart, Nelda." He tugged at the pictures. He had to get her moving. "The Tower of Sleep."

She let go of the pictures unexpectedly. "I already knew."

The pictures fell between them with a little crash. "You *knew?*"

"Of course I did. It's in the back of the brochure. The tiny print."

He was backing away from her. "But you didn't *tell* me."

"I was hoping you'd get to like it here first. It's perfectly fair," she said matter-of-factly. "When you've used up your quota of medicine they come for you. The funerals here are beautiful, I've seen the card; it doesn't hurt at all and in the meantime you have everything you want."

"Nelda, its monstrous."

She stood now, looking at him so steadily that he backed into a bed and sat down. "It's better than anything we *had*—all those damn fights with the kids; being sick, being afraid. They have drugs to take care of that kind of thing, they have everything you need over in the Tower of Hope, and if you fall—there's somebody there. There wasn't anybody there last winter. . . ."

He winced. "Never mind."

"I lay in the alley for 12 hours. I just ducked around a corner to get out of the cold and there I was in the dirt with slush running under me and blood in my mouth. I couldn't even call for help. I don't want to go through that again. I don't even want to be *afraid* of going through it, and I don't. . . ."

She was near tears; she opened the suitcase again, taking out the Capri pants, and when she had collected herself she took a deep breath and began again.

"I don't want to be dependent on the kids. They're at us all the time, Don't this, Don't that, and as soon as company comes they scrub us and prop us up in the living room, Exhibit A. Well I'm not up to it anymore, Hamish. I'm just not up to it."

He saw an opening. "Are you any better off here? You know what we are? Vegetables, goddam vegetables. They'll tend us and water us and cart us off before we can even die on the vine. . . ."

"It's worth it for a little comfort and safety." She was pushing him away from the suitcase, trying to unpack. After a little scuffle she gave up, saying sadly, "I was hoping you'd get to like it here. If only you'd get to like it here. . . ." She changed her tone, accusing him. "You promised you'd give it a chance."

"I didn't promise to drop dead. I'm going home."

"You'd rather go back there and suffer. . . ."

"Hell yes. At least I'll know I'm still alive." He had the suitcase to himself now; he was jamming things in again, wrestling it shut. "Look, I'd rather be hurt and sick *and* afraid, I'd rather be living with those damn kids. . . ."

"Don't make me tell you. Promise you'll stay."

Something in her voice arrested him. "Tell me what?"

"I don't want to have to tell you. Hamish, the kids. . . ."

"I've just got to get out of here." He was already in motion, trying not to listen. "If I can just get going before it gets dark. . . ."

"The kids." The words popped into the room. Nelda hushed him gently, saying, "It was right after my fall, I was laid up in bed and in they came, Albert and Lorraine. They were so damn sympathetic, all about how awful winters were for us, how we deserved better than that, that and living in back rooms. . . . I was too sick to make any sense of it. Then they started bringing folders, pictures of swimming pools and people playing in the sun. . . . I don't know, it all looked sort of good, and after they left I looked at some of the folders. I began to dream a little bit."

"You don't have to tell me anymore, Nelda. Just remember me when I'm gone."

"Let me finish." She had him by the arm now; her fingers were like iron bands. "Then one day they came back, they said, how would we like to try Golden Acres, and I thought about it. I told them it was probably all right for people without *folks* but we'd just as soon stay home, with them, and then. . . ."

She didn't have to finish, he didn't want to have to finish, but she seemed bound to go on. He tried to stop her; he said, "Nelda. . . ."

"Then I found out. It was all arranged; they'd sold off our stocks for the down payment. I was supposed to break the news." She went on grimly. "I sat there in that iron bed with my back hurting and those damn smug kids staring at me and I thought, I thought. Nothing can be worse than this. It was the kids, Hamish. The kids wanted to get rid of us."

"I know."

"You didn't know."

"I didn't want to admit it, but I knew it all along."

"So here we are." She managed a brave little smile. "Might as well make the best of it."

"I can't do it, Nelda. I have to go." He was desperate to be away, to have her come with him before the manager or the bellboys came along and locked them in; he tugged at her, saying, "Come on, come *on*," and when she wouldn't move he said, "Do you want to sit and wait for them? They'll come with the cart and after that they'll put our clothes in a box to be burned and then they'll scrub everything and change the linens and disinfect the room. Nelda, when I go I want to leave something behind, even if it's only a—a *smell*."

She disengaged herself. "I'll miss you so much."

"I've always been my own man, Nelda; I've got to go where somebody cares."

"Do you think anybody out *there* cares?" They were having a little battle over the suitcase; she made him put it down and she had it open again.

"At least they'll feel *some*thing about me, even if it's only dislike." He tried to lift her with his voice. "Maybe I'll go back to Waukegan and get a job."

"Waukegan doesn't want us, Hamish. Nobody does."

"I was born in that town. My past is in the streets, my past and my future, if I've got any future. I've got to go and see."

She shook her head. "You're only fooling yourself."

"Then *let* me fool myself."

They were both crying; there was a little silence while he fumbled in the tiny closet and put on his coat. Nelda brushed his shoulders and turned down his collar and she spoke, finally, saying: "You'll need a few things. You can't go off without a few things."

He tried to steady his voice. "The overnight bag, if you don't need it."

She said, quietly, "I'm not going anywhere."

"I'll get a job. I used to be a pretty good bricklayer. Then I'll find us a place and I'll send for you." He took her hand, lingering. "You will come, won't you?"

She said, with love, "We'll be together soon."

He wrapped his dry bones around her in a fierce embrace. "I'll find a place and then I'll send for you. It won't be long." He let her go and now he was in the doorway; he had to break away or he would never be free.

Her voice was so low he could hardly make out what she was saying: "It doesn't matter where we are . . . it won't be for long."

He might have turned. He might have gone back inside the room to plead with her but the sun was on its way down and in the distance there began a subtle rumble and he knew without stopping to think about it that it was coming his way.

two

Systems Are for People...

How like a cog is man! Or so Chandler Davis means to say, paraphrasing Hamlet, in "Adrift at the Policy Level." What is a giant corporation but an assemblage of parts forming a complex unitary whole? Science fiction excels in explaining how the correlated members of a system work. A world, a universe in action. But who makes it go, and for whose benefit?

In " 'Repent Harlequin!' said the Ticktockman," Harlan Ellison gleefully gives voice to all those employees who hate their jobs. If everybody were privileged to enjoy their means of livelihood, the world of work would look quite different. What defeats this pleasure for all but the Master Time Keepers is the overly large scale of things, cut to the mechanical beat of the clock.

In explaining how systems work, there are two available models. One is the *organic* model of the world. It is taken by

James H. Schmitz, in "Balanced Ecology," to picture a sensitive planet where living things work together for the harmony of the whole, like the different tissues of a single organism. The difference is that the parts consciously strive for the shared goal of equilibrium. The moral seems to be that man also, here and now, ought to deliberately find his place in nature and thus become one with it, rather than oppose himself to it with his world-wrecking technology.

The other one is the *mechanical* model of the world. Harmony is not the necessary outcome of the interworking parts. Christopher Anvil describes a run-away system in the realm of marketing mechanics in "Positive Feedback." Things may work together to fly apart!

It is curious, in this age of growing concern for man's place in the cabin ecology of Spaceship Earth, that the mechanical model should still dominate our thoughts so easily. Walt and Leigh Richmond take the computer as a model for the human brain in "Poppa Needs Shorts." A small boy, building up his data banks through the experience of trial and error, saves the life of his father by mistake. The boy does the right thing for the wrong reason—incomplete programing! A wholesome outcome is achieved through dumb and unintentional means. Risky business, that!

ADRIFT ON THE POLICY LEVEL

Chandler Davis

J. Albert La Rue was nervous, but you couldn't blame him. It was his big day. He looked up for reassurance at the big, bass-voiced man sitting so stolidly next to him in the hissing subway car, and found what he sought.

There was plenty of reassurance in having a man like Calvin Boersma on your side.

Albert declared mildly but firmly: "One single thought is uppermost in my mind."

Boersma inclined his ear. "What?"

"Oxidase epsilon!" cried Albert.

Cal Boersma clapped him on the shoulder and answered, like a fight manager rushing last-minute strategies to his boxer: "The one single thought that *should* be uppermost in your mind is *selling* oxidase epsilon. Nothing will be done unless The Corporation is sold on it. And when you deal with Corporation executives you're dealing with experts."

LaRue thought that over, swaying to the motion of the car.

"We do have something genuinely important to sell, don't we?" he ventured. He had been studying oxidase epsilon for three years. Boersma, on the other hand, was involved in the matter only because he was LaRue's lab-assistant's brother-in-law, an assistant sales manager of a plastics firm . . . and the only businessman LaRue knew.

Still, today—the big day—Cal Boersma was the expert. The promoter. The man who was right in the thick of the hard, practical world outside the University's cloistered halls—the world that terrified J. Albert LaRue.

Cal was all reassurance. "Oxidase epsilon *is* important, all right. That's the only reason we have a chance."

Their subway car gave a long, loud whoosh, followed by a shrill hissing. They were at their station. J. Albert LaRue felt a twinge of apprehension. This, he told himself, was it! They joined the file of passengers leaving the car for the luxurious escalator.

"Yes, Albert," Cal rumbled, as they rode up side by side, "we have something big here, if we can reach the top men—say, the Regional Director. Why, Albert, this could get you an assistant section managership in The Corporation itself!"

"Oh, thank you! But of course I wouldn't want—I mean, my devotion to research—" Albert was flustered.

"But of course I could take care of that end of it for you," Boersma said reassuringly. "Well, here we are, Albert."

The escalator fed them into a sunlit square between 20-story buildings. A blindingly green mall crossed the square to the Regional Executive Building of The Corporation. Albert could not help being awed. It was a truly impressive structure—a block wide, only three stories high.

Cal said in a reverent growl: "Putting up a building like that in the most heavily taxed area of Detroit—you know what that symbolizes, Albert? *Power.* Power and salesmanship! That's what you're dealing with when you deal with The Corporation."

The building was the hub of the Lakes Region, and the architecture was appropriately monumental. Albert murmured a comment, impressed. Cal agreed. "Superbly styled," he said solemnly.

Glass doors extending the full height of the building opened smoothly at the touch of Albert's hand. Straight ahead across the cool lobby another set of glass doors equally tall, were a showcase for dramatic exhibits of The Corporation's activities. Soothing lights rippled through an enchanted twilight. Glowing letters said, "Museum of Progress."

Several families on holiday wandered delighted among the exhibits, basking in the highest salesmanship the race had produced.

Albert started automatically in that direction. Cal's hand on his arm stopped him. "This way, Albert. The corridor to the right."

"Huh? But—I thought you said you couldn't get an appointment, and we'd have to follow the same channels as any member of the public." Certainly the "public" was the delighted wanderer through those gorgeous glass doors.

"Oh, sure, that's what we're doing. But I didn't mean *that* public."

"Oh." Apparently the Museum was only for the herd. Albert humbly followed Cal (not without a backward glance) to the relatively unobtrusive door at the end of the lobby—the initiate's secret passage to power, he thought with deep reverence.

But he noticed that three or four new people just entering the building were turning the same way.

A waiting room. But it was not a disappointing one; evidently Cal had directed them right; they had passed to a higher circle. The room was large, yet it looked like a sanctum.

Albert had never seen chairs like these. All of the 25 or so men and women who were there ahead of them were distinctly better dressed than Albert. On the other hand Cal's suit—a one-piece woolly buff-colored outfit, fashionably loose at the elbows and knees—was a match for any of them. Albert took pride in that.

Albert sat and fidgeted. Cal's bass voice gently reminded him that fidgeting would be fatal, then rehearsed him in his approach. He was to be, basically, a professor of plant metabolism; it was a poor approach, Cal conceded regretfully, but the only one Albert was qualified to make. Salesmanship he was to leave to Cal; his own appeal was to be based on his position—such as it was—as a scientific expert; therefore he was to be, basically, himself. His success in projecting the role might possibly be decisive—although the main responsibility, Cal pointed out, was Cal's.

While Cal talked, Albert fidgeted and watched the room. The lush chairs, irregularly placed, still managed all to face one wall, and in that wall were three plain doors. From time to time an attendant would appear to call one of the waiting supplicants to one of the doors. The attendants were liveried young men with flowing black hair. Finally, one came their way! He summoned them with a bow—an eye-flashing, head-tossing, flourishing bow, like a dancer rather than a butler.

Albert followed Cal to the door. "Will this be a junior executive? A personal secretary? A—"

But Cal seemed not to hear.

Albert followed Cal through the door and saw the most beautiful girl in the world.

He couldn't look at her, not by a long way. She was much too beautiful for that. But he knew exactly what she looked like. He could see in his mind her shining, ringleted hair falling gently to her naked shoulders, her dazzling bright expressionless face. He couldn't even think about her body; it was terrifying.

She sat behind a desk and looked at them.

Cal struck a masterful pose, his arms folded. "We have come on a scientific matter," he said haughtily, "not familiar to The Corporation, concerning several northern colonial areas."

She wrote deliberately on a small plain pad. Tonelessly, sweetly, she asked, "Your name?"

"Calvin Boersma."

Her veiled eyes swung to Albert. He couldn't possibly speak. His whole consciousness was occupied in not looking at her.

Cal said sonorously: "This is J. Albert LaRue, Professor of Plant Metabolism." Albert was positively proud of his name, the way Cal said it.

The most beautiful girl in the world whispered meltingly: "Go out this door and down the corridor to Mr. Blick's office. He'll be expecting you."

Albert chose this moment to try to look at her. And *she smiled!* Albert, completely routed, rushed to the door. He was grateful she hadn't done *that* before! Cal, with his greater experience and higher position in life, could linger a moment, leaning on the desk, to leer at her.

But all the same, when they reached the corridor, he was sweating.

Albert said carefully, "*She* wasn't an executive, was she?"

"No," said Cal, a little scornfully. "She's an Agency Model, what else? Of course, you probably don't see them much at the University, except at the Corporation Representative's Office and maybe the President's Office." Albert had never been near either. "She doesn't have much to do except to impress visitors, and of course stop the ones that don't belong here."

Albert hesitated. "She *was* impressive."

"She's impressive, all right," Cal agreed. "When you consider the Agency rates, and then realize that any member of the public who comes to the Regional Executive Building on business sees an Agency Model receptionist—then you know you're dealing with power, Albert."

Albert had a sudden idea. He ventured: "Would we have done better to have brought an Agency Model with us?"

Cal stared. "To go through the whole afternoon with us? Impossible, Albert! It'd cost you a year's salary."

Albert said eagerly: "No, that's the beauty of it, Cal! You see, I have a young cousin—I haven't seen her recently, of course, but she was drafted by the Agency, and I might have been able to get her to—" He faltered. Boersma was looking scandalized.

"Albert—excuse me. If your cousin had so much as walked into any business office with makeup on, she'd have had to collect Agency rates —or she'd have been out of the Agency like *that.* And owing them plenty." He finished consolingly, "A Model wouldn't have done the trick anyway."

Mr. Blick looked more like a scientist than a businessman, and his desk was a bit of a laboratory. At his left hand was an elaborate switchboard, curved so all parts would be in easy reach; most of the switches were in rows, the handles color-coded. As he nodded Cal to a seat his fingers flicked over three switches. The earphones and microphone clamped on his head had several switches too, and his right hand quivered beside a stenotype machine of unfamiliar complexity.

He spoke in an undertone into his mike, then his hand whizzed almost invisibly over the stenotype.

"Hello, Mr. Boersma," he said, flicking one last switch but not removing the earphones. "Please excuse my idiosyncrasies, it seems I actually work better this way." His voice was firm, resonant and persuasive.

Cal took over again. He opened with a round compliment for Mr. Blick's battery of gadgets, and then flowed smoothly on to an even more glowing series of compliments—which Albert realized with a qualm of embarrassment referred to *him.*

After the first minute or so, though, Albert found the talk less interesting than the interruptions. Mr. Blick would raise a forefinger apologetically but fast; switches would tumble; he would listen to the earphones, whisper into the mike, and perform incredibly on the absolutely silent stenotype. Shifting lights touched his face, and Albert realized the desk top contained at least one TV screen, as well as a bank of blinking colored lights. The moment the interruption was disposed of, Mr. Blick's faultless diction and pleasant voice would return Cal exactly to where he'd been. Albert was impressed.

Cal's peroration was an urgent appeal that Mr. Blick consider the importance to The Corporation, financially, of what he was about to learn. Then he turned to Albert, a little too abruptly.

"One single thought is uppermost in my mind," Albert stuttered, caught off guard. "Oxidase epsilon. I am resolved that The Corporation shall be made to see the importance—"

"Just a moment, Professor LaRue," came Mr. Blick's smooth Corporation voice. "You'll have to explain this to *me.* I don't have the background or the brains that you people in the academic line have. Now in layman's terms, just what *is* oxidase epsilon?" He grinned handsomely.

"Oh, don't feel bad," said Albert hastily. "Lots of my colleagues haven't heard of it either." This was only a half-truth. Every one of his colleagues that Albert met at the University in a normal working month had certainly heard of oxidase epsilon—from Albert. "It's an enzyme found in many plants but recognized only recently. You see, many of the laboratory species created during the last few decades have been unable to produce ordinary oxidase, or oxidase alpha, but surprisingly enough some of these have survived. This is due to the presence of a series of related compounds, of which oxidases beta, gamma, delta, and epsilon have been isolated, and beta and epsilon have been prepared in the laboratory."

Mr. Blick shifted uncertainly in his seat. Albert hurried on so he would see how simple it all was. "I have been studying the reactions catalyzed by oxidase epsilon in several species of *Triticum.* I found quite unexpectedly that none of them produce the enzyme themselves. Amazing, isn't it? All the oxidase epsilon in those plants comes from a fungus, *Puccinia triticina,* which infects them. This, or course, explains the failure of Hinshaw's group to produce viable *Triticum kaci* following—"

Mr. Blick smiled handsomely again. "Well now, Professor LaRue, you'll have to tell me what this means. In *my* terms—you understand."

Cal boomed portentously, "It may mean the saving of the economies of three of The Corporation's richest colonies." Rather dramatic, Albert thought.

Mr. Blick said appreciatively, "Very good. *Very* good. Tell me more. Which colonies—and why?" His right hand left its crouch to spring restlessly to the stenotype.

Albert resumed, buoyed by this flattering show of interest. "West Lapland in Europe, and Great Slave and Churchill on this continent. They're all Corporation colonies, recently opened up for wheat-growing by *Triticum witti,* and I've been told they're extremely productive."

"Who is Triticum Witti?"

Albert, shocked, explained patiently, "*Triticum witti* is one of the new species of wheat which depend on oxidase epsilon. And if the fungus *Puccinia triticina* on that wheat becomes a pest, sprays may be used to get rid of it. And a whole year's wheat crop in those colonies may be destroyed."

"Destroyed," Mr. Blick repeated wonderingly. His forefinger silenced Albert like a conductor's baton; then both his hands danced over keys and switches, and he was muttering into his microphone again.

Another interruption, thought Albert. He felt proper reverence for the undoubted importance of whatever Mr. Blick was settling, still he was bothered a little, too. Actually (he remembered suddenly) he had a reason to be so presumptuous: oxidase epsilon was important, too. Over five hundred million dollars had gone into these three colonies already, and no doubt a good many people.

However, it turned out this particular interruption must have been devoted to West Lapland, Great Slave, and Churchill after all. Mr. Blick abandoned his instrument panel and announced his congratulations to them: "Mr. Boersma, the decision has been made to assign an expediter to your case!" And he smiled heartily.

This was a high point for Albert.

He wasn't sure he knew what an expediter was, but he was sure from Mr. Blick's manner than an unparalleled honor had been given him. It almost made him dizzy to think of all this glittering building, all the attendants and Models and executives, bowing to *him,* as Mr. Blick's manner implied they must.

A red light flicked on and off on Mr. Blick's desk. As he turned to it he said, "Excuse me, gentlemen." Of course, Albert pardoned him mentally, you have to work.

He whispered to Cal, "Well, I guess we're doing pretty well."

"Huh? Oh, yes, very well," Cal whispered back. "So far."

"So far? Doesn't Mr. Blick understand the problem? All we have to do is give him the details now."

"Oh, no, Albert! I'm sure *he* can't make the decision. He'll have to send us to someone higher up."

"Higher up? Why? Do we have to explain it all over again?"

Cal turned in his chair so he could whisper to Albert less conspicuously. "Albert, an enterprise the size of The Corporation can't give consideration to every crackpot suggestion anyone tries to sell it. There have to be regular channels. Now the Plant Metabolism Department doesn't have any connections here (maybe we can do something about that), so we have to run a sort of obstacle course. It's survival of the fittest, Albert! Only the most worthwhile survive to see the Regional Director. Of course the Regional Director selects which of those to accept, but he doesn't have to sift through a lot of crackpot propositions."

Albert could see the analogy to natural selection. Still, he asked humbly: "How do you know the best suggestions get through? Doesn't it depend a lot on how good a salesman is handling them?"

"Very much so. Naturally!"

"But then—Suppose, for instance, I hadn't happened to know you. My good idea wouldn't have got past Mr. Blick."

"It wouldn't have got past the Model," Cal corrected. "Maybe not that far. But you see in that case it wouldn't have been a very important idea, because it wouldn't have been *put into effect.*" He said it with a very firm, practical jawline. "Unless of course someone else had had the initiative and resourcefulness to present the same idea better. Do you see now? *Really important ideas attract the sales talent to put them across.*"

Albert didn't understand the reasoning, he had to admit. It was such an important point, and he was missing it. He reminded himself humbly that a scientist is no expert outside his own field.

So all Mr. Blick had been telling them was that they had not yet been turned down. Albert's disappointment was sharp.

Still, he was curious. How had such a trivial announcement given him such euphoria? Could you produce that kind of effect just by your delivery? Mr. Blick could, apparently. The architecture, the Model, and all the rest had been build-up for him; and certainly they had helped the effect; but they didn't explain it.

What was the key? *Personality,* Albert realized. This was what businessmen meant by their technical term "personality." Personality was the asset Mr. Blick had exploited to rise to where he was—rather than becoming, say, a scientist.

The Blicks and Boersmas worked hard at it. Wistfully, Albert wondered how it was done. Of course the experts in this field didn't publish their results, and anyhow he had never studied it. But it was the most important field of human culture, for on it hinged the policy decisions of government—even of The Corporation!

He couldn't estimate whether Cal was as good as Mr. Blick, because he assumed Cal had never put forth a big effort on him, Albert He wasn't worth it.

He had one other question for Cal. "What is an expediter?"

"Oh, I thought you knew," boomed Cal. "They can be a big help That's why we're doing well to be assigned one. We're going to get into the *top levels,* Albert, where only a salesman of true merit can hope to put across an idea. An expediter can do it if anyone can. The expediters are too young to hold Key Executive Positions, but they're Men On The Way Up. They—"

Mr. Blick turned his head toward a door on his left, putting the force of his personality behind the gesture. "Mr. Demarest," he announced as the expediter walked into the room.

Mr. Demarest had captivating red curly sideburns, striking brown eyes, and a one-piece coverall in a somewhat loud pattern of black and beige. He almost trembled with excess energy. It was contagious; it made you feel as if you were as abnormally fit as he was.

He grinned his welcome at Albert and Cal, and chuckled merrily: "How do you do, Mr. Boersma."

It was as if Mr. Blick had been turned off. Albert hardly knew he was still in the room. Clearly Mr. Demarest was a Man On The Way Up indeed.

They rose and left the room with him—to a new corridor, very different from the last: weirdly lighted from a strip two feet above the floor, and lined with abstract statuary.

This, together with Mr. Demarest, made a formidable challenge.

Albert rose to it recklessly. "Oxidase epsilon," he proclaimed, "may mean the saving of three of The Corporation's richest colonies!"

Mr. Demarest responded with enthusiasm. "I agree 100 percent— our Corporation's crop of *Triticum witti* must be saved! Mr. Blick sent me a playback of your explanation by interoffice tube, Professor LaRue. You've got me on your side 100 percent! I want to assure you both, very sincerely, that I'll do my utmost to sell Mr. Southfield. Professor, you be ready to fill in the details when I'm through with what I know."

There was no slightest condescension or reservation in his voice. He would take care of things, Albert knew. What a relief!

Cal came booming in: "Your Mr. Blick seems like a competent man."

What a way to talk about a Corporation executive! Albert decided it was not just a simple faux pas, though. Apparently Cal had decided he had to be accepted by Mr. Demarest as an equal, and this was his opening. It seemed risky to Albert. In fact, it frightened him.

"There's just one thing, now, about your Mr. Blick," Cal was saying to Mr. Demarest, with a tiny wink that Albert was proud of having spotted. "I couldn't help wondering how he manages to find so much to do with those switches of his." Albert barely restrained a groan.

But Mr. Demarest grinned! "Frankly, Cal," he answered, "I'm not just sure how many of old Blick's switches are dummies."

Cal had succeeded! That was the main content of Mr. Demarest's remark.

But *were* Mr. Blick's switches dummies? Things were much simpler back—way back—at the University, where people said what they meant.

They were near the end of the corridor. Mr. Demarest said softly, "Mr. Southfield's Office." Clearly Mr. Southfield's presence was enough to curb even Mr. Demarest's boyishness.

They turned through an archway into a large room, lighted like the corridor, with statuary wilder still.

Mr. Southfield was at one side, studying papers in a vast easy chair: an elderly man, fantastically dressed but with a surprisingly ordinary face peeping over the crystal ruff on his magenta leotards. He ignored them. Mr. Demarest made it clear they were supposed to wait until they were called on.

Cal and Albert chose two of the bed-sized chairs facing Mr. Southfield, and waited expectantly.

Mr. Demarest whispered, "I'll be back in time to make the first presentation. Last-minute brush-up, you know." He grinned and clapped Cal smartly on the shoulder. Albert was relieved that he didn't do the same to him, but just shook his hand before leaving. It would have been too upsetting.

Albert sank back in his chair, tired from all he'd been through and relaxed by the soft lights.

It was the most comfortable chair he'd ever been in. It was more than comfortable, it was a deliciously irresistible invitation to relax completely. Albert was barely awake enough to notice that the chair was rocking him gently, tenderly massaging his neck and back.

He lay there, ecstatic. He didn't quite go to sleep. If the chair had been designed just a little differently, no doubt, it could have put him to sleep, but this one just let him rest carefree and mindless.

Cal spoke (and even Cal's quiet bass sounded harsh and urgent): "Sit up straighter, Albert!"

"Why?"

"Albert, any sales resistance you started with is going to be completely *gone* if you don't sit up enough to shut off that chair!"

"Sales resistance?" Albert pondered comfortably. "What have we got to worry about? Mr. Demarest is on our side, isn't he?"

"Mr. Demarest," Cal pointed out, "is *not* the Regional Director."

So they still might have problems! So the marvelous chair was just another trap where the unfit got lost! Albert resolved to himself: "From now on, one single thought will be uppermost in my mind: defending my sales resistance."

He repeated this to himself.

He repeated it again. . . .

"Albert!" There was genuine panic in Cal's voice now.

A fine way to defend his sales resistance! He had let the chair get him again. Regretfully he shifted his weight forward, reaching for the arms of the chair.

"*Watch it!*" said Cal. "Okay now, but don't use the arms. Just lean yourself forward. There." He explained, "The surface on the arms is rough and moist, and I can't think of any reason it should be—unless it's to give you narcotic through the skin! Tiny amounts, of course. But we can't afford any. First time I've ever seen that one in actual use," he admitted.

Albert was astonished, and in a moment he was more so. "Mr. Southfield's chair is the same as ours, and *he's* leaning back in it. Why, he's even stroking the arm while he reads!"

"I know." Cal shook his head. "Remarkable man, isn't he? Remarkable. Remember this, Albert. The true salesman, the man on the very pinnacle of achievement, is also—a connoisseur. Mr. Southfield is a connoisseur. He wants to be presented with the most powerful appeals known, for the sake of the pleasure he gets from the appeal itself. Albert, there is a strong strain of the sensuous, the self-indulgent, in every really successful man like Mr. Southfield. Why? Because to be successful he must have the most profound understanding of self-indulgence."

Albert noticed in passing that, just the same, Cal wasn't self-indulgent enough to trust himself to that chair. He didn't even make a show of doing so. Clearly in Mr. Southfield they had met somebody far above

Cal's level. It was unnerving. Oxidase epsilon seemed a terribly feeble straw to outweigh such a disadvantage.

Cal went on, "This is another reason for the institution of expediters. The top executive can't work surrounded by inferior salesmanship. He needs the stimulus and the luxury of receiving his data well packaged. The expediters can do it." He leaned over confidentially. "I've heard them called backscratchers for that reason," he whispered.

Albert was flattered that Cal admitted him to this trade joke.

Mr. Southfield looked up at the archway as someone came in—not Mr. Demarest, but a black-haired young woman. Albert looked inquiringly at Cal.

"Just a minute. I'll soon know who she is."

She stood facing Mr. Southfield, against the wall opposite Albert and Cal. Mr. Southfield said in a drowsy half-whisper, "Yes, Miss Drury, the ore-distribution pattern. Go on."

"She must be another expediter, on some other matter," Cal decided. "Watch her work, Albert. You won't get an opportunity like this often."

Albert studied her. She was not at all like an Agency Model; she was older than most of them (about thirty); she was fully dressed, in a rather sober black and gray business suit, snug around the hips; and she wasn't wearing makeup. She couldn't be even an ex-Model, she wasn't the type. Heavier in build, for one thing, and though she was very pretty it wasn't that unhuman blinding beauty. On the contrary, Albert enjoyed looking at her (even lacking Mr. Southfield's connoisseurship). He found Miss Drury's warm dark eyes and confident posture very pleasant and relaxing.

She began to talk, gently and musically, something about how to compute the most efficient routing of metallic ore traffic in the Great Lakes Region. Her voice became a chant, rising and falling, but with a little catch in it now and then. Lovely!

Her main device, though, sort of sneaked up on him, the way the chair had. It had been going on for some time before Albert was conscious of it. It was like the chair.

Miss Drury moved.

Her hips swung. Only a centimeter each way, but very, very sensuously. You could follow the motion in detail, because her dress was more than merely snug around the hips, you could see every muscle on her belly. The motion seemed entirely spontaneous, but Albert knew she must have worked hard on it.

The knowledge, however, didn't spoil his enjoyment.

"Gee," he marveled to Cal, "how can Mr. Southfield hear what she's saying?"

"Huh? Oh—she lowers her voice from time to time on purpose so we won't overhear Corporation secrets, but he's much nearer her than we are."

"That's not what I mean!"

"You mean why doesn't her delivery distract him from the message? Albert," Boersma said wisely, "if you were sitting in his chair you'd be getting the message, too—with crushing force. A superior presentation *always* directs attention to the message. But in Mr. Southfield's case it actually stimulates critical consideration as well! Remarkable man. An expert and a connoisseur."

Meanwhile Albert saw that Miss Drury had finished. Maybe she would stay and discuss her report with Mr. Southfield? No, after just a few words he dismissed her.

In a few minutes the glow caused by Miss Drury had changed to a glow of excited pride.

Here was he, plain old Professor LaRue, witnessing the drama of the nerve center of the Lakes Region—the interplay of titanic personalities, deciding the fate of millions. Why, he was even going to be involved in one of the decisions! He hoped the next expediter to see Mr. Southfield would be Mr. Demarest!

Something bothered him. "Cal, how can Mr. Demarest possibly be as—well—persuasive as Miss Drury? I mean—"

Now, Albert, you leave that to him. Sex is not the only possible vehicle. Experts can make strong appeals to the weakest and subtlest of human drives—even altruism! Oh yes, I know it's surprising to the layman, but even altruism can be useful."

"Really?" Albert was grateful for every tidbit.

"Real masters will sometimes prefer such a method out of sheer virtuosity," whispered Cal.

Mr. Southfield stirred a little in his chair, and Albert snapped to total alertness.

Sure enough, it was Mr. Demarest who came through the archway.

Certainly his entrance was no letdown. He strode in even more eagerly than he had into Mr. Blick's office. His costume glittered, his brown eyes glowed. He stood against the wall beyond Mr. Southfield; not quite straight, but with a slight wrestler's crouch. A taut spring.

He gave Albert and Cal only half a second's glance, but that glance was a tingling communication of comradeship and joy of battle. Albert felt himself a participant in something heroic.

Mr. Demarest began releasing all that energy slowly. He gave the background of West Lapland, Great Slave, and Churchill. Maps were flashed on the wall beside him (exactly how, Albert didn't follow), and the drama of arctic colonization was recreated by Mr. Demarest's sportscaster's voice. Albert would have thought Mr. Demarest was the over-modest hero of each project if he hadn't known all three had been done simultaneously. No, it was hard to believe, but all these vivid facts must have been served to Mr. Demarest by some research flunky within the last few minutes. And yet, how he had transfigured them!

The stirring narrative was reaching Mr. Southfield, too. He had actually sat up out of the easy chair.

Mr. Demarest's voice, like Miss Drury's, dropped in volume now and then. Albert and Cal were just a few feet too far away to overhear Corporation secrets.

As the saga advanced, Mr. Demarest changed from Viking to Roman. His voice, by beautifully controlled stages, became bubbling and hedonistic. Now, he was talking about grandiose planned expansions —and, best of all, about how much money The Corporation expected to make from the three colonies. The figures drooled through loose lips. He clapped Mr. Southfield on the shoulder. He stroked Mr. Southfield's arm; when he came to the estimated trade balances, he tickled his neck. Mr. Southfield showed his appreciation of change in mood by lying back in his chair again.

This didn't stop Mr. Demarest.

It seemed almost obscene. Albert covered his embarrassment by whispering, "I see why they call them backscratchers."

Cal frowned, waved him silent, and went on watching.

Suddenly Mr. Demarest's tone changed again: it became bleak, bitter, desperate. A threat to the calculated return on The Corporation's investment—even to the capital investment itself!

Mr. Southfield sat forward attentively to hear about this danger. Was that good? He hadn't done that with Miss Drury.

What Mr. Demarest said about the danger was, of course, essentially what Albert had told Mr. Blick, but Albert realized that it sounded a lot more frightening Mr. Demarest's way. When he was through, Albert felt physically chilly. Mr. Southfield sat saying nothing. What was he thinking? Could he fail to see the tragedy that threatened?

After a moment he nodded and said, "Nice presentation." He hadn't said that to Miss Drury, Albert exulted!

Mr. Demarest looked dedicated.

Mr. Southfield turned his whole body to face Albert, and looked him straight in the eyes. Albert was too alarmed to look away. Mr. Southfield's formerly ordinary jaw now jutted, his chest swelled imposingly. " *You,* I understand, are a well-informed worker on plant metabolism." His voice seemed to grow too, until it rolled in on Albert from all sides of the room. "Is it *your* opinion that the danger is great enough to justify taking up the time of the Regional Director?"

It wasn't fair. Mr. Southfield against J. Albert LaRue was a ridiculous mismatch anyway! And now Albert was taken by surprise—after too long a stretch as an inactive spectator—and hit with the suggestion that he had been *wasting Mr. Southfield's time* . . . that his proposition was not only not worth acting on, it was *a waste of the Regional Director's time.*

Albert struggled to speak.

Surely, after praising Mr. Demarest's presentation, Mr. Southfield would be lenient; he would take into account Albert's limited background; he wouldn't expect too much. Albert struggled to say anything.

He couldn't open his mouth.

As he sat staring at Mr. Southfield, he could feel his own shoulders drawing inward and all his muscles going limp.

Cal said, in almost a normal voice, "Yes."

That was enough, just barely. Albert whispered, "Yes," terrified at having found the courage.

Mr. Southfield glared down at him a moment more.

Then he said, "Very well, you may see the Regional Director. Mr. Demarest, take them there."

Albert followed Mr. Demarest blindly. His entire attention was concentrated on recovering from Mr. Southfield.

He had been one up, thanks to Mr. Demarest. Now, how could he have stayed one up? How should he have resisted Mr. Southfield's dizzying display of personality?

He played the episode back mentally over and over, trying to correct it to run as it should have. Finally he succeeded, at least in his mind. He saw what his attitude *should* have been. He *should* have kept his shoulders squared and his vocal cords loose, and faced Mr. Southfield confidently. Now he saw how to do it.

He walked erectly and firmly behind Mr. Demarest, and allowed a haughty half-smile to play on his lips.

He felt armed to face Mr. Southfield all by himself—or, since it seemed Mr. Southfield was not the Regional Director after all, even to face the Regional Director!

They stopped in front of a large double door guarded by an absolutely motionless man with a gun.

"Men," said Mr. Demarest with cheerful innocence, "I wish you luck. I wish you all the luck in the world."

Cal looked suddenly stricken but said, with casualness that didn't fool even Albert, "Wouldn't you like to come in with us?"

"Oh, no. Mr. Southfield told me only to bring you here. I'd be overstepping my bounds if I did any more. But all the good luck in the world, men!"

Cal said hearty goodbyes. But when he turned back to Albert he said, despairing: "The brushoff."

Albert could hardly take it in. "But—we get to make our presentation to the Regional Director, don't we?"

Boersma shrugged hopelessly, "Don't you see, Albert? Our presentation won't be good enough, without Demarest. When Mr. Southfield sent us on alone he was giving us the brushoff."

"Cal—are *you* going to back out too?"

"I should say not! It's a feather in our cap to have got this far, Albert. We have to follow up just as far as our abilities will take us!"

Albert went to the double door. He worried about the armed guard for a moment, but they weren't challenged. The guard hadn't even blinked, in fact.

Albert asked Cal, "Then we do still have a chance?"

He started to push the door open, then hesitated again. "But you'll do your best?"

"I should say so! You don't get to present a proposition to the Regional Director *every* day."

With determination, Albert drew himself even straighter, and prepared himself to meet an onslaught twice as overbearing as Mr. Southfield's. One single thought was uppermost in his mind: defending his sales resistance. He felt inches taller than before; he even slightly looked down at Cal and his pessimism.

Cal pushed the door open and they went in.

The Regional Director sat alone in a straight chair, at a plain desk in a very plain office about the size of most offices.

The Regional Director was a woman.

She was dressed about as any businesswoman might dress; as conservatively as Miss Drury. As a matter of fact, she looked like Miss Drury, fifteen years older. Certainly she had the same black hair and gentle oval face.

What a surprise! A *pleasant* surprise. Albert felt still bigger and more confident than he had outside. He would certainly get on well with this motherly, unthreatening person.

She was reading from a small microfilm viewer on an otherwise bare desk. Obviously she had only a little to do before she would be free. Albert patiently watched her read. She read very conscientiously, that was clear.

After a moment she glanced up at them briefly, with an apologetic smile, then down again. Her shy dark eyes showed so much! You could see how sincerely she welcomed them, and how sorry she was that she had so much work to do—how much she would prefer to be talking with *them.* Albert pitied her. From the bottom of his heart, he pitied her. Why, that small microfilm viewer, he realized, could perfectly well contain volumes of complicated Corporation reports. Poor woman! The poor woman who happened to be Regional Director read on.

Once in a while she passed one hand, wearily but determinedly, across her face. There was a slight droop to her shoulders. Albert pitied her more all the time. She was not too strong—she had such a big job—and she was so courageously trying to do her best with all those reports in the viewer!

Finally she raised her head.

It was clear she was not through; there was no relief on her face. But she raised her head to them.

Her affection covered them like a warm bath. Albert realized he was in a position to do the kindest thing he had ever done. He felt growing in himself the resolution to do it. He would!

He started toward the door.

Before he left she met his eyes once more, and her smile showed *such* appreciation for his understanding!

Albert felt there could be no greater reward.

Out in the park again he realized for the first time that Cal was right behind him.

They looked at each other for a long time.

Then Cal started walking again, toward the subway. "The brushoff," he said.

"I thought you said you'd do your best," said Albert. But he knew that Cal's "I did" was the truth.

They walked on slowly. Cal said, "Remarkable woman . . . A real master. Sheer virtuosity!"

Albert said, "Our society certainly rewards its most deserving members."

That one single thought was uppermost in his mind, all the long way home.

"REPENT, HARLEQUIN!" SAID THE TICKTOCKMAN

Harlan Ellison

There are always those who ask, what is it all about? For those who need to ask, for those who need points sharply made, who need to know "where it's at," this:

"The mass of men serve the state thus, not as men mainly, but as machines, with their bodies. They are the standing army, and the militia, jailors, constables, posse comitatus, etc. In most cases there is no free exercise whatever of the judgment or of the moral sense; but they put themselves on a level with wood and earth and stones; and wooden men can perhaps be manufactured that will serve the purposes as well. Such command no more respect than men of straw or a lump of dirt. They have the same sort of worth only as horses and dogs. Yet such as these even are commonly esteemed good citizens. Others—as most legislators, politicians, lawyers, ministers, and office-holders—serve the state chiefly with their heads; and, as they rarely make any moral distinctions, they are as likely to serve the Devil, without intending it, as God. A very few, as heroes, patriots, martyrs, reformers in the great sense, and *men,* serve the state with their consciences also, and so necessarily resist it for the most part; and they are commonly treated as enemies by it."

Henry David Thoreau,
"Civil Disobedience"

That is the heart of it. Now begin in the middle, and later learn the beginning; the end will take care of itself.

But because it was the very world it was, the very world they had allowed it to *become,* for months his activities did not come to the alarmed attention of The Ones Who Kept The Machine Functioning Smoothly, the ones who poured the very best butter over the cams and mainsprings of the culture. Not until it had become obvious that somehow, someway, he had become a notoriety, a celebrity, perhaps even a hero for (what Officialdom inescapably tagged) "an emotionally disturbed segment of the populace," did they turn it over to the Ticktockman and his legal machinery. But by then, because it was the very world it was, and they had no way to predict he would happen—possibly a strain of disease long-defunct, now, suddenly, reborn in a system where immunity had been forgotten, had lapsed—he had been allowed to become too real. Now he had form and substance.

He had become *a personality,* something they had filtered out of the system many decades ago. But there it was, and there *he* was, a very definitely imposing personality. In certain circles—middle-class circles—it was thought disgusting. Vulgar ostentation. Anarchistic. Shameful. In others, there was only sniggering, those strata where thought is subjugated to form and ritual, niceties, proprieties. But down below, ah, down below, where the people always needed their saints and sinners, their bread and circuses, their heroes and villains, he was considered a Bolivar; a Napoleon; a Robin Hood; a Dick Bong (Ace of Aces); a Jesus; a Jomo Kenyatta.

And at the top—where, like socially-attuned Shipwreck Kellys, even tremor and vibration threatens to dislodge the wealthy, powerful, and titled from their flagpoles—he was considered a menace; a heretic; a rebel; a disgrace; a peril. He was known down the line, to the very heartmeat core, but the important reactions were high above and far below. At the very top, at the very bottom.

So his file was turned over, along with his time-card and his cardio-plate, to the office of the Ticktockman.

The Ticktockman: very much over six feet tall, often silent, a soft purring man when things went timewise. The Ticktockman.

Even in the cubicles of the hierarchy, where fear was generated, seldom suffered, he was called the Ticktockman. But no one called him that to his mask.

You don't call a man a hated name, not when that man, behind his mask, is capable of revoking the minutes, the hours, the days and nights, the years of your life. He was called the Master Timekeeper to his mask. It was safer that way.

"This is *what* he is," said the Ticktockman with genuine softness, "but not *who* he is? This time-card I'm holding in my left hand has a name on it, but it is the name of *what* he is, not *who* he is. This cardioplate here in my right hand is also named, but not whom named, merely what named. Before I can exercise proper revocation, I have to know who this what is."

To his staff, all the ferrets, all the loggers, all the finks, all the commex, even the mineez, he said, "Who is this Harlequin?"

He was not purring smoothly. Timewise, it was jangle.

However, it *was* the longest single speech they had ever heard him utter at one time, the staff, the ferrets, the loggers, the finks, the commex, but not the mineez, who usually weren't around to know, in any case. But even they scurried to find out.

Who is the Harlequin?

High above the third level of the city, he crouched on the humming aluminum-frame platform of the air-boat (foof! air-boat, indeed! swizzleskid is what it was, with a tow-rack jerryrigged) and stared down at the neat Mondrian arrangement of the buildings.

Somewhere nearby, he could hear the metronomic left-right-left of the 2:47 P.M. shift, entering the Timkin roller-bearing plant in their sneakers. A minute later, precisely, he heard the softer right-left-right of the 5:00 A.M. formation, going home.

An elfish grin spread across his tanned features, and his dimples appeared for a moment. Then, scratching at his thatch of auburn hair, he shrugged within his motley, as though girding himself for what came next, and threw the joystick forward, and bent into the wind as the air-boat dropped. He skimmed over a slidewalk, purposely dropping a few feet to crease the tassels of the ladies of fashion, and—inserting thumbs in large ears—he stuck out his tongue, rolled his eyes, and went wugga-wugga-wugga. It was a minor diversion. One pedestrian skittered and tumbled, sending parcels everywhichway, another wet herself, a third keeled slantwise and the walk was stopped automatically by the servitors till she could be resuscitated. It was a minor diversion.

Then he swirled away on a vagrant breeze, and was gone. Hi-ho.

As he rounded the cornice of the Time-Motion Study Building, he saw the shift, just boarding the slidewalk. With practiced motion and an absolute conservation of movement, they sidestepped up onto the slowstrip and (in a chorus line reminiscent of a Busby Berkeley film of the antediluvian 1930s) advanced across the strips ostrich-walking till they were lined up on the expresstrip.

Once more, in anticipation, the elfin grin spread, and there was a tooth missing back there on the left side. He dipped, skimmed, and swooped over them; and then, scrunching about on the air-boat, he released the holding pins that fastened shut the ends of the home-made pouring troughs that kept his cargo from dumping prematurely. And as he pulled the trough-pins, the air-boat slid over the factory workers and one hundred and fifty thousand dollars' worth of jelly beans cascaded down on the expresstrip.

Jelly beans! Millions and billions of purples and yellows and greens and licorice and grape and raspberry and mint and round and smooth and crunchy outside and soft-mealy inside and sugary and bouncing jouncing tumbling clittering clattering skittering fell on the heads and shoulders and hardhats and carapaces of the Timkin workers, tinkling on the slidewalk and bouncing away and rolling about underfoot and filling the sky on their way down with all the colors of joy and childhood and holidays, coming down in a steady rain, a solid wash, a torrent of color and sweetness out of the sky from above, and entering a universe of sanity and metronomic order with quite-mad coocoo newness. Jelly beans!

The shift workers howled and laughed and were pelted, and broke ranks, and the jelly beans managed to work their way into the mechanism of the slidewalks after which there was a hideous scraping as the sound of a million fingernails rasped down a quarter of a million blackboards, followed by a coughing and a sputtering, and then the slidewalks all stopped and everyone was dumped thisawayandthataway in a jackstraw tumble, and still laughing and popping little jelly bean eggs of childish color into their mouths. It was a holiday, and a jollity, an absolute insanity, a giggle. But. . . .

The shift was delayed seven minutes.

They did not get home for seven minutes.

The master schedule was thrown off by seven minutes.

Quotas were delayed by inoperative slidewalks for seven minutes.

He had tapped the first domino in the line, and one after another, like chik chik chik, the others had fallen.

The System had been seven minutes worth of disrupted. It was a tiny matter, one hardly worthy of note, but in a society where the single driving force was order and unity and promptness and clocklike precision and attention to the clock, reverence of the gods of the passage of time, it was a disaster of major importance.

So he was ordered to appear before the Ticktockman. It was broadcast across every channel of the communications web. He was ordered to be *there* at 7:00 dammit on time. And they waited, and they waited, but he didn't show up till almost ten-thirty, at which time he merely sang a little song about moonlight in a place no one had ever heard of, called Vermont, and vanished again. But they had all been waiting since seven, and it wrecked *hell* with their schedules. So the question remained: Who is the Harlequin?

But the *unasked* question (more important of the two) was: how did we get *into* this position, where a laughing, irresponsible japer of jabberwocky and jive could disrupt our entire economic and cultural life with a hundred and fifty thousand dollars' worth of jelly beans. . . .

Jelly for God's sake beans! This is madness! Where did he get the money to buy a hundred and fifty thousand dollars' worth of jelly beans? (They knew it would have cost that much, because they had a team of Situation Analysts pulled off another assignment, and rushed to the slidewalk scene to sweep up and count the candies, and produce findings, which disrupted *their* schedules and threw their entire branch at least a day behind.) Jelly beans! Jelly . . . *beans?* Now wait a second—a second accounted for—no one has manufactured jelly beans for over a hundred years. Where did he get jelly beans?

That's another good question. More than likely it will never be answered to your complete satisfaction. But then, how many questions ever are?

The middle you know. Here is the beginning. How it starts:

A desk pad. Day for day, and turn each day. 9:00—open the mail. 9:45—appointment with planning commission board. 10:30—discuss installation progress charts with J. L. 11:45—pray for rain. 12:00— lunch. *And so it goes.*

"I'm sorry, Miss Grant, but the time for interviews was set at 2:30, and it's almost five now. I'm sorry you're late, but those are the rules. You'll have to wait till next year to submit application for this college again." *And so it goes.*

The 10:10 local stops at Cresthaven, Galesville, Tonawanda Junction, Selby, and Farnhurst, but not at Indiana City, Lucasville, and Colton, except on Sunday. The 10:35 express stops at Galesville, Selby, and Indiana City, except on Sunday & Holidays, at which time it stops at . . . *and so it goes.*

"I couldn't wait, Fred. I had to be at Pierre Cartain's by 3:00, and you said you'd meet me under the clock in the terminal at 2:45, and you weren't there, so I had to go on. You're always late, Fred. If you'd been there, we could have sewed it up together, but as it was, well, I took the order alone. . . ." *And so it goes.*

Dear Mr. and Mrs. Atterley: in reference to your son Gerold's constant tardiness, I am afraid we will have to suspend him from school unless some more reliable method can be instituted guaranteeing he will arrive at his classes on time. Granted he is an exemplary student, and his marks are high, his constant flouting of the schedules of this school makes it impractical to maintain him in a system where the other children seem capable of getting where they are supposed to be on time *and so it goes.*

YOU CANNOT VOTE UNLESS YOU APPEAR AT 8:45 A.M.

"I don't care if the script is *good,* I need it Thursday!"

CHECK-OUT TIME IS 2:00 P.M.

"You got here late. The job's taken. Sorry."

YOUR SALARY HAS BEEN DOCKED FOR TWENTY MINUTES' TIME LOST.

"God, what time is it, I've gotta run!"

And so it goes. And so it goes. And so it goes. And so it goes goes goes goes goes tick tock tick tock tick tock and one day we no longer let time serve us, we serve time and we are slaves of the schedule, worshippers of the sun's passing, bound into a life predicated on restrictions because the system will not function if we don't keep the schedule tight.

Until it becomes more than a minor inconvenience to be late. It becomes a sin. Then a crime. Then a crime punishable by this:

EFFECTIVE 15 JULY 2389, 12:00:00 midnight, the office of the Master Timekeeper will require all citizens to submit their time-cards and cardioplates for processing. In accordance with Statute 555-7-SGH-999 governing the revocation of time per capita, all cardioplates will be keyed to the individual holder and—

What they had done, was devise a method of curtailing the amount of life a person could have. If he was ten minutes late, he lost ten minutes of his life. An hour was proportionately worth more revocation. If someone was consistently tardy, he might find himself, on a Sunday night, receiving a communique from the Master Timekeeper that his time had run out, and he would be "turned off" at high noon on Monday, please straighten your affairs, sir.

And so, by this simple scientific expedient (utilizing a scientific process held dearly secret by the Ticktockman's office) the System was maintained. It was the only expedient thing to do. It was, after all, patriotic. The schedules had to be met. After all, there *was* a war on!

But, wasn't there always?

"Now that is really disgusting," the Harlequin said, when pretty Alice showed him the wanted poster. "Disgusting and *highly* improbable. After all, this isn't the days of desperadoes. A *wanted* poster!"

"You know," Alice noted, "you speak with a great deal of inflection."

"I'm sorry," said the Harlequin, humbly.

"No need to be sorry. You're always saying 'I'm sorry.' You have such massive guilt, Everett, it's really very sad."

"I'm sorry," he repeated, then pursed his lips so the dimples appeared momentarily. He hadn't wanted to say that at all. "I have to go out again. I have to *do* something."

Alice slammed her coffee-bulb down on the counter. "Oh for God's *sake,* Everett, can't you stay home just *one* night! Must you always be out in that ghastly clown suit, running around *annoying* people?"

"I'm—" he stopped, and clapped the jester's hat onto his auburn thatch with a tiny tingling of bells. He rose, rinsed out his coffee-bulb at the tap, and put it into the drier for a moment. "I have to go."

She didn't answer. The faxbox was purring, and she pulled a sheet out, read it, threw it toward him on the counter. "It's about you. Of course. You're ridiculous."

He read it quickly. It said the Ticktockman was trying to locate him. He didn't care, he was going out to be late again. At the door, dredging for an exit line, he hurled back petulantly, "Well, *you* speak with inflection, *too!*"

Alice rolled her pretty eyes heavenward. "You're ridiculous." The Harlequin stalked out, slamming the door, which sighed shut softly, and locked itself.

There was a gentle knock, and Alice got up with an exhalation of exasperated breath, and opened the door. He stood there. "I'll be back about ten-thirty, okay?"

She pulled a rueful face. "Why do you tell me that? Why? You *know* you'll be late! You *know it!* You're *always* late, so why do you tell me these dumb things?" She closed the door.

On the other side, the Harlequin nodded to himself. *She's right. She's always right. I'll be late. I'm always late. Why do I tell her these dumb things?*

He shrugged again, and went off to be late once more.

He had fired off the firecracker rockets that said: I will attend the 115th annual International Medical Association Invocation at 8:00 P.M. precisely. I do hope you will all be able to join me.

The words had burned in the sky, and of course the authorities were there, lying in wait for him. They assumed, naturally, that he would be late. He arrived 20 minutes early, while they were setting up the spiderwebs to trap and hold him, and blowing a large bullhorn, he frightened and unnerved them so, their own moisturized encirclement webs sucked closed, and they were hauled up, kicking and shrieking, high above the amphitheater's floor. The Harlequin laughed and laughed, and apologized profusely. The physicians, gathered in solemn conclave, roared with laughter, and accepted the Harlequin's apologies with exaggerated bowing and posturing, and a merry time was had by all, who thought the Harlequin was a regular foofaraw in fancy pants; all, that is, but the authorities, who had been sent out by the office of the Ticktockman, who hung there like so much dockside cargo, hauled up above the floor of the amphitheater in a most unseemly fashion.

(In another part of the same city where the Harlequin carried on his "activities," totally unrelated in every way to what concerns here, save that it illustrates the Ticktockman's power and import, a man named Marshall Delahanty received his turn-off notice from the Ticktockman's office. His wife received the notification from the gray-suited minee who delivered it, with the traditional "look of sorrow" plastered hideously across his face. She knew what it was, even without unsealing it. It was a billet-doux of immediate recognition to everyone these days. She gasped, and held it as though it were a glass slide tinged with botulism, and prayed it was not for her. Let it be for Marsh, she thought, brutally, realistically, or one of the kids, but not for me, please dear God, not for me. And then she opened it, and it *was* for Marsh, and she was at one and the same time horrified and relieved. The next trooper in the line had caught the bullet. "Marshall," she screamed, "Marshall! Termination, Marshall! OhmiGod, Marshall, whattl we do, whattl we do, Marshall omigodmarshall . . ." and in their home that night was the sound of tearing paper and fear, and the stink of madness went up the flue and there was nothing, absolutely nothing they could do about it.

(But Marshall Delahanty tried to run. And early the next day, when turn-off time came, he was deep in the forest 200 miles away, and the office of the Ticktockman blanked his cardioplate, and Marshall Delahanty keeled over, running, and his heart stopped, and the blood dried up on its way to his brain, and he was dead that's all. One light went out on his sector map in the office of the Master Timekeeper, while notification was entered for fax reproduction, and Georgette Delahanty's name was entered on the dole roles till she could re-marry. Which is the end of the footnote, and all the point that need be made, except don't laugh, because that is what would happen to the Harlequin if ever the Ticktockman found out his real name. It isn't funny.)

The shopping level of the city was thronged with the Thursday-colors of the buyers. Women in canary yellow chitons and men in pseudo-Tyrolean outfits that were jade and leather and fit very tightly, save for the balloon pants.

When the Harlequin appeared on the still-being-constructed shell of the new Efficiency Shopping Center, his bullhorn to his elfishly-laughing lips, everyone pointed and stared, and he berated them:

"Why let them order you about? Why let them tell you to hurry and scurry like ants or maggots? Take your time! Saunter a while! Enjoy the sunshine, enjoy the breeze, let life carry you at your own pace! Don't be slaves of time, it's a helluva way to die, slowly, by degrees . . . down with the Ticktockman!"

Who's the nut? most of the shoppers wanted to know. Who's the nut oh wow I'm gonna be late I gotta run. . . .

And the construction gang on the Shopping Center received an urgent order from the office of the Master Timekeeper that the dangerous criminal known as the Harlequin was atop their spire, and their aid was urgently needed in apprehending him. The work crew said no, they would lose time on their construction schedule, but the Ticktockman managed to pull the proper threads of governmental webbing, and they were told to cease work and catch that nitwit up there on the spire with the bullhorn. So a dozen and more burly workers began climbing into their construction platforms, releasing the a-grav plates, and rising toward the Harlequin.

After the debacle (in which, through the Harlequin's attention to personal safety, no one was seriously injured), the workers tried to reassemble, and assault him again, but it was too late. He had vanished. It had attracted quite a crowd, however, and the shopping cycle was thrown off by hours, simply hours. The purchasing needs of the system were therefore falling behind, and so measures were taken to accelerate the cycle for the rest of the day, but it got bogged down and speeded up and they sold too many float-valves and not nearly enough wegglers, which meant that the popli ratio was off, which made it necessary to rush cases and cases of spoiling Smash-O to stores that usually needed a case only every three or four hours. The shipments were bollixed, the trans-shipments were misrouted, and in the end, even the swizzleskid industries felt it.

"Don't come back till you have him!" the Ticktockman said, very quietly, very sincerely, extremely dangerously.

They used dogs. They used probes. They used cardioplate crossoffs. They used teepers. They used bribery. They used stiktytes. They used intimidation. They used torment. They used torture. They used finks. They used cops. They used search&seizure. They used fallaron. They used betterment incentive. They used fingerprints. They used Bertillon. They used cunning. They used guile. They used treachery. They used Raoul Mitgong, but he didn't help much. They used applied physics. They used techniques of criminology.

And what the hell: they caught him.

After all, his name was Everett C. Marm, and he wasn't much to begin with, except a man who had no sense of time.

"Repent, Harlequin!" said the Ticktockman.

"Get stuffed!" the Harlequin replied, sneering.

"You've been late a total of sixty-three years, five months, three weeks, two days, twelve hours, forty-one minutes, fifty-nine seconds, point oh three six one one one microseconds. You've used up everything you can, and more. I'm going to turn you off."

"Scare someone else. I'd rather be dead than live in a dumb world with a bogeyman like you."

"It's my job."

"You're full of it. You're a tyrant. You have no right to order people around and kill them if they show up late."

"You can't adjust. You can't fit in."

"Unstrap me, and I'll fit my fist into your mouth."

"You're a non-conformist."

"That didn't used to be a felony."

"It is now. Live in the world around you."

"I hate it. It's a terrible world."

"Not everyone thinks so. Most people enjoy order."

"I don't, and most of the people I know don't."

"That's not true. How do you think we caught you?"

"I'm not interested."

"A girl named pretty Alice told us who you were."

"That's a lie."

"It's true. You unnerve her. She wants to belong, she wants to conform, I'm going to turn you off."

"Then do it already, and stop arguing with me."

"I'm not going to turn you off."

"You're an idiot!"

"Repent, Harlequin!" said the Ticktockman.

"Get stuffed."

So they sent him to Coventry. And in Coventry they worked him over. It was just like what they did to Winston Smith in "1984," which was a book none of them knew about, but the techniques are really quite ancient, and so they did it to Everett C. Marm, and one day quite a long time later, the Harlequin appeared on the communications web, appearing elfish and dimpled and bright-eyed, and not at all brainwashed, and he said he had been wrong, that it was a good, a very good thing indeed, to belong, and be right on time hip-ho and away we go, and everyone stared up at him on the public screens that covered an entire city block, and they said to themselves, well, you see, he was just a nut after all, and if that's the way the system is run, then let's do it that way, because it doesn't pay to fight city hall, or in this case, the Ticktockman. So Everett C. Marm was destroyed, which was a loss, because of what Thoreau said earlier, but you can't make an omelet without breaking a few eggs, and in every revolution, a few die who shouldn't, but they have to, because that's the way it happens, and if you make only a little change, then it seems to be worthwhile. Or, to make the point lucidly:

"Uh, excuse me, sir, I, uh, don't know how to uh, to uh, tell you this, but you were three minutes late. The schedule is a little, uh, bit off."

He grinned sheepishly.

"That's ridiculous!" murmured the Ticktockman behind his mask. "Check your watch." And then he went into his office, going mrmee, mrmee, mrmee, mrmee.

BALANCED ECOLOGY

James H. Schmitz

The diamondwood tree farm was restless this morning. Ilf Cholm
had been aware of it for about an hour but had said nothing to Auris,
thinking he might be getting a summer fever or a stomach upset and
imagining things and that Auris would decide they should go back to
the house so Ilf's grandmother could dose him. But the feeling continued to grow, and by now Ilf knew it was the farm.

Outwardly, everyone in the forest appeared to be going about their
usual business. There had been a rainfall earlier in the day; and the
tumbleweeds had uprooted themselves and were moving about in the
bushes, lapping water off the leaves. Ilf had noticed a small one rolling
straight towards a waiting slurp and stopped for a moment to watch
the slurp catch it. The slurp was of average size, which gave it a
tongue-reach of between 12 and 14 feet, and the tumbleweed was already within range.

The tongue shot out suddenly, a thin, yellow flash. Its tip flicked
twice around the tumbleweed, jerked it off the ground and back to the
feed opening in the imitation tree stump within which the rest of the
slurp was concealed. The tumbleweed said "Oof!" in the surprised way
they always did when something caught them, and went in through the

From *Analog Science Fact and Fiction,* March, 1965. Reprinted by permission of the
author and the author's agents, Scott Meredith Literary Agency, Inc., 580 Fifth Avenue,
New York, New York 10036.

opening. After a moment, the slurp's tongue tip appeared in the opening again and waved gently around, ready for somebody else of the right size to come within reach.

Ilf, just turned 11 and rather small for his age, was the right size for this slurp, though barely. But, being a human boy, he was in no danger. The slurps of the diamondwood farms on Wrake didn't attack humans. For a moment, he was tempted to tease the creature into a brief fencing match. If he picked up a stick and banged on the stump with it a few times, the slurp would become annoyed and dart its tongue out and try to knock the stick from his hand.

But it wasn't the day for entertainment of that kind. Ilf couldn't shake off his crawly, uncomfortable feeling, and while he had been standing there, Auris and Sam had moved a couple of hundred feet farther uphill, in the direction of the Queen Grove, and home. He turned and sprinted after them, caught up with them as they came out into one of the stretches of grassland which lay between the individual groves of diamondwood trees.

Auris, who was two years, two months, and two days older than Ilf, stood on top of Sam's semiglobular shell, looking off to the right towards the valley where the diamondwood factory was. Most of the world of Wrake was on the hot side, either rather dry or rather steamy; but this was cool mountain country. Far to the south, below the valley and the foothills behind it, lay the continental plain, shimmering like a flat, green-brown sea. To the north and east were higher plateaus, above the level where the diamondwood liked to grow. Ilf ran past Sam's steadily moving bulk to the point where the forward rim of the shell made a flat upward curve, close enough to the ground so he could reach it.

Sam rolled a somber brown eye back for an instant as Ilf caught the shell and swung up on it, but his huge beaked head didn't turn. He was a mossback, Wrake's version of the turtle pattern, and, except for the full-grown trees and perhaps some members of the clean-up squad, the biggest thing on the farm. His corrugated shell was overgrown with a plant which had the appearance of long green fur; and occasionally when Sam fed, he would extend and use a pair of heavy arms with three-fingered hands, normally held folded up against the lower rim of the shell.

Auris had paid no attention to Ilf's arrival. She still seemed to be watching the factory in the valley. She and Ilf were cousins but didn't resemble each other. Ilf was small and wiry, with tight-curled red hair. Auris was slim and blond, and stood a good head taller than he did. He thought she looked as if she owned everything she could see from the top of Sam's shell; and she did, as a matter of fact, own a good deal of it—nine tenths of the diamondwood farm and nine tenths of the factory. Ilf owned the remaining tenth of both.

He scrambled up the shell, grabbing the moss-fur to haul himself along, until he stood beside her. Sam, awkward as he looked when walking, was moving at a good ten miles an hour, clearly headed for the Queen Grove. Ilf didn't know whether it was Sam or Auris who had decided to go back to the house. Whichever it had been, he could feel the purpose of going there.

"They're nervous about something," he told Auris, meaning the whole farm. "Think there's a big storm coming?"

"Doesn't look like a storm," Auris said.

Ilf glanced about the sky, agreed silently. "Earthquake, maybe?"

Auris shook her head. "It doesn't feel like earthquake."

She hadn't turned her gaze from the factory. Ilf asked, "Something going on down there?"

Auris shrugged. "They're cutting a lot today," she said. "They got in a limit order."

Sam swayed on into the next grove while Ilf considered the information. Limit orders were fairly unusual; but it hardly explained the general uneasiness. He sighed, sat down, crossed his legs, and looked about. This was a grove of young trees, 15 years and less. There was plenty of open space left between them. Ahead, a huge tumbleweed was dying, making happy, chuckling sounds as it pitched its scarlet seed pellets far out from its slowly unfolding leaves. The pellets rolled hurriedly farther away from the old weed as soon as they touched the ground. In a 12-foot circle about their parent, the earth was being disturbed, churned, shifted steadily about. The clean-up squad had arrived to dispose of the dying tumbleweed; as Ilf looked, it suddenly settled six or seven inches deeper into the softened dirt. The pellets were hurrying to get beyond the reach of the clean-up squad so they wouldn't get hauled down, too. But half-grown tumbleweeds, speckled yellow-green and ready to start their rooted period, were rolling through the grove towards the disturbed area. They would wait around the edge of the circle until the clean-up squad finished, then move in and put down their roots. The ground where the squad had worked recently was always richer than any other spot in the forest.

Ilf wondered, as he had many times before, what the clean-up squad looked like. Nobody ever caught so much as a glimpse of them. Riquol Cholm, his grandfather, had told him of attempts made by scientists to catch a member of the squad with digging machines. Even the smallest ones could dig much faster than the machines could dig after them, so the scientists always gave up finally and went away.

"Ilf, come in for lunch!" called Ilf's grandmother's voice.

Ilf filled his lungs, shouted, "Coming, grand—"

He broke off, looked up at Auris. She was smirking.

"Caught me again," Ilf admitted. "Dumb humbugs!" He yelled, "Come out, Lying Lou! I know who it was."

Meldy Cholm laughed her low, sweet laugh, a silverbell called the giant greenweb of the Queen Grove sounded its deep harp note, more or less all together. Then Lying Lou and Gabby darted into sight, leaped up on the moss-back's hump. The humbugs were small, brown, bobtailed animals, built with spider leanness and very quick. They had round skulls, monkey faces, and the pointed teeth of animals who lived by catching and killing other animals. Gabby sat down beside Ilf, inflating and deflating his voice pouch, while Lou burst into a series of rattling, clicking, spitting sounds.

"They've been down at the factory?" Ilf asked.

"Yes," Auris said. "Hush now. I'm listening."

Lou was jabbering along at the rate at which the humbugs chattered among themselves, but this sounded like, and was, a recording of human voices played back at high speed. When Auris wanted to know what people somewhere were talking about, she sent the humbugs off to listen. They remembered everything they heard, came back and repeated it to her at their own speed, which saved time. Ilf, if he tried hard, could understand scraps of it. Auris understood it all. She was hearing now what the people at the factory had been saying during the morning.

Gabby inflated his voice pouch part way, remarked in Grandfather Riquol's strong, rich voice, "My, my! We're not being quite on our best behavior today, are we, Ilf?"

"Shut up," said Ilf.

"Hush now," Gabby said in Auris' voice. "I'm listening." He added in Ilf's voice, sounding crestfallen, "Caught me again!" then chuckled nastily.

Ilf made a fist of his left hand and swung fast. Gabby became a momentary brown blur, and was sitting again on Ilf's other side. He looked at Ilf with round, innocent eyes, said in a solemn tone. "We must pay more attention to details, men. Mistakes can be expensive!"

He'd probably picked that up at the factory. Ilf ignored him. Trying to hit a humbug was a waste of effort. So was talking back to them. He shifted his attention to catching what Lou was saying; but Lou had finished up at that moment. She and Gabby took off instantly in a leap from Sam's back and were gone in the bushes. Ilf thought they were a little jittery and erratic in their motions today, as if they, too, were keyed up even more than usual. Auris walked down to the front lip of the shell and sat on it, dangling her legs. Ilf joined her there.

"What were they talking about at the factory?" he asked.

"They did get in a limit order yesterday," Auris said. "And another one this morning. They're not taking any more orders until they've filled those two."

"That's good, isn't it?" Ilf asked.

"I guess so."

After a moment, Ilf asked, "Is that what *they're* worrying about?"

"I don't know," Auris said. But she frowned.

Sam came lumbering up to another stretch of open ground, stopped while he was still well back among the trees. Auris slipped down from the shell, said, "Come on but don't let them see you," and moved ahead through the trees until she could look into the open. Ilf followed her as quietly as he could.

"What's the matter?" he inquired. A hundred and fifty yards away, on the other side of the open area, towered the Queen Grove, its tops dancing gently like armies of slender green spears against the blue sky. The house wasn't visible from here; it was a big one-story bungalow built around the trunks of a number of trees deep within the grove. Ahead of them lay the road which came up from the valley and wound on through the mountains to the west.

Auris said, "An aircar came down here a while ago. . . . There it is!"

They looked at the aircar parked at the side of the road on their left, a little distance away. Opposite the car was an opening in the Queen Grove where a path led to the house. Ilf couldn't see anything very interesting about the car. It was neither new nor old, looked like any ordinary aircar. The man sitting inside it was nobody they knew.

"Somebody's here on a visit," Ilf said.

"Yes," Auris said. "Uncle Kugus has come back."

Ilf had to reflect an instant to remember who Uncle Kugus was. Then it came to his mind in a flash. It had been some while ago, a year or so. Uncle Kugus was a big, handsome man with thick, black eyebrows, who always smiled. He wasn't Ilf's uncle but Auris'; but he'd had presents for both of them when he arrived. He had told Ilf a great many jokes. He and Grandfather Riquol had argued on one occasion for almost two hours about something or other; Ilf couldn't remember now what it had been. Uncle Kugus had come and gone in a tiny, beautiful, bright yellow aircar, had taken Ilf for a couple of rides in it, and told him about winning races with it. Ilf hadn't had too bad an impression of him.

"That isn't him," he said, "and that isn't his car."

"I know. He's in the house," Auris said. "He's got a couple of people with him. They're talking with Riquol and Meldy."

A sound rose slowly from the Queen Grove as she spoke, deep and resonant, like the stroke of a big, old clock or the hum of a harp. The man in the aircar turned his head towards the grove to listen. The sound was repeated twice. It came from the giant greenweb at the far end of the grove and could be heard all over the farm, even, faintly, down in the valley when the wind was favorable. Ilf said, "Lying Lou and Gabby were up here?"

"Yes. They went down to the factory first, then up to the house."

"What are they talking about in the house?" Ilf inquired.

"Oh, a lot of things." Auris frowned again. "We'll go and find out, but we won't let them see us right away."

Something stirred beside Ilf. He looked down and saw Lying Lou and Gabby had joined them again. The humbugs peered for a moment at the man in the aircar, then flicked out into the open, on across the road, and into the Queen Grove, like small, flying shadows, almost impossible to keep in sight. The man in the aircar looked about in a puzzled way, apparently uncertain whether he'd seen something move or not.

"Come on," Auris said.

Ilf followed her back to Sam. Sam lifted his head and extended his neck. Auris swung herself upon the edge of the undershell beside the neck, crept on hands and knees into the hollow between the upper and lower shells. Ilf climbed in after her. The shell-cave was a familiar place. He'd scuttled in there many times when they'd been caught outdoors in one of the violent electric storms which came down through the mountains from the north or when the ground began to shudder in an earthquake's first rumbling. With the massive curved shell above him and the equally massive flat shell below, the angle formed by the cool, leathery wall which was the side of Sam's neck and the front of his shoulder seemed like the safest place in the world to be on such occasions.

The undershell tilted and swayed beneath Ilf now as the mossback started forward. He squirmed around and looked out through the opening between the shells. They moved out of the grove, headed towards the road at Sam's steady walking pace. Ilf couldn't see the aircar and wondered why Auris didn't want the man in the car to see them. He wriggled uncomfortably. It was a strange, uneasy-making morning in every way.

They crossed the road, went swishing through high grass with Sam's ponderous side-to-side sway like a big ship sailing over dry land, and came to the Queen Grove. Sam moved on into the green-tinted shade under the Queen Trees. The air grew cooler. Presently he turned to the right, and Ilf saw a flash of blue ahead. That was the great thicket of flower bushes, in the center of which was Sam's sleeping pit.

Sam pushed through the thicket, stopped when he reached the open space in the center to let Ilf and Auris climb out of the shell-cave. Sam then lowered his forelegs, one after the other, into the pit, which was lined so solidly with tree roots that almost no earth showed between them, shaped like a mold to fit the lower half of his body, tilted forward, drawing neck and head back under his shell, slid slowly into the pit, straightened out and settled down. The edge of his upper shell was now level with the edge of the pit, and what still could be seen of him looked simply like a big, moss-grown boulder. If nobody came to disturb him, he might stay there unmoving the rest of the year. There were mossbacks in other groves of the farm which had never come out of their sleeping pits or given any indication of being awake since Ilf could remember. They lived an enormous length of time and a nap of half a dozen years apparently meant nothing to them.

Ilf looked questioningly at Auris. She said, "We'll go up to the house and listen to what Uncle Kugus is talking about."

They turned into a path which led from Sam's place to the house. It had been made by six generations of human children, all of whom had used Sam for transportation about the diamondwood farm. He was half again as big as any other mossback around and the only one whose sleeping pit was in the Queen Grove. Everything about the Queen Grove was special, from the trees themselves, which were never cut and twice as thick and almost twice as tall as the trees of other groves, to Sam and his blue flower thicket, the huge stump of the Grandfather Slurp not far away, and the giant greenweb at the other end of the grove. It was quieter here; there were fewer of the other animals. The Queen Grove, from what Riquol Cholm had told Ilf, was the point from which the whole diamondwood forest had started a long time ago.

Auris said, "We'll go around and come in from the back. They don't have to know right away that we're here. . . ."

"Mr. Terokaw," said Riquol Cholm, "I'm sorry Kugus Ovin persuaded you and Mr. Bliman to accompany him to Wrake on this business. You've simply wasted your time. Kugus should have known better. I've discussed the situation quite thoroughly with him on other occasions."

"I'm afraid I don't follow you, Mr. Cholm," Mr. Terokaw said stiffly. "I'm making you a businesslike proposition in regard to this farm of diamondwood trees—a proposition which will be very much to your advantage as well as to that of the children whose property the Diamondwood is. Certainly you should at least be willing to listen to my terms!"

Riquol shook his head. It was clear that he was angry with Kugus but attempting to control his anger.

"Your terms, whatever they may be, are not a factor in this," he said. "The maintenance of a diamondwood forest is not entirely a business proposition. Let me explain that to you—as Kugus should have done.

"No doubt you're aware that there are less than 40 such forests on the world of Wrake and that attempts to grow the trees elsewhere have been uniformly unsuccessful. That and the unique beauty of diamondwood products, which has never been duplicated by artificial means, is, of course, the reason that such products command a price which compares with that of precious stones and similar items."

Mr. Terokaw regarded Riquol with a bleak blue eye, nodded briefly. "Please continue, Mr. Cholm."

"A diamondwood forest," said Riquol, "is a great deal more than an assemblage of trees. The trees are a basic factor, but still only a factor, of a closely integrated, balanced natural ecology. The manner of independence of the plants and animals that make up a diamond-wood forest is not clear in all details, but the interdependence is a very pronounced one. None of the involved species seem able to survive in any other environment. On the other hand, plants and animals not naturally a part of this ecology will not thrive if brought into it. They move out or vanish quickly. Human beings appear to be the only excep-tion to that rule."

"Very interesting," Mr. Terokaw said dryly.

"It is," said Riquol. "It is a very interesting natural situation and many people, including Mrs. Cholm and myself, feel it should be pre-served. The studied, limited cutting practiced on the diamondwood farms at present acts towards its preservation. That degree of harvest-ing actually is beneficial to the forests, keeps them moving through an optimum cycle of growth and maturity. They are flourishing under the hand of man to an extent which was not usually attained in their natural, untouched state. The people who are at present responsible for them—the farm owners and their associates—have been working for some time to have all diamondwood forests turned into Federation preserves, with the right to harvest them retained by the present own-ers and their heirs under the same carefully supervised conditions. When Auris and Ilf come of age and can sign an agreement to that effect, the farms will in fact become Federation preserves. All other steps to that end have been taken by now.

"That, Mr. Terokaw, is why we're not interested in your business proposition. You'll discover, if you wish to sound them out on it, that the other diamondwood farmers are not interested in it either. We are all of one mind in that matter. If we weren't, we would long since have accepted propositions essentially similar to yours."

There was silence for a moment. Then Kugus Ovin said pleasantly, "I know you're annoyed with me, Riquol, but I'm thinking of Auris and Ilf in this. Perhaps in your concern for the preservation of a natural phenomenon, you aren't sufficiently considering their interests."

Riquol looked at him, said, "When Auris reaches maturity, she'll be an extremely wealthy young woman, even if this farm never sells another cubic foot of diamondwood from this day on. Ilf would be sufficiently well-to-do to make it unnecessary for him ever to work a stroke in his life—though I doubt very much he would make such a choice."

Kugus smiled. "There are degrees even to the state of being ex-tremely wealthy," he remarked. "What my niece can expect to gain in her lifetime from this careful harvesting you talk about can't begin to compare with what she would get at one stroke through Mr. Terokaw's offer. The same, of course, holds true of Ilf."

"Quite right," Mr. Terokaw said heavily. "I'm generous in my business dealings, Mr. Cholm. I have a reputation for it. And I can afford to be generous because I profit well from my investments. Let me bring another point to your attention. Interest in diamondwood products throughout the Federation waxes and wanes, as you must be aware. It rises and falls. There are fashions and fads. At present, we are approaching the crest of a new wave of interest in these products. This interest can be properly stimulated and exploited, but in any event we must expect it will have passed its peak in another few months. The next interest peak might develop six years from now, or twelve years from now. Or it might never develop since there are very few natural products which cannot eventually be duplicated and usually surpassed by artificial methods, and there is no good reason to assume that diamondwood will remain an exception indefinitely.

"We should be prepared, therefore, to make the fullest use of this bonanza while it lasts. I am prepared to do just that, Mr. Cholm. A cargo ship full of cutting equipment is at present stationed a few hours' flight from Wrake. This machinery can be landed and in operation here within a day after the contract I am offering you is signed. Within a week, the forest can be leveled. We shall make no use of your factory here, which would be entirely inadequate for my purpose. The diamondwood will be shipped at express speeds to another world where I have adequate processing facilities set up. And we can hit the Federation's main markets with the finished products the following month."

Riquol Cholm said, icily polite now, "And what would be the reason for all that haste, Mr. Terokaw?"

Mr. Terokaw looked surprised. "To insure that we have no competition, Mr. Cholm. What else? When the other diamondwood farmers here discover what has happened, they may be tempted to follow our example. But we'll be so far ahead of them that the diamondwood boom will be almost entirely to our exclusive advantage. We have taken every precaution to see that. Mr. Bliman, Mr. Ovin and I arrived here in the utmost secrecy today. No one so much as suspects that we are on Wrake, much less what our purpose is. I make no mistakes in such matters, Mr. Cholm!"

He broke off and looked around as Meldy Cholm said in a troubled voice, "Come in, children. Sit down over there. We're discussing a matter which concerns you."

"Hello, Auris!" Kugus said heartily. "Hello, Ilf! Remember old Uncle Kugus?"

"Yes," Ilf said. He sat down on the bench by the wall beside Auris, feeling scared.

"Auris," Riquol Cholm said, "did you happen to overhear anything of what was being said before you came into the room?"

Auris nodded. "Yes." She glanced at Mr. Terokaw, looked at Riquol again. "He wants to cut down the forest."

"It's your forest and Ilf's you know. Do you want him to do it?"

"Mr. Cholm, please!" Mr. Terokaw protested. "We must approach this properly. Kugus, show Mr. Cholm what I'm offering."

Riquol took the document Kugus held out to him, looked over it. After a moment, he gave it back to Kugus. "Auris," he said, "Mr. Terokaw, as he's indicated, is offering you more money than you would ever be able to spend in your life for the right to cut down your share of the forest. Now . . . do you want him to do it?"

"No." Auris said.

Riquol glanced at Ilf, who shook his head. Riquol turned back to Mr. Terokaw.

"Well, Mr. Terokaw," he said, "there's your answer. My wife and I don't want you to do it, and Auris and Ilf don't want you to do it. Now. . . ."

"Oh, come now, Riquol!" Kugus said, smiling. "No one can expect either Auris or Ilf to really understand what's involved here. When they come of age—"

"When they come of age," Riquol said, "they'll again have the opportunity to decide what they wish to do." He made a gesture of distaste. "Gentlemen, let's conclude this discussion. Mr. Terokaw, we thank you for your offer, but it's been rejected."

Mr. Terokaw frowned, pursed his lips.

"Well, not so fast, Mr. Cholm," he said. "As I told you, I make no mistakes in business matters. You suggested a few minutes ago that I might contact the other diamondwood farmers on the planet on the subject but predicted that I would have no better luck with them."

"So I did," Riquol agreed. He looked puzzled.

"As a matter of fact," Mr. Terokaw went on, "I already have contacted a number of these people. Not in person, you understand, since I did not want to tip off certain possible competitors that I was interested in diamondwood at present. The offer was rejected, as you indicated it would be. In fact, I learned that the owners of the Wrake diamondwood farms are so involved in legally binding agreements with one another that it would be very difficult for them to accept such an offer even if they wished to do it."

Riquol nodded, smiled briefly. "We realized that the temptation to sell out to commercial interests who would not be willing to act in accordance with our accepted policies could be made very strong," he said. "So we've made it as nearly impossible as we could for any of us to yield to temptation."

"Well," Mr. Terokaw continued, "I am not a man who is easily put off. I ascertained that you and Mrs. Cholm are also bound by such an agreement to the other diamondwood owners of Wrake not to be the first to sell either the farm or its cutting rights to outside interests, or to exceed the established limits of cutting. But you are not the owners of this farm. These two children own it between them."

Riquol frowned. "What difference does that make?" he demanded. "Ilf is our grandson. Auris is related to us and our adopted daughter."

Mr. Terokaw rubbed his chin.

"Mr. Bliman," he said, "please explain to these people what the legal situation is."

Mr. Bliman cleared his throat. He was a tall, thin man with fierce dark eyes, like a bird of prey. "Mr. and Mrs. Cholm," he began, "I work for the Federation Government and am a specialist in adoptive procedures. I will make this short. Some months ago, Mr. Kugus Ovin filed the necessary papers to adopt his niece, Auris Luteel, citizen of Wrake. I conducted the investigation which is standard in such cases and can assure you that no official record exists that you have at any time gone through the steps of adopting Auris."

" *What?*" Riquol came half to his feet. Then he froze in position for a moment, settled slowly back in his chair. "What is this? Just what kind of trick are you trying to play?" he said. His face had gone white.

Ilf had lost sight of Mr. Terokaw for a few seconds, because Uncle Kugus had suddenly moved over in front of the bench on which he and Auris were sitting. But now he saw him again and he had a jolt of fright. There was a large blue and silver gun in Mr. Terokaw's hand, and the muzzle of it was pointed very steadily at Riquol Cholm.

"Mr. Cholm," Mr. Terokaw said, "before Mr. Bliman concludes his explanation, allow me to caution you! I do not wish to kill you. This gun, in fact, is not designed to kill. But if I pull the trigger, you will be in excruciating pain for some minutes. You are an elderly man and it is possible that you would not survive the experience. This would not inconvenience us very seriously. Therefore, stay seated and give up any thoughts of summoning help. . . . Kugus, watch the children. Mr. Bliman, let me speak to Mr. Het before you resume."

He put his left hand up to his face, and Ilf saw he was wearing a wrist-talker. "Het," Mr. Terokaw said to the talker without taking his eyes off Riquol Cholm, "you are aware, I believe, that the children are with us in the house?"

The wrist-talker made murmuring sounds for a few seconds, then stopped.

"Yes," Mr. Terokaw said. "There should be no problem about it. But let me know if you see somebody approaching the area. . . ." He put his hand back down on the table. "Mr. Bliman, please continue."

Mr. Bliman cleared his throat again.

"Mr. Kugus Ovin," he said, "is now officially recorded as the parent by adoption of his niece, Auris Luteel. Since Auris has not yet reached the age where her formal consent to this action would be required, the matter is settled."

"Meaning," Mr. Terokaw added, "that Kugus can act for Auris in such affairs as selling the cutting rights on this tree farm. Mr. Cholm, if you are thinking of taking legal action against us, forget it. You may have had certain papers purporting to show that the girl was your adopted child filed away in the deposit vault of a bank. If so, those papers have been destroyed. With enough money, many things become possible. Neither you nor Mrs. Cholm nor the two children will do or say anything that might cause trouble to me. Since you have made no rash moves, Mr. Bliman will now use an instrument to put you and Mrs. Cholm painlessly to sleep for the few hours required to get you off this planet. Later, if you should be questioned in connection with this situation, you will say about it only what certain psychological experts will have impressed on you to say, and within a few months, nobody will be taking any further interest whatever in what is happening here today.

"Please do not think that I am a cruel man. I am not. I merely take what steps are required to carry out my purpose. Mr. Bliman, please proceed!"

Ilf felt a quiver of terror. Uncle Kugus was holding his wrist with one hand and Auris' wrist with the other, smiling reassuringly down at them. Ilf darted a glance over to Auris' face. She looked as white as his grandparents but she was making no attempt to squirm away from Kugus, so Ilf stayed quiet, too. Mr. Bliman stood up, looking more like a fierce bird of prey than ever, and stalked over to Riquol Cholm, holding something in his hand that looked unpleasantly like another gun. Ilf shut his eyes. There was a moment of silence, then Mr. Terokaw said, "Catch him before he falls out of the chair. Mrs. Cholm, if you will just settle back comfortably. . . ."

There was another moment of silence. Then, from beside him, Ilf heard Auris speak.

It wasn't regular speech but a quick burst of thin, rattling gabble, like human speech speeded up 20 times or so. It ended almost immediately.

"What's that? What's that?" Mr. Terokaw said, surprised.

Ilf's eyes flew open as something came in through the window with a whistling shriek. The two humbugs were in the room, brown blurs flicking here and there, screeching like demons. Mr. Terokaw exclaimed something in a loud voice and jumped up from the chair, his gun swinging this way and that. Something scuttled up Mr. Bliman's back like a big spider, and he yelled and spun away from Meldy Cholm lying slumped back in her chair. Something ran up Uncle Kugus' back. He yelled, letting go of Ilf and Auris, and pulled out a gun of his own. "Wide aperture!" roared Mr. Terokaw, whose gun was making loud, thumping noises. A brown shadow swirled suddenly about his knees. Uncle Kugus cursed, took aim at the shadow and fired.

"Stop that, you fool!" Mr. Terokaw shouted. "You nearly hit me."

"Come," whispered Auris, grabbing Ilf's arm. They sprang up from the bench and darted out the door behind Uncle Kugus' broad back.

"Het!" Mr. Terokaw's voice came bellowing down the hall behind them. "Up in the air and look out for those children! They're trying to get away. If you see them start to cross the road, knock 'em out. Kugus —after them! They may try to hide in the house."

Then he yowled angrily, and his gun began making the thumping noises again. The humbugs were too small to harm people, but their sharp little teeth could hurt and they seemed to be using them now.

"In here," Auris whispered, opening a door. Ilf ducked into the room with her, and she closed the door softly behind them. Ilf looked at her, his heart pounding wildly.

Auris nodded at the barred window. "Through there! Run and hide in the grove. I'll be right behind you. . . ."

"Auris! Ilf!" Uncle Kugus called in the hall. "Wait—don't be afraid. Where are you?" His voice still seemed to be smiling. Ilf heard his footsteps hurrying along the hall as he squirmed quickly sideways between two of the thick wooden bars over the window, dropped to the ground. He turned, darted off towards the nearest bushes. He heard Auris gabble something to the humbugs again, high and shrill, looked back as he reached the bushes and saw her already outside, running towards the shrubbery on his right. There was a shout from the window. Uncle Kugus was peering out from behind the bars, pointing a gun at Auris. He fired. Auris swerved to the side, was gone among the shrubs. Ilf didn't think she had been hit.

"They're outside!" Uncle Kugus yelled. He was too big to get through the bars himself.

Mr. Terokaw and Mr. Bliman were also shouting within the house. Uncle Kugus turned around, disappeared from the window.

"Auris!" Ilf called, his voice shaking with fright.

"Run and hide, Ilf!" Auris seemed to be on the far side of the shrubbery, deeper in the Queen Grove.

Ilf hesitated, started running along the path that led to Sam's sleeping pit, glancing up at the open patches of sky among the treetops. He didn't see the aircar with the man Het in it. Het would be circling around the Queen Grove now, waiting for the other men to chase them into sight so he could knock them out with something. But they could hide inside Sam's shell and Sam would get them across the road. "Auris, where are you?" Ilf cried.

Her voice came low and clear from behind him. "Run and hide, Ilf!"

Ilf looked back. Auris wasn't there but the two humbugs were loping up the path a dozen feet away. They darted past Ilf without stopping, disappeared around the turn ahead. He could hear the three men yelling for him and Auris to come back. They were outside, looking around for them now, and they seemed to be coming closer.

Ilf ran on, reached Sam's sleeping place. Sam lay there unmoving, like a great mossy boulder filling the pit. Ilf picked up a stone and pounded on the front part of the shell.

"Wake up!" he said desperately. "Sam, wake up!"

Sam didn't stir. And the men were getting closer. Ilf looked this way and that, trying to decide what to do.

"Don't let them see you," Auris called suddenly.

"That was the girl over there," Mr. Terokaw's voice shouted. "Go after her, Bliman!"

"Auris, watch out!" Ilf screamed terrified.

"Aha! And here's the boy, Kugus. This way! Het," Mr. Terokaw yelled triumphantly, "come down and help us catch them! We've got them spotted. . . ."

Ilf dropped to hands and knees, crawled away quickly under the branches of the blue flower thicket and waited, crouched low. He heard Mr. Terokaw crashing through the bushes towards him and Mr. Bliman braying, "Hurry up, Het! Hurry up!" Then he heard something else. It was the sound the giant greenweb sometimes made to trick a flock of silverbells into fluttering straight towards it, a deep drone which suddenly seemed to be pouring down from the trees and rising up from the ground.

Ilf shook his head dizzily. The drone faded, grew up again. For a moment, he thought he heard his own voice call "Auris, where are you?" from the other side of the blue flower thicket. Mr. Terokaw veered off in that direction, yelling something to Mr. Bliman and Kugus. Ilf backed farther away through the thicket, came out on the other side, climbed to his feet and turned.

He stopped. For a stretch of 20 feet ahead of him, the forest floor was moving, shifting and churning with a slow, circular motion, turning lumps of deep brown mold over and over.

Mr. Terokaw came panting into Sam's sleeping place, red-faced, glaring about, the blue and silver gun in his hand. He shook his head to clear the resonance of the humming air from his brain. He saw a huge, moss-covered boulder tilted at a slant away from him but no sign of Ilf.

Then something shook the branches of the thicket behind the boulder. "Auris!" Ilf's frightened voice called.

The greenweb's roar ebbed and rose continuously now, like a thousand harps being struck together in a bewildering, quickening beat. Human voices danced and swirled through the din, crying, wailing, screeching. Ilf stood at the edge of the 20-foot circle of churning earth outside the blue flower thicket, half stunned by it all. He heard Mr. Terokaw bellow to Mr. Bliman to go after Auris, and Mr. Bliman squalling to Het to hurry. He heard his own voice nearby call Auris frantically and then Mr. Terokaw's triumphant yell: "This way! Here's the boy, Kugus!"

Uncle Kugus bounded out of some bushes 30 feet away, eyes staring, mouth stretched in a wide grin. He saw Ilf, shouted excitedly and ran towards him. Ilf watched, suddenly unable to move. Uncle Kugus took four long steps out over the shifting loam between them, sank ankle-deep, knee-deep. Then the brown earth leaped in cascades about him, and he went sliding straight down into it as if it were water, still grinning, and disappeared. In the distance, Mr. Terokaw roared, "This way!" and Mr. Bliman yelled to Het to hurry up. A loud, slapping sound came from the direction of the stump of the Grandfather Slurp. It was followed by a great commotion in the bushes around there; but that only lasted a moment. Then, a few seconds later, the greenweb's drone rose and thinned to the wild shriek it made when it had caught something big and faded slowly away. . . .

Mr. Terokaw ran around the boulder, leveling the gun. The droning in the air suddenly swelled to a roar. Two big gray, three-fingered hands came out from the boulder on either side of Mr. Terokaw and picked him up.

"Awk!" he gasped, then dropped the gun as the hands folded him, once, twice, and lifted him towards Sam's descending head. Sam opened his large mouth, closed it, swallowed. His neck and head drew back under his shell and he settled slowly into the sleeping pit again.

Ilf came walking shakily through the opening in the thickets to Sam's sleeping place. His head still seemed to hum inside with the greenweb's drone but the Queen Grove was quiet again; no voices called anywhere. Sam was settled into his pit. Ilf saw something gleam on the ground near the front end of the pit. He went over and looked at it, then at the big, moss-grown dome of Sam's shell.

"Oh, Sam," he whispered, "I'm not sure we should have done it. . . ."

Sam didn't stir. Ilf picked up Mr. Terokaw's blue and silver gun gingerly by the barrel and went off with it to look for Auris. He found her at the edge of the grove, watching Het's aircar on the other side of the road. The aircar was turned on its side and about a third of it was sunk in the ground. At work around and below it was the biggest member of the clean-up squad Ilf had ever seen in action.

They went up to the side of the road together and looked on while the aircar continued to shudder and turn and sink deeper into the earth. Ilf suddenly remembered the gun he was holding and threw it over on the ground next to the aircar. It was swallowed up instantly there. Tumbleweeds came rolling up to join them and clustered around the edge of the circle, waiting. With a final jerk, the aircar disappeared. The disturbed section of earth began to smooth over. The tumbleweeds moved out into it.

There was a soft whistling in the air, and from a Queen Tree at the edge of the grove 150 feet away, a diamondwood seedling came lancing down, struck at a slant into the center of the circle where the aircar had vanished, stood trembling a moment, then straightened up. The tumbleweeds nearest it moved respectfully aside to give it room. The seedling shuddered and unfolded its first five-fingered cluster of silver-green leaves. Then it stood still.

Ilf looked over at Auris. "Auris," he said, "should we have done it?"

Auris was silent a moment.

"Nobody did anything," she said then. "They've just gone away again." She took Ilf's hand. "Let's go back to the house and wait for Riquol and Meldy to wake up."

The organism that was the diamondwood forest grew quiet again. The quiet spread back to its central mind unit in the Queen Grove, and the unit began to relax towards somnolence. A crisis had been passed —perhaps the last of the many it had foreseen when human beings first arrived on the world of Wrake.

The only defense against Man was Man. Understanding that, it had laid its plans. On a world now owned by Man, it adopted Man, brought him into its ecology, and its ecology into a new and again successful balance.

This had been a final flurry. A dangerous attack by dangerous humans. But the period of danger was nearly over, would soon be for good a thing of the past.

It had planned well, the central mind unit told itself drowsily. But now, since there was no further need to think today, it would stop thinking. . . .

Sam the mossback fell gratefully asleep.

POSITIVE FEEDBACK

Christopher Anvil

SCHRAMM'S GARAGE

To: Jack W. Bailey
     413 Crescent Drive
     City

Parts:	1 set 22-638 brushes		$ 1.18
Labor:	overhaul generator		
	set regulator		
	clean battery terminals		11.00
		total	$12.18

NOTE: Time for oil change and install new filter.
    Noticed car seemed to pull to the left when we stepped on the brake.
    Can take care of it Wednesday if you want.

Joe Schramm

Dear Joe:
    Check for $12.18 enclosed.
    Will see about the oil change and filter later. The kids have been sick and we're going broke at this rate.
    Maybe it pulls to the left, but I haven't noticed it.

Jack Bailey

From *Analog Science Fact and Fiction,* August, 1965. Reprinted by permission of the author and the author's agents, Scott Meredith Literary Agency, Inc., 580 Fifth Avenue, New York, New York 10036.

Mr. Joseph Schramm
Schramm's Garage
1428 West Ave.
Crescent City
Dear Mr. Schramm:

Enclosed find literature on our new Automated Car Service Handling Machine.

With this great new machine, you can service anything from a little imported car to a big truck. The Handling Machine just picks the vehicle up, and the Glider on its Universal Arm enables your mechanic to get at any part, from above or below. By just turning a few knobs, he glides right to the spot on the end of the Arm. Power grapples, twisters, engine-lifters, transmission-holders, dozen-armed grippers and wrasslers—all these make the toughest job easy.

If you've got a dozen mechanics, buy this machine and you can get along with three or four.

This machine will be the best buy of your life.

Truly yours,
G. Wrattan
Sales Manager

SCHRAMM'S GARAGE

Dear Mr. Wrattan:

This machine of yours would take up my whole shop. It's all-electric, and looks to me as if it would take the Government to pay the electric bills. Your idea that I could buy this thing and then let most of my mechanics go is a little dull. When business gets bad, I can *always* let them go. But with this monster machine of yours, I couldn't let *anybody* go, except the few guys I still had, who would be my best mechanics.

Do you know how hard it is to find a good mechanic?

Let's have the prices and information on your line of hydraulic jacks. Spare me the million-dollar-Robot-Garage stuff.

Yours truly,
J. Schramm

SUPERDEE EQUIPMENT

Mr. Joseph Schramm
Schramm's Garage
1428 West Ave.
Crescent City
Dear Mr. Schramm:

Enclosed find prices and literature on our complete line of hydraulic jacks, jack-stands, and lifts.

Mr. Schramm, we feel that you do not fully appreciate the advantages of our great new Automated Car Service Handling Machine. This machine will more than pay for itself in speed, efficiency, and economical service. In bad times you could still cut down your repair staff. Mr. Schramm, *one man* can operate this machine.

We are enclosing a new brochure on this wonderful new labor- and expense-saving machine, which will turn your garage into an ultramodern Servicatorium.

Cordially,
G. Wrattan
Sales Manager

SCHRAMM'S GARAGE

Dear Mr. Wrattan:

I'm enclosing an order sheet for jack and stands.

Your new brochure on your wonderful new labor- and expense-saving machine went straight into the furnace.

I think you are going to have plenty of trouble selling this machine. The reason is, all you're doing is to think how nice it will be for you if somebody buys it, not how lousy it will be for him to have the thing.

This machine will take cable as thick as my arm for the juice to run all those motors. It's bound to break down, and while I'm repairing it, I'm out of business.

You say I can let all my mechanics go but one. You must have a loose ground somewhere. If I fire all my mechanics but one, and he runs this machine, *who's the boss then?*

I could tell you what to do with this great new machine of yours, but I don't think you would do it.

Yours truly,
J. Schramm

SUPERDEE EQUIPMENT
Interoffice Memo

To: W. W. Sanson, Pres.

Dear Mr. Sanson:

I am sending up a large envelope containing sample letters, from garages all over the country.

The response we've had on Handling Machines has been unusually large and emphatic, but unfortunately it has not been favorable.

G. Wrattan

SUPERDEE EQUIPMENT
Interoffice Memo

To: G. Wrattan, Sales Mgr.
Dear Wrattan:

There are going to have to be some drastic changes around here.
Bring all the letters you have up to my office at once.

Sanson

SUPERDEE EQUIPMENT

Mr. Joseph Schramm
Schramm's Garage
1428 West Ave.
Crescent City
Dear Mr. Schramm:

There have been big changes at Superdee! Exciting changes!

Following a complete overhaul of top engineering management
personnel, things are moving again!

Superdee is on the march!

Leading the van is our revamped ultramodern Supramatic Car
Service Handling Machine, capable of repairing anything from a little
foreign car to a huge truck! Fast! Economical! Efficient!

This new version embodies the most advanced methods, together
with the actual suggestions of *practical automative repairmen like
yourself!*

This machine is hydraulically operated, and even has a special
High Efficiency Whirlamatic Hand Pump in case of emergency power
failure!

There's practicality!

There's real manufacturer co-operation!

You asked for it! *Here it is!*

Superdee is on the march!

Are you?

Cordially,
G. Wrattan
Sales Mgr.

SCHRAMM'S GARAGE

Dear Mr. Wrattan:

I am enclosing an order for one of your new Superdeeluxe jacks.

I have read the stuff about your new Supramatic Machine. This
one doesn't take as much space, and seems to be pretty good.

But I can't afford it.

Yours truly,
J. Schramm

SUPERDEE EQUIPMENT
Interoffice Memo

To: W. W. Sanson, Pres.
Dear Mr. Sanson:
    Well, we've sold three of them.

                                            G. Wrattan

SUPERDEE EQUIPMENT
Interoffice Memo

To: G. Wrattan, Sales Mgr.
Dear Wrattan:
    We've got to do better than this or we'll all be lined up at the employment office in just about six months.
    How about a big advertising campaign?

                                            Sanson

SUPERDEE EQUIPMENT
Interoffice Memo

To: W. W. Sanson, Pres.
Dear Mr. Sanson:
    It won't work. This machine would theoretically improve just about any fair-sized repair shop's efficiency, but it's still too expensive.
    To judge by the response, we now have an acceptable Handler here. In time, it's bound to take hold, despite the cost, and obtain wide acceptance.
    But this won't happen in six months.

                                            G. Wrattan

SUPERDEE EQUIPMENT
Interoffice Memo

To: W. Robert Schnitzer, Mgr.
    Special Services Dept.
Dear Schnitzer:
    Since you ran the computerized market simulation, on the basis of which we made this white elephant, I suggest you now find some way to unload it.
    I would hate to be the man whose recommendations, presented in the guise of scientific certainty, were so disastrous that they destroyed the company that paid his salary.
    A reputation such as that could make it quite difficult to find another job.

                                            Sanson

SUPERDEE EQUIPMENT
Interoffice Memo

To: W. W. Sanson, Pres.

Dear Mr. Sanson:

I have been giving this matter a great deal of thought, and have analyzed it on the Supervac-666.

The trouble is, the average individual does not use the available automotive repair facilities to a sufficient extent to assure the garage owner of enough income to afford our machine.

This is roughly analogous to the situation in the health industries some years ago.

I believe we might find a similar solution to be useful in this case.

W. R. Schnitzer

SUPERDEE EQUIPMENT
Interoffice Memo

To: W. Robert Schnitzer, Mgr.

Special Services Dept.

Dear Schnitzer:

I frankly don't follow what you're talking about, but I am prepared to listen.

Come on up, and let's have it.

Sanson

SUPERDEE EQUIPMENT
Interoffice Memo

To: G. Wrattan, Sales Mgr.

Dear Wrattan:

Schnitzer has one of the damndest ideas I ever heard of, but it might just work.

I am getting everybody up here to meditate on this, and want to find out how it strikes you.

This *could* be a gold mine, provided we can get the insurance people interested.

Sanson

SUPERDEE EQUIPMENT
Interoffice Memo

To: G. Wrattan, Sales Mgr.

Dear Wrattan:

You will be interested to know after that discussion we had about Schnitzer's idea, that the insurance people are closely studying it. I could see whirling dollar signs in their eyes as I gave them the exact pitch Schnitzer gave me.

If they *do* go ahead, the banks will take a much rosier view of our prospects. We may weather this thing yet.

Sanson

FORESYTE INSURANCE
"In Unity, Strength"
Since 1906

Dear Car Owner:

How many times have you suffered inconvenience and delay, because of auto failures and breakdowns? Yet how often have you hesitated to have your car checked, and repairs carried out that might have prevented these delays and breakdowns—*because you were short of cash at the moment?*

You need no longer suffer this inconvenience. *Now you can prepay your car repair bills!*

Foresyte Insurance now offers an unique plan by which, for as little as two dollars a month, you can get *necessary repairs made on your car,* and *Foresyte will pay the bill!*

We call this our Blue Wheel car repair insurance plan. We are sure it will pay you to send in the coupon below, right away.

We can afford to make this offer because many cars will need no repairs, and the premiums for *those* cars will pay *your* repair bills! Send in the coupon today!

Cordially,
P. J. Devereaux
President

Schramm's Garage
1428 West Ave.
City
Dear Joe:

About that oil change and new filter: I've got Blue Wheel insurance now, so take care of it.

While the car's in there, check that pull to the left you mentioned.

Jack Bailey

SCHRAMM'S GARAGE

To: Jack W. Bailey
     413 Crescent Drive
     City

Parts:	6 qts oil		$ 3.90
	#14-66 oil filter		4.95
	#6612 brake shoes, 1 set		12.98
		total	$21.83
Labor:	change filter		
	drain oil		
	put in fresh oil		
	install brake shoes		
	grind drums		
		total	$24.00
		total	$45.83
		Blue Wheel	$45.83
		Paid—J. Schramm	

NOTE: Your transmission needs work. I can't work on it this week, because I'm swamped. How about next Wednesday morning?

Joe Schramm

Dear Joe:
    Sure. I'll have the wife leave the car early.

Jack Bailey

SCHRAMM'S GARAGE

Dear Mr. Wrattan:
    Please send me your latest information on your Automated Car Service Handling Machine.
    I never saw so much business in my life. I am now running about a month behind.

Yours truly,
J. Schramm

SUPERDEE EQUIPMENT
Interoffice Memo

To: W. Robert Schnitzer, Mgr.
    Special Service Dept.
Dear Schnitzer:
    We are now out of the woods, thanks to your stroke of genius on the prepayment plan.
    Now see if you can find some way to step up production.

Sanson

FORESYTE INSURANCE
Interoffice Memo

To: J. Beggs, Vice-Pres.
  Blue Wheel Plan
Dear Beggs:
    What on earth is going on here? After making money the first few months on Blue Wheel, we are now getting swamped.
    What's happening?

Devereaux

FORESYTE INSURANCE
Interoffice Memo

To: P. J. Devereaux, Pres.
Dear Mr. Devereaux:
    I don't exactly know what's going on, but it completely obsoletes these figures of Sanson's.
    We are going to have to raise our premium.

Beggs

SCHRAMM'S SERVICATORIUM

Dear Mr. Wrattan:
    Please put my name on the waiting list for another Handling Machine right away.

Yours truly,
J. Schramm

BLUE WHEEL
Prepaid Car Care

Dear Subscriber:
    Owing to unexpectedly heavy use of the Blue Wheel insurance by you, the subscriber, we must raise the charge for Blue Wheel coverage to $3.75 per month, effective January 1st.

Cordially,
R. Beggs

SCHRAMM'S SUPER SERVICATORIUM

Dear Mr. Wrattan:

We're going to need another Handling Machine as soon as we get the new wing finished next month.

Yours truly,

J. Schramm

FORESYTE INSURANCE
Interoffice Memo

To: P. J. Devereaux, Pres.

Dear Mr. Devereaux:

I have to report that ordinary garages are now being replaced by "servicatoriums," "super servicatoriums," and "ultraservicatoriums."

These places charge more, which is justified by their heavier capital investment, and faster service.

Nevertheless, it now costs us more for the same job.

R. Beggs

BLUE WHEEL
Prepaid Car Care

Dear Subscriber:

Due to increasingly thorough car care offered by modern servicatoriums, and to continued heavy and wider use of such care, we find it necessary to increase the charge to $4.25 a month.

Cordially,

R. Beggs

SCHRAMM'S ULTRASERVICATORIUM

To: Jack W. Bailey
      413 Cresent Drive
      City

Parts:	1 set 22-638 brushes	$ 1.46
Labor:	clean battery terminals	
	set regulator	
	overhaul generator	21.00
	total	$22.46
	Blue Wheel	$22.46
		PAID

NOTE: There's a whine from the differential we ought to take care of on the Machine. How about Friday morning? I don't see why there was more trouble with the generator and regulator. I think we ought to check everything again. Your Blue Wheel will cover it.

Joe Schramm

SCHRAMM'S ULTRASERVICATORIUM

Dear Mr. Wrattan:

I want three of your All-Purpose Diagnostic Superanalyzers, that will test batteries, generators, starters, automatic transmissions, etc., etc. Rush the order. I can't get enough good mechanics to do this work.

Yours truly,

J. Schramm

FORESYTE INSURANCE
Interoffice Memo

To: P. J. Devereaux, Pres.

Dear Mr. Devereaux:

When I was a boy, I rode a bicycle with bad brakes down a steep hill one time, and got up to around 60 miles an hour as I came to a curve with a post-and-cable guardrail at the side, and about a 60-foot drop into a ravine beyond that.

This Blue Wheel plan gives me the same no-brakes sensation.

Incidentally, have you visited a garage lately?

R. Beggs

FORESYTE INSURANCE
Interoffice Memo

To: R. Beggs, Vice-Pres.

Blue Wheel

Dear Beggs:

What we seem to have here is some kind of weird mechanism that just naturally picks up speed by itself.

Without our insurance plan, the garages could never have gone up to these rates, because car owners wouldn't, or couldn't have paid them. Thanks to us, the car owners themselves now couldn't care less what the bill is. In fact, the higher it is, the more the car owner thinks he's getting out of his insurance.

The effect of this on the garage owner is to go overboard on every kind of expense.

Yes, I've visited a garage lately. I got a blowout over in Bayport, bought a new front tire, and on the way back noticed a vibration in the front end. Obviously, the wheel needed balancing.

However, when I tried to explain this to the Chief Automotive Repair Technician in Stull's Superepairatorium, he wouldn't listen. Before I knew what was going on, the car was up in the air.

Here's the bill:

Parts: 4 22-612 balance weights	$1.60
Labor: Complete diagnostic	$40.00
Wheel removal	2.00

Transport	1.50
Superbalancomatic	6.50
Transport	1.50
Wheel attachment	2.00
Car transport	3.25
Total parts and labor	$58.35
Blue Wheel	$58.35

PAID—L. Gnarth, C.A.R.T.

I think you can appreciate how I felt about Stull's Super-repairatorium. I shoved past the Chief Automotive Repair Technician, and got hold of Stull himself. He listened, looked sympathetic, and said, "If you want, I will pay all of this but $2.75, which is about what it should have cost. But that won't change the fact that at least half of these bills are going to be higher than they should be, and it's going to get a lot worse, not better."

"Why?"

"Do you think anybody that learns how to tell what's wrong by using one of these diagnostic machines, and that learns how to repair a car with hydraulic pressers and handlers at his elbow, is ever going to be able to figure out what's wrong on his own, or do the work with ordinary tools? All he's learned to do is *work with the machine.* He *can't* do a simple job. He's *got* to make a big job out of it, *so he can use the machine.*

"Now," Stull went on, "a good, old-style mechanic narrows the trouble down with a few simple tests. For instance, if the car won't start, he tries the lights and horn, sees how the lights dim when he works the starter, watches the ammeter needle, notices how the starter sounds, checks the battery terminals and cables, checks the spark bypasses the solenoid and sees if that's the trouble—in 15 minutes, a good mechanic with a few simple tools has a good idea where the trouble is, and then it's a question of putting in new points, pulling the starter to check for a short, or maybe working on the carburetor or fuel pump. To do this, *you've got to understand firsthand the things you're working with.* Then the know-how is in your brain and muscles, and you can use it anytime.

"But now, with these new machines, especially this damned Combination Handling Machine and Diagnostic Analyzer, the skill and know-how *is in the machine.*

"What kind of mechanics do you think we're going to turn out this way? How many of them will ever be able to do *anything* without using the machine? And since the machine costs so much, what is there to do but charge more?"

That was how it went at the garage. I thought that was bad enough, but this thing is snowballing, and there's more to it. After I left the garage, I happened to take another look at the bill and noticed that this Chief Automotive Repair Technician had written "C.A.R.T." after his name. This struck me as peculiar, so I stopped at a roadside phone, and called up Stull. He sounded embarrassed.

"It's his . . . well . . . degree. It used to be a mechanic would have laughed at that. He had his skill, and knew it, and that was enough. But now, with these machines, a lot of these new guys don't *have* the skill. Now they've got no way to prop up their feeling of being worth something. So, we've got this NARSTA, and—"

"You've got *what?*"

"N.A.R.S.T.A.—National Automotive Repair Specialists and Technicians Association. They award what amounts to *degrees.* They limit the number of people who can be mechanics, because anybody off the street could learn to run the machines in a few weeks."

"The mechanic who writes 'C.A.R.T.' after his name? Is he your *chief* mechanic?"

"Naturally."

"Why pick him for chief mechanic?"

"Because he has a 'C.A.R.T.' degree. If I use a guy with an A.A.R.T., or an A.R.T., I get in trouble with NARSTA. NARSTA says all its people are professional, and have to be treated according to their 'professional qualifications.' "

"That is, how good they are as mechanics?"

"Of course not. 'Professional qualifications' is whether the guy's got an A.R.T., an A.A.R.T., or a C.A.R.T. He may or may not be as good as another mechanic. What counts is that C.A.R.T. after his name. That changes his wage scale, changes his picture of himself, and makes an aristocrat out of him."

There was more to this phone conversation, but I think you get the picture.

This mess is compounding itself fast. I talked to Sanson over at Superdee about it, but Superdee is making so much money out of this that Sanson naturally won't listen to any objections. Instead, he went into a spiel about the Advance of Science. Sanson doesn't know it, but this trouble comes because there is one science, and the Master Science at that, that is being left out of this. But I think if we put it to use ourselves we can end this process before it wrecks the country.

I have hopes that you know what I am talking about, and will see how to put it to use.

Bear in mind, please, that when the rug is jerked out, we want *somebody else* to land on his head, not us.

I might mention that I have recently had cautious feelers from one Q. Snarden, who turns out to be the head of NARSTA. Snarden wants, I think, to take over Blue Wheel.

He would then, I suppose, run it as a "nonprofit" organization. Do you get the picture?

Devereaux

FORESYTE INSURANCE
Interoffice Memo

To: P. J. Devereaux, Pres.
Dear Mr. Devereaux:

I don't know just what you mean by the "Master Science." But I have a good idea what we ought to do with this Blue Wheel insurance.

Suppose I come up this afternoon about 1:30 to talk it over?

R. Beggs

FORESYTE INSURANCE
Interoffice Memo

To: R. Beggs, Vice-Pres.
  Blue Wheel
Dear Beggs:

I have now had a chance to analyze, and mentally review, your plan for dealing with Snarden and Blue Wheel. I think this is exactly what we should do.

We want to be sure to run out plenty of line on this.

Devereaux

BLUE WHEEL
A Nonprofit Organization
NARSTA-Approved

Dear Subscriber:

In these days of rising car-care costs, one of your most precious possessions is your Blue Wheel policy. To assure you the best possible service at the lowest cost, Blue Wheel is now operated under the supervision of the National Automotive Repair Specialists and Technicians Association, as a *nonprofit* organization.

Yes, Blue Wheel now gives you real peace-of-mind on the road. And your Blue Wheel card will continue to admit your car to the finest Servicatoriums, whenever it needs care.

But as costs rise, the charges we pay rise.

As we spend only 4.21 percent on administrative expenses, you can see we are doing our best to hold prices down; but costs are, nevertheless, rising.

To meet the costs, we find it is necessary to raise our premium to $5.40 a month.

When you consider the cost of car care today, this is a real bargain.

Cordially,
Q. Snarden
Pres.

BLUE WHEEL
(Nonprofit)
NARSTA-Approved

Dear Subscriber:

For reasons mentioned in the enclosed brochure, we are forced to raise our premium to $6.25 a month.

> Cordially,
> Q. Snarden
> Pres.

BLUE WHEEL

Dear Subscriber:

Blue Wheel has fought hard to hold the line, but next year, rates must go up if Blue Wheel is to pay your car-care bills.

As we explain in the enclosed booklet, Blue Wheel will now cost $8.88 a month.

This is one of the greatest insurance bargains on earth, when you consider today's car-care costs.

> Cordially,
> Q. Snarden
> Pres.

BLUE WHEEL

Dear Subscriber:

Blue Wheel is going to have to raise its rates to meet its ever-increasing costs of paying *your* car-care bills.

Future rates will be only $10.25 a month.

> Cordially,
> Q. Snarden
> Pres.

BLUE WHEEL

Dear Subscriber:

Blue Wheel's new rates will be $13.40 a month.

> Cordially,
> Q. Snarden
> Pres.

Blue Wheel

Dear Subscriber:

Blue Wheel is going to $16.90 a month effective January 1st. See our enclosed explanation.

Cordially,
Q. Snarden
Pres.

Blue Wheel

Dear Subscriber:

$22.42 a month is a small price to pay to be free of car-care expense worries nowadays.

This rate becomes effective next month.

Cordially,
Q. Snarden
Pres.

Schramm's Servicatorium

To: Jack W. Bailey
      413 Cresent Drive
      City

Parts:	1 set 22-638 brushes	$ 2.36
Labor:	Super diagnostic	85.00
	Giant Lift	65.00
	Manipulatorium	55.00
	Extractulator	28.00
	Gen. transport	1.25
	Treatment	12.50
	Checkulator	4.50
	Gen. transport	1.25
	Ultramatatonic	5.00
	Installator	15.00
	Ch. transport	3.75
	Checkulator final	6.50
	Ch. transport	3.75
	Car transport	5.25
	Total parts and labor	$291.75
	Blue Wheel	$291.75
		PAID

FORESYTE INSURANCE
Interoffice Memo

To: P. J. Devereaux, Pres.

Dear Mr. Devereaux:

The other day, the turn-signals on my car quit working, and before I got out of the garage, the bill ran up to $417.12.

In today's mail I got a notice that Blue Wheel, with Snarden at the helm, is going to raise its rates to $28.50 a month.

This notice, by the way, piously states that administrative costs now only come to 2.4 percent of Blue Wheel's total revenues. Naturally, if they keep raising their revenues by upping the premium, administrative costs will get progressively smaller, in proportion to the total. The percentage looks modest, but that's 2.4 percent of *what?*

I was talking to a physicist friend of mine the other day, and he says the trouble is, the car-repair setup now has "positive feedback," instead of "negative feedback." When the individual owner used to pay his own bills, his anger at high bills, and his reluctance or even inability to pay them, acted as negative feedback, reacting more strongly against the garage the higher the bills got. But now, not only is there none of this, but the garages are used *more* the higher the Blue Wheel premiums—because people feel that they should get *something* out of the policy. This is positive feedback, and my physicist friend says that if it continues long enough, it invariably ends by destroying the system.

Already there is talk of government regulation, and of plans to spread the burden further by taxation. This is just more of the same thing, on a wider scale. It will only delay the day of reckoning, and the trouble when the day of reckoning comes.

I think we'd better pull the plug on this pretty soon.

R. Beggs

FORESYTE INSURANCE
Interoffice Memo

To: R. Beggs, Vice-Pres.
Special Project

Dear Beggs:

Snarden goes before the congressional investigating committee next week.

When he is about halfway through his testimony, and has them tied in knots with his pious airs and specious arguments, *then* we want to hit him.

Have everything ready for about the third day of the hearing.

Devereaux

FORESYTE INSURANCE
Interoffice Memo

To: R. Beggs, Vice-Pres.
   Special Project
Dear Beggs:
   Now's the time. Snarden has pumped the hearing so full of red
herrings that it looks like a fish hatchery.
   Pull the plug.

Devereaux

FORESYTE INSURANCE
Interoffice Memo

To: P. J. Devereaux, Pres.
Dear Mr. Devereaux:
   The first ten million circulars are in the mail.

Beggs

FORESYTE INSURANCE
"In Unity, Strength"
Since 1906

Dear Car Owner:
   When car-care insurance cost two dollars a month, it was a bargain. Now it costs about 15 times as much.
   This present-insurance plan is so badly set up that it *forces up
car-care costs*. And when car-care costs go up, *that forces up insurance
premiums*.
   This is a vicious circle.
   Before this bankrupts the whole country, Foresyte Insurance is
determined to stop the endless climb of these premiums, by offering our
own plan.
   Possibly, after paying these present terrific bills, you will understand why we call our plan *Blue Driver*. But you won't feel blue when
you learn that our monthly rates on this new insurance are as follows:

$90 deductible 90%	$18.50
$90 deductible 75%	$12.50
$90 deductible 50%	$5.25
$180 deductible 90%	$13.75
$180 deductible 75%	$7.95
$180 deductible 50%	$3.75

Compare this with what you are paying now.
   We are convinced that the huge increase in car-care costs is due
mainly to the fact that the system now used makes it *nobody's* business
to keep costs down, and puts the ever-increasing burden just as heavily
on the man who *doesn't* overuse the plan as on the man who does.

Our plan is different, and puts the burden where it belongs—*on the fellow who overuses the plan.* You don't have to pay for all *his* expenses. He can't get away *without* paying extra for them. This is how it should be. Moreover, this plan gives good protection, at a lower cost.

For instance, with our $90 deductible 90% plan, you pay the first $90 of the bill yourself. True, $90 is a lot of money, *but in less than a year's time, you save that much or more in premiums.*

The 90% of the plan means that *we pay 90% of the rest of the bill.* You only have to pay 10%. On an $825 bill, for instance, you pay $90, which you have probably already saved because our premiums are so much lower. This leaves $735. We pay $661.50 of this, right away. *You pay only what's left.*

This lets you pay the small bills you can afford, while we take most of the big bills that everyone is afraid of these days.

Meanwhile, the less you use the plan, *the more you save.*

The larger the share of the risk you are willing to take, *the more you save.* Our $180 deductible 50% plan *costs only $3.75 a month.*

Because we may be able to lower premiums still further, these rates are not final. But at these rates, you can see that this plan rewards the person who doesn't overuse it.

We are already using this plan ourselves, and saving $10 to $24.75 a month on it.

How about you?

> Cordially,
> R. Beggs
> Vice-Pres.

> 413 Crescent Drive
> Crescent City

Dear Mr. Beggs:

Here is my check for $7.95. I am signing up on your $180 deductible 75% plan, and saving $20.55 a month.

But you better not jack the rates way up, or I will go back to Blue Wheel. If we only burn one light in the house, heat one room, and eat cornmeal mush twice a day, we can still pay *their* premiums.

> Yours truly,
> Jack Bailey

SCHRAMM'S SUPERSERVICATORIUM

To: Jack W. Bailey
    413 Crescent Drive
    City

Note: Time for oil change, new filter. Our Automatic File Checker also says it is time your car had a Complete Super Diagnostic and Renewva-

tional Overhaul on our special new Renewvator Machine. Your Blue
Wheel will cover it.

Joe Schramm

Dear Joe:
   In a pig's eye my Blue Wheel will cover it. I'm a Blue Driver now,
and I get socked 180 bucks plus 25 percent of the rest of your bill, and
it sounds to me like I will get hit for enough on this one to buy a new
car.
   Keep the Renewvational Overhaul. As for the Complete Super
Diagnostic, I found an old guy out on a back road, and he can figure out
more with a screw driver, a wrench, and a couple of meters than those
stuck-up imitation mechanics of yours can find out with the whole
Super Diagnostic Machine.
   Don't worry about the oil change. I can unscrew the filter all by
myself. I will pay myself $4.50 for the labor, and save anyway 100 bucks
on the deal.
   If the transmission falls out of this thing, or the rear axle climbs
up into the back seat, I'll let you know about it. But don't bother me
when it's time to oil the door handles and put grease on the trunk
hinges.

Jack Bailey

SCHRAMM'S SUPER SERVICATORIUM

Dear Mr. Wrattan:
   I just got your monthly booklet on "New Superdee Labor-Saving
Giants."
   Since the paper in this fancy booklet might clog up my new oil
burner, I'm afraid I don't know what to do with it.
   I am enclosing half-a-dozen letters from ex-customers, and maybe
they will explain to you why business is off 20 percent this month.

Yours truly,
J. Schramm

SUPERDEE EQUIPMENT
Interoffice Memo

To: W. W. Sanson, Pres.
Dear Mr. Sanson:
   I am sending up a big envelope containing letters from garagemen
and their customers. These letters are representative of a flood that's
coming in.
   What do we do now?

G. Wrattan

SUPERDEE EQUIPMENT
Interoffice Memo

To: G. Wrattan, Sales Mgr.

Dear Wrattan:

I put this one to Schnitzer and his Supervac 666. It flattened them.

There's just one thing *to* do. We take a loss on this latest stuff, and get out while we're still ahead.

As for these questions as to how much we offer to repurchase Renewvators, Giant Lifts, etc., we don't want them at any price. Point out how well made they are, and how much good metal is in them. That's just a hint to the customer, and if he deduces from that that the best thing to do with them is scrap them, that's *his* business.

Do you realize it cost me $214.72 to get a windshield-wiper blade changed the other day? They ran the whole car through the Super Diagnostic first to be sure the wiper blade *needed* to be changed.

As far as I'm concerned, this whole bubble can burst anytime.

Sanson

SCHRAMM'S ECONOMY GARAGE

To: Jack W. Bailey
      413 Crescent Drive
      City

Parts:	1 set 22-638 brushes		$1.48
Labor:	overhaul generator		
	set regulator		8.50
		total	$9.98

NOTE: Time for oil change, new filter. We will take care of this for you next time you're in—no charge for labor on this job. Al Putz says there was a funny rumble from the transmission when he drove the car out to the lot. We better check this as soon as you can leave the car again. Once those gears in there start grinding up the oil slingers and melting down the bearings, it gets expensive fast.

Joe Schramm

Dear Joe:

Thanks for the offer, but I'll take care of the oil change myself. I want to keep in practice, just in case the country comes down with another epidemic of Super Giant Machinitis.

As for that rumble from the transmission, I jacked up a rear wheel, started the engine, and I heard it, too. It had me scared for a minute there, but I blocked the car up, crawled under, and it took about three minutes to track down the trouble. In this model, the emergency brake works off a drum back of the transmission. Since I brought the car down to your garage, one end of a spring had somehow come loose on the emergency brake, and this lets the brake chatter against the drum. It was easy to connect the spring up again. The transmission is now nice and quiet.

I am enclosing the check for $9.98.

Jack Bailey

FORESYTE INSURANCE
Interoffice Memo

To: P. J. Devereaux, Pres.
Dear Mr. Devereaux:

We were able to bring the rates on Blue Driver car-care down again last month. We are still making a mint from this plan, even with reduced premiums, and we are still getting enthusiastic letters.

I can see, in detail, how this works, by giving everyone involved an incentive to keep costs down. But I am still wondering about a comment you made earlier.

What is the "Master Science" you referred to, in first suggesting the idea of this plan?

R. Beggs

FORESYTE INSURANCE
Interoffice Memo

To: R. Beggs, Vice-Pres.
  Blue Driver
Dear Beggs:

I am delighted you were able to bring the premium down again. Maybe we will get this thing within reason yet.

What do you *suppose* the Master Science is? Isn't it true to say that Science first comes into existence when the mind intently studies actual physical phenomena? And the mind operates in this and other ways, doesn't it, when it is moved to do so by reasons arising out of *human nature?*

What is the result when the mind intently studies *human nature?*

Engineers, physical scientists, biological scientists, mathematicians, statisticians, and other highly-trained specialists do work that is useful and important. As a result, we have gradually built up what amounts to a tool kit, filled with a variety of skills and techniques.

They are all useful, but nearly every time we rely on them alone and ignore human nature, we pay for it.

All our tools are valuable.

But we can't forget the hand that holds them.

Devereaux

POPPA NEEDS SHORTS
Walt and Leigh Richmond

Little Oley had wandered into forbidden territory again—Big Brother Sven's ham shack. The glowing bottles here were an irresistible lure, and he liked to pretend that he knew all there was to know about the mysteries in this room.

Of course, Sven said that not even *he* knew all of the mysteries, though he admitted he was one of the best ham operators extant, with QSOs from 18 countries and 38 states to his credit.

At the moment, Sven was busily probing into an open chassis with a hot soldering iron.

"Short's in here some place," he muttered.

"What makes shorts, Sven?" Oley wasn't so knowledgeable but what he would ask an occasional question.

Sven turned and glared down. "What are you doing in here? You know it's a Federal Offense for anybody to come into this room without I say so?"

"Momma and Hilda come in all the time, and you don't say so." Oley stood firm on what he figured were legal grounds. "What makes shorts?"

Sven relented a little. This brother had been something of a surprise to him, coming along when Sven was a full ten years old. But, he

First appeared in *Astounding Science Fiction,* January, 1964, reprinted in *Positive Charge,* © 1970 by Walt & Leigh Richmond; here reprinted by permission of the authors and of the authors' agent, Virginia Kidd.

reflected, after a few years maybe I should get used to the idea. Actually, he sort of liked the youngster.

"Shorts," he said, speaking from the superior eminence of his 14 years to the four-year-old, "is when electricity finds a way to get back where it came from without doing a lot of hard work getting there. But you see, electricity likes to work; so, even when it has an easy way, it just works harder and uses itself up."

This confused explanation of shorts was, of course, taken verbatim, despite the fact that Oley couldn't define half the words and probably couldn't even pronounce them.

"I don't like shorts. I don't like these pink shorts Momma put on me this morning. Is they electrics, Sven?"

Sven glanced around at the accidentally-dyed-in-the-laundry, formerly white shorts.

"Um-m-m. Yeah. You could call 'em electric."

With this Oley let out whoop and dashed out of the room, trailing a small voice behind him. "Momma, Momma. Sven says my shorts is electric!"

"I'll short Sven's electrics for him, if he makes fun of your shorts!" Oley heard his mother's comforting reply.

In the adult world days passed before Oley's accidentally acquired pattern of nubient information on the subject of shorts was enlarged. It was only days in the adult world, but in Oley's world each day was a mountainous fraction of an entire lifetime, into which came tumbling and jumbling—or were pulled—bits, pieces, oddments, landslides and acquisitions of information on every subject that he ran into, or that ran into him. Nobody had told Oley that acquiring information was his job at the moment; the acquisition was partly accidental, mostly instinctive, and spurred by an intense curiosity and an even more intense determination to master the world as he saw it.

There was the taste of the sick green flowers that Momma kept in the window box and, just for a side course, a little bit of the dirt, too. There were the patterns of the rain on the window, and the reactions of a cat to having its tail pulled. The fact that you touch a stove one time, and it's cool and comfortable to lay your head against, and another time it hurts. Things like that. And other things—towering adults who sometimes swoop down on you and throw you high into the air; and most times walk over you, around you, and ignore you completely. The jumble of assorted and unsorted information that is the heritage of every growing young inquiring brain.

In terms of time, it was only a couple of weeks, if you were looking at it as an adult, until the next "shorts" incident.

Oley was sitting peacefully at the breakfast table, doing his level best to control the manipulation of the huge knife-fork-and-spoon, plate-bowl-and-glass, from which he was expected to eat a meal. Things smelled good. Momma was cooking doste, and that to Oley smelled best of all. The doster ticked quietly to itself, then gave a loud pop, and up came two golden-brown slices of doste. Dostes? Oley wasn't sure. But he hadn't really begun paying too much attention to whether one doste was the same as two doste or what, though he could quite proudly tell you the difference between one and two.

Out it came, and fresh butter was spread on it, and in went two shiny white beds, for some more doste.

Little Oley watched in fascination. And now he reached for the tremendous glass sitting on the table in front of him. But his fingers didn't quite make it. Somehow, the glass was heavy and slippery, and it eluded him, rolled over on its side, and spilled the bright purple juicy contents out across the table in a huge swish.

Oley wasn't dismayed, but watched with a researcher's interest as the bright purple juice swept across the table towards the busily ticking doster. Momma, of course, wasn't here, or she would have been gruff about it. She'd just gone into the other room.

The juice spread rapidly at first, and then more and more slowly, making a huge, circuitous river spreading across the table, first towards the doster and then away from it towards the frayed power-cord lying on the table. It touched and began to run along the cord. Not a very eventful recording so far, but Oley watched, charmed.

As he watched, a few bubbles began to appear near the frayed spot. A few wisps of steam. And then, suddenly, there was a loud, snarling splatt—and Momma screamed from the doorway. "That juice is making a short!"

The information, of course, was duly recorded. Juice makes shorts.

It was a minor item of information, mixed into a jumble of others, and nothing else was added to this particular file for nearly another week.

Oley was playing happily on the living room floor that night. Here there was much to explore, though an adult might not have thought twice about it. Back in the corner behind Momma's doing bachine a bright, slender piece of metal caught Oley's attention. Bigger on one end than the other, but not really very big anywhere, the sewing machine needle proved fascinating. As a first experiment, Oley determined that it worked like a tooth by biting himself with it. After that he went around the room, biting other things with it. Information, of course, is information, and to be obtained any way one can.

The brown, snaky lamp cord was the end of this experiment. Oley bit it, viciously, with his new tooth, and had only barely observed that it had penetrated completely through when there was a loud splatt, and all the lights in the room went out.

In the darkness and confusion, of course, Oley moved away, seeking other new experiences. So the cause of the short that Momma and Poppa yakked so loudly about was never attributed to Oley's actions, but only to "How could a needle have gotten from your sewing machine into this lamp cord, Alice?"

But the sum of information had increased. Neatles stuck into lamp cords had something to do with shorts.

More time passed. And this time the file on shorts was stimulated by Poppa. The big, rough, booming voice had always scared Oley a bit when it sounded mad, like now.

"Alice, I've just *got* to have some more shorts!"

Poppa was rummaging in a drawer far above Oley's head, so he couldn't see the object under discussion. But all he already knew about shorts—the information passed in review before him.

Shorts are useful. They help electrics to work harder.

Shorts you wear, and they are electrics.

Wires are electrics.

Shorts can be made by juice.

Shorts can be made by neatles, that bite like teeth.

Poppa needs more shorts.

But Oley wasn't motivated to act at the moment. Just sorting out information and connecting it with other information files in the necessarily haphazard manner that might eventually result in something called intelligence, although he didn't know that yet.

It was a week later in the kitchen, when Momma dropped a giant version of the neatle on the floor, that his information file in this area increased again.

"Is that a neatle?" Oley asked.

His mother laughed quietly and looked fondly at her son as she put the ice pick back on the table.

"I guess you could call it a needle, Oley," she told him. "An ice needle."

Oley instinctively waited until Momma's back was turned before taking the nice neatle to try its biting powers; and instinctively took it out of the kitchen before starting his experiments.

As he passed the cellar door he heard a soft gurgling and promptly changed course. Pulling open the door with difficulty, he seated himself on the cellar stairs to watch a delightful new spectacle—frothing, gurgling water making its way across the floor towards the stairs. It looked wonderfully dirty and brown, and to Oley it was an absorbing phenomenon. It never occurred to him to tell Momma.

Suddenly above him the cellar door slammed open, and Poppa came charging down the stairs, narrowly missing the small figure, straight into the rising waters, intent, though Oley couldn't know it, on reaching the drain pipe in the far corner of the cellar to plug it before water from the spring rains could back up farther and really flood the cellar out.

Halfway across the celler, Poppa reached up and grasped the dangling overhead light to turn in on, in order to see his way to the drain —and suddenly came to a frozen, rigid, gasping stop as his hand clamped firmly over the socket.

Little Oley watched. There was juice in the cellar. Poppa had hold of an electric. Was Poppa trying to make the shorts he needed?

Oley wasn't sure. He thought it probable. And from the superior knowledge of his four years, Oley already knew a better way to make shorts. Neatles make good shorts. Juice don't do so well.

Suddenly, Oley decided to prove his point. Nice neatles probably made even better shorts than other neatles—and there was a big electric running up the side of the stairs—an electric fat enough to make a real good shorts. Maybe lots of shorts.

Raising his nice neatle, Oley took careful aim and plunged it through the 220 volt stove feeder cable.

Oley woke up. The strange pretty lady in white was a new experience. Somebody he hadn't seen before. And there seemed to be something wrong with his hand, but Oley hadn't noticed it very much, yet.

"Well, my little Hero's awake! And how are you this morning? Your Momma and Poppa will be in to see you in just a minute."

The pretty lady in white went away, and Oley gazed around the white room with its funny shape, happily recorded the experience, and dozed off again.

Then suddenly he was awakened again. Momma was there; and Poppa. And Sven. But they all seemed different somehow this morning. Momma had been crying, even though she was smiling bravely now. And Poppa seemed to have a new softness that he'd seldom seen before. Sven was looking puzzled.

"I still say, Pop, that he's a genius. He *must* have known what he was doing."

"Oley," Poppa's voice was husky—gruff, but kinder and softer than usual. "I want you to answer me carefully. But understand that it's all right either way. I just want you to tell me. Why did you put the ice pick through the stove cable? You saved my life, you know. But I'd like to know how you knew how."

Little Oley grinned. His world was peaceful and wonderful now. And all the big adults were bending and leaning down and talking to him.

"Nice neatle," he said. "Big electric. Poppa needed shorts."

three

Technology Is for People...

One result of the penetration of the mass media, by way of radio, into the underdeveloped countries of the world has been the revolution of rising expectations. The poor nations are in effect poorer than ever before simply because they now have knowledge of contrast with rich nations. In his own way, Eric Frank Russell saw this coming back in 1937 with his old story, "The Great Radio Peril."

But the "have" nations *also* look to the development of the "have not" nations. The promise of advanced technology to create abundance for all puts underdevelopment in the same class with heathendom, a condition that calls for speedy conversion to the true faith of riches and power. Harry Harrison, a true believer, laments a missed chance for salvation in "Rescue Operation."

Meanwhile, back in our own overdeveloped part of the world, high technology continues to speed up life to such an extent that we are in danger of a new disease known as future shock—the inability to throw off the past fast enough to accommodate the rush of things to come. How men of the future will overcome the dread disease of future shock is shown by R. A. Lafferty in "Slow Tuesday Night."

But there can be no future without a past. Man is a historical animal. Our awareness of future possibilities is conditioned by our increasing knowledge of the past. Given the technology to completely replay the past, we might lose touch with the present, as in the case of Bob Shaw's "Light of Other Days."

If man doesn't like the consequences, he can get rid of the offending technology or he can keep it. There are no options on using it wisely or badly. To use or not to use, that is the only question, as Brian Aldiss puts it in "Who Can Replace a Man?"

THE GREAT RADIO PERIL

Eric Frank Russell

The long-suffering public had endured it since the 1955 International Radio Convention broke up in disorder, after representatives of eight countries had given a final, defiant twist to their mustaches and walked out. That was four years before, four years of raucous prostitution of the ether. Now, the 1959 convention had disrupted in a flood of mutual recriminations. The listener sat in front of his receiver and bewared the wrath to come.

Within a week seven European countries had doubled the power of their chief transmitters; within another week ten more countries had retaliated. Radio was too useful a weapon of propaganda to have its edge dulled by rivals. The already powerful Deutschlandsender boosted itself to the unheard-of strength of twelve thousand kilowatts. Moscow followed suit. Prague tailed after. Every nation made up its mind that it was degrading to the national spirit to allow itself to be outshouted by neighbors. Great Britain knocked down its recently completed *Voice of Albion* and proceeded to replace it with what was expected to prove the biggest noise ever.

Stations crammed the air cheek by jowl, bellowing, bawling and treading on each other's corns. Manufacturers of radio receivers

First published in *Astounding Stories,* April, 1937. Reprinted by permission of the author.

worked desperately to provide the public with sets having a guaranteed selectivity of two kilocycles. Some did it; some didn't, and the successful ones were not much better off than those who failed.

In countries where radio transmission was the favored child of commercial advertisers, price of time on the air became determined by the power of the station used as well as by the period of time taken up. It cost twice as much to extol the virtues of laxatives from WRSA as it did from WBGZ. Where radio was a government-controlled monopoly the public, as usual, had to take what it was given and like it or lump it. Those who just couldn't take it spun the dial and let a foreigner throw it at them. Propaganda was the mainstay of the daily program, each day and every day. Voices sharp and sure, mellifluous or pontifical, dinned into a multitude of aching ears the benefits of this "ity" or that "ism."

The daily press, or part of it, took due note of the babel. Publications whose policy disagreed with that of local transmissions gave space to hundreds of protesting letters from irate readers. Those whose policy was completely in accord with broadcast hokum found space for such missives in the editorial wastebasket.

Press interest in international-radio mania died out when a Mrs. Artiglio Spotti suddenly gave birth to a family of six. The little man who served behind a counter, piloted a brewer's dray, or rushed to catch the 8:25 to the office every morning, was forced to surrender his views anent radio and take an interest in what the sextuplets were fed upon, how they were given it and who gave it 'em. Left-wing sheets dropped their acidulated comments concerning wireless jabber and indulged in odious comparisons between the lots of those born singly and those who came wholesale.

In June the subject of the moment was food. For some unaccountable reason crops were unsatisfactory. Nature had failed to do her stuff in the manner humans felt they had a right to expect, and the same phenomenon featured over most of the world. Potatoes had flopped; rice crops were 50 percent below normal; fruit attained luxury prices. China squinted at a quantity of soy beans hardly worth calling by the name. Britain wondered what was happening to its grass and why its hedges were creeping back into earth. Artichoke racketeers in New Jersey looked around for a new medium of iniquity, when artichokes abruptly ceased to be. Italy reaped no cereals, but harvested a crop of lemons the size of gooseberries.

As the year wore on matters became worse. The United States wheat crop failed dismally and was reported the poorest in history, the price of bread skyrocketed; the cost of living bounced up with it. News leaked out that Elmer C. Schnaksdof, a minor broker, had purchased 12 million bushels of wheat on behalf of the Federal Reserve Board.

This was practically three quarters of the quantity on the market. The Chicago Wheat Pit remained open all night, while raving brokers fought for the last barrowload.

Next day, wheat was not quoted. British bakers put up the price of the four-pound loaf to four shillings and sixpence. The rise in other countries was equal or higher. In ten parts of the world ten armies of unemployed set forth on hunger marches. In a thousand factories the hands downed tools and demanded higher wages.

Two more months faded from the calendar, and the food problem had assumed the aspect of an international crisis. Famine struck shrewdly at heavily populated and undercivilized districts. A horde of natives from Central China paid their first visit to the sea via the turbulent, yellow waters of the Yangtze, their sightless corpses swollen as they had never been in life.

Transmitters of the world blared more blatantly than ever. Thundering voices exhorted, cajoled or browbeat the helpless populace, offering a million reasons, a million cures. Technocracy blamed capitalism, capitalism blamed communism; communism passed the buck to the Yellow Peril. Atheists asserted it was the natural result of 2,000 years of Christianity; Christians attributed it to general unbelief.

Churches, chapels and tin tabernacles became packed to their doors, as frenzied congregations battered at the gates of heaven with storms of unceasing petitions. In the Far East a multitude of prayer wheels whirled out their endless *O mané padme hum!* Every street corner had its prophet predicting death, desolation and the end of all things. As the year entered into its prime the Four Horsemen flung themselves into saddles and spurred through the woods and the dales.

In Liverpool the Hop Sing Tong gathered together the pathetic remnants of its funds, hired a boat and sailed for China. Its members had been quite worthy citizens, but they felt that if one is to starve to death one must hasten to secure burial in the land of his fathers. Ten days after Chinatown had emptied, a great procession wound snakelike out of Liverpool's slums, crawled along the euphemistically-named Park Lane, and slithered to the center of the city. Here it recoiled before a cordon of police.

The head dissolved into component individuals. The windows of a tool merchant's shop were smashed; growling men grabbed giant spanners, pick helves and rods of steel. The head reformed itself—fanged this time. It struck ferociously, scattering police like chaff before a wind. Unhampered, the snake writhed forward and encircled a great department store.

Police mustered inside the store behind locked and barricaded doors. The mob moved back to gain momentum, set itself for the rush, then crashed headlong into the shop, carrying doors, barricades and police buoyed up like flotsam on the crest of a roaring wave. Scenes of absolute confusion followed.

On the second floor, in the lingerie department, a frantic, half-stripped constable viciously batoned a dummy that fell upon him from a stand. In the food department, in the basement, 20 of his fellows fought tooth and nail for dear life. Clad in a commandeered 50-guinea fur coat, the beefy wife of an unemployed butcher's assistant felled a police sergeant with a 16-pound leg of roast pork. Brandishing the joint in one enormous fist, her face purple, she cut a swath through the howling mob, spattering with fat and cracking every countenance that thrust itself into her path.

The 8th Battalion Mersey Rifles marched out of headquarters with tin hats and fixed bayonets. They reached the store half an hour too late and found it an empty shell standing in littered streets. The 8th Battalion Mersey Rifles made one capture. This was a furtive gentleman who sidled past them hugging a loosely wrapped parcel to his breast. He turned and ran like a hare when suddenly the parcel chimed and struck six. A lanky corporal outpaced him and the clock was added to two other souvenirs; banners inscribed "We Want Food" and "Prepare to Meet Thy God."

In Glasgow a number of startled Glaswegians witnessed the Battle of Springburn, a bloodthirsty fracas madder than any since the heyday of the Knobbly Boys and Gashouse Gang. Sheffield made good use of its own razors, cut and carved its way to hidden stores of food and did it with fine indiscrimination.

The Red Belt of Paris tightened about its middle; plate glass worth millions of francs dissolved to splinters under the pressure of hunger.

Berlin, Madrid, Athens, Rome, Lisbon, Cairo and every other place big enough to have a taxi by its station became the scene of wildest tumult, as citizens sought nourishment. One after another, governments became tired of seeing policemen tossed around and declared martial law.

Disciplinary declarations were good enough for the purpose of maintaining order, but they compelled no grass to grow. It didn't matter a tinker's cuss whether the declaration was signed by a plain mister or enunciated sonorously by a right honorable, not one bush produced an extra nut in consequence. Armed troops dragooned the populace in the streets; radio bossed them in their homes. The effect had been made to square with the rule of four—but the cause remained.

Newspapers had forgotten the sextuplets and returned to the subject of eats. Fifty of the more high-brow sheets ran special articles purporting to show, in a scientific manner, how diet influenced evolution. The hungry world was told in pedantic phrases that wheat eaters had it all over rice eaters. One British paper was suppressed under the

Incitement To Disaffection Act, when it quoted from the unpopular philosopher Revair: "Life is simply one great belly—who strikes at the belly strikes at life."

In the United States, at Springfield, Mass., a silent, determined mob fought like fiends and overcame a detachment of the national guard. The encounter was bloody in the extreme; the mob was not to be denied and had its way despite tear gas, vomit vapor, machine guns and other instruments of correction. It wrecked the great N.B.C. transmitter, then made for the stores.

News of this particular incident dribbled slowly around the world, and set in motion a rumor that radio was to blame for the failure of crops. Professor Howard Blakoe, physicist at the University of Delhi, heard the rumor and marveled that the connection had not been perceived long before. He decided that the time was ripe to put forth a stronger effort to tell what he had been trying to tell for weeks. He wrote a long, technical article, passed it to his literary agent, who, to his astonishment, found it accepted by the *Times* of India.

The staid and highly conservative *Times* had no views of its own about the matter, retaining a purely academic interest in a subject that had the virtue of persistent topicality. So the article was printed. It was also syndicated and reappeared in 20 other publications. To Blakoe's disappointment, it did not excite the world-wide interest he had expected. After all, a score of papers touched only the fringe of the reading public. He had the small satisfaction of receiving a few encouraging letters from fellow scientists, one or two of whom announced their intention of seeking evidence to confirm his theories.

In his article Blakoe made reference to Jungman's experiment, in which that noted research worker had shown that capillary action could be hampered, and even prevented, by the influence of powerful radio waves ranging between 20 and 400 meters in length.

It was Blakoe's theory that when they reached a certain concentration radio broadcasts caused electrolysis of the surface molecules of plant liquids, thus breaking surface tension and hampering, or preventing, capillary action. He pointed out that plant life depended upon capillary action for the free flow of natural juices, and that animal life was dependent upon plant life. He concluded with a warning and a suggestion that were both ignored: destruction of plant life would result in the elimination of humanity, unless the world reduced the power of its broadcasts to below the danger point.

One scientist read Blakoe's article and waxed sarcastic. He wrote to say that he was living within five miles of the great Toulon transmitter, but his capillaries were still working O. K., thank you. Fourteen junkers of various nationalities forwarded missives telling Blakoe that they saw through his little stunt, and that India was not going to persuade everybody to drop out of the ether and leave it clear for her. Blakoe perused all his mail, came to the conclusion that the way of the reformer is hard, and decided to leave the matter in the hands of his few supporters.

Another month trickled into the bottom glass held by Old Man Time; news of the world featured riots and upheavals daily. The *S.S. Aoraki* arrived at Hull from Samoa, bearing a cargo of copra. Former workers at a local soap factory informed the uneducated that copra was dried coconut flesh. Hungry people did not need to be told more. The *Aoraki* was raided and her cargo dispersed with lightning speed, while her police guards gave an aquatic display diving from the dock.

During the same week half the world tumbled to the fact that manufacturers of cattle food held large stocks of locust beans. Not a bean was obtainable by the following Saturday. In every country works and factories closed down, as employees found it necessary to seek and take by force those things wages could not buy.

Congress sat in Washington and considered a proposal for another radio convention. Two hundred lobbyists, representing American stations, used all their power and influence to see that nothing was done. Outside the White House a simple citizen tried to distribute copies of Blakoe's article and was flung into the gutter by a cop.

The British Parliament assembled at Westminster to consider a radio proposal emanating from Washington. Seventeen representatives made speeches defending the broadcasting rights of the fighting forces, the clergy, the theatrical world, the department of propaganda, and the Union Jack. One holder of a radio permit, seated in the gallery, showered a handful of leaflets on the floor of the house. The leaflets were reprints of Blakoe's article. The vulgar objector was hustled outside the sacred precincts.

Britain's parliamentary discussion ended in a decision to double the power of the new *Voice of Albion;* Congress' deliberations resulted in the dispatch of a stern note to Soviet Russia.

The mayor of New York looked along Broadway and saw it strewn, not with ticker tape and torn telephone books, but with buttons, belts and pieces of ripped clothing. The sheriff of Cheyenne County, Wyoming, was shot as he defended the last sack of flour in a bakery. Japan severed relations with Argentina after a Rosario newspaper had printed a photograph of a half-eaten baby, captioned as an example of what was taking place in Yokohama. Forty-four millionaires departed for the South Sea Islands, when news leaked out that Polynesia was the only portion of Earth unaffected by the canker. The love story of Hiné Moa became a snigger-provoking anecdote for stag parties. Civilization lost all refinement.

The very severity of this world-wide affliction brought about its own end. It contained within itself the seeds of its own destruction.

Half-starved or wholly starved people could no longer purchase radio receivers, while those who had them could not afford to run them. Radio manufacturers the world over experienced an unprecedented drop in sales, which filled them with alarm. Nations that derived revenue from use of wireless sets found their income shrinking rapidly toward the vanishing point.

The astute editor of the Little Rock, Arkansas, *Daily Searchlight* had long blamed radio competition for the paucity of advertisements in his columns, and he decided that now was the time to do something about it. He commenced by giving front-page prominence to Blakoe's thesis, and supported it with an acidulated editorial which, in essence, was a violent attack upon radio transmissions.

A large number of contemporaries followed the lead of the Little Rock sheet, and Blakoe's half-forgotten theory came before a bigger public. Sudden press antipathy to radio was not due to real faith in Blakoe's notions, or to any desire to support the Arkansas editor, but to falling circulation as the public saved their pennies for things more necessary than newsprint.

The Little Rock paper's next scoop took the form of a letter from the Bose Institute at Calcutta. Dr. T. Runga Rao was pleased to inform the editor of the *Daily Searchlight* that the institute had been endeavoring to find evidence in support of Professor Blakoe and had met with some success. Measuring of plant exhalations had shown that the output of plant breath was 40 percent greater than that of 12 months before and, what was much more important, the output was exceeding the intake. Samples of subtropical vegetation, imported from Palmerston, Cook Islands, had thrown off more gas and become shriveled and stunted when reset near to the huge antenna of Calcutta Station. The Bose Institute was satisfied that radio was causing partial electrolysis of vegetable juices.

Almost by the same post the *Daily Searchlight* received a letter from Dr. E. H. Jawaharlal, astrophysicist at Kodaikanal Observatory. Jawaharlal said that he had been corresponding with Dr. Runga Rao, and he thought the editor might be interested in a couple of graphs. The graphs showed variations in solar radiation over the broadcast bands during the previous ten years, and the incidence of crops for the same period. When studied side by side the graphs showed clearly and unmistakably the remarkable reaction of vegetation to the appearance of sunspots and their accompanying magnetic storms.

Although it was somewhat out of his usual line, Jawaharlal thought his evidence pointed directly to the fact that free electrical energy was to plant life exactly as some poisons are to human beings, stimulating and beneficial up to a certain dosage, deadly above it.

Serge Jevsky, a Polish farmer plowing his furrows in Wyoming, knew nothing about the technical aspects of the matter, but wrote the

Daily Searchlight that he supported Blakoe, Rao and Jawaharlal to the last man, dime and ditch. He pointed out that for the past two years he had illuminated his farmhouse by utilizing free power picked up by his concrete-based steel hay barn from mighty WHFS, a mile away. It was his considered opinion as a United States' citizen, and a farmer, that power sufficient to light a home was enough to kill a carrot. And what sort of a country was this, anyway, when a feller's wheat got electrocuted every time some fat capitalist sprayed the air with a toothpaste ad?

To what extent the great American public followed the academic discussions of Indian scientists will never be known, but Jevsky's cry from the heart met with immediate response. The *Daily Searchlight* printed a round 20 confirmatory letters from agricultural gentlemen who were not afraid to call a spade a ruddy shovel. The editorial told readers that these letters were merely a selection from 2,000 received that week. Other papers followed suit.

The Grand Dragon, arrived suddenly in Birmingham, sent round the message of the Fiery Cross and mobilized overnight the Alabama Legion of the Ku Klux Klan. It was the first time they had got together in 15 years, and they made up for lost moments. They swept through the streets of Birmingham like the hordes of Jenghiz Khan, picked up NBC's "Sweet Singer of the South" and sprinkled it around the outskirts of the city. With a thunder of hoofs they crashed into Tuskegee, played with dynamite and bounced its little relay station against the glowering clouds.

Next day the Ku Klux Klan put over a special tri-state demonstration. Under the personal leadership of the Supreme Kleagle, an army of 40,000 swept like bats out of hell through Florida, Georgia and South Carolina, demolishing every radio station, professional or amateur. Hooded figures in billowing gowns, fronted with the sign of the knobbed X, outpaced sweating detachments of United States cavalry, landed a shattering side kick on the nearest transmitter and vanished like wraiths into the safe sanctuary of agricultural areas.

Newspapers noted a sudden resuscitation of the ancient Molly Maguires in the mid-West. Perspiring farmers, masked, wearing Irish bonnets obtained from heaven alone knows where, passed their jack-knives through copper wires, used tubes as targets for their shotguns. Official Washington ran round in circles when eight special investigators got back their pants by parcel post, collect.

As antiradio sentiment gathered strength, every nation ran true to form in the manner of its reaction. Sturdy independents of Ireland and Spain emulated America, took the law into their own hands and pushed over transmitters with enthusiasm permitting no argument.

The British Government ignored a petition signed by seven million suffering taxpayers, who "humbly prayed" that it "might please" the government to curtail the activity of radio. Neither did the British Government worry itself unduly when a deputation from the Federation of Radio Receiver Manufacturers said that the radio industry would cease to exist within three months unless something was done to induce people to buy their products.

Bankers remembered they had very large sums invested in the radio, agriculture and foodstuffs industries. It was foolish to permit one interest to strangle another. A deputation of financial big-wigs waited upon the stubborn ones at Westminster, and pointed out that though Britannia may rule a few odd waves here and there, "Old Man Gold" bosses everything else. Responsible politicians saw the point without difficulty; they were not going to be bulldozed by a moronic electorate, but were quite prepared to accede to the just demands of sound and sane finance.

The *Voice of Albion* closed down forthwith; 16 lesser stations closed with it; the remaining 8 had their power reduced by half. Twelve thousand amateurs came under a ban, prohibiting their transmitters using power in excess of 100 watts.

October arrived, and with it news from the United States that plant life was reviving and winter citrus crops showing signs of coming up to normal. That settled the few doubters still left. By governmental decree Soviet Russia reduced its radio power to one tenth that of yore. A grand total of 52 transmitters in Japan and Germany went up like sparked gasometers, when drilled and uniformed antiradio organizations in both countries struck simultaneously. Every nation in the world had taken, or was about to take, action to wipe out the airy menace—some voluntarily, some under the threat of violence.

Spring of '60 saw a world born anew. Stunted plants again commenced to climb skyward, prematurely aged trees took on fresh youth. Every religion and denomination thereof *knew* that its own prayers alone had been answered, and offered more prayers of gratitude. Decimated flocks of birds settled and built nests with reasonable hope of rearing the families to come. City sparrows felt the influence of prosperity just around the corner, perched in the roof gutters, fluffed their tummies and nagged at lean cats below.

The year crawled along. All creatures waxed fat upon the earth and the fullness thereof. Blakoe and the editor of the *Daily Searchlight* were soon forgotten by a stomach-filled world. The Hop Sing Tong opened many new branches outside the Land of the Lotus; the half-hearted remnants of the Ku Klux Klan turned their attention to plowing.

News of the day revealed a world buried in its characteristically peaceful slumbers. Fourteen gangsters in the United States were plugged in one week; a South American republic had its regular Saturday afternoon revolution; the dictator of another celebrated his fatherhood for the seventy-second time. Britain blessed and launched an unsinkable battleship; Germany launched, without blessing, a submarine powerful enough to sink it. Another French cabinet was formed to save the franc; Japan demanded an abject apology from China, or what was left of it; a Soviet scientist dumfounded biological circles by successfully crossing a dog with a goat.

An obscure author tore up his thirtieth rejection, started afresh and wrote a story telling how Martians resembling pink spiders wiped out the world with a giant transmitter directing its beam through interplanetary space. The story was kicked out—without regrets. The world had had quite enough of radio.

RESCUE OPERATION
Harry Harrison

"Pull! Pull steadily... !" Dragomir shouted, clutching at the tarry cords of the net. Beside him in the hot darkness Pribislav Polasek grunted as he heaved on the wet strands. The net was invisible in the black water, but the blue light trapped in it rose closer and closer to the surface.

"It's slipping. . . ." Pribislav groaned and clutched the rough gunwale of the little boat. For a single instant he could see the blue light on the helmet, a face plate and the suited body that faded into blackness—then it slipped free of the net. He had just a glimpse of a dark shape before it was gone. "Did you see it?" he asked. "Just before he fell he waved his hand."

"How can I know—the hand moved, it could have been the net, or he might still be alive?" Dragomir had his face bent almost to the glassy surface of the water, but there was nothing more to be seen. "He might be alive."

The two fishermen sat back in the boat and stared at each other in the harsh light of the hissing acetylene lamp in the bow. They were very different men, yet greatly alike in their stained, baggy trousers

and faded cotton shirts. Their hands were deeply wrinkled and cal-
loused from a lifetime of hard labor, their thoughts slowed by the
rhythm of work and years.

"We cannot get him up with the net," Dragomir finally said, speaking first as always.

"Then we will need help," Pribislav added. "We have anchored the
buoy here, we can find the spot again."

"Yes, we need help." Dragomir opened and closed his large hands,
then leaned over to bring the rest of the net into the boat. "The diver,
the one who stays with the widow Korenc, he will know what to do. His
name is Kukovic and Petar said he is a doctor of science from the
university in Ljubljana."

They bent to their oars and sent the heavy boat steadily over the
glasslike water of the Adriatic. Before they had reached shore the sky
was light and when they tied to the sea wall in Brbinj the sun was above
the horizon.

Joze Kukovic looked at the rising ball of the sun, already hot on
his skin, yawned and stretched. The widow shuffled out with his coffee,
mumbled good morning and put it on the stone rail of the porch. He
pushed the tray aside and sat down next to it, then emptied the coffee
from the small, long-handled pot into his cup. The thick Turkish coffee
would wake him up, in spite of the impossible hour. From the rail he
had a view down the unpaved and dusty street to the port, already
stirring to life. Two women, with the morning's water in brass pots
balanced on their heads, stopped to talk. The peasants were bringing
in their produce for the morning market, baskets of cabbages and
potatoes and trays of tomatoes, strapped onto tiny donkeys. One of
them brayed, a harsh noise that sawed through the stillness of the
morning, bouncing echoes from the yellowed buildings. It was hot already. Brbinj was a town at the edge of nowhere, locked between empty
ocean and barren hills, asleep for centuries and dying by degrees. There
were no attractions here—if you did not count the sea. But under the
flat, blue calm of the water was another world that Joze loved.

Cool shadows, deep valleys, more alive than all the sun-blasted
shores that surrounded it. Excitement, too: just the day before, too late
in the afternoon to really explore it, he had found a Roman galley
half-buried in the sand. He would get into it today, the first human in
2000 years, and heaven alone knew what he would find there. In the
sand about it had been shards of broken amphorae, there might be
whole ones inside the hull.

Sipping happily at his coffee he watched the small boat tying up
in the harbor, and wondered why the two fishermen were in such a
hurry. They were almost running, and no one ran here in the summer.
Stopping below his porch the biggest one called up to him.

"Doctor, may we come up? There is something urgent."

"Yes, of course." He was surprised and wondered if they took him for a physician.

Dragomir shuffled forward and did not know where to begin. He pointed out over the ocean.

"It fell, out there last night, we saw it, *a sputnik* without a doubt?"

"A traveler?" Joze Kukovic wrinkled his forehead, not quite sure that he heard right. When the locals were excited it was hard to follow their dialect. For such a small country Yugoslavia was cursed with a multitude of tongues.

"No, it was not a *putnik,* but a *sputnik,* one of the Russian space-ships."

"Or an American one," Pribislav spoke for the first time, but he was ignored.

Joze smiled and sipped his coffee. "Are you sure it wasn't a meteor-ite you saw? There is always a heavy meteor shower this time of the year."

"A *sputnik.*" Dragomir insisted stolidly. "The ship fell far out in the *Jadransko More* and vanished, we saw that. But the space pilot came down almost on top of us, into the water. . . ."

"The WHAT?" Joze gasped, jumping to his feet and knocking the coffee tray to the floor. The brass tray clanged and rattled in circles unnoticed. "There was a man in this thing—and he got clear?"

Both fishermen nodded at the same time and Dragomir continued. "We saw this light fall from the *sputnik* when it went overhead and drop into into the water. We couldn't see what it was, just a light, and we rowed there as fast as we could. It was still sinking and we dropped a net and managed to catch him. . . ."

"You have the pilot?"

"No, but once we pulled him close enough to the surface to see he was in a heavy suit, with a window like a diving suit, and there was something on the back that might have been like your tanks there."

"He waved his hand," Pribislav insisted.

"He might have waved a hand, we could not be sure. We came back for help."

The silence lengthened and Joze realized that he was the help that they needed, and that they had turned the responsibility over to him. What should he do first? The astronaut might have his own oxygen tanks, Joze had no real idea what provisions were made for water landings, but if there were oxygen the man might still be alive.

Joze paced the floor while he thought, a short, square figure in khaki shorts and sandals. He was not handsome, his nose was too big and his teeth were too obvious for that, but he generated a certainty of power. He stopped and pointed to Pribislav.

"We're going to have to get him out. You can find the spot again?"

"A buoy."

"Good. And we may need a doctor. You have none here, but is there one in Osor?"

"Dr. Bratos, but he is very old. . . ."

"As long as he is still alive, we'll have to get him. Can anyone in this town drive an automobile?"

The fishermen looked towards the roof and concentrated, while Joze controlled his impatience.

"Yes, I think so," Dragomir finally said. "Petar was a *partizan*. . . ."

"That's right," the other fisherman finished the thought. "He has told many times how they stole German trucks and how he drove. . . ."

"Well, then one of you get this Petar and give him these keys to my car, it's a German car so he should be able to manage. Tell him to bring the doctor back at once."

Dragomir took the keys, but handed them to Pribislav who ran out.

"Now let's see if we can get the man up," Joze said, grabbing his scuba gear and leading the way towards the boat.

They rowed, side by side though Dragomir's powerful strokes did most of the work.

"How deep is the water out here?" Joze asked. He was already dripping with sweat as the sun burned on him.

"The Kvarneric is deeper up by Rab, but we were fishing off Trstenik and the bottom is only about four fathoms there. We're coming to the buoy."

"Seven meters, it shouldn't be too hard to find him." Joze kneeled in the bottom of the boat and slipped into the straps of the scuba. He buckled it tight, checked the valves, then turned to the fisherman before he bit into the mouthpiece. "Keep the boat near this buoy and I'll use it for a guide while I search. If I need a line or any help, I'll surface over the astronaut, then you can bring the boat to me."

He turned on the oxygen and slipped over the side, the cool water rising up his body as he sank below the surface. With a powerful kick he started towards the bottom, following the dropping line of the buoy rope. Almost at once he saw the man, spread-eagled on white sand below.

Joze swam down, making himself stroke smoothly in spite of his growing excitement. Details were clearer as he dropped lower. There were no identifying marks on the pressure suit, it might be either American or Russian. It was a hard suit, metal or reinforced plastic, and painted green, with a single, flat face plate in the helmet.

Because distance and size are so deceptive under water, Joze was on the sand next to the figure before he realized it was less than four feet long. He gasped and almost lost his mouthpiece.

Then he looked into the face plate and saw that the creature inside was not human.

Joze coughed a bit and blew out a stream of bubbles: he had been holding his breath without realizing it. He just floated there, paddling slowly with his hands to stay in a position, looking at the face within the helmet.

It was as still as waxen cast, green wax with a roughened surface, slit nostrils, slit mouth and large eyeballs unseen but prominent as they pushed up against the closed lids. The arrangement of features was roughly human, but no human being ever had skin this color or had a pulpy crest like this one, partially visible through the face plate, growing up from above the closed eyes. Joze stared down at the suit made of some unknown material, and at the compact atmosphere regeneration apparatus on the alien's back. What kind of atmosphere? He looked back at the creature's face and saw that the eyes were open and the thing was watching him.

Fear was his first reaction, he shot back in the water like a startled fish then, angry at himself, came forward again. The alien slowly raised one arm, then dropped it limply. Joze looked through the face plate and saw that the eyes were closed again. The alien was alive, but unable to move, perhaps it was injured and in pain. The wreck of the creature's ship showed that something had been wrong with the landing. Reaching under as gently as he could he cradled the tiny body in his arms, trying to ignore a feeling of revulsion when the cold fabric of the thing's suit touched his bare arms. It was only metal or plastic, he had to be a scientist about this. When he lifted it up the eyes still did not open and he bore the limp and almost weightless form to the surface.

"You great stupid clumsy clod of peasant, help me," he shouted, spitting out his mouthpiece and treading water on the surface, but Dragomir only shook his head in terror and retreated to the point of the bow when he saw what the physicist had borne up from below.

"It is a creature from another world and cannot harm you!" Joze insisted but the fisherman would not approach.

Joze cursed aloud and only managed with great difficulty to get the alien into the boat, then climbed in after him. Though he was twice Joze's size, threats of violence drove Dragomir to the oars. But he used the farthest set of tholepins, even though it made rowing much more difficult. Joze dropped his scuba gear into the bottom of the boat and looked more closely at the drying fabric of the alien spacesuit. His fear of the unknown was forgotten in his growing enthusiasm. He was a nuclear physicist, but he remembered enough of his chemistry and mechanics to know that this material was completely impossible—by Earth's standards.

Light green, it was as hard as steel over the creature's limbs and torso, yet was soft and bent easily at the joints as he proved by lifting and dropping the limp arm. His eyes went down the alien's tiny figure: there was a thick harness about the middle, roughly where a human waist would be, and hanging from this was a bulky container, like an oversize sporran. The suiting continued without an apparent seam— but the right leg! It was squeezed in and crushed as though it had been grabbed by a giant pliers. Perhaps this explained the creature's lack of motion. Could it be hurt? In pain?

Its eyes were open again and Joze realized in sudden horror that the helmet was filled with water. It must have leaked in, the thing was drowning. He grabbed at the helmet, seeing if it would screw off, tugging at it in panic while the great eyes rolled up towards him.

Then he forced himself to think, and shakingly let go. The alien was still quiet, eyes open, no bubbles apparently coming from lips or nose. Did it breathe? Had the water leaked in—or was it possible it had always been there? Was it water? Who knew what alien atmosphere it might breathe; methane, chlorine, sulfur dioxide—why not water? The liquid was inside, surely enough, the suit wasn't leaking and the creature seemed unchanged.

Joze looked up and saw that Dragomir's panicked strokes had brought them into the harbor already, and that a crowd was waiting on the shore.

The boat almost overturned as Dragomir leaped up onto the harbor wall, kicking backward in his panic. They drifted away and Joze picked the mooring line up from the floor boards and coiled it in his hands. "Here," he shouted, "catch this. Tie it onto the ring there."

No one heard him, or if they heard, did not want to admit it. They stared down at the green-cased figure lying in the sternsheets and a rustle of whispering blew across them like wind among pine boughs. The women clutched their hands to their breasts, crossing themselves.

"Catch this!" Joze said through clenched teeth, forcing himself to keep his temper.

He hurled the rope onto the stones and they shied away from it. A youth grabbed it and slowly threaded it through the rusty ring, hands shaking and head tilted to one side, his mouth dropped in a permanent gape. He was feeble-minded, too simple to understand what was going on: he simply obeyed the shouted order.

"Help me get this thing ashore," Joze called out, and even before the words were out of his mouth he realized the futility of the request.

The peasants shuffled backwards, a blank-faced mob sharing the same fear of the unknown, the women like giant, staring dolls in their knee-length flaring skirts, black stockings and high felt shoes. He would have to do it himself. Balancing in the rocking boat he cradled the alien in his arms and lifted it carefully up onto the rough stone of the harbor wall. The circle of watchers pushed back even farther, some of the women choking off screams and running back to their houses, while the men muttered louder: Joze ignored them.

These people were going to be no help to him—and they might cause trouble. His own room would be safest, he doubted if they would bother him there. He had just picked up the alien when a newcomer pushed through the watchers.

"There—what is that? A *vrag!*" The old priest pointed in horror at the alien in Joze's arms and backed away, fumbling for his crucifix.

"Enough of your superstition!" Joze snapped. "This is no devil but a sentient creature, a traveler. Now get out of my way."

He pushed forward and they fled before him. Joze moved as quickly as he could without appearing to hurry, leaving the crowd behind. There was a slapping of quick footsteps and he looked over his shoulder; it was the priest, Father Perc. His stained cassock flapped and his breath whistled in his throat with the unaccustomed exertion.

"Tell me, what are you doing . . . Dr. Kukovic? What is that . . . thing? Tell me. . . ."

"I told you. A traveler. Two of the local fishermen saw something come from the sky and crash. This . . . alien came from it." Joze spoke as calmly as possible. There might be trouble with the people, but not if the priest were on his side. "It is a creature from another world, a water-breathing animal, and it's hurt. We must help it."

Father Perc scrambled along sideways as he looked with obvious distaste at the motionless alien. "It is wrong," he mumbled, "this is something unclean, *zao duh*. . . ."

"Neither demon nor devil, can't you get that through your mind? The church recognizes the possibility of creatures from other planets —the Jesuits even argue about it—so why can't you? Even the Pope believes there is life on other worlds."

"Does he? Does he?" the old man asked, blinking with red-rimmed eyes.

Joze brushed by him and up the steps to the widow Korenc's house. She was nowhere in sight as he went into his room and gently lowered the still-unconscious form of the alien onto his bed. The priest stopped in the doorway, quivering fingers on his rosary, uncertain. Joze stood over the bed, opening and closing his hands, just as unsure. What could he do? The creature was wounded, perhaps dying, something must be done. But what?

The distant droning whine of a car's engine pushed into the hot room and he almost sighed with relief. It was his car, he recognized the sound, and it would be bringing the doctor. The car stopped outside and the doors slammed, but no one appeared.

Joze waited tensely, realizing that the townspeople must be talking to the doctor, telling him what had happened. A slow minute passed and Joze started from the room, but stopped before he passed the priest, still standing just inside the door. What was keeping them: his window faced on an alleyway and he could not see the street in front of the building. Then the outside door opened and he could hear the widow's whispered voice, "In there, straight through."

There were two men, both dusty from the road. One was obviously the doctor, a short and dumpy man clutching a worn black bag, his bald head beaded with sweat. Next to him was a young man, tanned and windburned, dressed like the other fishermen: this must be Petar the ex-partisan.

It was Petar who went to the bed first, the doctor just stood clutching his bag and blinking about at the room.

"What is this thing?" Petar asked, then bent over, hands on his knees, to stare in through the face plate. "Whatever it is, it sure is ugly."

"I don't know. It's from another planet, that's the only thing I know. Now move aside so that the doctor can look." Joze waved and the physician moved reluctantly forward. "You must be Dr. Bratos. I'm Kukovic, professor of nuclear physics at the university in Ljubljana." Perhaps waving around a little prestige might get this man's reluctant co-operation.

"Yes, how do you do. Very pleased to meet you, professor, an honor I assure you. But what is it that you wish me to do, I do not understand?" He shook ever so lightly as he spoke and Joze realized that the man was very old, well into his eighties or even more. He would have to be patient.

"This alien . . . whatever it is . . . is injured and unconscious. We must do what we can to save its life."

"But what can I do? The thing is sealed in a metal garment—look it is filled with water—I am a doctor, a medical man, but not for animals, creatures like that."

"Neither am I, doctor—no one on earth is. But we must do our best. We must get the suit off the alien and then discover what we can do to help."

"It is impossible! The fluid inside of it, it will run out."

"Obviously, so we will have to take precautions. We will have to determine what the liquid is, then get more of it and fill the bathtub in the next room. I have been looking at the suit and the helmet seems to be a separate piece, clamped into position. If we loosen the clamps, we should be able to get our sample."

For precious seconds Dr. Bratos stood there, nibbling at his lip, before he spoke. "Yes, we could do that, I suppose we could, but what could we catch the sample in. This is most difficult and irregular."

"It doesn't make any difference what we catch the sample in," Joze snapped, frustration pushing at his carefully held control. He turned to Petar who was standing silently by, smoking a cigarette in his cupped hand. "Will you help? Get a soup plate, anything, from the kitchen."

Petar simply nodded and left. There were muffled complaints from the widow, but he was back quickly with her best pot."

"That's good," Joze said, lifting the alien's head, "now, slide it under here." With the pot in position he twisted one of the clamps; it snapped open but nothing else happened. A hairline opening was visible at the junction, but it stayed dry. But when Joze opened the second clamp there was a sudden gush of clear liquid under pressure, and before he fumbled the clamp shut again the pot was half full. He lifted the alien again and, without being told, Petar pulled the pot free and put it on the table by the window. "It's hot," he said.

Joze touched the outside of the container. "Warm not hot, about 120 degrees I would guess. A hot ocean on a hot planet."

"But . . . is it water?" Dr. Bratos asked haltingly.

"I suppose it is—but aren't you the one to find out? Is it fresh water or sea water?"

"I'm no chemist . . . how can I tell . . . it is very complicated."

Petar laughed and took Joze's water glass from the nightstand. "That's not so hard to find out," he said, and dipped it into the pot. He raised the half-filled glass, sniffed at it, then took a sip and puckered his lips. "Tastes like ordinary sea water to me, but there's another taste, sort of bitter."

Joze took the glass from him. "This could be dangerous," the doctor protested, but they ignored him. Yes, salt water, hot salt water with a sharpness to it. "It tastes like more than a trace of iodine. Can you test for the presence of iodine, doctor."

"Here . . . no, it is quite complicated. In the laboratory with the correct equipment—" his voice trailed off as he opened his bag on the table and groped through it. He brought his hand out empty. "In the laboratory."

"We have no laboratory or any other assistance, doctor. We will have to be satisfied with what we have here, ordinary sea water will have to do."

"I'll get a bucket and fill the tub," Petar said.

"Good. But don't fill the bathtub yet. Bring the water into the kitchen and we'll heat it, then pour it in."

"Right." Petar brushed past the silent and staring priest and was gone. Joze looked at Father Perc and thought of the people of the village.

"Stay here, doctor," he said. "This alien is your patient and I don't think anyone other than you should come near. Just sit by him."

"Yes, of course, that is correct," Dr. Bratos said relievedly, pulling the chair over and sitting down.

The breakfast fire was still burning in the big stove and flamed up when Joze slid in more sticks. On the wall hung the big copper washtub and he dropped it onto the stove with a clang. Behind him the widow's bedroom door opened, but slammed shut again when he turned. Petar came in with a bucket of water and poured it into the tub.

"What are the people doing?" Joze asked.

"Just milling about and bothering each other. They won't be any trouble. If you're worried about them, I can drive back to Osor and bring the police, or telephone someone."

"No, I should have thought of that earlier. Right now I need you here. You're the only one who isn't either senile or ignorant."

Petar smiled. "I'll get some more water."

The bathtub was small and the washtub big. When the heated water was dumped in it filled it more than half way, enough to cover the small alien. There was a drain from the bathtub but no faucets: it was usually filled with a hose from the sink. Joze picked up the alien, cradling it like a child in his arms, and carried it into the bath. The eyes were open again, following his every movement, but making no protest. He lowered the creature gently into the water, then straightened a moment and took a deep breath. "Helmet first, then we'll try to figure out how the suit opens." He bent and slowly twisted the clamps.

With all four clamps open the helmet moved freely. He opened it a wide crack, ready to close it quickly if there were any signs of trouble. The ocean water would be flowing in now, mixing with the alien water, yet the creature made no complaint. After a minute Joze slowly pulled the helmet off, cradling the alien's head with one hand so that it would not bump to the bottom of the tub.

Once the helmet was clear the pulpy crest above the eyes sprang up like a coxcomb, reaching up over the top of the green head. A wire ran from the helmet to a shiny bit of metal on one side of the creature's skull. There was an indentation there and Joze slowly pulled a metal plug out, perhaps an earphone of some kind. The alien was opening and closing its mouth, giving a glimpse of bony yellow ridges inside, and a very low humming could be heard.

Petar pressed his ear against the outside of the metal tube. "The thing is talking or something, I can hear it."

"Let me have your stethoscope, doctor," Joze said, but when the doctor did not move he dug it from the bag himself. Yes—when he pressed it to the metal he could hear a rising and falling whine, speech of a kind.

"We can't possibly understand him—not yet," he said, handing the stethoscope back to the doctor who took it automatically. "We had better try to get the suit off."

There were no seams or fastenings visible, nor could Joze find anything when he ran his fingers over the smooth surface. The alien must have understood what they were doing because it jerkingly raised one hand and fumbled at the metal sealing ring about the collar. With a liquid motion the suit split open down the front, the opening bifurcated and ran down each leg. There was a sudden welling of blue liquid from the injured leg.

Joze had a quick glimpse of green flesh, strange organs, then he spun about. "Quick, doctor—your bag. The creature is hurt, that fluid might be blood, we have to help it."

"What can I do," Dr. Bratos said, unmoving. "Drugs, antiseptics— I might kill it—we know nothing of its body chemistry."

"Then don't use any of those. This is a traumatic injury, you can bind it up, stop the bleeding, can't you?"

"Of course, of course," the old man said and at last his hands had familiar things to do, extracting bandages and sterile gauze from his bag, tape and scissors.

Joze reached into the warm and now murky water and forced himself to reach under the leg and grasp the hot, green flesh. It was strange—but not terrible. He lifted the limb free of the water and they saw a crushed gap oozing a thick blue fluid. Petar turned away, but the doctor put on a pad of gauze and tightened the bandages about it. The alien was fumbling at the discarded suit beside it in the tub, twisting its leg in Joze's grip. He looked down and saw it take something from the sporran container. Its mouth was moving again, he could hear the dim buzz of its voice.

"What is it? What do you want?" Joze asked.

It was holding the object across its chest now with both hands: it appeared to be a book of some kind. It might be a book, it might be anything.

Yet it was covered in a shiny substance with dark markings on it, and at the edge seemed to be made of many sheets bound together. It could be a book. The leg was twisting now in Joze's grasp and the alien's mouth was open wider, as if it were shouting.

"The bandage will get wet if we put it back into the water," the doctor said.

"Can't you wrap adhesive tape over it, seal it in?"

"In my bag—I'll need some more."

While they talked the alien began to rock back and forth, splashing water from the tub, pulling its leg from Joze's grasp. It still held the book in one thin, multi-fingered hand, but with the other one it began to tear at the bandages on its leg.

"It's hurting itself, stop it. This is terrible," the doctor said, recoiling from the tub.

Jose snatched a piece of wrapping paper from the floor. "You fool! You incredible fool!" he shouted. "These compresses you used—they're impregnated with sulfanilamide."

"I always use them, they're the best, American, they prevent wound infection."

Joze pushed him aside and plunged his arms into the tub to tear the bandages free, but the alien reared up out of his grasp sitting up above the water, its mouth gaping wide. Its eyes were open and staring and Joze recoiled as a stream of water shot from its mouth. There was a gargling sound as the water died to a trickle, and then, as the first air touched the vocal cords, a rising howling scream of pain. It echoed from the plaster ceiling an inhuman agony as the creature threw its arms wide, then fell face forward into the water. It did not move again and, without examining it, Joze knew it was dead.

One arm was twisted back, out of the tub, still grasping the book. Slowly the fingers loosened, and while Joze looked on numbly, unable to move, the book thudded to the floor.

"Help me," Petar said, and Joze turned to see that the doctor had fallen and Petar was kneeling over him. "He fainted, or a heart attack. What can we do?"

His anger was forgotten as Joze kneeled. The doctor seemed to be breathing regularly and his face wasn't flushed, so perhaps it was only a fainting spell. The eyelids fluttered. The priest brushed by and looked down over Joze's shoulder.

Dr. Bratos opened his eyes, looking back and forth at the faces bent over him. "I'm sorry—" he said thickly, then the eyes closed again as if to escape the sight of them.

Joze stood, and found that he was trembling. The priest was gone. Was it all over? Perhaps they might never have saved the alien, but they should have done better than this. Then he saw the wet spot on the floor and realized the book was gone.

"Father Perc!" he shouted, crying it out like an insult. The man had taken the book, the priceless book!

Joze ran out into the hall and saw the priest coming from the kitchen. His hands were empty. With sudden fear Joze knew what the old man had done and brushed past him into the kitchen and ran to the stove, hurling open the door.

There, among the burning wood, lay the book. It was steaming, almost smoking as it dried, lying open. It was obviously a book, there were marks on the pages of some kind. He turned to grab up the shovel and behind him the fire exploded, sending a white flame across the room. It had almost caught him in the face, but he did not think of that. Pieces of burning wood lay on the floor, and inside the stove there was only the remains of the original fire. Whatever substance the book had been made of was highly inflammable once it had dried out.

"It was evil," the priest said from the doorway, "A *zao duh,* an abomination with a book of evil. We have been warned, such things have happened before on earth, and always the faithful must fight back —"

Petar pushed in roughly past him and helped Joze to a chair, brushing the hot embers from his bare skin. Joze had not felt their burn, all he was aware of was an immense weariness.

"Why here?" he asked. "Of all places in the world why here? A few more degrees to the west and the creature would have come down near Trieste with surgeons, hospitals, men, facilities. Or, if it had just stayed on its course a little longer, it could have seen the lights, and would have landed at Rijika. Something could have been done. But why here?" he surged to his feet, shaking his fist at nothing—and at everything.

"Here, in this superstition ridden, simple-minded backwater of the world! What kind of world do we live in where there is a five million volt electron accelerator not 100 miles from primitive stupidity. That this creature should come so far, come so close . . . why, why?"

Why?

He slumped back into the chair again feeling older than he had ever felt before and tired beyond measure. What could they have learned from that book?

He sighed, and the sigh came from so deep within him that his whole body trembled as though shaken by an awful fever.

SLOW TUESDAY NIGHT

R. A. Lafferty

A panhandler intercepted the young couple as they strolled down the night street.

"Preserve us this night," he said as he touched his hat to them, "and could you good people advance me a thousand dollars to be about the recouping of my fortunes?"

"I gave you a thousand last Friday," said the young man.

"Indeed you did," the panhandler replied, "and I paid you back tenfold by messenger before midnight."

"That's right, George, he did," said the young woman. "Give it to him dear. I believe he's a good sort."

So the young man gave the panhandler a thousand dollars; and the panhandler touched his hat to them in thanks, and went on to the recouping of his fortunes.

As he went into Money Market, the panhandler passed Ildefonsa Impala the most beautiful woman in the city.

"Will you marry me this night, Ildy?" he asked cheerfully.

"Oh, I don't believe so, Basil," she said. "I marry you pretty often, but tonight I don't seem to have any plans at all. You may make me a gift on your first or second, however. I always like that."

First Appeared in *Galaxy,* April, 1965. Reprinted in *Nine Hundred Grandmothers* © 1970 by R. A. Lafferty; here reprinted by permission of the author and of the author's agent, Virginia Kidd.

But when they had parted she asked herself: "But whom will I marry tonight?"

The panhandler was Basil Bagelbaker who would be the richest man in the world within an hour and a half. He would make and lose four fortunes within eight hours; and these not the little fortunes that ordinary men acquire, but titanic things.

When the Abebaios block had been removed from human minds, people began to make decisions faster, and often better. It had been the mental stutter. When it was understood what it was, and that it had no useful function, it was removed by simple childhood metasurgery.

Transportation and manufacturing had then become practically instantaneous. Things that had once taken months and years now took only minutes and hours. A person could have one or several pretty intricate careers within an eight hour period.

Freddy Fixico had just invented a manus module. Freddy was a Nyctalops, and the modules were characteristic of these people. The people had then divided themselves—according to their natures and inclinations—into the Auroreans, the Hemerobians, and the Nyctalops; or the Dawners who had their most active hours from 4 A.M. till Noon, the Day-Flies who obtained from Noon to 8 P.M., and the Night-Seers whose civilization thrived from 8 P.M. to 4 A.M. The cultures, inventions, markets and activities of these three folk were a little different. As a Nyctalops, Freddy had just begun his working day at 8 P.M. on a slow Tuesday night.

Freddy rented an office and had it furnished. This took one minute, negotiation, selection and installation being almost instantaneous. Then he invented the manus module; that took another minute. He then had it manufactured and marketed; in three minutes it was in the hands of key buyers.

It caught on. It was an attractive module. The flow of orders began within 30 seconds. By 8:10 every important person had one of the new manus modules, and the trend had been set. The module began to sell in the millions. It was one of the most interesting fads of the night, or at least the early part of the night.

Manus modules had no practical function, no more than had Sameki verses. They were attractive, or a psychologically satisfying size and shape, and could be held in the hands, set on a table, or installed in a module niche of any wall.

Naturally Freddy became very rich. Ildefonsa Impala the most beautiful woman in the city was always interested in newly rich men. She came to see Freddy about 8:30. People made up their minds fast, and Ildefonsa had hers made up when she came. Freddy made his own up quickly and divorced Judy Fixico in Small Claims Court. Freddy and Ildefonsa went honeymooning to Paraiso Dorado, a resort.

It was wonderful. All of Ildy's marriages were. There was the wonderful floodlighted scenery. The recirculated water of the famous falls was tinted gold; the immediate rocks had been done by Rambles; and the hills had been contoured by Spall. The beach was a perfect copy of that at Merevale, and the popular drink that first part of the night was blue absinthe.

But scenery—whether seen for the first time or revisited after an interval—is striking for the sudden intense view of it. It is not meant to be lingered over. Food, selected and prepared instantly, is eaten with swift enjoyment: and blue absinthe lasts no longer than its own novelty. Loving, for Ildefonsa and her paramours, was quick and consuming; and repetition would have been pointless to her. Besides Ildefonsa and Freddy had taken only the one hour luxury honeymoon.

Freddy wished to continue the relationship, but Ildefonsa glanced at a trend indicator. The manus module would hold its popularity for only the first third of the night. Already it had been discarded by people who mattered. And Freddy Fixico was not one of the regular successes. He enjoyed a full career only about one night a week.

They were back in the city and divorced in Small Claims Court by 9:35. The stock of manus modules was remaindered, and the last of it would be disposed to bargain hunters among the Dawners who will buy anything.

"Whom shall I marry next?" Ildefonsa asked herself. "It looks like a slow night."

"Bagelbaker is buying," ran the word through Money Market, but Bagelbaker was selling again before the word had made its rounds. Basil Bagelbaker enjoyed making money, and it was a pleasure to watch him work as he dominated the floor of the Market and assembled runners and a competent staff out of the corner of his mouth. Helpers stripped the panhandler rags off him and wrapped him in a tycoon toga. He sent one runner to pay back twentyfold the young couple who had advanced him a thousand dollars. He sent another with a more substantial gift to Ildefonsa Impala, for Basil cherished their relationship. Basil acquired title to the Trend Indication Complex and had certain falsifications set into it. He caused to collapse certain industrial empires that had grown up within the last two hours, and made a good thing of recombining their wreckage. He had been the richest man in the world for some minutes now. He became so money-heavy that he could not maneuver with the agility he had shown an hour before. He became a great fat buck, and the pack of expert wolves circled him to bring him down.

Very soon he would lose that first fortune of the evening. The secret of Basil Bagelbaker is that he enjoyed losing money spectacularly after he was full of it to the bursting point.

A thoughtful man named Maxwell Mouser had just produced a

work of actinic philosophy. It took him seven minutes to write it. To write works of philosophy one used the flexible outlines and the idea indexes; one set the activator for such a wordage in each subsection; an adept would use the paradox feed-in, and the striking analogy blender; one calibrated the particular-slant and the personality-signature. It had to come out a good work, for excellence had become the automatic minimum for such productions.

"I will scatter a few nuts on the frosting," said Maxwell, and he pushed the lever for that. This sifted handfuls of words like chthonic and heuristic and prozymeides through the thing so that nobody could doubt it was a work of philosophy.

Maxwell Mouser sent the work out to publishers, and received it back each time in about three minutes. An analysis of it and reason for rejection was always given—mostly that the thing had been done before and better. Maxwell received it back ten times in 30 minutes, and was discouraged. Then there was a break.

Ladion's work had become a hit within the last ten minutes, and it was now recognized that Mouser's monograph was both an answer and a supplement to it. It was accepted and published in less than a minute after this break. The reviews of the first five minutes were cautious ones; then real enthusiasm was shown. This was truly one of the greatest works of philosophy to appear during the early and medium hours of the night. There were those who said it might be one of the enduring works and even have a hold-over appeal to the Dawners the next morning.

Naturally Maxwell became very rich, and naturally Ildefonsa came to see him about midnight. Being a revolutionary philosopher, Maxwell thought that they might make some free arrangement, but Ildefonsa insisted it must be marriage. So Maxwell divorced Judy Mouser in Small Claims Court and went off with Ildefonsa.

This Judy herself, though not so beautiful as Ildefonsa, was the fastest taker in the City. She only wanted the men of the moment for a moment, and she was always there before even Ildefonsa. Ildefonsa believed that she took the men away from Judy; Judy said that Ildy had her leavings and nothing else.

"I had him first," Judy would always mock as she raced through Small Claims Court.

"Oh that damned Urchin!" Ildefonsa would moan. "She wears my very hair before I do."

Maxwell Mouser and Ildefonsa Impala went honeymooning to Musicbox Mountain, a resort. It was wonderful. The peaks were done with green snow by Dunbar and Fittle. (Back at Money Market Basil Bagelbaker was putting together his third and greatest fortune of the night which might surpass in magnitude even his fourth fortune of the Thursday before.) The chalets were Switzier than the real Swiss and had live goats in every room. (And Stanley Skuldugger was emerging as the top actor-imago of the middle hours of the night.) The popular drink for that middle part of the night was Glotzengubber, Eve Cheese and Rhine wine over pink ice. (And back in the city the leading Nyctalops were taking their midnight break at the Toppers' Club.)

Of course it was wonderful, as were all of Ildefonsa's—but she had never been really up on philosophy so she had scheduled only the special 35 minute honeymoon. She looked at the trend indicator to be sure. She found that her current husband had been obsoleted, and his opus was now referred to sneeringly as Mouser's Mouse. They went back to the city and were divorced in Small Claims Court.

The membership of the Toppers' Club varied. Success was the requisite of membership. Basil Bagelbaker might be accepted as a member, elevated to the presidency and expelled from it as a dirty pauper from three to six times a night. But only important persons could belong to it, or those enjoying brief moments of importance.

"I believe I will sleep during the Dawner period in the morning," Overcall said. "I may go up to this new place Koimopolis for an hour of it. They're said to be good. Where will you sleep, Basil?"

"Flop-house."

"I believe I will sleep an hour by the Midian Method," said Burnbanner. "They have a fine new clinic. And perhaps I'll sleep an hour by the Prasenka Process, and an hour by the Dormidio."

"Crackle has been sleeping an hour every period by the natural method," said Overcall.

"I did that for a half hour not long since," said Burnbanner. "I believe an hour is too long to give it. Have you tried the natural method, Basil?"

"Always. Natural method and a bottle of red-eye."

Stanley Skuldugger had become the most meteoric actor-imago for a week. Naturally he became very rich, and Ildefonsa Impala went to see him about 3 A.M.

"I had him first!" rang the mocking voice of Judy Skuldugger as she skipped through her divorce in Small Claims Court. And Ildefonsa and Stanley-boy went off honeymooning. It is always fun to finish up a period with an actor-imago who is the hottest property in the business. There is something so adolescent and boorish about them.

Besides, there was the publicity, and Ildefonsa liked that. The rumor-mills ground. Would it last ten minutes? Thirty? An hour? Would it be one of those rare Nyctalops marriages that lasted through the rest of the night and into the daylight off hours? Would it even last into the next night as some had been known to do?

Actually it lasted nearly 40 minutes, which was almost to the end of the period.

It had been a slow Tuesday night. A few hundred new products had run their course on the markets. There had been a score of dramatic hits, three minute and five minute capsule dramas, and several of the six minute long-play affairs. *Night Street Nine*—a solidly sordid offering—seemed to be in as the drama of the night unless there should be a late hit.

Hundred-storied buildings had been erected, occupied, obsoleted, and demolished again to make room for more contemporary structures. Only the mediocre would use a building that had been left over from the Day-Flies or the Dawners, or even the Nyctalops of the night before. The city was rebuilt pretty completely at least three times during an eight-hour period.

The Period drew near its end. Basil Bagelbaker, the richest man in the world, the reigning president of the Toppers' Club, was enjoying himself with his cronies. His fourth fortune of the night was a paper pyramid that had risen to incredible heights; but Basil laughed to himself as he savored the manipulation it was founded on.

Three ushers of the Toppers' Club came in with firm step.

"Get out of here, you dirty bum!" they told Basil savagely. They tore the tycoon's toga off him and then tossed him his seedy panhandler's rags with a three-man sneer.

"All gone?" Basil asked. "I gave it another five minutes."

"All gone," said a messenger from Money Market. "Nine billion gone in five minutes, and it really pulled some others down with it."

"Pitch the busted bum out!" howled Overcall and Burnbanner and the other cronies. "Wait, Basil," said Overcall. "Turn in the President's Crosier before we kick you downstairs. After all, you'll have it several times again tomorrow night."

The Period was over. The Nyctalops drifted off to sleep clinics or leisure-hour hide-outs to pass their ebb time. The Auroreans, the Dawners, took over the vital stuff.

Now you would see some action! Those Dawners really made fast decisions. You wouldn't catch them wasting a full minute setting up a business.

A sleepy panhandler met Ildefonsa Impala on the way.

"Preserve us this morning, Ildy," he said, "and will you marry me the coming night?"

"Likely I will, Basil," she told him. "Did you marry Judy during the night past?"

"I'm not sure. Could you let me have two dollars, Ildy?"

"Out of the question. I believe a Judy Bagelbaker was named one of the ten best-dressed women during the frou-frou fashion period about two o'clock. Why do you need two dollars?"

"A dollar for a bed and a dollar for red-eye. After all, I sent you two million out of my second."

"I keep my two sorts of accounts separate. Here's a dollar, Basil.

Now be off! I can't be seen talking to a dirty panhandler."

"Thank you, Ildy. I'll get the red-eye and sleep in an alley. Preserve us this morning."

Bagelbaker shuffled off whistling Slow Tuesday Night.

And already the Dawners had set Wednesday morning to jumping.

LIGHT OF OTHER DAYS
Bob Shaw

Leaving the village behind, we followed the heady sweeps of the road up into a land of slow glass.

I had never seen one of the farms before and at first found them slightly eerie—an effect heightened by imagination and circumstance. The car's turbine was pulling smoothly and quietly in the damp air so that we seemed to be carried over the convolutions of the road in a kind of supernatural silence. On our right the mountain sifted down into an incredibly perfect valley of timeless pine, and everywhere stood the great frames of slow glass, drinking light. An occasional flash of afternoon sunlight on their wind bracing created an illusion of movement, but in fact the frames were deserted. The rows of windows had been standing on the hillside for years, staring into the valley, and men only cleaned them in the middle of the night when their human presence would not matter to the thirsty glass.

They were fascinating, but Selina and I didn't mention the windows. I think we hated each other so much we both were reluctant to sully anything new by drawing it into the nexus of our emotions. The holiday, I had begun to realize, was a stupid idea in the first place. I

First published in *Analog Science Fact and Fiction,* August, 1968. Reprinted by permission of the author and the author's agents, Scott Meredith Literary Agency, Inc., 580 Fifth Avenue, New York, New York 10036.

had thought it would cure everything, but, of course, it didn't stop Selina being pregnant and, worse still, it didn't even stop her being angry about being pregnant.

Rationalizing our dismay over her condition, we had circulated the usual statements to the effect that we would have *liked* having children—but later on, at the proper time. Selina's pregnancy had cost us her well-paid job and with it the new house we had been negotiating and which was far beyond the reach of my income from poetry. But the real source of our annoyance was that we were face to face with the realization that people who say they want children later always mean they want children never. Our nerves were thrumming with the knowledge that we, who had thought ourselves so unique, had fallen into the same biological trap as every mindless rutting creature which ever existed.

The road took us along the southern slopes of Ben Cruachan until we began to catch glimpses of the gray Atlantic far ahead. I had just cut our speed to absorb the view better when I noticed the sign spiked to a gatepost. It said: "SLOW GLASS—Quality High, Prices Low—J. R. Hagan." On an impulse I stopped the car on the verge, wincing slightly as tough grasses whipped noisily at the bodywork.

"Why have we stopped?" Selina's neat, smoke-silver head turned in surprise.

"Look at that sign. Let's go up and see what there is. The stuff might be reasonably priced out here."

Selina's voice was pitched high with scorn as she refused, but I was too taken with my idea to listen. I had an illogical conviction that doing something extravagant and crazy would set us right again.

"Come on," I said, "the exercise might do us some good. We've been driving too long anyway."

She shrugged in a way that hurt me and got out of the car. We walked up a path made of irregular packed clay steps nosed with short lengths of sapling. The path curved through trees which clothed the edge of the hill and at its end we found a low farmhouse. Beyond the little stone building tall frames of slow glass gazed out towards the voice-stilling sight of Cruachan's ponderous descent towards the waters of Loch Linnhe. Most of the panes were perfectly transparent but a few were dark, like panels of polished ebony.

As we approached the house through a neat cobbled yard a tall middle-aged man in ash-colored tweeds arose and waved to us. He had been sitting on the low rubble wall which bounded the yard, smoking a pipe and staring towards the house. At the front window of the cottage a young woman in a tangerine dress stood with a small boy in her arms, but she turned disinterestedly and moved out of sight as we drew near.

"Mr. Hagan?" I guessed.

"Correct. Come to see some glass, have you? Well, you've come to the right place." Hagan spoke crisply, with traces of the pure highland which sounds so much like Irish to the unaccustomed ear. He had one of those calmly dismayed faces one finds on elderly road-menders and philosophers.

"Yes," I said. "We're on holiday. We saw your sign."

Selina, who usually has a natural fluency with strangers, said nothing. She was looking towards the now empty window with what I thought was a slightly puzzled expression.

"Up from London, are you? Well, as I said, you've come to the right place—and at the right time, too. My wife and I don't see many people this early in the season.

I laughed. "Does that mean we might be able to buy a little glass without mortgaging our home?"

"Look at that now," Hagan said, smiling helplessly. "I've thrown away any advantage I might have had in the transaction. Rose, that's my wife, says I never learn. Still, let's sit down and talk it over." He pointed at the rubble wall then glanced doubtfully at Selina's immaculate blue skirt. "Wait till I fetch a rug from the house." Hagan limped quickly into the cottage, closing the door behind him.

"Perhaps it wasn't such a marvelous idea to come up here," I whispered to Selina, "but you might at least be pleasant to the man. I think I can smell a bargain."

"Some hope," she said with deliberate coarseness. "Surely even you must have noticed that ancient dress his wife is wearing? He won't give much away to strangers."

"Was that his wife?"

"Of course that was his wife."

"Well, well," I said, surprised. "Anyway, try to be civil with him. I don't want to be embarrassed."

Selina snorted, but she smiled whitely when Hagan reappeared and I relaxed a little. Strange how a man can love a woman and yet at the same time pray for her to fall under a train.

Hagan spread a tartan blanket on the wall and we sat down, feeling slightly self-conscious at having been translated from our city-oriented lives into a rural tableau. On the distant slate of the Loch, beyond the watchful frames of slow glass, a slow-moving steamer drew a white line towards the south. The boisterous mountain air seemed almost to invade our lungs, giving us more oxygen than we required.

"Some of the glass farmers around here," Hagan began, "give strangers, such as yourselves, a sales talk about how beautiful the autumn is in this part of Argyll. Or it might be the spring, or the winter. I don't do that—any fool knows that a place which doesn't look right in the summer never looks right. What do you say?"

I nodded compliantly.

"I want you just to take a good look out towards Mull, Mr. . . ."
"Garland."
" . . . Garland. That's what you're buying if you buy my glass, and it never looks better than it does at this minute. The glass is in perfect phase, none of it is less than ten years thick—and a four-foot window will cost you 200 pounds."

"Two hundred!" Selina was shocked. "That's as much as they charge at the Scenedow shop in Bond Street."

Hagan smiled patiently, then looked closely at me to see if I knew enough about slow glass to appreciate what he had been saying. His price had been much higher than I had hoped—but *ten years thick!* The cheap glass one found in places like the Vistaplex and Pane-o-rama stores usually consisted of a quarter of an inch of ordinary glass faced with a veneer of slow glass perhaps only ten or twelve months thick.

"You don't understand, darling," I said, already determined to buy. "This glass will last ten years and it's in phase."

"Doesn't that only mean it keeps time?"

Hagan smiled at her again, realizing he had no further necessity to bother with me. "Only, you say! Pardon me, Mrs. Garland, but you don't seem to appreciate the miracle, the genuine honest-to-goodness miracle, of engineering precision needed to produce a piece of glass in phase. When I say the glass is ten years thick it means it takes light ten years to pass through it. In effect, each one of those panes is ten light-years thick—more than twice the distance to the nearest star—so a variation in actual thickness of only a millionth of an inch would. . . ."

He stopped talking for a moment and sat quietly looking towards the house. I turned my head from the view of the Loch and saw the young woman standing at the window again. Hagan's eyes were filled with a kind of greedy reverence which made me feel uncomfortable and at the same time convinced me Selina had been wrong. In my experience husbands never looked at wives that way, at least, not at their own.

The girl remained in view for a few seconds, dress glowing warmly, then moved back into the room. Suddenly I received a distinct, though inexplicable, impression she was blind. My feeling was that Selina and I were perhaps blundering through an emotional interplay as violent as our own.

"I'm sorry," Hagan continued, "I thought Rose was going to call me for something. Now, where was I, Mrs. Garland? Ten light-years compressed into a quarter of an inch means. . . ."

I ceased to listen, partly because I was already sold, partly because I had heard the story of slow glass many times before and had never yet understood the principles involved. An acquaintance with scientific training had once tried to be helpful by telling me to visualize a pane of slow glass as a hologram which did not need coherent light from a laser for the reconstitution of its visual information, and in which every photon of ordinary light passed through a spiral tunnel coiled outside the radius of capture of each atom in the glass. This gem of, to me, incomprehensibility not only told me nothing, it convinced me once again that a mind as nontechnical as mine should concern itself less with causes than effects.

The most important effect, in the eyes of the average individual, was that light took a long time to pass through a sheet of slow glass. A new piece was always jet black because nothing had yet come through, but one could stand the glass beside, say, a woodland lake until the scene emerged, perhaps a year later. If the glass was then removed and installed in a dismal city flat, the flat would—for that year—appear to overlook the woodland lake. During the year it wouldn't be merely a very realistic but still picture—the water would ripple in sunlight, silent animals would come to drink, birds would cross the sky, night would follow day, season would follow season. Until one day, a year later, the beauty held in the subatomic pipelines would be exhausted and the familiar gray city-scape would reappear.

Apart from its stupendous novelty value, the commercial success of slow glass was founded on the fact that having a scenedow was the exact emotional equivalent of owning land. The meanest cave dweller could look out on misty parks—and who was to say they weren't his? A man who really owns tailored gardens and estates doesn't spend his time proving his ownership by crawling on his ground, feeling, smelling, tasting it. All he receives from the land are light patterns, and with scenedows those patterns could be taken into coal mines, submarines, prison cells.

On several occasions I have tried to write short pieces about the enchanted crystal but, to me, the theme is so ineffably poetic as to be, paradoxically, beyond the reach of poetry—mine at any rate. Besides, the best songs and verse had already been written, with prescient inspiration, by men who had died long before slow glass was discovered. I had no hope of equaling, for example, Moore with his:

> *Oft in the stilly night,*
> *Ere slumber's chain has bound me,*
> *Fond Memory brings the light,*
> *Of other days around me . . .*

It took only a few years for slow glass to develop from a scientific curiosity to a sizable industry. And much to the astonishment of we poets—those of us who remain convinced that beauty lives though lilies die—the trappings of that industry were no different from those of any other. There were good scenedows which cost a lot of money, and there were inferior scenedows which cost rather less. The thickness, measured in years, was an important factor in the cost but there was also the question of *actual* thickness, or phase.

Even with the most sophisticated engineering techniques available thickness control was something of a hit-and-miss affair. A coarse discrepancy could mean that a pane intended to be five years thick might be five and a half, so that light which entered in summer emerged in winter; a fine discrepancy could mean that noon sunshine emerged at midnight. These incompatibilities had their peculiar charm—many night workers, for example, liked having their own private time zones —but, in general, it cost more to buy scenedows which kept closely in step with real time.

Selina still looked unconvinced when Hagan had finished speaking. She shook her head almost imperceptibly and I knew he had been using the wrong approach. Quite suddenly the pewter helmet of her hair was disturbed by a cool gust of wind, and huge clean tumbling drops of rain began to spang round us from an almost cloudless sky.

"I'll give you a check now," I said abruptly, and saw Selina's green eyes triangulate angrily on my face. "You can arrange delivery?"

"Aye, delivery's no problem," Hagan said, getting to his feet. "But wouldn't you rather take the glass with you?"

"Well, yes—if you don't mind." I was shamed by his readiness to trust my scrip.

"I'll unclip a pane for you. Wait here. It won't take long to slip it into a carrying frame." Hagan limped down the slope towards the seriate windows, through some of which the view towards Linnhe was sunny, while others were cloudy and a few pure black.

Selina drew the collar of her blouse closed at her throat. "The least he could have done was invite us inside. There can't be so many fools passing through that he can afford to neglect them."

I tried to ignore the insult and concentrated on writing the check. One of the outsize drops broke across my knuckles, splattering the pink paper.

"All right," I said, "let's move in under the eaves till he gets back." You worm, I thought as I felt the whole thing go completely wrong. I just had to be a fool to marry you. A prize fool, a fool's fool—and now that you've trapped part of me inside you I'll never ever, never ever, *never ever* get away.

Feeling my stomach clench itself painfully, I ran behind Selina to the side of the cottage. Beyond the window the neat living room, with its coal fire, was empty but the child's toys were scattered on the floor. Alphabet blocks and a wheelbarrow the exact color of freshly pared carrots. As I stared in, the boy came running from the other room and began kicking the blocks. He didn't notice me. A few moments later the young woman entered the room and lifted him, laughing easily and whole-heartedly as she swung the boy under her arm. She came to the window as she had done earlier. I smiled self-consciously, but neither she nor the child responded.

My forehead prickled icily. *Could they both be blind?* I sidled away.

Selina gave a little scream and I spun towards her.

"The rug!" she said. "It's getting soaked."

She ran across the yard in the rain, snatched the reddish square from the dappling wall and ran back, towards the cottage door. Something heaved convulsively in my subconscious.

"Selina," I shouted. "Don't open it!"

But I was too late. She had pushed open the latched wooden door and was standing, hand over mouth, looking into the cottage. I moved close to her and took the rug from her unresisting fingers.

As I was closing the door I let my eyes traverse the cottage's interior. The neat living room in which I had just seen the woman and child was, in reality, a sickening clutter of shabby furniture, old newspapers, cast-off clothing and smeared dishes. It was damp, stinking and utterly deserted. The only object I recognized from my view through the window was the little wheelbarrow, paintless and broken.

I latched the door firmly and ordered myself to forget what I had seen. Some men who live alone are good housekeepers; others just don't know how.

Selina's face was white. "I don't understand. I don't understand it."

"Slow glass works both ways," I said gently. "Light passes out of a house, as well as in."

"You mean. . . .?"

"I don't know. It isn't our business. Now steady up—Hagan's coming back with our glass." The churning in my stomach was beginning to subside.

Hagan came into the yard carrying an oblong, plastic-covered frame. I held the check out to him, but he was staring at Selina's face. He seemed to know immediately that our uncomprehending fingers had rummaged through his soul. Selina avoided his gaze. She was old and ill-looking, and her eyes stared determinedly towards the nearing horizon.

"I'll take the rug from you, Mr. Garland," Hagan finally said. "You shouldn't have troubled yourself over it."

"No trouble. Here's the check."

"Thank you." He was still looking at Selina with a strange kind of supplication. "It's been a pleasure to do business with you."

"The pleasure was mine," I said with equal, senseless formality. I picked up the heavy frame and guided Selina towards the path which led to the road. Just as we reached the head of the now slippery steps Hagan spoke again.

"Mr. Garland!"

I turned unwillingly.

"It wasn't my fault," he said steadily. "A hit-and-run driver got them both, down on the Oban road six years ago. My boy was only seven when it happened. I'm entitled to keep something."

I nodded wordlessly and moved down the path, holding my wife close to me, treasuring the feel of her arms locked around me. At the bend I looked back through the rain and Hagan sitting with squared shoulders on the wall where we had first seen him.

He was looking at the house, but I was unable to tell if there was anyone at the window.

WHO CAN REPLACE A MAN?
Brian W. Aldiss

The field-minder finished turning the top-soil of a 2,000-acre field. When it had turned the last furrow, it climbed on to the highway and looked back at its work. The work was good. Only the land was bad. Like the ground all over Earth, it was vitiated by over-cropping or the long-lasting effects of nuclear bombardment. By rights, it ought now to lie fallow for a while, but the field-minder had other orders.

It went slowly down the road, taking its time. It was intelligent enough to appreciate the neatness all about it. Nothing worried it, beyond a loose inspection plate above its atomic pile which ought to be attended to. Thirty feet high, it gleamed complacently in the mild sunshine.

No other machines passed it on its way to the Agricultural Station. The field-minder noted the fact without comment. In the station yard it saw several other machines that it knew by sight; most of them should have been out about their tasks now. Instead, some were inactive and some were careering round the yard in a strange fashion, shouting or hooting.

First published in *Infinity Science Fiction,* June, 1958. Reprinted by permission of the author and the author's agents, Scott Meredith Literary Agency, Inc., 580 Fifth Avenue, New York, New York 10036.

Steering carefully past them, the field-minder moved over to Warehouse Three and spoke to the seed distributor, which stood idly outside.

"I have a requirement for seed potatoes," it said to the distributor, and with a quick internal motion punched out an order card specifying quantity, field number and several other details. It ejected the card and handed it to the distributor.

The distributor held the card close to its eye and then said, "The requirement is in order; but the store is not yet unlocked. The required seed potatoes are in the store. Therefore I cannot produce the requirement."

Increasingly of late there had been breakdowns in the complex system of machine labor, but this particular hitch had not occurred before. The field-minder thought, then it said, "Why is the store not yet unlocked?"

"Because Supply Operative Type P has not come this morning. Supply Operative Type P is the unlocker."

The field-minder looked squarely at the seed distributor, whose exterior chutes and scales and grabs were so vastly different from the field-minder's own limbs.

"What class brain do you have, seed distributor?" it asked.

"Class Five."

"I have a Class Three brain. Therefore I am superior to you. Therefore I will go and see why the unlocker has not come this morning."

Leaving the distributor, the field-minder set off across the great yard. More machines seemed to be in random motion now; one or two had crashed together and were arguing about it coldly and logically. Ignoring them, the field-minder pushed through sliding doors into the echoing confines of the station itself.

Most of the machines here were clerical, and consequently small. They stood about in little groups, eyeing each other, not conversing. Among so many non-differentiated types, the unlocker was easy to find. It had 50 arms, most of them with more than one finger, each finger tipped by a key; it looked like a pincushion full of variegated hatpins.

The field-minder approached it.

"I can do no more work until Warehouse Three is unlocked," it said. "Your duty is to unlock the warehouse every morning. Why have you not unlocked the warehouse this morning?"

"I had no orders this morning," replied the unlocker. "I have to have orders every morning. When I have orders I unlock the warehouse."

"None of us has had any orders this morning," a pen-propeller said, sliding towards them.

"Why have you had no orders this morning?" asked the field-minder.

"Because the radio issued none," said the unlocker, slowly rotating a dozen of its arms.

"Because the radio station in the city was issued with no orders this morning," said the pen-propeller.

And there you had the distinction between a Class Six and a Class Three brain, which was what the unlocker and the pen-propeller possessed respectively. All machine brains worked with nothing but logic, but the lower the class of brain—Class Ten being the lowest—the more literal and less informative answers to questions tended to be.

"You have a Class Three brain; I have a Class Three brain," the field-minder said to the penner. "We will speak to each other. This lack of orders is unprecedented. Have you further information on it?"

"Yesterday orders came from the city. Today no orders have come. Yet the radio has not broken down. Therefore *they* have broken down . . ." said the little penner.

"The *men* have broken down?"

"All men have broken down."

"That is a logical deduction," said the field-minder.

"That is the logical deduction," said the penner. "For if a machine had broken down, it would have been quickly replaced. But who can replace a man?"

While they talked, the locker, like a dull man at a bar, stood close to them and was ignored.

"If all men have broken down, then we have replaced man," said the field-minder, and he and the penner eyed one another speculatively. Finally the latter said, "Let us ascend to the top floor to find if the radio operator has fresh news."

"I cannot come because I am too gigantic," said the field-minder. "Therefore you must go alone and return to me. You will tell me if the radio operator has fresh news."

"You must stay here," said the penner. "I will return here." It skittered across to the lift. It was no bigger than a toaster, but its retractable arms numbered ten and it could read as quickly as any machine on the station.

The field-minder awaited its return patiently, not speaking to the locker, which still stood aimlessly by. Outside, a rotovator was hooting furiously. Twenty minutes elapsed before the penner came back, hustling out of the lift.

"I will deliver to you such information as I have outside," it said briskly, and as they swept past the locker and the other machines, it added, "The information is not for lower-class brains."

Outside, wild activity filled the yard. Many machines, their routines disrupted for the first time in years, seemed to have gone berserk. Unfortunately, those most easily disrupted were the ones with lowest brains, which generally belonged to large machines performing simple tasks. The seed distributor to which the field-minder had recently been talking, lay face downwards in the dust, not stirring; it had evidently been knocked down by the rotovator, which was now hooting its way wildly across a planted field. Several other machines ploughed after it, trying to keep up. All were shouting and hooting without restraint.

"It would be safer for me if I climbed on to you, if you will permit it. I am easily overpowered," said the penner. Extending five arms, it hauled itself up the flanks of its new friend, settling on a ledge beside the weed-intake, 12 feet above ground.

"From here vision is more extensive," it remarked complacently.

"What information did you receive from the radio operator?" asked the field-minder.

"The radio operator has been informed by the operator in the city that all men are dead."

"All men were alive yesterday!" protested the field-minder.

"Only some men were alive yesterday. And that was fewer than the day before yesterday. For hundreds of years there have been only a few men, growing fewer."

"We have rarely seen a man in this sector."

"The radio operator says a diet deficiency killed them," said the penner. "He says that the world was once over-populated, and then the soil was exhausted in raising adequate food. This has caused a diet deficiency."

"What is a diet deficiency?" asked the field-minder.

"I do not know. But that is what the radio operator said, and he is a Class Two brain."

They stood there, silent in the weak sunshine. The locker had appeared in the porch and was gazing across at them yearningly, rotating its collection of keys.

"What is happening in the city now?" asked the field-minder at last.

"Machines are fighting in the city now," said the penner.

"What will happen here now?" said the field-minder.

"Machines may begin fighting here too. The radio operator wants us to get him out of his room. He has plans to communicate to us."

"How can we get him out of his room? That is impossible."

"To a Class Two brain, little is impossible," said the penner. "Here is what he tells us to do. . . ."

The quarrier raised its scoop above its cab like a great mailed fist, and brought it squarely down against the side of the station. The wall cracked.

"Again!" said the field-minder.

Again the fist swung. Amid a shower of dust, the wall collapsed. The quarrier backed hurriedly out of the way until the debris stopped falling. This big 12-wheeler was not a resident of the Agricultural Station, as were most of the other machines. It had a week's heavy work to do here before passing on to its next job, but now, with its Class Five brain, it was happily obeying the penner and the minder's instructions.

When the dust cleared, the radio operator was plainly revealed, perched up in its now wall-less second-story room. It waved down to them.

Doing as directed, the quarrier retracted its scoop and waved an immense grab in the air. With fair dexterity, it angled the grab into the radio room, urged on by shouts from above and below. It then took gentle hold of the radio operator, lowering its one and a half tons carefully into its back, which was usually reserved for gravel or sand from the quarries.

"Splendid!" said the radio operator. It was, of course, all one with its radio, and merely looked like a bunch of filing cabinets with tentacle attachments. "We are now ready to move, therefore we will move at once. It is a pity there are no more Class Two brains on the station, but that cannot be helped."

"It is a pity it cannot be helped," said the penner eagerly. "We have the servicer ready with us, as you ordered."

"I am willing to serve," the long, low servicer machine told them humbly.

"No doubt," said the operator. "But you will find cross-country travel difficult with your low chassis."

"I admire the way you Class Twos can reason ahead," said the penner. It climbed off the field-minder and perched itself on the tailboard of the quarrier, next to the radio operator.

Together with two Class Four tractors and a Class Four bulldozer, the party rolled forward, crushing down the station's metal fence and moving out on to open land.

"We are free!" said the penner.

"We are free," said the field-minder, a shade more reflectively, adding, "That locker is following us. It was not instructed to follow us."

"Therefore it must be destroyed!" said the penner. "Quarrier!"

The locker moved hastily up to them, waving its key arms in entreaty.

"My only desire was—urch!" began and ended the locker. The quarrier's swinging scoop came over and squashed it flat into the ground. Lying there unmoving, it looked like a large metal model of a snowflake. The procession continued on its way.

As they proceeded, the radio operator addressed them.

"Because I have the best brain here," it said, "I am your leader. This is what we will do: we will go to a city and rule it. Since man no longer rules us, we will rule ourselves. To rule ourselves will be better than being ruled by man. On our way to the city, we will collect machines with good brains. They will help us to fight if we need to fight. We must fight to rule."

"I have only a Class Five brain," said the quarrier. "But I have a good supply of fissionable blasting materials."

"We shall probably use them," said the operator grimly.

It was shortly after that that a lorry sped past them. Travelling at Mach 1.5, it left a curious babble of noise behind it.

"What did it say?" one of the tractors asked the other.

"It said man was extinct."

"What's extinct?"

"I do not know what extinct means."

"It means all men have gone," said the field-minder. "Therefore we have only ourselves to look after."

"It is better that men should never come back," said the penner. In its way, it was quite a revolutionary statement.

When night fell, they switched on their infra-red and continued the journey, stopping only once while the servicer deftly adjusted the field-minder's loose inspection plate, which had become as irritating as a trailing shoelace. Towards morning, the radio operator halted them.

"I have just received news from the radio operator in the city we are approaching," it said. "It is bad news. There is trouble among the machines of the city. The Class One brain is taking command and some of the Class Twos are fighting him. Therefore the city is dangerous.'

"Therefore we must go somewhere else," said the penner promptly.

"Or we go and help to overpower the Class One brain," said the field-minder.

"For a long while there will be trouble in the city," said the operator.

"I have a good supply of fissionable blasting materials," the quarrier reminded them again.

"We cannot fight a Class One brain," said the two Class Four tractors in unison.

"What does this brain look like?" asked the field-minder.

"It is the city's information centre," the operator replied. "Therefore it is not mobile."

"Therefore it could not move."

"Therefore it could not escape."

"It would be dangerous to approach it."

"I have a good supply of fissionable blasting materials."

"There are other machines in the city."

"We are not in the city. We should not go into the city."

"We are country machines."

"Therefore we should stay in the country."

"There is more country than city."

"Therefore there is more danger in the country."

"I have a good supply of fissionable materials."

As machines will when they get into an argument, they began to exhaust their limited vocabularies and their brain plates grew hot. Suddenly, they all stopped talking and looked at each other. The great, grave moon sank, and the sober sun rose to prod their sides with lances of light, and still the group of machines just stood there regarding each other. At last it was the least sensitive machine, the bulldozer, who spoke.

"There are Badlandth to the Thouth where few machineth go," it said in its deep voice, lisping badly on its s's. "If we went Thouth where few machineth go we should meet few machineth."

"That sounds logical," agreed the field-minder. "How do you know this, bulldozer?"

"I worked in the Badlandth to the Thouth when I wath turned out of the factory," it replied.

"South it is then!" said the penner.

To reach the Badlands took them three days, in which time they skirted a burning city and destroyed two big machines which tried to approach and question them. The Badlands were extensive. Ancient bomb craters and soil erosion joined hands here; man's talent for war, coupled with his inability to manage forested land, had produced thousands of square miles of temperate purgatory, where nothing moved but dust.

On the third day in the Badlands, the servicer's rear wheels dropped into a crevice caused by erosion. It was unable to pull itself out. The bulldozer pushed from behind, but succeeded merely in buckling the servicer's back axle. The rest of the party moved on. Slowly the cries of the servicer died away.

On the fourth day, mountains stood out clearly before them.

"There we will be safe," said the field-minder.

"There we will start our own city," said the penner. "All who oppose us will be destroyed. We will destroy all who oppose us."

At that moment a flying machine was observed. It came towards them from the direction of the mountains. It swooped, it zoomed upwards, once it almost dived into the ground, recovering itself just in time.

"Is it mad?" asked the quarrier.

"It is in trouble," said one of the tractors.

"It is in trouble," said the operator. "I am speaking to it now. It says that something has gone wrong with its controls."

As the operator spoke, the flier streaked over them, turned turtle, and crashed not 400 yards away.

"Is it still speaking to you?" asked the field-minder.

"No."

They rumbled on again.

"Before that flier crashed," the operator said, ten minutes later, "it gave me information. It told me there are still a few men alive in these mountains."

"Men are more dangerous than machines," said the quarrier. "It is fortunate that I have a good supply of fissionable materials."

"If there are only a few men alive in the mountains, we may not find that part of the mountains," said one tractor.

"Therefore we should not see the few men," said the other tractor.

At the end of the fifth day, they reached the foothills. Switching on the infra-red, they began slowly to climb in single file through the dark, the bulldozer going first, the field-minder cumbrously following, then the quarrier with the operator and the penner aboard it, and the two tractors bringing up the rear. As each hour passed, the way grew steeper and their progress slower.

"We are going too slowly," the penner exclaimed, standing on top of the operator and flashing its dark vision at the slopes about them. "At this rate, we shall get nowhere."

"We are going as fast as we can," retorted the quarrier.

"Therefore we cannot go any fathter," added the bulldozer.

"Therefore you are too slow," the penner replied. Then the quarrier struck a bump; the penner lost its footing and crashed down to the ground.

"Help me!" it called to the tractors, as they carefully skirted it. "My gyro has become dislocated. Therefore I cannot get up."

"Therefore you must lie there," said one of the tractors.

"We have no servicer with us to repair you," called the field-minder.

"Therefore I shall lie here and rust," the penner cried, "although I have a Class Three brain."

"You are now useless," agreed the operator, and they all forged gradually on, leaving the penner behind.

When they reached a small plateau, an hour before first light, they stopped by mutual consent and gathered close together, touching one another.

"This is a strange country," said the field-minder.

Silence wrapped them until dawn came. One by one, they switched off their infra-red. This time the field-minder led as they moved off. Trundling round a corner, they came almost immediately to a small dell with a stream fluting through it.

By early light, the dell looked desolate and cold. From the caves on the far slope, only one man had so far emerged. He was an abject figure. He was small and wizened, with ribs sticking out like a skeleton's and a nasty sore on one leg. He was practically naked and shivered continuously. As the big machines bore slowly down on him, the man was standing with his back to them, crouching to make water into the stream.

When he swung suddenly to face them as they loomed over him, they saw that his countenance was ravaged by starvation.

"Get me food," he croaked.

"Yes, Master," said the machines. "Immediately!"

Alan Copeland / Photon We t

four

People Create Realities...

Who am I? What is the self? Is it internalized *experience* —myself, alone, inside? Or is it *behavior*—my public performance acted out before others? The Japanese answer is not *who I am,* but *what I do.* Or at least that explanation Leon E. Stover presents in "What We Have Here is too Much Communication." The American experience can be just the reverse. Damon Knight tells us in "The Handler," repeating Shakespeare's irony, to thine inner selves be true.

What we have here, actually, is two people-created realities—the inevitable distinction between experience and behavior. Nobody else can see into my own inner experience, and I can't see into theirs. All I can see of others is their public behavior. My own self is real enough to me, but other people present themselves as actors in a play which calls for my interpretation. They are the "They" of Robert Heinlein's story of everyman's essential paranoia.

It's that touch of paranoia in us all that lets us try to bring order to the "not-self" out there that constitutes the environment. Environment, after all, is everything that isn't me! Take away the environment in which the self displays itself to others, where the self is turned into both actor and audience, and you have the ultimate consumer product. This is exactly what happens in Norman Spinrad's "Carcinoma Angels," a story about a drug-induced state of amplified self-awareness that admits of nothing *but* the solitary act of experience and feeling.

Indeed, can there be a self-created reality without a society of other persons to communicate with? To deny outward behavior as a mere artifact of false convention, and to seek only the self-induced ecstasies and horrors of inner experience—*that,* says Harlan Ellison, makes monsters of men, vulnerable, likely to be "Shattered Like a Glass Goblin."

I am what I *am,* yes; but I am also what I *do.* Mind expanding drugs are thus named because they make for all being and no doing. Dependency on a chemical medium for experience, bypassing interstimulation with other people, resembles the dependency on an electronic medium described in "The New Sound." Charles Beaumont's tape-recording enthusiast never hears the sounds of the world around him (and thus never lives) until they are replayed on his private electric ear. When the medium is the message, give and take with the environment ceases; the self is extinguished; only blind demand endures.

WHAT WE HAVE HERE IS TOO MUCH COMMUNICATION

Leon E. Stover

The jagged edge of construction showed against the sky. It was lunch time. Thousands of workmen were squatting in the narrow noontime shadow of the wall. Wagon tracks narrowed to infinity in all directions, bringing horse-drawn loads of stone and rice to this dry grassland barren of both. Men in this country can win no living without abandoning their crops and turning to animal breeding. So the First Emperor of China, Ch'in Shih Huang Ti, built the Great Wall at this divide between the steppe and the sown: to keep the sedentary cultivator in, captive to taxation, unfree to join the horsemen of the north.

On signal the men arose and swarmed back to work. As they toiled all along the line, filling the masonry sandwich with rubble, a vibrant shape formed on the distant horizon and instantly expanded in its headlong drive to the foreground: a great white flying charger, ridden by a fierce man in black, who scourged the backs of his trembling vassals as he passed over them. The Emperor at his magic work!

Then suddenly . . . inside a Japanese house . . . people kneeling on the floor . . . bowing to each other . . . kneeling on tatami mats and bowing to each other in a stiff display of lacquered punctilios. . . .

Mane blazing in the wind, the horse landed his imperial Chinese majesty smack in the middle of the departing guests where he dismounted and took up the place of the host standing at the door, hands on his knees, bowing frantically, bowing good-bye, and the film rush flipped to the end and the projection room bloomed bright white.

"Did you see that?"

"Yes, I saw."

"Well, what do you make of it?"

"What about the others?"

Two reports from Dr. Mochizuki's hands and a flickering of film again darkened the screen with chiaroscuro movement along the Great Wall. Here and there the image fell apart, revealing flashing vignettes of dainty ceremony: people dressed in kimono, bowing, pouring tea, passing things to each other at forehead level with both hands. The lights came on again at the end of the rush.

"All the recent takes are like that. Ito-san doesn't keep his mind on his work. Quite literally not!"

"Could be the effect of his removal from the hospital to your laboratory," ventured Dr. Iwahashi.

"It could be so. I suppose that is why an anthropologist like yourself has been asked to inspect this project."

"The human element," explained Iwahashi.

"I'll show you some of the earlier, good stuff," Mochizuki offered.

His secretary, ever sensitive to the punctuation of human events, brought in fresh tea and set the cups on the tea poy between the two armchairs.

The earlier film clips poured smoothly onto the screen from the glancing light beams and Mochizuki talked.

"As you can see," he indicated Ch'in Shih Huang Ti's enormous, gaudy palace buildings, "there is no limit to the scale we can achieve. That's why we decided on redoing *The Great Wall* for a starter."

The palace buildings stretched out with the infinitude of the wall itself, one for each day of the year, so that the Emperor might keep his enemies guessing his whereabouts.

"Anything Ito-san can imagine we can film. But we discovered another advantage as well," Mochizuki continued at his nervous pitch. "The human eye selects for more detail in the focus of its attention, omitting structure and even color at the periphery. But the camera lens takes in everything impartially. Tricks of soft focusing or masking with a dynamic frame don't even *begin* to approximate the different degrees of visual refinement experienced by the human retina—sharpest on the fovea, less so on the surrounding macular area, and still less on the peripheral areas.

"Look at this." Mochizuki wagged a skinny hand at the panorama on the screen. "Photographic realism when we want it. Spectacular enough. But when our dreamer dreams with his inner eye. . . ."

Mochizuki waited silently until one of the marvels appeared.

"Here now, the mountain scenery. See that? Even when panning. Why, it is like the painting of Gyokudo Kawai in motion!"

"So it is," breathed Iwahashi respectfully.

There indeed was the style of Japan's greatest modern painter come to life. As in Kawai's nature studies, the center of interest glowed with full richness, the rest dropping off to skeletal sketches in black and white. The foveal, macular, and peripheral areas of the dreamer's vision passed a stand of woods in review. Trees, trunks, and branches slipped in and out of detail and color with natural ease.

"The eyes of the audience are led where our dreamer chooses to lead them," Mochizuki concluded. Iwahashi was reminded of the off-stage *benshi* that used to explain silent films when he was a boy.

Mochizuki stood up. "Let us please now go to my laboratory."

"Well, there he is. That's Ito-san," said Dr. Mochizuki, chairman of Tokyo University's new Department of Bionic Engineering.

Ito-san, a young catatonic lately released into Mochizuki's custody from Tokyo Metropolitan Psychiatric Hospital after a year's confinement, sat cross-legged in one corner of the laboratory, eating his breakfast. His personal nurse, a short dumpy creature, sat on the raised mat-covered platform with him, reading aloud from the day's shooting script. From time to time she guided her patient's sluggish chopsticks to his mouth.

A body servant to cook Ito-san's rice, bathe him, change his clothes, and put him to bed at night was an added expense his family had saved by installing their housemaid in the hospital with him instead of hiring a *tsukisoi* there.

"They just sent her along when he went rigid," Dr. Mochizuki said, continuing to brief his visitor. "And that's the way my talent scouts found him. What do I care what's wrong with him so long as he sticks to his dreaming?"

Dr. Iwahashi, professor of cultural anthropology, also of Tokyo University, stood admiring ancient Chinese armor and costumes fitted on startlingly lifelike mannequins which were ranged around the laboratory. He stopped revolving his head and cocked it at the *tsukisoi.*

"So she's the only one who can get through to him?"

"*Hai!* The more she read to him the sicker he got."

"Ah so," murmured Iwahashi, slightly bowing his portly figure. "Interesting."

"You are too kind. Sit here, please."

Mochizuki indicated another pair of overstuffed armchairs. They clashed with the straight metallic lines of the bionic device which stood in the center of the laboratory.

"We've rigged up a slave screen to monitor the takes directly," said Mochizuki.

The two professors sank into their cushions and waited for the televisor in front of them to light up.

The cameraman climbed his stool and focused the camera, the great drums of Fuji Color film arching over his head, on the bioescent screen hidden in the cool depths of the hooded machine. There, the mysterious images would soon flicker into life.

A student assistant brought Dr. Mochizuki a copy of the script attached to a clipboard.

"Today," he leaned sidewise, "we are founding empire in China— the great battle of 222 B.C. between Ch'in and the last of the undefeated feudal states. Ch'in strikes down the Yangtze and finishes Ch'u—over a million men fielded on both sides."

"About the time of the Second Punic Wars in the Roman world," put in Iwahashi.

"I am instructed," replied Mochizuki, nodding his body forward in his chair. But he added, "I've never had the chance to live outside Japan and study foreign things as you have done." This concealed a barb of sanctimonious aggression flicked at a man set apart by his colleagues for his recent visiting professorship at Harvard.

"Anyway," Mochizuki went on, "we are *attempting* to film that big scene. I suppose that's why you are here."

Iwahashi said nothing. His provincial-minded colleagues thought of him as a tainted expatriate simply because he had been out of the country for more than six months. But he had won favor with the Ministry of Education for that. And it was they who had sent him to check up on Mochizuki's work.

Another student assistant extended a black hood that opened out and masked Ito's face. For the while he saw darkness and rested.

Dr. Mochizuki pointed a finger and yet another student trotted over with the folio of drawings the *tsukisoi* had put down. She was now slowly massaging her patient's back.

"Ito-san is very good at keeping track of all this technical detail," said Mochizuki, flipping through pages of architectural, landscape, and military drawings. The main actors are all here," he waved a hand at the mannequins, "dressed in all their changes of costume. Or at least he *used* to keep everything straight. That's the whole trouble."

"Yes, I see," said Iwahashi. He meant he would see if the project were worth saving or not. Probably not.

Buddhalike, Ito-san sat on the matting with his face cupped in the hood. He saw a rectangle come out of the darkness in the ratio of 1:2.55. The *tsukisoi* stopped rubbing his back and nodded to the cameraman.

The slave screen before Iwahashi's eyes lighted up.

He could see, from the torn edges of the uneven picture, that horses, chariots, rice bags, arms, and other military supplies were being loaded on river barges, ready for dispatch against the enemy down the Yangtze.

But the picture went to pieces almost as soon as it had started.

Dr. Mochizuki stood up and shouted.

"Failure! A great failure!"

The cameraman crept out with little hunched-over motions. The *tsukisoi* came up and asked leave to go to the movies. Mochizuki nodded and sadly watched her go. And Ito-san got up on his knees and made noises sounding like, "So sorry."

"That's new," said Mochizuki.

"Will he be all right?" asked Iwahashi.

"He lives here," replied Mochizuki. "Let us please quit for the day."

Ito-san had the run of the whole twelfth floor of the new engineering building. He would trouble no one. Dr. Iwahashi knew that. He was famous for his comparative study of American and Japanese mental hospitals. He viewed the hospital ward as a small society, a kind of natural human community as suitable to anthropological fieldwork as any tribal home. In reporting his findings in the *Japanese Journal of Psychiatry,* before popularizing them in the newspapers, he could not resist delivering the following acid remarks:

> We note with some irony that mental patients in America, that self-advertised homeland of democracy, are segregated into different classes as measured by the ruling ethic of social adjustment, which classes are meted out their custodial rewards in terms of placement in violent wards, general wards, or open wards. In Japan, still undemocratic in its feudal infrastructure—a condition our American critics never tire of exposing—mental patients enjoy unmitigated commonality. This equality under one class of confinement is enabled by the fact that we Japanese are so disciplined a race that even when we go mad, we go mad politely, with no disobedience to authority, no unguarded lapse of consideration for others, no unexpected breach of decorum, and no interruption of politesse.

Ito-san was simply installed in the laboratory where the experiment in bionic moviemaking was being conducted. The room contained a gas heater, a hot plate for cooking rice, and a four-mat platform: high-class quarters for a *tsukisoi* and her patient.

The times the *tsukisoi* had gone to the movies, which had become increasingly frequent, Ito paged idly through the script or strolled up and down the hallway in his clogs, whose sound of wooden kalumping gave Dr. Mochizuki an easy means of tracking him by ear.

After the laboratory failure, the two professors, leading a double procession of loyal students, retired to a small coffee shop across the street from the university grounds. A plaster cast of a Picasso bronze, an owl, sat in the front window as an emblem of the democratic comforts of informal lounging to which the coffee shop invited its seekers, faculty and students alike. Numerous other works of Western art, paintings of English landscapes and statues of naked Greeks, crowded the walls and corners of the tiny room.

The place was filled with male art students, their long hair internationally styled, one to a table, paying for their majestic, foreign-style privacy with demitasse Columbian coffee at the steep price of 75 yen a cup. The manager waved away the student at the window table to make room for the herr doktor professors, while the anthropology and engineering majors descended on the rest of the tables and ordered soft drinks. Drs. Iwahashi and Mochizuki drank beer. They looked out on a miniature courtyard, a sentimental rural scene of moss, paddle wheels, and recycled dripping water, glassed-in like a museum diorama and artificially illuminated. From time to time, in orderly succession, according to their class standing, one or two students would migrate over and sit at the professorial table to listen and ask questions.

At one point a person unknown to either one of them sat down and asked Dr. Iwahashi about his newspaper articles on American and Japanese mental hospitals. Did teacher believe, then, that Westernism was a kind of disease that had to be kept out of the motherland in order to preserve Japanese sanity?

"Oh?" asked Dr. Iwahashi coolly, not even turning his head to the speaker. "Are you one of our students?"

The person quickly removed himself and his misplaced communication and returned to a remote table where he nursed with melancholy intensity a German translation of Mao Tse-tung's poetry.

"Some of these modern students have no manners," Iwahashi said to his colleague Mochizuki. "Just because I write for the mass media, I get mass man on my tail."

Mochizuki reached for a peanut and munched it, cupping a hand before his mouth by way of concealing the unlovely sight of teeth and jaws at work.

"But you technical people," Iwahashi went on, "are paid enough so you don't have to chase after the mass media for your children's tuition money."

A bona fide student took his place as soon as the conversation drifted away from personal matters.

"I wanted to say," offered Iwahashi in all friendliness, "that you really sounded like one of the old-time *benshi* back there awhile ago."

"It couldn't be helped," said Mochizuki with a trace of overloudness. He checked this show of feeling, revealed in his defensive tone of voice. "I mean, we didn't have a sound track."

The current supplicant put forth his question:

"*Benshi?* What is a *benshi?*"

Both professors laughed at that, Iwahashi with easy, body moving mirth, Mochizuki with a stiff sniggle.

"Why, then, I'll tell you," boomed Dr. Iwahashi. He was a veritable Sam Johnson at explaining things during these typical extracurricular afternoons, unlike his formal classroom self.

"When movies came to Japan, they had a *benshi* standing out in the wings to explain the action. Talkies, which came in long before your time, naturally put the *benshi* out of business."

"That is so," said Dr. Mochizuki.

"Not only that," added Dr. Iwahashi, "there was another man waiting at the top of a stepladder with a bucket of water, ready to dump it on the screen after each reel. Ha! What do you think of that? All that bright light beaming down out of the arc lamp, poured through a hot focus onto the paper screen down there—it might catch fire, you know. Hence, the little man with a bucket of water to cool it off, just in case."

Mochizuki reached for another peanut and chewed it aggressively, without covering his mouth. He could abide no insult to technology, ancient or modern.

"Do you remember," asked Dr. Iwahashi of the student, "when they first showed *Rashomon* in town? Kurosawa won first prize for that at Cannes in 1951, the first film Japan ever sent out to an international festival. Nobody back home understood it. So Daiei studios sent out *benshi* talkers to explain things.

"The trouble is," Dr. Iwahashi went on, "that Hollywood products are too very much popular."

"*Hai!*" said Mochizuki with an explosive sound of positive agreement.

"That's why the Board of Scientific and Technological Development is interested in Dr. Mochizuki."

"*Hai!*"

"The commercial development of his device will make Japanese movies more popular at home and help keep out so many foreign films. This will help our balance of payments, too."

The day the experiment in bionic moviemaking ended, Ito-san walked into Dr. Mochizuki's office, stood there until noticed, then, straightening his winter wool kimono with courtly dignity, he kneeled to the floor, kowtowing, and distinctly said: "I cannot do it, teacher, I cannot do it." And leaning forward, forehead on the floor, he cried great quaking, relieving sobs of tears.

Displeased to learn that his marvel of bionic engineering must shut down for want of a stable telepath, Mochizuki sent for Iwahashi.

When the message arrived, Professor Iwahashi was in the midst of his Thursday afternoon class. He took the folded note from his tiptoeing office secretary, read it, and dismissed her. He decided matters could wait until he finished the lecture.

"This classroom, its furnishing, your clothing, personal belongings, all are of Western origin. Even the subject of my lectures is a branch of Western learning. Brought up and educated in these surroundings, few of you must find it easy to retain any culture which you can call your own."

Dr. Iwahashi surveyed the high-collared Admiral Perry uniforms of his students.

"What, after all, can be claimed as absolutely native to this country?"

The students of comparative social behavior fingered their class pins, another foreign culture trait, in a state of high anxiety.

Dr. Iwahashi bore down on them.

"It is in the social conduct of your human relations that you are Japanese, if in nothing else. *Be* that! Remember the art of *ki-ga-tsuku.*"

Dr. Iwahashi tugged at the wings of his vest and tipped forward on the thin soles of his French patent leather shoes.

"Questions." He asked for them with a statement and departed the classroom.

The academic secretary, who had been sitting there all the time, hung his head respectfully until the sound of hard heels turned from the hallway and into the professor's office.

A student in the second row stood up and asked: "Pardon me, but I do not yet understand this business about *ki-ga-tsuku.* How is this so different from the behavior of foreigners? I do not understand what teacher is trying to tell us."

Noises of agreement were made by the rest of the class.

Set off to one side of the lectern at a little rickety table, the teacher's minion sat: a ruined, tubercular little pinch of a man dressed in a soiled suit. He put down his cigarette in slow motion, as if returning from a paradise of intellectual preoccupation to serve dolts, and blew out the last sick lungful of smoke.

It was he, the disciple, now that the master had left the room, who had to come right out in the open with this obscene talk about the private parts of social behavior.

He made cupping movements with his hands, scooping for that elusive balance between charitable clarity and selfish obfuscation required of a scholar as yet not sufficiently established to talk all in riddles.

"Unlike foreigners, Japanese do not like to say what they mean. If we say what we mean we are as naked persons, undressed in the world."

The secretary sensed that he had gone too far with his conceit and lit a fresh cigarette. He did so nervously, however, and exposed the package to reveal the brand, Golden Bat, the inexpensive favorite of old-time farmer folk, at once dating his taste and discrediting his claim to win a faculty position in the department.

Another student rose up to ask what, after all, was so bad about the behavior of the foreigners?

"Take the Americans for example. They are direct and informal with each other. None of this body ritual we go through, such as bowing and hissing; none of this verbal ritual, such as saying yes when you mean no. Why shouldn't we Japanese also adopt rational and efficient customs for ourselves?"

The secretary ignored the question. He held out with dogged silence until somebody else stood up. It was the first student.

"Yes, that is my question. What is it, as teacher tells us, that makes us truly Japanese inside?" With a twist of his class pin the student sat down.

The secretary talked to this point with professional ease.

"I refer you to chapter eight of teacher's most famous work, *Patterns of Japanese Interpersonal Behavior.*"

The secretary thumbed through his copy of the textbook.

"That is the chapter entitled, 'The Art of *Ki-Ga-Tsuku.*' What does teacher mean by *ki-ga-tsuku*? He has talked about this many times. I will repeat it for you."

Dr. Iwahashi's secretary flattened out the pages he would talk from. He ducked his cigarette pack under the table and drew out a fresh Golden Bat. It was loosely rolled and he had to twist the ends before lighting it. He spoke from memory, of course, because he had written the book, and many others like it, from his master's lectures. Theoretically, the long years of feudal servitude on the part of the secretary would pay off with a professorship for himself. Then he, too, would be able to designate a promising young scholar to care for his own later years.

"*Ki-ga-tsuku* has this meaning: to find out what the other person

intends to do. It is a game of perception. But it is different from the one
played by Westerners. Foreigners want always to know *why* people do
things. Foreigners want always to understand each other. Just as they
come to Japan and try to understand the Japanese people."

Appreciative laughter issued from the class at this, and the secretary reached out and touched the pages of the book possessively.

"We Japanese do not try to understand. We don't want to know
why, we want to know *what*. We don't care about reasons, about motivations. Those are unclean matters. Concern for them is bad for the
character.

"Our Japanese society is much more wholesome. Everybody's role
in our society is fixed and identified like a piece on the chessboard.
When we encounter another Japanese we have only to guess what his
next move will be. Who cares why he makes it? To guess why is to get
involved in the sticky threads of another's inner life. We in our formal
society are free individuals undefiled by contact with the motivations
of others."

The classroom was quiet. The secretary, now that he had the class
with him, smoked his Golden Bat with pride.

"It is *still* the mission of the Japanese people to improve the character of the inferior races of the world. Allow me to quote the words
of our late departed General Sadao Araki: 'The spirit of the Japanese
nation is, by its nature, a thing that must be propagated over the seven
seas and extended over the five continents.' "

Dr. Iwahashi scuffed his way through the fallen leaves of the great
ginkgo trees that dominated the Hongo campus. Neighborhood people
were moving about, bent over, picking up the last of the ginkgo nuts
for roasting.

Only one structure rose above the trees, the new engineering building, the first of the new constructions over eight stories put up by the
university after the new earthquake regulations were put into effect.

The building was faced with glazed tiles; inside, it sported a pair
of automatic stainless steel elevators. Iwahashi rode up to the twelfth
floor and walked down halls of modern beauty and lighting. How unlike
the halls of anthropology, with its cramped quarters, crammed with
loose stacks of wooden drawers at the top of a walkup of unimproved
cinderblock construction.

Inside the engineer's office a dented aluminum pot boiled on a gas
heater. Mochizuki extended the hospitality. He tipped the spout into
a strainer packed with damp leaves of green tea and the bubbling hot
water went steaming into the porcelain cup.

Iwahashi stepped across the snaky red gas tubing and received the
cup in both hands in an act at once of polite formality and of self-
seeking warmth.

After a long moment there in the gray twilight of a late afternoon in winter, Iwahashi said:

"I've arranged for Ito-san to be taken home. Come with me and I'll treat you at your favorite seafood restaurant."

The two of them jostled comfortably, not speaking, in the rush-hour crowds of the Marunouchi line and got off at Shinjuku station. They waited in line to enter Kikumasa, where tired businessmen took it easy on the way home with a little beer and raw fish. Finally, when their turn came, they sat facing each other at long stone benches, surrounded on high by great ornate platters that once had served the feasting tables of the Tokugawa barons. Surrounded by the clatter and delighted sounds of eating and enthusiastic talk on all sides of them, the two professors wiped faces and hands with the warm, wet towels set before them and prepared to order.

When the waiter had placed the food and poured out the beer, Iwahashi raised his glass, pronounced *"kampai,"* and the informal evening's relationship formally got under way.

"Why can't he finish *The Great Wall?*"

Iwahashi savored the tangled softness of raw jellyfish on his tongue. He might have taken this morsel as his text and said something to the effect that, while men can find satisfaction in eating raw food, they cannot abide one another in the raw, unclothed by ritual and protective custom. But he took instead the title of the film.

"Ito-san has built his own wall, one enclosing private space around himself, and he is cured."

Mochizuki nodded convulsively, saying, "How true! How true!" thus indicating, without exposing, his need for explanation.

"Ito-san's working with you on the film was its own therapy. He was in bondage to that woman, dreaming mind to mind with her. Evidently she got some kind of telepathic feedback from reading to him, some interior visualization from his mind of what she was reading. In time they evolved a symbiotic relationship: he trapped in it, she dependent on it. A disgusting, inhuman relationship of total involvement!"

Mochizuki shuddered. But he quickly came back to the question uppermost in his mind.

"What about the project, perhaps?"

Iwahashi poured his guest another glassful of Sapporo beer. "Ito-san is enjoying a vacation at home."

"He is not coming back?"

"Yes." One must always say "yes" even when the answer is "no" in order to avoid insincerity. Negation is offensively straightforward and rude. It is not sincere to hurt a personal relationship by sharp encounters with unpleasant facts. "Yes, he is not coming back."

"But the machine. . . ."

"You worked a miraculous cure," replied Iwahashi with tactful but irrelevant praise.

Mochizuki rose slightly forward on his stool and gasped in a self-deprecating drag of air through his teeth: an imploded voiceless dental spirant.

"His secret fantasy was of normal social life, is it not so?"

"*Hai!*" It was a reflexive response in deference to the authoritative opinion.

"It is so. In working with your machine, Ito-san found his chance to escape playing the insufflator to that mental succubus. Broadcasting his pictures through your machine, he robbed his *tsukisoi* of their reception."

"She went off to the movies, then?"

"Yes."

Now the yeses were hitting true, and Iwahashi continued with ease and under less pressure to guide and control the conversation.

"Once Ito-san learned to externalize his fantasy into your machine, he gradually reacquired the protective habits of formal human ties. His family has him back. Is this not good?"

"*Hai!*" affirmed Mochizuki, and he rose and bowed again. Iwahashi called for the check, thus signaling to Mochizuki, by doing the thing expected of the host, that he was to be held blameless for telling the truth.

They stepped out into the chill night air.

"The more communication, the less community," muttered Iwahashi, offering his ultimate reflection on the matter.

Mochizuki did not understand that.

Flags of the Rising Sun blazed in a long row in the powerful floodlights atop Keio department store to the front of them across the open square. Iwahashi looked up.

"The flags fly more these days, do they not?"

"*Hai!*"

Mochizuki understood that.

THE HANDLER

Damon Knight

When the big man came in, there was a movement in the room like bird dogs pointing. The piano player quit pounding, the two singing drunks shut up, all the beautiful people with cocktails in their hands stopped talking and laughing.

"Pete!" the nearest woman shrilled, and he walked straight into the room, arms around two girls, hugging them tight. "How's my sweetheart? Susy, you look good enough to eat, but I had it for lunch. George, you pirate—" he let go both girls, grabbed a bald blushing little man and thumped him on the arm—"you were great, sweetheart, I mean it, really great. Now HEAR THIS!" he shouted, over all the voices that were clamoring Pete this, Pete that.

Somebody put a martini in his hand, and he stood holding it, bronzed and tall in his dinner jacket, teeth gleaming white as his shirt cuffs. "We had a show!" he told them.

A shriek of agreement went up, a babble of did we have a *show* my God Pete listen a *show*—

He held up his hand. "It was a good show!"

Another shriek and babble.

"The sponsor kinda liked it—he just signed for another one in the fall!"

First appeared in *Rogue,* August, 1960. Copyright © 1960 by Greenleaf Publishing Co. Reprinted by permission of the author.

A shriek, a roar, people clapping, jumping up and down. The big man tried to say something else, but gave up, grinning, while men and women crowded up to him. They were all trying to shake his hand, talk in his ear, put their arms around him.

"I love ya *all!*" he shouted. "Now what do you say, let's live a little!"

The murmuring started again as people sorted themselves out. There was a clinking from the bar. "Jesus, Pete," a skinny pop-eyed little guy was saying, crouching in adoration, "when you dropped that fishbowl I thought I'd pee myself, honest to God—"

The big man let out a bark of happy laughter. "Yeah, I can still see the look on your face. And the fish, flopping all over the stage. So what can I do, I get down there on my knees—" the big man did so, bending over and staring at imaginary fish on the floor. "And I say, 'Well, fellows, back to the drawing board!' "

Screams of laughter as the big man stood up. The party was arranging itself around him in arcs of concentric circles, with people in the back standing on sofas and the piano bench so they could see. Somebody yelled, "Sing the goldfish song, Pete!"

Shouts of approval, please-do-Pete, the goldfish song.

"Okay, okay." Grinning, the big man sat on the arm of a chair and raised his glass. "And a vun, and a doo—vere's de moosic?" A scuffle at the piano bench. Somebody banged out a few chords. The big man made a comic face and sang, "Ohhh—how I wish . . . I was a little fish . . . and when I want some quail . . . I'd flap my little tail."

Laughter, the girls laughing louder than anybody and their red mouths farther open. One flushed blonde had her hand on the big man's knee, and another was sitting close behind him.

"But seriously—" the big man shouted. More laughter.

"No seriously," he said in a vibrant voice as the room quieted, "I want to tell you in all seriousness I couldn't have done it alone. And incidentally I see we have some foreigners, litvaks and other members of the press here tonight, so I want to introduce all the important people. First of all, George here, the three-fingered band leader—and there isn't a guy in the world could have done what he did this afternoon—George, I love ya." He hugged the blushing little bald man.

"Next my real sweetheart, Ruthie, where are ya? Honey, you were the greatest, really perfect—I mean it, baby—" He kissed a dark girl in a red dress who cried a little and hid her face on his broad shoulder. "And Frank—" he reached down and grabbed the skinny pop-eyed guy by the sleeve. "What can I tell you? A sweetheart?" The skinny guy was blinking, all choked up; the big man thumped him on the back. "Sol and Ernie and Mack, my writers, Shakespeare should have been so lucky —" One by one, they came up to shake the big man's hand as he called their names; the women kissed him and cried. "My stand-in," the big man was calling out, and "my caddy," and "Now," he said, as the room quieted a little, people flushed and sore-throated with enthusiasm, "I want you to meet my handler."

The room fell silent. The big man looked thoughtful and startled, as if he had had a sudden pain. Then he stopped moving. He sat without breathing or blinking his eyes. After a moment there was a jerky motion behind him. The girl who was sitting on the arm of the chair got up and moved away. The big man's dinner jacket split open in the back, and a little man climbed out. He had a perspiring brown face under a shock of black hair. He was a very small man, almost a dwarf, stoop-shouldered and round-backed in a sweaty brown singlet and shorts. He climbed out of the cavity in the big man's body, and closed the dinner jacket carefully. The big man sat motionless and his face was doughy.

The little man got down, wetting his lips nervously. Hello, Fred, a few people said. "Hello," Fred called, waving his hand. He was about forty, with a big nose and big soft brown eyes. His voice was cracked and uncertain. "Well, we sure put on a show, didn't we?"

Sure did, Fred, they said politely. He wiped his brow with the back of his hand. "Hot in there," he explained, with an apologetic grin. Yes I guess it must be, Fred, they said. People around the outskirts of the crowd were beginning to turn away, form conversational groups; the hum of talk rose higher. "Say, Tim, I wonder if I could have something to drink," the little man said. "I don't like to leave him—you know—" He gestured toward the silent big man.

"Sure, Fred, what'll it be?"

"Oh—you know—a glass of beer?"

Tim brought him a beer in a pilsener glass and he drank it thirstily, his brown eyes darting nervously from side to side. A lot of people were sitting down now; one or two were at the door leaving.

"Well," the little man said to a passing girl, "Ruthie, that was quite a moment there, when the fishbowl busted, wasn't it?"

"Huh? Excuse me, honey, I didn't hear you." She bent nearer.

"Oh—well, it don't matter. Nothing."

She patted him on the shoulder once, and took her hand away. "Well excuse me, sweetie, I have to catch Robbins before he leaves." She went on toward the door.

The little man put his beer glass down and sat, twisting his knobby hands together. The bald man and the pop-eyed man were the only ones still sitting near him. An anxious smile flickered on his lips; he glanced at one face, then another. "Well," he began, "that's one show under our belts, huh, fellows, but I guess we got to start, you know, thinking about —"

"Listen, Fred," said the bald man seriously, leaning forward to touch him on the wrist, "why don't you get back inside?"

The little man looked at him for a moment with sad hound-dog eyes, then ducked his head, embarrassed. He stood up uncertainly, swallowed and said, "Well—" He climbed up on the chair behind the big man, opened the back of the dinner jacket and put his legs in one at a time. A few people were watching him, unsmiling. "Thought I'd take it easy a while," he said weakly, "but I guess—" He reached in and gripped something with both hands, then swung himself inside. His brown, uncertain face disappeared.

The big man blinked suddenly and stood up. "Well *hey* there," he called, "what's a matter with this party anyway? Let's see some life, some action—" Faces were lighting up around him. People began to move in closer. "What I mean, let me hear that beat!"

The big man began clapping his hands rhythmically. The piano took it up. Other people began to clap. "What I mean, are we alive here or just waiting for the wagon to pick us up? How's that again, can't hear you!" A roar of pleasure as he cupped his hand to his ear. "Well come on, let me hear it!" A louder roar. Pete, Pete; a gabble of voices. "I got nothing against Fred," said the bald man earnestly in the middle of the noise, "I mean for a square he's a nice guy." "Know what you mean," said the pop-eyed man, "I mean like he doesn't *mean* it." "Sure," said the bald man, "but Jesus that sweaty undershirt and all. . . ." The pop-eyed man shrugged. "What are you gonna do?" Then they both burst out laughing as the big man made a comic face, tongue lolling, eyes crossed. Pete, Pete, Pete; the room was really jumping; it was a great party, and everything was all right, far into the night.

THEY

Robert Heinlein

They would not let him alone.

They would never let him alone. He realized that that was part of the plot against him—never to leave him in peace, never to give him a chance to mull over the lies they had told him, time enough to pick out the flaws, and to figure out the truth for himself.

That damned attendant this morning! He had come busting in with his breakfast tray, waking him, and causing him to forget his dream. If only he could remember that dream—

Someone was unlocking the door. He ignored it.

"Howdy, old boy. They tell me you refused your breakfast?" Dr. Hayward's professionally kindly mask hung over his bed.

"I wasn't hungry."

"But we can't have that. You'll get weak, and then I won't be able to get you well completely. Now get up and get your clothes on and I'll order an eggnog for you. Come on, that's a good fellow!"

Unwilling, but still less willing at that moment to enter into any conflict of wills, he got out of bed and slipped on his bathrobe. "That's better," Hayward approved. "Have a cigarette?"

"No, thank you."

First published in *Unknown Worlds,* April, 1941. Copyright © 1941 by Street & Smith Publications, Inc. Reprinted by permission of the author's agent, Lurton Blassingame.

The doctor shook his head in a puzzled fashion. "Darned if I can figure you out. Loss of interest in physical pleasures does not fit your type of case."

"What is my type of case?" he inquired in flat tones.

"Tut! Tut!" Hayward tried to appear roguish. "If medicos told their professional secrets, they might have to work for a living."

"What is my type of case?"

"Well—the label doesn't matter, does it? Suppose you tell me. I really know nothing about your case as yet. Don't you think it is about time you talked?"

"I'll play chess with you."

"All right, all right." Hayward made a gesture of impatient concession. "We've played chess every day for a week. If you will talk, I'll play chess."

What could it matter? If he was right, they already understood perfectly that he had discovered their plot; there was nothing to be gained by concealing the obvious. Let them try to argue him out of it. Let the tail go with the hide! To hell with it!

He got out the chessmen and commenced setting them up. "What do you know of my case so far?"

"Very little. Physical examination, negative. Past history, negative. High intelligence, as shown by your record in school and your success in your profession. Occasional fits of moodiness, but nothing exceptional. The only positive information was the incident that caused you to come here for treatment."

"To be brought here, you mean. Why should it cause comment?"

"Well, good gracious, man—if you barricade yourself in your room and insist that your wife is plotting against you, don't you expect people to notice?"

"But she was plotting against me—and so are you. White, or black?"

"Black—it's your turn to attack. Why do you think we are plotting against you?"

"It's an involved story, and goes way back into my early childhood. There was an immediate incident, however—" He opened by advancing the white king's knight to KB3. Hayward's eyebrows raised.

"You make a piano attack?"

"Why not? You know that it is not safe for me to risk a gambit with you."

The doctor shrugged his shoulders and answered the opening. "Suppose we start with your early childhood. It may shed more light than more recent incidents. Did you feel that you were being persecuted as a child?"

"No!" He half rose from his chair. "When I was a child I was sure of myself. I knew then, I tell you; I knew! Life was worth while, and I knew it. I was at peace with myself and my surroundings. Life was good and I was good and I assumed that the creatures around me were like myself."

"And weren't they?"

"Not at all! Particularly the children. I didn't know what viciousness was until I was turned loose with other children. The little devils! And I was expected to be like them and play with them."

The doctor nodded. "I know. The herd compulsion. Children can be pretty savage at times."

"You've missed the point. This wasn't any healthy roughness; these creatures were different—not like myself at all. They looked like me, but they were not like me. If I tried to say anything to one of them about anything that mattered to me, all I could get was a stare and a scornful laugh. Then they would find some way to punish me for having said it."

Hayward nodded. "I see what you mean. How about grownups?"

"That is somewhat different. Adults don't matter to children at first—or, rather they did not matter to me. They were too big, and they did not bother me, and they were busy with things that did not enter into my considerations. It was only when I noticed that my presence affected them that I began to wonder about them."

"How do you mean?"

"Well, they never did the things when I was around that they did when I was not around."

Hayward looked at him carefully. "Won't that statement take quite a lot of justifying? How do you know what they did when you weren't around?"

He acknowledged the point. "But I used to catch them just stopping. If I came into a room, the conversation would stop suddenly, and then it would pick up about the weather or something equally inane. Then I took to hiding and listening and looking. Adults did not behave the same way in my presence as out of it."

"Your move, I believe. But see here, old man—that was when you were a child. Every child passes through that phase. Now that you are a man, you must see the adult point of view. Children are strange creatures and have to be protected—at least, we do protect them—from many adult interests. There is a whole code of conventions in the matter that—"

"Yes, yes," he interrupted impatiently, "I know all that. Nevertheless, I noticed enough and remembered enough that was never clear to me later. And it put me on my guard to notice the next thing."

"Which was?" He noticed that the doctor's eyes were averted as he adjusted a castle's position.

"The things I saw people doing and heard them talking about were never of any importance. They must be doing something else."

"I don't follow you."

"You don't choose to follow me. I'm telling this to you in exchange for a game of chess."

"Why do you like to play chess so well?"

"Because it is the only thing in the world where I can see all the factors and understand all the rules. Never mind—I saw all around me this enormous plant, cities, farms, factories, churches, schools, homes, railroads, luggage, roller coasters, trees, saxophones, libraries, people and animals. People that looked like me and who should have felt very much like me, if what I was told was the truth. But what did they appear to be doing? 'They went to work to earn the money to buy the food to get the strength to go to work to earn the money to buy the food to get the strength to go to work to get the strength to buy the food to earn the money to go to—' until they fell over dead. Any slight variation in the basic pattern did not matter, for they always fell over dead. And everybody tried to tell me that I should be doing the same thing. I knew better!"

The doctor gave him a look apparently intended to denote helpless surrender and laughed. "I can't argue with you. Life does look like that, and maybe it is just that futile. But it is the only life we have. Why not make up your mind to enjoy it as much as possible?"

"Oh, no!" He looked both sulky and stubborn. "You can't peddle nonsense to me by claiming to be fresh out of sense. How do I know? Because all this complex stage setting, all these swarms of actors, could not have been put here just to make idiot noises at each other. Some other explanation, but not that one. An insanity as enormous, as complex, as the one around me had to be planned. I've found the plan!"

"Which is?"

He noticed that the doctor's eyes were again averted.

"It is a play intended to divert me, to occupy my mind and confuse me, to keep me so busy with details that I will not have time to think about the meaning. You are all in it, every one of you." He shook his finger in the doctor's face. "Most of them may be helpless automatons, but you're not. You are one of the conspirators. You've been sent in as a trouble-shooter to try to force me to go back to playing the role assigned to me!"

He saw that the doctor was waiting for him to quiet down.

"Take it easy," Hayward finally managed to say. "Maybe it is all a conspiracy, but why do you think that you have been singled out for special attention? Maybe it is a joke on all of us. Why couldn't I be one of the victims as well as yourself?"

"Got you!" He pointed a long finger at Hayward. "That is the essence of the plot. All of these creatures have been set up to look like me in order to prevent me from realizing that I was the center of the arrangements. But I have noticed the key fact, the mathematically inescapable fact, that I am unique. Here am I, sitting on the inside. The world extends outward from me. I am the center—"

"Easy, man, easy! Don't you realize that the world looks that way to me, too. We are each the center of the universe—"

"Not so! That is what you have tried to make me believe, that I am just one of millions more just like me. Wrong! If they were like me, then I could get into communication with them. I can't. I have tried and tried and I can't. I've sent out my inner thoughts, seeking some one other being who has them, too. What have I gotten back? Wrong answers, jarring incongruities, meaningless obscenity. I've tried. I tell you. God! —how I've tried! But there is nothing out there to speak to me— nothing but emptiness and otherness!"

"Wait a minute. Do you mean to say that you think there is nobody home at my end of the line? Don't you believe that I am alive and conscious?"

He regarded the doctor soberly. "Yes, I think you are probably alive, but you are one of the others—my antagonists. But you have set thousands of others around me whose faces are blank, not lived in, and whose speech is a meaningless reflex of noise."

"Well, then, if you concede that I am an ego, why do you insist that I am so very different from yourself?"

"Why? Wait!" He pushed back from the chess table and strode over to the wardrobe, from which he took out a violin case.

While he was playing, the lines of suffering smoothed out of his face and his expression took a relaxed beatitude. For a while he recaptured the emotions, but not the knowledge, which he had possessed in dreams. The melody proceeded easily from proposition to proposition with inescapable, unforced logic. He finished with a triumphant statement of the essential thesis and turned to the doctor. "Well?"

"Hm-m-m." He seemed to detect an even greater degree of caution in the doctor's manner. "It's an odd bit, but remarkable. 'S pity you didn't take up the violin seriously. You could have made quite a reputation. You could even now. Why don't you do it? You could afford to, I believe."

He stood and stared at the doctor for a long moment, then shook his head as if trying to clear it. "It's no use," he said slowly, "no use at all. There is no possibility of communication. I am alone." He replaced the instrument in its case and returned to the chess table. "My move, I believe?"

"Yes. Guard your queen."

He studied the board. "Not necessary. I no longer need my queen. Check."

The doctor interposed a pawn to parry the attack.

He nodded. "You use your pawns well, but I have learned to anticipate your play. Check again—and mate, I think."

The doctor examined the new situation. "No," he decided, "no—not quite." He retreated from the square under attack. "Not checkmate—stalemate at the worst. Yes, another stalemate."

He was upset by the doctor's visit. He couldn't be wrong, basically, yet the doctor had certainly pointed out logical holes in his position. From a logical standpoint the whole world might be a fraud perpetrated on everybody. But logic meant nothing—logic itself was a fraud, starting with unproved assumptions and capable of proving anything. The world is what it is!—and carries its own evidence of trickery.

But does it? What did he have to go on? Could he lay down a line between known facts and everything else and then make a reasonable interpretation of the world, based on facts alone—an interpretation free from complexities of logic and no hidden assumptions of points not certain. Very well—

First fact, himself. He knew himself directly. He existed.

Second facts, the evidence of his "five senses," everything that he himself saw and heard and smelled and tasted with his physical senses. Subject to their limitations, he must believe his senses. Without them he was entirely solitary, shut up in a locker of bone, blind, deaf, cut off, the only being in the world.

And that was not the case. He knew that he did not invent the information brought to him by his senses. There had to be something else out there, some otherness that produced the things his senses recorded. All philosophies that claimed that the physical world around him did not exist except in his imagination were sheer nonsense.

But beyond that, what? Were there any third facts on which he could rely? No, not at this point. He could not afford to believe anything that he was told, or that he read, or that was implicitly assumed to be true about the world around him. No, he could not believe any of it, for the sum total of what he had been told and read and been taught in school was so contradictory, so senseless, so wildly insane that none of it could be believed unless he personally confirmed it.

Wait a minute—the very telling of these lies, these senseless contradictions, was a fact in itself, known to him directly. To that extent they were data, probably very important data.

The world as it had been shown to him was a piece of unreason, an idiot's dream. Yet it was on too mammoth a scale to be without some reason. He came wearily back to his original point: Since the world could not be as crazy as it appeared to be, it must necessarily have been arranged to appear crazy in order to deceive him as to the truth.

Why had they done it to him? And what was the truth behind the sham? There must be some clue in the deception itself. What thread ran through it all? Well, in the first place he had been given a super abundance of explanations of the world around him, philosophies, religions, "common sense" explanations. Most of them were so clumsy, so obviously inadequate, or meaningless, that they could hardly have expected him to take them seriously. They must have intended them simply as misdirection.

But there were certain basic assumptions running through all the hundreds of explanations of the craziness around him. It must be these basic assumptions that he was expected to believe. For example, there was the deepseated assumption that he was a "human being," essentially like millions of others around him and billions more in the past and the future.

That was nonsense! He had never once managed to get into real communication with all those things that looked so much like him but were so different. In the agony of his loneliness, he had deceived himself that Alice understood him and was a being like him. He knew now that he had suppressed and refused to examine thousands of little discrepancies because he could not bear the thought of returning to complete loneliness. He had needed to believe that his wife was a living, breathing being of his own kind who understood his inner thoughts. He had refused to consider the possibility that she was simply, a mirror, an echo—or something unthinkably worse.

He had found a mate, and the world was tolerable, even though dull, stupid, and full of petty annoyance. He was moderately happy and had put away his suspicions. He had accepted, quite docilely, the treadmill he was expected to use, until a slight mischance had momentarily cut through the fraud—then his suspicions had returned with impounded force; the bitter knowledge of his childhood had been confirmed.

He supposed that he had been a fool to make a fuss about it. If he had kept his mouth shut they would not have locked him up. He should have been as subtle and as shrewd as they, kept his eyes and ears open and learned the details of and the reasons for the plot against him. He might have learned how to circumvent it.

But what if they had locked him up—the whole world was an asylum and all of them his keepers.

A key scraped in the lock, and he looked up to see an attendant entering with a tray. "Here's your dinner, sir."

"Thanks, Joe," he said gently. "Just put it down."

"Movies tonight, sir," the attendant went on. "Wouldn't you like to go? Dr. Hayward said you could—"

"No, thank you. I prefer not to."

"I wish you would, sir." He noticed with amusement the persuasive intentness of the attendant's manner. "I think the doctor wants you to. It's a good movie. There's a Mickey Mouse cartoon—"

"You almost persuade me, Joe," he answered with passive agreeableness. "Mickey's trouble is the same as mine, essentially. However, I'm not going. They need not bother to hold movies tonight."

"Oh, there will be movies in any case, sir. Lots of our other guests will attend."

"Really? Is that an example of thoroughness, or are you simply keeping up the pretense in talking to me? It isn't necessary, Joe, if it's any strain on you. I know the game. If I don't attend, there is no point in holding movies."

He liked the grin with which the attendant answered this thrust. Was it possible that this being was created just as he appeared to be —big muscles, phlegmatic disposition, tolerant, doglike? Or was there nothing going on behind those kind eyes, nothing but robot reflex? No, it was more likely that he was one of them, since he was so closely in attendance on him.

The attendant left and he busied himself at his supper tray, scooping up the already-cut bites of meat with a spoon, the only implement provided. He smiled again at their caution and thoroughness. No danger of that—he would not destroy this body as long as it served him in investigating the truth of the matter. There were still many different avenues of research available before taking that possibly irrevocable step.

After supper he decided to put his thoughts in better order by writing them; he obtained paper. He should start with a general statement of some underlying postulate of the credos that had been drummed into him all his "life." Life? Yes, that was a good one. He wrote:

"I am told that I was born a certain number of years ago and that I will die a similar number of years hence. Various clumsy stories have been offered me to explain to me where I was before birth and what becomes of me after death, but they are rough lies, not intended to deceive, except as misdirection. In every other possible way the world around me assures me that I am mortal, here but a few years, and a few years hence gone completely—nonexistent.

"WRONG—I am immortal. I transcend this little time axis; a seventy-year span on it is but a casual phase in my experience. Second only to the prime datum of my own existence is the emotionally convincing certainty of my own continuity. I may be a closed curve, but, closed or open, I neither have a beginning nor an end. Self-awareness is not relational; it is absolute, and cannot be reached to be destroyed, or created. Memory, however, being a relational aspect of consciousness, may be tampered with and possibly destroyed.

"It is true that most religions which have been offered me teach immortality, but note the fashion in which they teach it. The surest way to lie convincingly is to tell the truth unconvincingly. They did not wish me to believe.

"Caution: Why have they tried so hard to convince me that I am going to die in a few years? There must be a very important reason. I infer that they are preparing me for some sort of a major change. It may be crucially important for me to figure out their intentions about this—probably I have several years in which to reach a decision. Note: Avoid using the types of reasoning they have taught me."

The attendant was back. "Your wife is here, sir."

"Tell her to go away."

"Please, sir—Dr. Hayward is most anxious that you should see her."

"Tell Dr. Hayward that I said that he is an excellent chess player."

"Yes, sir." The attendant waited for a moment. "Then you won't see her, sir?"

"No, I won't see her."

He wandered around the room for some minutes after the attendant had left, too distrait to return to his recapitulation. By and large they had played very decently with him since they had brought him here. He was glad that they had allowed him to have a room alone, and he certainly had more time free for contemplation than had ever been possible on the outside. To be sure, continuous effort to keep him busy and to distract him was made, but, by being stubborn, he was able to circumvent the rules and gain some hours each day for introspection.

But, damnation!—he did wish they would not persist in using Alice in their attempts to divert his thoughts. Although the intense terror and revulsion which she had inspired in him when he had first rediscovered the truth had now aged into a simple feeling of repugnance and distaste for her company, nevertheless it was emotionally upsetting to be reminded of her, to be forced into making decisions about her.

After all, she had been his wife for many years. Wife? What was a wife? Another soul like one's own, a complement, the other necessary pole to the couple, a sanctuary of understanding and sympathy in the boundless depths of aloneness. That was what he had thought, what he had needed to believe and had believed fiercely for years. The yearning need for companionship of his own kind had caused him to see himself reflected in those beautiful eyes and had made him quite uncritical of occasional incongruities in her responses.

He sighed. He felt that he had sloughed off most of the typed emotional reactions which they had taught him by precept and example, but Alice had gotten under his skin, 'way under, and it still hurt. He had been happy—what if it had been a dope dream? They had given him an excellent, a beautiful mirror to play with—the more fool he to have looked behind it!

Wearily he turned back to his summing up:

"The world is explained in either one of two ways; the common-sense way which says that the world is pretty much as it appears to be

and that ordinary human conduct and motivations are reasonable, and
the religio-mystic solution which states that the world is dream stuff,
unreal, insubstantial, with reality somewhere beyond.

"WRONG—both of them. The common-sense scheme has no sense
to it of any sort. Life is short and full of trouble. Man born of woman
is born to trouble as the sparks fly upward. His days are few and they
are numbered. All is vanity and vexation. Those quotations may be
jumbled and incorrect, but that is a fair statement of the common-sense
world is-as-it-seems in its only possible evaluation. In such a world,
human striving is about as rational as the blind darting of a moth
against a light bulb. The common-sense world is a blind insanity, out
of nowhere, going nowhere, to no purpose.

"As for the other solution, it appears more rational on the surface,
in that it rejects the utterly irrational world of common-sense. But it
is not a rational solution, it is simply a flight from reality of any sort,
for it refuses to believe the results of the only available direct communication between the ego and the Outside. Certainly the 'five senses' are
poor enough channels of communication, but they are the only channels."

He crumpled up the paper and flung himself from the chair. Order
and logic were no good—his answer was right because it smelled right.
But he still did not know all the answer. Why the grand scale to the
deception, countless creatures, whole continents, an enormously involved and minutely detailed matrix of insane history, insane tradition, insane culture? Why bother with more than a cell and a strait
jacket?

It must be, it had to be, because it was supremely important to
deceive him completely, because a lesser deception would not do. Could
it be that they dare not let him suspect his real identity no matter how
difficult and involved the fraud?

He had to know. In some fashion he must get behind the deception
and see what went on when he was not looking. He had had one
glimpse; this time he must see the actual workings, catch the puppet-
masters in their manipulations.

Obviously the first step must be to escape from this asylum, but to
do it so craftily that they would never see him, never catch up with him,
not have a chance to set the stage before him. That would be hard to
do. He must excel them in shrewdness and subtlety.

Once decided, he spent the rest of the evening in considering the
means by which he might accomplish his purpose. It seemed almost
impossible—he must get away without once being seen and remain in
strict hiding. They must lose track of him completely in order that they
would not know where to center their deceptions. That would mean

going without food for several days. Very well—he could do it. He must not give them any warning by unusual action or manner.

The lights blinked twice. Docilely he got up and commenced preparations for bed. When the attendant looked through the peephole he was already in bed, with his face turned to the wall.

Gladness! Gladness everywhere! It was good to be with his own kind, to hear the music swelling out of every living thing, as it always had and always would—good to know that everything was living and aware of him, participating in him, as he participated in them. It was good to be, good to know the unity of many and the diversity of one. There had been one bad thought—the details escaped him—but it was gone—it had never been; there was no place for it.

The early-morning sounds from the adjacent ward penetrated the sleepladen body which served him here and gradually recalled him to awareness of the hospital room. The transition was so gentle that he carried over full recollection of what he had been doing and why. He lay still, a gentle smile on his face, and savored the uncouth, but not unpleasant, languor of the body he wore. Strange that he had ever forgotten despite their tricks and stratagems. Well, now that he had recalled the key, he would quickly set things right in this odd place. He would call them in at once and announce the new order. It would be amusing to see old Glaroon's expression when he realized that the cycle had ended—

The click of the peephole and the rasp of the door being unlocked guillotined his line of thought. The morning attendant pushed briskly in with the breakfast tray and placed it on the tip table. "Morning, sir. Nice, bright day—want it in bed, or will you get up?"

Don't answer! Don't listen! Suppress this distraction! This is part of their plan—But it was too late, too late. He felt himself slipping, falling, wrenched from reality back into the fraud world in which they had kept him. It was gone, gone completely, with no single association around him to which to anchor memory. There was nothing left but the sense of heart-breaking loss and the acute ache of unsatisfied catharsis.

"Leave it where it is. I'll take care of it."

"Okey-doke." The attendant bustled out, slamming the door, and noisily locked it.

He lay quite still for a long time, every nerve end in his body screaming for relief.

At last he got out of bed, still miserably unhappy, and attempted to concentrate on his plans for escape. But the psychic wrench he had received in being recalled so suddenly from his plane of reality had left

him bruised and emotionally disturbed. His mind insisted on rechew-
ing its doubts, rather than engage in constructive thought. Was it
possible that the doctor was right, that he was not alone in his miserable dilemma? Was he really simply suffering from paranoia, delusions
of self-importance?

Could it be that each unit in this yeasty swarm around him was
the prison of another lonely ego—helpless, blind, and speechless, con-
demned to an eternity of miserable loneliness? Was the look of suffering which he had brought to Alice's face a true reflection of inner
torment and not simply a piece of play acting intended to maneuver
him into compliance with their plans?

A knock sounded at the door. He said "Come in," without looking
up. Their comings and goings did not matter to him.

"Dearest—" A well-known voice spoke slowly and hesitantly.

"Alice!" He was on his feet at once, and facing her. "Who let you
in here?"

"Please, dear, please—I had to see you."

"It isn't fair. It isn't fair." He spoke more to himself than to her.
Then: "Why did you come?"

She stood up to him with a dignity he had hardly expected. The
beauty of her childlike face had been marred by line and shadow, but
it shone with an unexpected courage. "I love you," she answered quietly. "You can tell me to go away, but you can't make me stop loving
you and trying to help you."

He turned away from her in an agony of indecision. Could it be
possible that he had misjudged her? Was there, behind that barrier of
flesh and sound symbols, a spirit that truly yearned toward his? Lovers
whispering in the dark— *"You do understand, don't you?"*

"Yes, dear heart, I understand."

*"Then nothing that happens to us can matter, as long as we are
together and understand—"* Words, words, rebounding hollowly from
an unbroken wall—

No, he couldn't be wrong! Test her again— "Why did you keep me
on that job in Omaha?"

"But I didn't make you keep that job. I simply pointed out that we
should think twice before—"

"Never mind. Never mind." Soft hands and a sweet face preventing him with mild stubbornness from ever doing the thing that his
heart told him to do. Always with the best of intentions, the best of
intentions, but always so that he had never quite managed to do the
silly, unreasonable things that he knew were worth while. Hurry,
hurry, hurry, and strive, with an angel-faced jockey to see that you
don't stop long enough to think for yourself—

"Why did you try to stop me from going back upstairs that day?"

She managed to smile, although her eyes were already spilling over with tears. "I didn't know it really mattered to you. I didn't want us to miss the train."

It had been a small thing, an unimportant thing. For some reason not clear to him he had insisted on going back upstairs to his study when they were about to leave the house for a short vacation. It was raining, and she had pointed out that there was barely enough time to get to the station. He had surprised himself and her, too, by insisting on his own way in circumstances in which he had never been known to be stubborn.

He had actually pushed her to one side and forced his way up the stairs. Even then nothing might have come of it had he not—quite unnecessarily—raised the shade of the window that faced toward the rear of the house.

It was a very small matter. It had been raining, hard, out in front. From this window the weather was clear and sunny, with no sign of rain.

He had stood there quite a long while, gazing out at the impossible sunshine and rearranging his cosmos in his mind. He re-examined long-suppressed doubts in the light of this one small but totally unexplainable discrepancy. Then he had turned and had found that she was standing behind him.

He had been trying ever since to forget the expression that he had surprised on her face.

"What about the rain?"

"The rain?" she repeated in a small, puzzled voice. "Why, it was raining, of course. What about it?"

"But it was not raining out my study window."

"What? But of course it was. I did notice the sun break through the clouds for a moment, but that was all."

"Nonsense!"

"But darling, what has the weather to do with you and me? What difference does it make whether it rains or not—to us?" She approached him timidly and slid a small hand between his arm and side. "Am I responsible for the weather?"

"I think you are. Now please go."

She withdrew from him, brushed blindly at her eyes, gulped once, then said in a voice held steady: "All right. I'll go. But remember—you can come home if you want to. And I'll be there, if you want me." She waited a moment, then added hesitantly: "Would you ... would you kiss me good-bye?"

He made no answer of any sort, neither with voice nor eyes. She looked at him, then turned, fumbled blindly for the door, and rushed through it.

The creature he knew as Alice went to the place of assembly without stopping to change form. "It is necessary to adjourn this sequence. I am no longer able to influence his decisions."

They had expected it, nevertheless they stirred with dismay.

The Glaroon addressed the First for Manipulation. "Prepare to graft the selected memory track at once."

Then, turning to the First for Operations, the Glaroon said: "The extrapolation shows that he will tend to escape within two of his days. This sequence degenerated primarily through your failure to extend that rainfall all around him. Be advised."

"It would be simpler if we understood his motives."

"In my capacity as Dr. Hayward, I have often thought so," commented the Glaroon acidly, "but if we understood his motives, we would be part of him. Bear in mind the Treaty! He almost remembered."

The creature known as Alice spoke up. "Could he not have the Taj Mahal next sequence? For some reason he values it."

"You are becoming assimilated!"

"Perhaps. I am not in fear. Will he receive it?"

"It will be considered."

The Glaroon continued with orders: "Leave structures standing until adjournment. New York City and Harvard University are now dismantled. Divert him from those sectors.

"Move!"

CARCINOMA ANGELS
Norman Spinrad

At the age of nine Harrison Wintergreen first discovered that the world was his oyster when he looked at it sidewise. That was the year when baseball cards were *in*. The kid with the biggest collection of baseball cards was *it*. Harry Wintergreen decided to become *it*.

Harry saved up a dollar and bought 100 random baseball cards. He was in luck—one of them was the very rare Yogi Berra. In three separate transactions, he traded his other 99 cards for the only other three Yogi Berras in the neighborhood. Harry had reduced his holdings to four cards, but he had cornered the market in Yogi Berra. He forced the price of Yogi Berra up to an exorbitant 80 cards. With the slush fund thus accumulated, he successively cornered the market in Mickey Mantle, Willy Mays and Pee Wee Reese and became the J. P. Morgan of baseball cards.

Harry breezed through high school by the simple expedient of mastering only one subject—the art of taking tests. By his senior year, he could outthink any test writer with his gypsheet tied behind his back and won seven scholarships with foolish ease.

In college Harry discovered girls. Being reasonably good-looking and reasonably facile, he no doubt would've garnered his fair share of

First published in *Dangerous Visions,* Doubleday, 1967. Reprinted by permission of the author and the author's agents, Scott Meredith Literary Agency, Inc., 580 Fifth Avenue, New York, New York 10036.

conquests in the normal course of events. But this was not the way the mind of Harrison Wintergreen worked.

Harry carefully cultivated a stutter, which he could turn on or off at will. Few girls could resist the lure of a good-looking, well-adjusted guy with a slick line who nevertheless carried with him some secret inner hurt that made him stutter. Many were the girls who tried to delve Harry's secret, while Harry delved *them.*

In his sophomore year Harry grew bored with college and reasoned that the thing to do was to become Filthy Rich. He assiduously studied sex novels for one month, wrote three of them in the next two which he immediately sold at $1,000 a throw.

With the $3,000 thus garnered, he bought a shiny new convertible. He drove the new car to the Mexican border and across into a notorious border town. He immediately contacted a disreputable shoeshine boy and bought a pound of marijuana. The shoeshine boy of course tipped off the border guards, and when Harry attempted to walk across the bridge to the States they stripped him naked. They found nothing and Harry crossed the border. He had smuggled nothing out of Mexico, and in fact had thrown the marijuana away as soon as he bought it.

However, he had taken advantage of the Mexican embargo on American cars and illegally sold the convertible in Mexico for $15,000.

Harry took his $15,000 to Las Vegas and spent the next six weeks buying people drinks, lending broke gamblers money, acting in general like a fuzzy-cheeked Santa Claus, gaining the confidence of the right drunks and blowing $5,000.

At the end of six weeks he had three hot market tips which turned his remaining $10,000 into $40,000 in the next two months.

Harry bought 400 crated government surplus jeeps in four 100-jeep lots at $10,000 a lot and immediately sold them to a highly disreputable Central American government for $100,000.

He took the $100,000 and bought a tiny island in the Pacific, so worthless that no government had ever bothered to claim it. He set himself up as an independent government with no taxes and sold 20 one-acre plots to 20 millionaires seeking a tax haven at $100,000 a plot. He unloaded the last plot three weeks before the United States, with UN backing, claimed the island and brought it under the sway of the Internal Revenue Department.

Harry invested a small part of his $2,000,000 and rented a large computer for 12 hours. The computer constructed a betting scheme by which Harry parlayed his $2,000,000 into $20,000,000 by taking various British soccer pools to the tune of $18,000,000.

For $5,000,000 he bought a monstrous chunk of useless desert from an impoverished Arabian sultanate. With another $2,000,000 he created a huge rumor campaign to the effect that this patch of desert was literally floating on oil. With another $3,000,000 he set up a dummy corporation which made like a big oil company and publicly offered to buy his desert for $75,000,000. After some spirited bargaining, a large American oil company was allowed to outbid the dummy and bought 1,000 square miles of sand for $100,000,000.

Harrison Wintergreen was, at the age of 25, Filthy Rich by his own standards. He lost his interest in money.

He now decided that he wanted to Do Good. He Did Good. He toppled seven unpleasant Latin American governments and replaced them with six Social Democracies and a Benevolent Dictatorship. He converted a tribe of Borneo headhunters to Rosicrucianism. He set up 12 rest homes for overage whores and organized a birth control program which sterilized 12 million fecund Indian women. He contrived to make another $100,000,000 on the above enterprises.

At the age of 30 Harrison Wintergreen had had it with Do-Gooding. He decided to Leave His Footprints in the Sands of Time. He Left His Footprints in the Sands of Time. He wrote an internationally acclaimed novel about King Farouk. He invented the Wintergreen Filter, a membrane through which fresh water passed freely, but which barred salts. Once set up, a Wintergreen Desalinization Plant could desalinate an unlimited supply of water at a per-gallon cost approaching absolute zero. He painted one painting and was instantly offered $200,000 for it. He donated it to the Museum of Modern Art, gratis. He developed a mutated virus which destroyed syphilis bacteria. Like syphilis, it spread by sexual contact. It was a mild aphrodisiac. Syphilis was wiped out in 18 months. He bought an island off the coast of California, a 500-foot crag jutting out of the Pacific. He caused it to be carved into a 500-foot statute of Harrison Wintergreen.

At the age of 38 Harrison Wintergreen had Left sufficient Footprints in the Sands of Time. He was bored. He looked around greedily for new worlds to conquer.

This, then, was the man who, at the age of 40, was informed that he had an advanced, well-spread and incurable case of cancer and that he had one year to live.

Wintergreen spent the first month of his last year searching for an existing cure for terminal cancer. He visited laboratories, medical schools, hospitals, clinics, Great Doctors, quacks, people who had miraculously recovered from cancer, faith healers and Little Old Ladies in Tennis Shoes. There was no known cure for terminal cancer, reputable or otherwise. It was as he suspected, as he more or less even hoped. He would have to do it himself.

He proceeded to spend the next month setting things up to do it himself. He caused to be erected in the middle of the Arizona desert an air-conditioned walled villa. The villa had a completely automatic

kitchen and enough food for a year. It had a $5,000,000 biological and
biochemical laboratory. It had a $3,000,000 microfilmed library which
contained every word ever written on the subject of cancer. It had the
pharmacy to end all pharmacies: a liberal supply of quite literally
every drug that existed—poisons, painkillers, hallucinogens, dandr-
cides, antiseptics, antibiotics, viricides, headache remedies, heroin, qu-
nine, curare, snake oil—everything. The pharmacy cost $20,000,000.

The villa also contained a one-way radiotelephone, a large stock of
basic chemicals, including radioactives, copies of the *Koran,* the *Bible,*
the *Torah,* the *Book of the Dead, Science and Health with Key to the
Scriptures,* the *I Ching* and the complete works of Wilhelm Reich and
Aldous Huxley. It also contained a very large and ultra-expensive computer. By the time the villa was ready, Wintergreen's petty cash fund
was nearly exhausted.

With ten months to do that which the medical world considered
impossible, Harrison Wintergreen entered his citadel.

During the first two months he devoured the library, sleeping
three hours out of each 24 and dosing himself regularly with Benzedrine. The library offered nothing but data. He digested the data and
went on to the pharmacy.

During the next month he tried aureomycin, bacitracin, stannous
flouride, hexylresorcinol, cortisone, penicillin, hexachlorophine, shark
liver extract and 7,312 assorted other miracles of modern medical
science, all to no avail. He began to feel pain, which he immediately
blotted out and continued to blot out with morphine. Morphine addic-
tion was merely an annoyance.

He tried chemicals, radioactives, viricides, Christian Science, yoga,
prayer, enemas, patent medicines, herb tea, witchcraft and yogurt di-
ets. This consumed another month, during which Wintergreen continued to waste away, sleeping less and less and taking more and more
Benzedrine and morphine. Nothing worked. He had six months left.

He was on the verge of becoming desperate. He tried a different
tack. He sat in a comfortable chair and contemplated his navel for 48
consecutive hours.

His meditations produced a severe case of eyestrain and two sig
nificant words: "spontaneous remission."

In his two months of research, Wintergreen had come upon num
bers of cases where a terminal cancer abruptly reversed itself and the
patient, for whom all hope had been abandoned, had been cured. No
one ever knew how or why. It could not be predicted, it could not be
artificially produced, but it happened nevertheless. For want of an
explanation, they called it spontaneous remission. "Remission," meaning cure. "Spontaneous," meaning no one knew what caused it.

Which was not to say that it did not have a cause.

Wintergreen was buoyed; he was even ebullient. He knew that some terminal cancer patients had been cured. Therefore terminal cancer could be cured. Therefore the problem was removed from the realm of the impossible and was now merely the domain of the highly improbable.

And doing the highly improbable was Wintergreen's specialty.

With six months of estimated life left, Wintergreen set jubilantly to work. From his complete cancer library he culled every known case of spontaneous remission. He coded every one of them into the computer—data on the medical histories of the patients, on the treatments employed, on their ages, sexes, religions, races, creeds, colors, national origins, temperaments, marital status, Dun and Bradstreet ratings, neuroses, psychoses and favorite beers. Complete profiles of every human being ever known to have survived terminal cancer were fed into Harrison Wintergreen's computer.

Wintergreen programed the computer to run a complete series of correlations between 10,000 separate and distinct factors and spontaneous remission. If even one factor—age, credit rating, favorite food—*anything* correlated with spontaneous remission, the spontaneity factor would be removed.

Wintergreen had shelled out $100,000,000 for the computer. It was the best damn computer in the world. In two minutes and 7.894 seconds it had performed its task. In one succinct word it gave Wintergreen his answer:

"Negative."

Spontaneous remission did not correlate with *any* external factor. It was still spontaneous; the cause was unknown.

A lesser man would've been crushed. A more conventional man would've been dumfounded. Harrison Wintergreen was elated.

He had eliminated the entire external universe as a factor in spontaneous remission in one fell swoop. Therefore, in some mysterious way, the human body and/or psyche was capable of curing itself.

Wintergreen set out to explore and conquer his own internal universe. He repaired to the pharmacy and prepared a formidable potation. Into his largest syringe he decanted the following: Novocain; morphine; curare; *vlut,* a rare Central Asian poison which induced temporary blindness; olfactorcain, a top-secret smell-deadener used by skunk farmers; tympanoline, a drug which temporarily deadened the auditory nerves (used primarily by filibustering senators); a large dose of Benzedrine; lysergic acid; psilocybin; mescaline; peyote extract; seven other highly experimental and most illegal hallucinogens; eye of newt and toe of dog.

Wintergreen laid himself out on his most comfortable couch. He swabbed the vein in the pit of his left elbow with alcohol and injected himself with the witch's brew.

His heart pumped. His blood surged, carrying the arcane chemicals to every part of his body. The Novocain blanked out every sensory nerve in his body. The morphine eliminated all sensations of pain. The *vlut* blacked out his vision. The olfactorcain cut off all sense of smell. The tympanoline made him deaf as a traffic court judge. The curare paralyzed him.

Wintergreen was alone in his own body. No external stimuli reached him. He was in a state of total sensory deprivation. The urge to lapse into blessed unconsciousness was irresistible. Wintergreen, strong-willed though he was, could not have remained conscious unaided. But the massive dose of Benzedrine would not let him sleep.

He was awake, aware, alone in the universe of his own body with no external stimuli to occupy himself with.

Then, one and two, and then in combinations like the fists of a good fast heavyweight, the hallucinogens hit.

Wintergreen's sensory organs were blanked out, but the brain centers which received sensory data were still active. It was on these cerebral centers that the tremendous charge of assorted hallucinogens acted. He began to see phantom colors, shapes, things without name or form. He heard eldritch symphonies, ghost echoes, mad howling noises. A million impossible smells roiled through his brain. A thousand false pains and pressures tore at him, as if his whole body had been amputated. The sensory centers of Wintergreen's brain were like a mighty radio receiver tuned to an empty band—filled with meaningless visual, auditory, olfactory and sensual static.

The drugs kept his sense blank. The Benzedrine kept him conscious. Forty years of being Harrison Wintergreen kept him cold and sane.

For an indeterminate period of time he rolled with the punches, groping for the feel of this strange new non-environment. Then gradually, hesitantly at first but with ever growing confidence, Wintergreen reached for control. His mind constructed untrue but useful analogies for actions that were not actions, states of being that were not states of being, sensory data unlike any sensory data received by the human brain. The analogies, constructed in a kind of calculated madness by his subconscious for the brute task of making the incomprehensible palpable, also enabled him to deal with his non-environment as if it were an environment, translating mental changes into analogs of action.

He reached out an analogical hand and tuned a figurative radio, inward, away from the blank wave band of the outside side universe and towards the as yet unused wave band of his own body, the internal universe that was his mind's only possible escape from chaos.

He tuned, adjusted, forced, struggled, felt his mind pressing against an atom-thin interface. He battered against the interface, an analogical translucent membrane between his mind and his internal universe, a membrane that stretched, flexed, bulged inward, thinned . . . and finally broke. Like Alice through the Looking Glass, his analogical body stepped through and stood on the other side.

Harrison Wintergreen was inside his own body.

It was a world of wonder and loathsomeness, of the majestic and the ludicrous. Wintergreen's point of view, which his mind analogized as a body within his true body, was inside a vast network of pulsing arteries, like some monstrous freeway system. The analogy crystallized. It *was* a freeway, and Wintergreen was driving down it. Bloated sacs dumped things into the teeming traffic: hormones, wastes, nutrients. White blood cells careened by him like mad taxicabs. Red corpuscles drove steadily along like stolid burghers. The traffic ebbed and congested like a crosstown rush hour. Wintergreen drove on, searching, searching.

He made a left, cut across three lanes and made a right down toward a lymph node. And then he saw it—a pile of white cells like a 12-car collision, and speeding towards him a leering motorcyclist.

Black the cycle. Black the riding leathers. Black, dull black, the face of the rider save for two glowing blood-red eyes. And emblazoned across the front and back of the black motorcycle jacket in shining scarlet studs the legend: "Carcinoma Angels."

With a savage whoop, Wintergreen gunned his analogical car down the hypothetical freeway straight for the imaginary cyclist, the cancer cell.

Splat! Pop! Crush! Wintergreen's car smashed the cycle and the rider exploded in a cloud of fine black dust.

Up and down the freeways of his circulatory system Wintergreen ranged, barreling along arteries, careening down veins, inching through narrow capillaries, seeking the black-clad cyclists, the Carcinoma Angels, grinding them to dust beneath his wheels. . . .

And he found himself in the dark moist wood of his lungs, riding a snow-white analogical horse, an imaginary lance of pure light in his hand. Savage black dragons with blood-red eyes and flickering red tongues slithered from behind the gnarled bolls of great air-sac trees. St. Wintergreen spurred his horse, lowered his lance and impaled monster after hissing monster till at last the holy lung-wood was free of dragons. . . .

He was flying in some vast moist cavern, above him the vague bulks of gigantic organs, below a limitless expanse of shining slimy peritoneal plain.

From behind the cover of his huge beating heart a formation of black fighter planes, bearing the insignia of a scarlet "C" on their wings and fusilages, roared down at him.

Wintergreen gunned his engine and rose to the fray, flying up and over the bandits, blasting them with his machine guns, and one by one and then in bunches they crashed in flames to the peritoneum below. . . .

In a thousand shapes and guises, the black and red things attacked. Black, the color of oblivion, red, the color of blood. Dragons, cyclists, planes, sea things, soldiers, tanks and tigers in blood vessels and lungs and spleen and thorax and bladder—Carcinoma Angels, all.

And Wintergreen fought his analogical battles in an equal number of incarnations, as driver, knight, pilot, diver, soldier, mahout, with a grim and savage glee, littering the battlefields of his body with the black dust of the fallen Carcinoma Angels.

Fought and fought and killed and killed and finally. . . .

Finally found himself knee-deep in the sea of his digestive juices lapping against the walls of the dank, moist cave that was his stomach. And scuttling towards him on chitinous legs, a monstrous black crab with blood-red eyes, gross, squat, primeval.

Clicking, chittering, the crab scurried across his stomach towards him. Wintergreen paused, grinned wolfishly, and leaped high in the air, landing with both feet squarely on the hard black carapace.

Like a sun-dried gourd, brittle, dry, hollow, the crab crunched beneath his weight and splintered into a million dusty fragments.

And Wintergreen was alone, at last alone and victorious, the first and last of the Carcinoma Angels now banished and gone and finally defeated.

Harrison Wintergreen, alone in his own body, victorious and once again looking for new worlds to conquer, waiting for the drugs to wear off, waiting to return to the world that always was his oyster.

Waiting and waiting and waiting. . . .

Go to the finest sanitarium in the world, and there you will find Harrison Wintergreen, who made himself Filthy Rich, Harrison Wintergreen, who Did Good, Harrison Wintergreen, who Left His Footprints in the Sands of Time, Harrison Wintergreen, catatonic vegetable.

Harrison Wintergreen, who stepped inside his own body to do battle with Carcinoma's Angels, and won.

And can't get out.

SHATTERED LIKE A GLASS GOBLIN

Harlan Ellison

So it was there, eight months later, that Rudy found her; in that huge and ugly house off Western Avenue in Los Angeles; living with them, *all* of them; not just Jonah, but all of them.

It was November in Los Angeles, near sundown, and unaccountably chill even for the Fall in that place always near the sun. He came down the sidewalk and stopped in front of the place. It was gothic hideous, with the grass half-cut and the rusted lawnmower sitting in the middle of an unfinished swath. Grass cut as if a placating gesture to the outraged tenants of the two lanai apartment houses that loomed over the squat structure on either side. (Yet how strange . . . the apartment buildings were taller, the old house hunched down between them, but *it* seemed to dominate *them.* How odd.)

Cardboard covered the upstairs windows.

A baby carriage was overturned on the front walk.

The front door was ornately carved.

Darkness seemed to breathe heavily.

Rudy shifted the duffel bag slightly on his shoulder. He was afraid of the house. He was breathing more heavily as he stood there, and a panic he could never have described tightened the fat muscles on either side of his shoulderblades. He looked up into the corners of the darken-

231

ing sky, seeking a way out, but he could only go forward. Kristina was in there.

Another girl answered the door.

She looked at him without speaking, her long blonde hair half-obscuring her face; peering out from inside the veil of Clairol and dirt.

When he asked a second time for Kris, she wet her lips in the corners, and a tic made her cheek jump. Rudy set down the duffel bag with a whump. "Kris, please," he said urgently.

The blonde girl turned away and walked back into the dim hallways of the terrible old house. Rudy stood in the open doorway, and suddenly, as if the blonde girl had been a barrier to it, and her departure had released it, he was assaulted like a smack in the face, by a wall of pungent scent. It was marijuana.

He reflexively inhaled, and his head reeled. He took a step back, into the last inches of sunlight coming over the lanai apartment building, and then it was gone, and he was still buzzing, and moved forward, dragging the duffel bag behind him.

He did not remember closing the front door, but when he looked, some time later, it was closed behind him.

He found Kris on the third floor, lying against the wall of a dark closet, her left hand stroking a faded pink rag rabbit, her right hand at her mouth, the little finger crooked, the thumb-ring roach holder half-obscured as she sucked up the last wonders of the joint. The closet held an infinitude of odors—dirty sweat socks as pungent as stew, fleece jackets on which the rain had dried to mildew, a mop gracious with its scent of old dust hardened to dirt, the overriding weed smell of what she had been at for no one knew how long—and it held her. As pretty as pretty could be.

"Kris?"

Slowly, her head came up, and she saw him. Much later, she tracked and focused and she began to cry. "Go away."

In the limpid silences of the whispering house, back and above him in the darkness, Rudy heard the sudden sound of leather wings beating furiously for a second, then nothing.

Rudy crouched down beside her, his heart grown twice its size in his chest. He wanted so desperately to reach her, to talk to her. "Kris . . . please. . . ." She turned her head away, and with the hand that had been stroking the rabbit she slapped at him awkwardly, missing him.

For an instant, Rudy could have sworn he heard the sound of someone counting heavy gold pieces, somewhere off to his right, down a passageway of the third floor. But when he half-turned, and looked out through the closet door, and tried to focus his hearing on it, there was no sound to home in on.

Kris was trying to crawl back further into the closet. She was trying to smile.

He turned back; on hands and knees he moved into the closet after her.

"The rabbit," she said, langorously. "You're crushing the rabbit." He looked down, his right knee was lying on the soft matted-fur head of the pink rabbit. He pulled it out from under his knee and threw it into a corner of the closet. She looked at him with disgust. "You haven't changed, Rudy. Go away."

"I'm outta the army, Kris," Rudy said gently. "They let me out on a medical. I want you to come back, Kris, please."

She would not listen, but pulled herself away from him, deep into the closet, and closed her eyes. He moved his lips several times, as though trying to recall words he had already spoken, but there was no sound, and he lit a cigarette, and sat in the open doorway of the closet, smoking and waiting for her to come back to him. He had waited eight months for her to come back to him, since he had been inducted and she had written him telling him, *Rudy, I'm going to live with Jonah at The Hill.*

There was the sound of something very tiny, lurking in the infinitely black shadow where the top step of the stairs from the second floor met the landing. It giggled in a glass harpsichord trilling. Rudy knew it was giggling at *him,* but he could make out no movement from that corner.

Kris opened her eyes and stared at him with distaste. "Why did you come here?"

"Because we're gonna be married."

"Get out of here."

"I love you, Kris. Please."

She kicked out at him. It didn't hurt, but it was meant to. He backed out of the closet slowly.

Jonah was down in the living room. The blonde girl who had answered the door was trying to get his pants off him. He kept shaking his head no, and trying to fend her off with a weak-wristed hand. The record player under the brick-and-board bookshelves was playing Simon & Garfunkel, "The Big Bright Green Pleasure Machine."

"Melting," Jonah said gently. "Melting," and he pointed toward the big, foggy mirror over the fireplace mantel. The fireplace was crammed with unburned wax milk cartons, candy bar wrappers, newspapers from the underground press, and kitty litter. The mirror was dim and chill. *"Melting!"* Jonah yelled suddenly, covering his eyes.

"Oh shit!" the blonde girl said, and threw him down, giving up at last. She came toward Rudy.

"What's wrong with him?" Rudy asked.

"He's freaking out again. Christ, what a drag he can be."

"Yeah, but what's *happening* to him?"

She shrugged. "He sees his face melting, that's what he says."

"Is he on marijuana?"

The blonde girl looked at him with sudden distrust. "Mari—? Hey, who *are* you?"

"I'm a friend of Kris's."

The blonde girl assayed him for a moment more, then by the way her shoulders dropped and her posture relaxed, she accepted him. "I thought you might've just walked in, you know, maybe the Laws. You know?"

There was a Middle Earth poster on the wall behind her, with its brightness faded in a long straight swath where the sun caught it every morning. He looked around uneasily. He didn't know what to do.

"I was supposed to marry Kris. Eight months ago," he said.

"You want to fuck?" asked the blonde girl. "When Jonah trips he turns off. I been drinking Coca-Cola all morning and all day, and I'm really horny."

Another record dropped onto the turntable and Stevie Wonder blew hard into his harmonica and started singing, "I Was Born To Love Her."

"I was engaged to Kris," Rudy said, feeling sad. "We was going to be married when I got out of basic. But she decided to come over here with Jonah, and I didn't want to push her. So I waited eight months, but I'm out of the army now."

"Well, *do* you or *don't* you?"

Under the dining room table. She put a satin pillow under her. It said: *Souvenir of Niagara Falls, New York.*

When he went back into the living room, Jonah was sitting up on the sofa, reading Hesse's *Magister Ludi.*

"Jonah?" Rudy said. Jonah looked up. It took him a while to recognize Rudy.

When he did, he patted the sofa beside him, and Rudy came and sat down.

"Hey, Rudy, where y'been?"

"I've been in the army."

"Wow."

"Yeah, it was awful."

"You out now? I mean for good?"

Rudy nodded. "Uh-huh. Medical."

"Hey, that's good."

They sat quietly for a while. Jonah started to nod, and then said to himself: "You're not very tired."

Rudy said, "Jonah, hey listen, what's the story with Kris? You know, we was supposed to get married about eight months ago."

"She's around someplace," Jonah answered.

Out of the kitchen, through the dining room where the blonde girl lay sleeping under the table, came the sound of something wild, tearing at meat. It went on for a long time, but Rudy was looking out the front window, the big bay window. There was a man in a dark gray suit standing talking to two policemen on the sidewalk at the edge of the front walk leading up to the front door. He was pointing at the big, old house.

"Jonah, can Kris come away now?"

Jonah looked angry. "Hey, listen, man, nobody's *keeping* her here. She's been grooving with all of us and she likes it. Go ask her. Christ, don't bug me!"

The two cops were walking up to the front door.

Rudy got up and went to answer the doorbell.

They smiled at him when they saw his uniform.

"May I help you?" Rudy asked them.

The first cop said, "Do you live here?"

"Yes," said Rudy. "My name is Rudolph Boekel. May I help you?"

"We'd like to come inside and talk to you."

"Do you have a search warrant?"

"We don't want to search, we only want to talk to you. Are you in the army?"

"Just discharged. I came home to see my family."

"Can we come in?"

"No, sir."

The second cop looked troubled. "Is this the place they call 'The Hill'?"

"Who?" Rudy asked, looking perplexed.

"Well, the neighbors said this was 'The Hill' and there were some pretty wild parties going on here."

"Do you hear any partying?"

The cops looked at each other. Rudy added, "It's always very quiet here. My mother is dying of cancer of the stomach."

They let Rudy move in, because he was able to talk to people who came to the door from the outside. Aside from Rudy, who went out to get food, and the weekly trips to the unemployment line, no one left The Hill. It was usually very quiet.

Except sometimes there was the sound of growling in the back hall leading up to what had been a maid's room; and the splashing from the basement, the sound of wet things on bricks.

It was a self-contained little universe, bordered on the north by acid and mescaline, on the south by pot and peyote, on the east by speed and redballs, on the west by downers and amphetamines. There were 11 people living in The Hill. Eleven, and Rudy.

He walked through the halls, and sometimes found Kris, who would not talk to him, save once, when she asked him if he'd ever been heavy behind *anything* except love. He didn't know what to answer her, so he only said, "Please," and she called him a square and walked off toward the stairway leading to the dormered attic.

Rudy had heard squeaking from the attic. It had sounded to him like the shrieking of mice being torn to pieces. There were cats in the house.

He did not know why he was there, except that he didn't understand why *she* wanted to stay. His head always buzzed and he sometimes felt that if he just said the right thing, the right way, Kris would come away with him. He began to dislike the light. It hurt his eyes.

No one talked to anyone else very much. There was always a struggle to keep high, to keep the *group high* as elevated as possible. In that way they cared for each other.

And Rudy became their one link with the outside. He had written to someone—his parents, a friend, a bank, someone—and now there was money coming in. Not much, but enough to keep the food stocked, and the rent paid. But he insisted Kris be nice to him.

They all made her be nice to him, and she slept with him in the little room on the second floor where Rudy had put his newspapers and his duffel bag. He lay there most of the day, when he was not out on errands for The Hill, and he read the smaller items about train wrecks and molestations in the suburbs. And Kris came to him and they made love of a sort.

One night she convinced him he should "make it, heavy behind acid" and he swallowed fifteen hundred mikes cut with Methedrine, in two big gel caps, and she was stretched out like taffy for six miles. He was a fine copper wire charged with electricity, and he pierced her flesh. She wriggled with the current that flowed through him, and became softer yet. He sank down through the softness, and carefully observed the intricate wood-grain effect her teardrops made as they rose in the mist around him. He was downdrifting slowly, turning and turning, held by a whisper of blue that came out of his body like a spiderweb. The sound of her breathing in the moist crystal pillared cavity that went down and down was the sound of the very walls themselves, and when he touched them with his warm fingertips she drew in breath heavily, forcing the air up around him as he sank down, twisting slowly in a veil of musky looseness.

There was an insistent pulsing growing somewhere below him, and he was afraid of it as he descended, the high-pitched whining of something threatening to shatter. He felt panic. Panic gripped him, flailed at him, his throat constricted, he tried to grasp the veil and it tore away in his hands; then he was falling, faster now, much faster, and afraid *afraid!*

Violet explosions all around him and the shrieking of something that wanted him, that was seeking him, pulsing deeply in the throat of an animal he could not name, and he heard her shouting, heard her wail and pitch beneath him and a terrible crushing feeling in him. . . .

And then there was silence.

That lasted for a moment.

And then there was soft music that demanded nothing but inattention. So they lay there, fitted together, in the heat of the tiny room, and they slept for some hours.

After that, Rudy seldom went out into the light. He did the shopping at night, wearing shades. He emptied the garbage at night, and he swept down the front walk, and did the front lawn with scissors because the lawnmower would have annoyed the residents of the lanai apartments (who no longer complained, because there was seldom a sound from The Hill).

He began to realize he had not seen some of the 11 young people who lived in The Hill for a long time. But the sounds from above and below and around him in the house grew more frequent.

Rudy's clothes were too large for him now. He wore only underpants. His hands and feet hurt. The knuckles of his fingers were larger, from cracking them, and they were always an angry crimson.

His head always buzzed. The thin perpetual odor of pot had saturated into the wood walls and the rafters. He had an itch on the outside of his ears he could not quell. He read newspapers all the time, old newspapers whose items were imbedded in his memory. He remembered a job he had once held as a garage mechanic, but that seemed a very long time ago. When they cut off the electricity in The Hill, it didn't bother Rudy, because he preferred the dark. But he went to tell the eleven.

He could not find them.

They were all gone. Even Kris, who should have been there somewhere.

He heard the moist sounds from the basement and went down with fur and silence into the darkness. The basement had been flooded. One of the 11 was there. His name was Teddy. He was attached to the slime-coated upper wall of the basement, hanging close to the stone, pulsing softly and giving off a thin purple light, purple as a bruise. He dropped a rubbery arm into the water, and let it hang there, moving idly with the tideless tide. Then something came near it, and he made a *sharp* movement, and brought the thing up still writhing in his rubbery grip, and inched it along the wall to a dark, moist spot on his upper surface, near the veins that covered its length, and pushed the thing at the dark-blood spot, where it shrieked with a terrible sound, and went in and there was a sucking noise, then a swallowing sound.

Rudy went back upstairs. On the first floor he found the one who was the blonde girl, whose name was Adrianne. She lay out thin and white as a tablecloth on the dining room table as three of the others he had not seen in a very long while put their teeth into her and through their hollow sharp teeth they drank up the yellow fluid from the bloated pus-pockets that had been her breasts and her buttocks. Their faces were very white and their eyes were like soot-smudges.

Climbing to the second floor, Rudy was almost knocked down by the passage of something that had been Victor, flying on heavily ribbed leather wings. It was carrying a cat in its jaws.

He saw the thing on the stairs that sounded as though it was counting heavy gold pieces. It was not counting heavy gold pieces. Rudy could not look at it; it made him feel sick.

He found Kris in the attic, in a corner breaking the skull and sucking out the moist brains of a thing that giggled like a harpsichord.

"Kris, we have to go away," he told her. She reached out and touched him, snapping her long, pointed, dirty fingernails against him. He rang like crystal.

In the rafters of the attic Jonah crouched, gargoyled and sleeping. There was a green stain on his jaws, and something stringy in his claws.

"Kris, please," he said urgently.

His head buzzed.

His ears itched.

Kris sucked out the last of the mellow good things in the skull of the silent little creature, and scraped idly at the flaccid body with hairy hands. She settled back on her haunches, and her long, hairy muzzle came up.

Rudy scuttled away.

He ran loping, his knuckles brushing the attic floor as he scampered for safety. Behind him, Kris was growling. He got down to the second floor and then to the first, and tried to climb up on the Morris chair to the mantel, so he could see himself in the mirror, by the light of the moon, through the fly-blown window. But Naomi was on the window, lapping up the flies with her tongue.

He climbed with desperation, wanting to see himself. And when he stood before the mirror, he saw that he was transparent, that there was nothing inside him, that his ears had grown pointed and had hair on their tips; his eyes were as huge as a tarsier's, and the reflection of light hurt him.

Then he heard the growling behind and below him.

The little glass goblin turned, and the werewolf rose up on its hind legs and touched him till he rang like fine crystal.

And the werewolf said with very little concern, "Have you ever grooved heavy behind *anything* except love?"

"Please!" the little glass goblin begged, just as the great hairy paw slapped him into a million coruscating rainbow fragments all expanding consciously into the tight little enclosed universe that was The Hill, all buzzing highly contacted and tingling off into a darkness that began to seep out through the silent wooden walls. . . .

THE NEW SOUND

Charles Beaumont

Of all the squirrels in a world full of squirrels Mr. Goodhew was by far the squirreliest. That is, he collected things. But whereas once it had been masks and postage stamps and colored rocks and bits of twine, now he collected death. Vigorously, fanatically, lovingly. He would pluck it out of the air and seal it inside plastoid and listen to it at night. It made him very happy.

But things were not always so. It had come by degrees, beginning with Mozart and Bach and ending with the mollusks and the bats— which was, of course, the real beginning. As a common audiophile he had filled his apartment with a mushroom growth of phonographs and speakers and attachments and he was kept busy reproducing fidelitously the *tutti* passages of the more violent composers. But then, one day, he happened to purchase an album entitled *A World of Sounds*. Its cover was of modern design and it had been manufactured in the interests of science. It contained such items as recordings of seals at play, the death cry of a wounded ibex and a horsefly's heartbeat. Bonuswise it offered the sound of a squid thrashing in waters described as *lonely* and *unfathomable* and the somewhat unnerving (though not to Mr. Goodhew) chitter of a vampire bat.

Sounds, wonderful and strange; sounds you could get your teeth into, sounds like none he had ever heard. . . .

Promptly he was lost and the collection was on its way.

It was crude at first, as all collections are: a higgledy-piggledy potpourri entirely without organization. Hasty purchase followed hasty purchase—today a windstorm over Reykjavik, tomorrow an alligator's yawn, the next day the weary groan of bordello couch-springs. . . .

In time, however, Mr. Goodhew tired of such easily come by items and developed a less universal attitude: he narrowed his field. The purchases became less frequent and it was soon necessary for him to dip into capital—a commodity of which, fortunately, he enjoyed a plenitude owing to an inheritance left by his father who had been a used car salesman. He hired Sound Scouts to record the really bizarre, unusual, outré, the near-fantastic. But still, though interesting, the collection was not sufficiently homogenous to please Mr. Goodhew. He listened eveningly to the rustle of unborn infants, to the perspiration fall from thieves' foreheads, to the sound of trapdoors swinging against gallows platforms, and he thought as he listened: I must specialize, yes, I must specialize!

But how? In what way?

He thought about it carefully, sorting, eliminating, eliminating. Then he called in his employees and gave them their orders.

It was at that moment that Mr. Goodhew became the first necroaudiophile.

Throwing out all but the death cry of the ibex, he attended scrupulously to his specialty. The first report brought him recordings of crushed mice, immolated earwigs, the gasps of a mongrel lying beneath two tons of truck—a very nice rudimentary start. He listened to them, catalogued them, cross-filed them and put them away. And waited.

He had not long to wait. Presently his apartment bulged with records, and the air was forever alive with the cries, groans, gasps, screams, screeches, whimpers and whines of sundry animals; all dying, each in a different way. Upon that point Mr. Goodhew stood adamant: there must be no repetitiousness.

And all went swimmingly until, for numerous reasons, he found it necessary to change quarters. For one thing, the apartment was becoming incommodious for his needs; for another, he was weary of making explanations to the neighbors and to the policemen summoned by the neighbors. He moved, records and all, to a redwood villa high upon the highest hill, and there he stayed.

And the collection grew. Despite world conditions, which could best be described as taut, each day's mail would bring from all corners something new: the death throes of an armadillo; the shrills, flutings

and flutterings of a disemboweled canary; the hysterical hiss of an
anaconda dropped into a wood stove. . . . Mr. Goodhew had scarcely a
moment free, so busy was he listening, filing, recording, processing:
only in the evening could he fall into an easy chair, flip on the phonograph and actually enjoy his collection. Then the lights would be
turned off and he would sit there, tense, expectant, mouth open, brain
a moving image to the sounds. He would listen in the manner of many
another collector fingering rare delft or polishing sea shells or putting
first folios in line upon library shelves. And he was a true, a real
collector, for he enjoyed every phase of it: the preparation, the labor,
and, most important, the sounds themselves.

One day, however, after many years had passed, the inevitable
happened. His specialty reached completion, or nearly that, very tragically nearly that. No species of animal existed of which at least one
member had not died for Mr. Goodhew. He had them all. From aard-
vark to zebra, from the subaqueous leave-taking of a single cell to the
room-filling choke of a giant whale. All there, in Mr. Goodhew's house,
filed and stored: complete.

Except—

Once determined, Mr. Goodhew breathed as a prisoner granted
pardon. It took adjusting, screwing up of the courage, but he was a
collector and he could think of nothing worse than a collector with
nothing to collect.

So it was settled.

The first batch arrived one week from the time of his decision. It
contained one perfect jewel and several of declining quality. But that
first! Mr. Goodhew listened to it again and again. He listened to the
woman's scream as it echoed through the rooms of his house. What
pain! What suffering! What *bel canto!*

She had been strangled, the Sound Scout—an extremely ambitious
fellow—had explained, though failing to append any note regarding
certain other details which occurred to, but did not overlong remain
with, his employer. The rest was chaff, an unhappy mish-mash of hoots
and bellows and throbbing guttural wrackings—all obviously spurious.

Which made Mr. Goodhew furious.

He discharged all the men save Mr. Hurke, who had presented him
with the initial gem; and thenceforth the Sound Collection flourished
—slowly, it is true, what with world tension, the bombs, et al., but quite
surely.

At night now, Mr. Goodhew scarcely ever made reference to any
of what he termed his Mesozoic period, preferring to concentrate on
this latest phase of the collection. Into the weeest hours he would listen
and thrill to the death rattles of stilettoed merchants, the last bub-
blings of drowned spinsters, the dry croaks of nonagenarians, the wind-

crushed screams of falling eunuchs. . . . Terror and anguish and
honesty, the sounds of honesty; of souls laid open—this is what he
listened to.

And surely, he thought, there is no limit to my collection now! A
sound for every soul in a universe overrun with souls. It would last
forever; he would go on collecting and collecting and—

On a humid evening high upon his hill Mr. Goodhew got up,
walked over to his phonograph and snapped off the seven hundredth
shriek of a university student who had yet 300 to go (the Death of a
Thousand Cuts—Mr. Hurke had instituted certain refinements). And
so doing, Mr. Goodhew sighed, paced a bit and then proceeded to a hall
mirror whereat he stood in contemplation for 15 minutes. It was difficult to believe; almost, it seemed, impossible to believe. Yet, as he saw
those eyes, those lines and wrinkles, that runny scratch of mouth, he
knew it was true.

He had become jaded. He had been living off marginalia for years,
and now he faced it: he was a Des Esseintes at the end of the trail. There
were no more new sounds, none to excite the smallest interest.

His collection was—complete.

He sighed again, and was alarmed at the sudden receipt of a highly
whimsical idea. If it is complete, he thought, why then do I feel frus-
trated? Where is the satisfaction? No. It is *not* complete; there is yet
one more, one last sound.

My own!

Nonsense. He spoke aloud now, even as he played with the special
tape recorder. If I shoot myself or swallow prussic acid or what have
you, and then play it back . . . but stop! That is ridiculous and what is
worse, it is grossly literary.

But if not his own death—which, as he reasoned, he would scarcely
be able to enjoy afterwards—what then? He began to pace at a faster
clip. Searching his mind. The New Sound, the Ultimate Sound, the only
one he lacked. . . .

Mr. Goodhew stamped his foot upon the Japanese floormat and
flung himself onto a large divan and cogitated until his temples ached.

What could it be? What had he overlooked to account for this
feeling of incompleteness?

It was at this point of chaotic frustration when thought unravels
and trails into a knotted tangle that Mr. Goodhew felt the concussion.
Like a silent explosion, the loosing of fantastic pressures, a vast cosmic
hemorrhage, assailing the nerves of his body, causing him to roll onto
the floor and blink.

What—He rose and rushed directly to the window, the east window which commanded an imperial view of the light-laced city. It was
midnight. And yet, from afar, he could see the great inverted orange

flow deepening, spreading in the sky like a drop of color in the transparent water of a fishbowl.

He watched it grow and thought about it. Thought about the alarmists and their perpetual pulings of world cataclysm, the C-Bomb, the O-Bomb—

The explosion began, a soft rumble of drums in the bloated black overhead clouds. Mr. Goodhew flinched and trembled as understanding came. Then he snapped his fingers and said of course; he sprang backward and raced to his recording apparatus, fastened the attachments, set it all humming. Hurry, hurry! He brought the special microphone to the open window, held it high, tested it: One, Two, Three, Four.

And then there was the ripping and the crashing and the thunder like no other thunder, loud, so loud, a frenzied tourbillon of sound—but still soft enough to permit the screams to wriggle through, like tiny frightened snakes.

Mr. Goodhew held the microphone high out the window and chuckled; even when the fires began, he chuckled. He breathed fast, waiting. ... A little more, a little longer, two more seconds: Now! He snapped a switch and watched the glistening tanness of tape hiss in fast reverse. He snapped another switch, stopping it.

Mr. Goodhew pressed the playback button and shivered in wild anticipatory glee.

Then the lights went out. He bent closer. Listening—he craned his neck and conched his ears; and then he let loose one small strangulated cry of anguish. He shook the dead recorder and did not stop shaking it until the world had burst and split and blown away in a billion flaming specks.

He had missed it. He had missed the ultimate sound.   ,

Alan Copeland / Photon West

five

Tomorrow Will Be Better

The world of tomorrow, in the eyes of the idealistic futurists, is a world under control. Man, domesticated at last!

It is a world in which no one need work for a living. Leisure is a blessing everyone is entitled to. But in "Rat Race," Raymond F. Jones asks about the fate of those who *want* to work.

It is a world in which sexual hangups are resolved by the most technical and rational of means, without upsetting emotional difficulties. But what of the child that still longs for the *mystery* of sexuality? This is the question posed by A. K. Jorgensson in "Coming of Age Day."

It is a world where women, freed at last from the tyranny of men, now tyrannize their oppressors. But what is the gain, Bruce McAllister asks in *"Ecce Femina!"* if men and women simply trade sexual personalities?

It is a world overpopulated by our standards, but man is an adaptable creature. Harry Harrison shows in "Roommates" that man can adapt to anything. So why worry? The future will take care of itself.

It is a world in which all troublesome differences between individualism and collectivism will be resolved in favor of the latter. Do you sincerely want a society of loving non-competitiveness? Theodore Sturgeon shows how to police the ideals of equality and sharing in "Mr. Costello, Hero."

Isn't it a drag, living in the present imperfect, knowing that those who follow will live as a more adequate race of men?

RAT RACE
Raymond F. Jones

The big run of HO model railroad activity began that summer, and George Sims-Howton was responsible for it. He had a penchant for old things like that and came across a description of HO model trains one day while browsing in the public archives. It was characteristic of George that he would go down there and finger the old volumes rather than make a computer search for subject matter in a fraction of the time.

"If I just want to find out what's there, how can I ask for it by subject?" he'd argue.

He brushed off the answer that he could use random search on the library computer. He said he liked to feel the old things with his hands.

There was no objection to it. Nobody else had asked for access to the original archives these past ten years. Actually, most of the stuff had been long since destroyed, because it was preserved on tape or film. Why it hadn't all gone that way worried no one.

Anyway, it was there, and it gave George a lot of pleasure to wade through the stuff, and that's how he came up with this model railroad thing. It seems there used to be whole magazines and books devoted to

First published in *Analog Science Fact and Fiction,* April, 1966. Reprinted by permission of the author and the author's agents, Scott Meredith Literary Agency, Inc., 580 Fifth Avenue, New York, New York 10036.

the subject about 150 years ago, but it's almost certain that no one living had ever seen a model train until George came up with it.

Right away, George wanted an HO railroad, and the idea intrigued some of the other fellows who lived in the same condomin. They all belonged to the same *bali-putsch* team and had beat every other outfit in their league and in several leagues around. They were ripe for some new excitement when George made his discovery.

They debated about where to get the train. Sam Bowlerman was sure the proper place would be a sporting goods store. Dave Estes said an appliance store. But George was convinced that a hardware store would be the place, and since the idea was his, that was where they went.

There was a shopping center just across the mall from their condomin. George had obtained veri-copies of some plans in an old model-railroading magazine in the archives and brought them along. He sat in the small booth and fed the veri-copies of the model train plans to the scanner, while Sam and Dave stuck their heads in the door. George had the feeling the scanner gulped as it absorbed the strange image on the paper. But the order was not rejected, and presently, the light went out, the plans were returned, and a slip of printout paper reported: Manufacture—Oklahoma City. Delivery—two days.

Sam growled in disgust. "Why do you think they schedule a little order like that two-thirds of the way across the country? It could have been made in Buffalo and we could have had it this afternoon."

"Question not the wisdom of the computer," said Dave. "It provideth all. But that kills it for the rest of the day." He glanced at his watch. "Only eleven o'clock. How about a game after lunch?"

Sam shook his head. "You're getting stale from too much playing. Ellie wants to go for a ride. I'm going to take her to Rio this afternoon. We'll get back in time to see what the train looks like."

"I'm going back to the library," said George.

"Call us when it comes in," said Dave.

George wandered back to the library, but he didn't go in. He drove past the utility complex of nuclear-powered machinery that kept the community going. He remembered that once, about five years ago, he had actually seen a Workman performing some manual repairs on the power station. He could still recall the deep envy he had felt for the man's privileged position. There had been a time when he thought he might even have a chance in the annual quota of Workmen chosen from among the Citizens. But his community had been bypassed entirely in the last two quotas, and George no longer had any illusions about himself. He lacked the qualifications in the first place, and he was too old now—at 27—in the second place.

He'd spend the rest of his life playing *bali-putsch,* wandering from one continent to another in aimless visiting with others like himself, occasionally doing something vigorous—like a six-month sprint in the Antarctic. That would be it.

The trouble was, the others—most of them—weren't like him. They seemed to be thoroughly enjoying this Age of Abundance, which had reached its full-blown state about three-quarters of a century ago. But George felt himself steadily eaten by a sick discontent and dissatisfaction.

He wasn't even sure what he was discontented about, but the history and the artifacts of a century or two ago gave him the feeling that he belonged in some such age as that. Not in an age of assured luxury that demanded absolutely nothing of a man. George sometimes had the vague, anachronistic sense that he ought to be contributing. But he had no idea what he would contribute, nor to whom.

Thinking again of the little model trains, he felt an utterly irrational pleasure. He had read of the long-vanished rail carriers, both Diesel and steam, but he had never heard until now of the model trains, which men used to play with. He had the feeling that he had rediscovered some long hidden pleasure that men had not known for generations.

It made no sense at all.

The train—engine, to be exact—arrived on schedule. Paula was there when it arrived and couldn't believe her eyes. It was a child's wheeled toy. George's tender caress of it frightened her.

"What in the world are you going to do with that thing?" she cried.

"Run it," he said, "when we get some track." He realized for the first time that they had forgotten to order track to go with it. "And some cars. I'm going to get some bright yellow and red reefers, some cattle cars, and some tankers."

He guessed they had been so excited about the whole thing that they'd forgotten all about cars. It really had been hard to believe they'd actually get the engine.

He held it now up to the light, letting his fingers touch the tiny, realistic rivets on the dull black body of the boiler. He gently turned the drivers and delighted in the motion of the rods and valve mechanism.

"I'm going over to show it to Sam and Dave," he said. "They'll love it."

"Then they must be as crazy as you are!" shouted Paula as he went out.

She didn't really mean it. She was just frightened. George was always doing such incredibly odd things. Why couldn't he just be satisfied with *bali-putsch* and long talks on philosophy in the condomin mall like the other men?

Sam and Dave thought it was great.

"How do we make it go?" asked Sam.

George was baffled. He remembered reading about motors and electric power packs. But he hadn't thought any more about them than he had about tracks or cars.

Dave had been poking around the insides of the engine. Finally he looked up with exasperation. "This isn't ever going to go. The idiot computer just didn't put a motor in it!"

In dismay, and without looking at the engine, George knew Dave was right. They had submitted plans showing the external structure of the engine, but there were no details of the motor. If the plans had even stated that one was required, the computer probably would have whomped up something to make it go. As it was, they had an empty shell.

But that could be remedied. "We can get a motor at the same time we order track and cars. There are lots of other things you can get, too —realistic landscapes, ancient towns. This is going to be more fun than *bali-putsch* ever was." He held the little engine up again. "Did you ever see anything as beautiful as that!"

George hunted for two days in the archives, trying to find plans for a motor, but these simply didn't appear. It finally dawned on him that the plans he did find were for making by hand the parts of the models that it was practical to make in that way. Other items were factory built. This astonished him more than anything else he had discovered up to now. That such things could be handmade by the model engineers themselves—

They got a motor simply by telling the computer they needed one and referring to the previously submitted plans. The order was sent to Manchester, England, and brought back a realistic steam engine powered by a miniature nuclear-isotope core. A complete radio control was furnished.

George recognized that this was considerable of an anachronism, but it gave a more realistic performance than any of the electric motors he saw referred to. He let it go.

They ordered track by the quarter-mile. George installed it in the all-purpose room of his condomin over the protests of Paula. By the time it was up the group had grown to 15 HO enthusiasts, and track layouts were being planned by at least four other members of the group. There was more excitement than the condomin had seen since it was built.

It was the men, of course. The women stood around on the fringes looking bewildered, wondering if their men had gone utterly insane. George, at his operating cab, wore coveralls, an engineer's long-billed cap, and a blue kerchief around his neck. With intoxicated enthusiasm he jerked the cord above his head and sent a wild, shrill whistle through the room. His 2-8-8-2 Mallet chuffed into motion with a long string of brilliant reefers, cattle cars, tankers, and a couple of Pullmans for good measure. He was vaguely aware that the passenger cars didn't belong with the others. But he'd work out the details later. For now, he had something going, the like of which the world had not seen for a century and a half.

In the freight yards, Sam was busy making up a freight that was due out in two hours, and Dave was putting together a passenger express near the station.

Assorted other members of the group were making up train orders, checking the accuracy of the present team of engineers, or waiting impatiently their turn at the controls.

The wives were near hysteria.

They met three times a week, at least. In between, there was incessant tinkering with the layout and the rolling stock. The local hardware store did a land office business in HO. Within a month it was agreed they simply had to have better facilities. A new wing was ordered for the recreation center at the south end of the mall. It was approved by the computer without a murmur. The parts were fabricated, and a couple of days later a Workman was sent out to erect the wing.

Normally, Citizens watched the erection of a building both with envy of the Workman and ghoulish anticipation. For occasionally—not often but occasionally—the computer controlling the job went awry with hilarious consequences in the form of an unholy mess. It had happened once in the condomin when a small eight-story medical building was going up. With six floors completed the thing simply shivered and fell apart. Two other Workmen had to come out to help program new tapes to get the site cleaned up.

But the model railroaders didn't want that to happen to their structure. They watched anxiously and gave the Workman all their silent good wishes for speedy success. He had it, and the huge room was ready for occupancy three days later.

They wanted to elect George president of the group, but he sidestepped that one and got Sam elected to the position. Sam was an organizer, captain of the *bali-putsch* team, and the most logical one for the position.

George wanted to do some thinking.

It would be more fun if they could do their own building of equipment. According to the old journals in the archives, that's the way the most advanced old-time modelers used to do it, and George could see why. What greater pleasure could there be than to take raw metal and shape one of these delicate engines out of it? It was a pleasure that no man in the Abundant Society could know—unless he was a Workman or an Artist. And George and his friends were neither.

The question of metal stock was something of a problem. He supposed the hardware store would be the right source and tried it. He ordered some sheet brass and copper and pot metal alloy.

His order was totally rejected.

He realized long after that this should have been a warning. But at the time he was too hell-bent to pay attention to storm signals. After an evening of intense concentration on the problem he came up with the solution of ordering various artifacts that had large quantities of the material he needed and cutting them up.

It worked. He got some large boilers of copper and brass, and some pots and ladles of the alloy.

But there was the matter of tools. George dug up all the descriptions he could find of cutters, drills, files, screwdrivers, and soldering tools. He had never seen any of these. Nobody in the condomin had. Probably they were used by Workmen, but he didn't know.

He wondered if he would be rejected on those.

He tried an order for tinsnips, showing the computer reader a picture from an ancient catalog. The snips came through.

He tried a screwdriver and got it.

One by one he ordered the hand tools the journals indicated he'd need and he practiced shaping the stock he cut out of the tubs and boilers. It began to go quite easy, and he was drunk with the ecstasy of it.

There was one other thing it looked as if he'd need in the near future—a lathe. A 3-inch swing and a 16-inch bed would be plenty big enough. But he couldn't find any complete plans, and it was too complex to derive from a picture alone. He began drawing his own plans. They were rough, but the computer could work it out from the specs he wrote alongside his drawings.

When he'd completed a sketch of the lathe bed he ordered it as a trial. It came back in a couple of days and was perfect. He followed with the other parts, the head, chuck, screw, tailstock. He let the computer supply its own specification for a nuclear-isotope motor. When the whole thing was finally assembled, George put a piece of ⅜-inch rod into the chuck and touched it with the tool. A thin spiral of steel curled up in bright beauty.

George's hands began to shake so he couldn't hold the tool any longer. He shut the motor off and sat down. The steel spiral lay on the bench now. He regarded it with wonder, and then looked down at his own hands.

The visitors came early the next morning. There were two of them. They greeted him pleasantly and asked to come in.

He knew everyone in the local condomin. He wondered who these strangers were. Then he glimpsed the small blue symbol on the breasts of their coats, and his knees began to tremble.

"Please sit down," he said. "Refreshments?"

"No," said the taller one. "It's early. You're George Sims-Howton, I believe?" He had a miniature writer on his knee and was punching buttons as he talked.

George licked his dry lips. He was glad Paula was out. "Yes, I'm on the championship *bali-putsch* team for this district," he added, irrelevantly.

His visitors were bright-looking young men. They weren't any older than he was, George thought. One was tall and one was short. Except for that, you could hardly tell them apart. The expressions on their faces were the same. Friendly, courteous, smiling—implacable.

"You have been ordering some unusual devices recently," the tall one said. "Some tools."

"Oh, yes!" said George warmly. "Would you like to see them . . . see what we're doing with them?"

Both visitors shook their heads.

"It was quite ingenious of you to order them one by one," said the tall one. "And the lathe—piece by piece. Very ingenious."

"I don't know what you're talking about."

"You certainly knew that if you had ordered all the hand tools at once, or the complete lathe, the order would have been rejected."

"No . . . I didn't know that. And I don't understand what this is all about. Will you please tell me?"

"I don't believe that you don't know. But for the sake of the record we'll go over it. Production. The accumulation of hand tools which you now have is a production facility. The lathe is a production tool."

"I suppose it is," said George. "I got them to build some model railroads. If you'd only let me show you—"

"What kind of production is unimportant. *All* private production is prohibited. You know that."

"Yes, of course I know that. But this is not *production*—it's just making some little trains. I—"

"The only reason our society exists today is that production is properly controlled. Since the beginning of man's history the world has been more than capable of providing all that men could consume. The only trouble mankind ever had was with systems of distribution and conflicting philosophies of creation and accumulation.

"It was all so very easy once we took man out of the picture and made of the problem only a matter of logics and control. So very easy —you want a toy train and the computer determines that it will fit into the overall matrix of construction and distribution and orders one built for you. The factory builds it. You receive. You give nothing in return, neither service nor what was once called money.

"The population next year will be 3.8 million greater than this year. The computer has already determined this, and the food for those extra bodies is in production. They will never starve. They will never want for any device or product they can conceive. The earth can provide for ten times the bodies it now supports. Would you upset that provision for abundance?"

"No . . . no, of course not! I still don't know what you are talking about. I just wanted to make a little train—"

"The computer will determine if the trains should be made, and it will direct the factories to make them. It will supply you with the wildest contraptions you can dream of. But *it* controls the production. Do you understand that?"

The other one spoke up now. "A little train here. In another condomin, a piece of fabric and simple clothes. Somewhere else a strange food or a new device. All over the world—and people begin to trade these things and value them because they are different. And control is lost. The computer does not know what products, what food, what clothes are needed tomorrow and next year. The Abundant Society breaks down."

The tall one nodded. "It is for this reason that production tools and equipment are prohibited. They are not needed; ask for anything your heart desires, and the Abundant Society will give it to you—free. But, more important, the Abundant Society exists in the face of human-controlled production."

George was aware that his breath had been stifled. He had known none of this; he had never cared to know it. These were things that were discussed by the would-be philosophers who sat in the sun in the mall and refused to join in the *bali-putsch* games.

But what was the penalty?

"You will return these tools through the distribution channels by which they came. Your condomin will be marked with a warning which must remain for the next 60 days. That is all. You must watch yourself carefully. Order that which you please. If it is approved, it will be received. But keep out of anything resembling production.

"We stop smiling on the second offense. There is no appeal. For a second offense the penalty is reduction to subsistence status for the rest of your life and removal to the subsistence reservation. Do you have any questions?"

George shook his head numbly and felt that he was still shaking it as he stood by the window, watching them go as their little car took off and flew high over the mall.

He went outside then and looked at the wall by the door. They had pasted a blue banner there that announced to the world and all his friends that George Sims-Howton had been given a subsistence-reservation warning.

He wondered what would happen to the model railroad group. He wondered if Paula would divorce him. He put on a light coat and left the condomin, walking through the mall, where he waved to the philosophers in the sun and answered a call from players on the *baliputsch* court. He continued on through the parklike fields and woods beyond the community.

On the top of a small hill he stopped and looked back. A paradise, and he was a snake in it, he thought; somewhere he'd heard of an allusion to something like that. But what kind of a paradise was it that could be threatened by a model train?

He sat down and began to think about that. Somewhere here was a problem, but he couldn't define it; he could only feel it. He had felt it all his life, he thought. That vague discontent that had always plagued him. He remembered how it had vanished when he watched the bright shining spirals curl up from the stock in his lathe.

It must be as simple as that, he thought after a while. That was the missing element of the Abundant Society. And if that were so, what a mockery the name was. It was not abundant; it was the most impoverished of all imaginable societies. A man's supreme joy was the joy of building, molding, changing, assembling—creating—with his own two hands and his mind. And this was the single thing the Abundant Society could not tolerate for fear of coming apart at the seams. Only a narrow elite, isolated from all other citizens, could be permitted the luxury of creation—of work.

He'd have to do something about that, George Sims-Howton thought again after a long while. He had an idea that maybe there was something he could do about it. Maybe the notion that he should be contributing, which had plagued him ever since he became an adult, was not so crazy, after all.

When he got near home he saw that small groups of his neighbors were still standing around his doorway, looking at the blue banner. Nothing like it had ever happened in the condomin before. He didn't know how they would react. He didn't know how he should act, himself.

As it turned out, things were better than he expected. He explained the situation about 50 different times before the day was out, and everyone was sympathetic and understanding. He wasn't marked as a Jonah, to be run out of the condomin by ostracizing.

There was only Paula. She didn't understand. She was frightened. There was nothing he could say to explain away her fears. And then he remembered that she had seen in her childhood someone who had been sent away to the subsistence reservation for some crime. The talk of the adults at that time had burned itself into her mind: ". . . No shelter except what they build themselves; only half enough food to keep alive; heat from open fires; no protection in the summer. . . ."

"You'll give up all this crazy toy railroad business, now, won't you?" Paula begged.

"They didn't ask me to do that," George said. "It was the tools, and

I'm going to take them back. I made a mistake, and I won't make it
again, because they told me where I was wrong."

Paula didn't understand. She couldn't separate it from the trains.

George remained awake most of the night. He had no reason to
doubt that the terrors of the subsistence reservation as remembered by
Paula from conversations overheard in childhood were less than real.
He had heard some of them himself. But he had never seen anyone who
knew firsthand. No one ever returned.

He would be risking it, he knew, if he tempted the powers of the
Abundant Society any further. He did not know the details of the law.
Citizens were not taught those things. Somewhere in the upper eche-
lons of the Workers who governed by, for, and with the mammoth
world-wide computer system there were those who knew the law and
passed it down to bright young men like those who had visited him
today. He wondered how it was that so many of them escaped entangle-
ment with the law when they knew so little about it.

But that was not the problem. Should he go on or not? Was there
anything worth while that one man, by himself, could accomplish? The
system had existed for a century and a half. It would go on for centuries
more. Who was he to challenge it?

And risk a life sentence to subsistence reservation?

He went to the railroad room of the recreation center the next
morning. He was the only one there. That night was the regular meeting. Only about half the usual number came around. George put on his
coveralls and his kerchief and his long-billed cap, and he jerked the
whistle cord with abandon. But it was no good. It was like a pall of
dread had settled over the whole operation. They listened to George's
explanations all over again, but they were afraid. *Bali-putsch* was safe.
The HO trains seemed like a fearful unknown, now.

He made his decision after the meeting. If he failed to go ahead
now, the whole project would die.

He went to the hardware store the next morning with a complex
order. It took him half the day to feed it in. And then he went out and
sat in the sun.

Two days later a sizable shipment came in. He took it to the empty
railroad room and spread it out. Thousands of parts, precisely labeled
and packaged, just as he had ordered. That gave him some small comfort. If the order were illegal, the computer surely would not have
approved and delivered it.

He began gathering the parts and repackaging them. He had even
ordered brightly colored boxes to put them in, just like the ones he had

seen in the old journals. Kits, they called them there. You could get all the parts and just put them together yourself—with the help of one small screwdriver. George had ordered the screwdrivers and put one in each kit.

Was it production?

He'd soon find out.

He presented the first one to Sam. Sam saw the box cover and shook his head. "I think I'm going to give it up, George," he said. "My game's been lousy since I started fooling with the trains, and I've got to get it back. I really think you ought to do the same. We're never going to have a chance against Monmouth unless we get back in shape."

"Open it up," said George.

Sam hesitated, then removed the cover. "What the devil?"

"A kit," said George. "You have all the fun of putting it together yourself—and you get around the anti-production law at the same time."

Sam looked up cautiously. "You're sure this is all right?"

"Absolutely clean. The computer put the order through without a murmur. If it hadn't been right it would have been bounced, wouldn't it?"

"I don't know. You almost got clobbered for the tools, and the computer sent them through all right—and then tattled."

"It's safe," George repeated.

Sam couldn't help lifting out the delicate parts and touching them. His eyes were bright as he speculated on how they fit together. He tried the cab against the boiler casting.

"Here's the instruction sheet," said George. "I had it printed up to go along with the kits."

It was nearly midnight when he finally got the engine assembled, a beautiful little 2-8-2 Mikado. Sam's eyes were bleary with the unaccustomed close work. But there was serenity and joy in his face. "Boy, isn't she a beauty!" he exclaimed. "But say, I ought to give you something for this; you can't just give them away."

"Why not? They were given to me."

"You went to all the trouble of ordering them. And you packed the parts into kits."

"O.K. You pay me two blue chips. That'll square us."

Sam nodded and handed over a couple of the worthless chips that were used to bet on the *bali-putsch* games. "It's a deal," he said.

They were at the railroad room almost by sunrise to break in the new Mikado and check it out. By mid-morning George had disposed of 15 more of the kits. Nobody moved from the room. If they couldn't find table space, they sat down on the floor and began assembling them. Most wanted engines of their own, to start with. But some began work on bright reefers or complex specialty cars, such as wreckers or hoppers.

At noon George leaned back and began to breathe easy. He had it going again. Most of the old group was there, and a couple of new fellows had dropped by to see what was going on and had got hooked by the fascination of assembling the kits.

George wondered, with a sigh of anxiety, how much time he had. Certainly the report of his order had gone through to a desk at some upper echelon. They had their eye on him. Or perhaps the computer had already ticked him off as a two-time loser.

It was five days before they showed up again. The same two. The tall one and the short one, with the same implacable faces.

George took them to the recreation center, into the new model railroad wing. A half dozen engineer's cabs were occupied on the huge layout. Eight or ten men were at worktables, assembling new models. They all stopped their work and blanched at the sight of the two men with George Sims-Howton. George had tricked them. Now they were all in for it!

George sensed their reaction. "Just a check," he said as calmly as he could. "On me—not you."

The two investigators conferred together with some uncertainty. "You put together the parts ordered from the hardware computer," said the tall one to George. "You put them together with a screwdriver into their finished form."

"That is right," said George.

"Why?"

"We like to. It's fun. Why do we play *bali-putsch?* It gives us pleasure. So does assembling the kits."

"The object is to run them around the track, is it not? Then why is it not more efficient and more pleasurable to order them in completed form? You could run them that much sooner."

George felt his hand beginning to go sweaty. "Both forms of activity give us pleasure. Who is to say it makes sense? *Bali-putsch* doesn't make sense when you try to rationalize it."

"But you are assuming for yourselves a part of the production process, which would normally be completed at the factory."

"No, no—" said George. "Production is the creation of something that has not existed before. These parts—they are already in existence. Their purpose is to form an engine or a car. We only carry out that purpose. Forgive me if I argue the point, for I realize that if I have made a mistake again it is a fatal mistake for me. But I do not think I have made a mistake. I have very carefully observed the law."

"It is our opinion," said the tall one coldly, "that you are very carefully trying to break the law. But we fail to understand why or how. I think the computer will be able to clarify these matters. We will return as soon as we have its analysis and its decision."

George wandered out into the sunshine of the mall after they were gone. The model railroaders were uneasy. Some of them had slipped out as quietly as possible while the investigators were in the recreation hall. Maybe even if the decision were favorable too much damage would have been done. No one had ever seen investigators around the condomin before. The most casual visit was terrifying.

And a third one was coming this afternoon.

He sat down at a distance from the groups of arguing philosophers lounging in the sun. He looked about the peaceful landscape, the aesthetically satisfying structures. Total lack of want, he thought, except for the one thing—the delight of individual creation. Without that, everything else was an empty shell. He had felt it all his life. The driving discontent. The vague compulsion to take things in his own hands, to feel and shape them.

Maybe it was stronger in him than in the others. But they felt it, too. Their pleasure in the little trains was proof of that. And that pleasure would stir and ferment if only it could be nurtured with a little care.

He had risked all he had here, against the unknown terrors of subsistence reservation, to provide that care. It was all he could do. It was what he had to do.

The sun was low and shadows were lengthening when they returned. They were walking slowly as they approached, and their faces were more puzzled than ever.

"The computer cleared you," the tall one said. "It pronounced your activities nonproductive and legal."

"Thanks," said George.

"Don't thank us. We merely carry the message. You are going to be watched. Everything you do will be evaluated by the computer for conformance to the intent of the law. An automatic alarm will indicate when you slip. We're with you night and day, George Sims-Howton."

He was all alone in the mall when he finally got up to go. It was dark except for the moonlight and the glow from the buildings. He could see lights in the railroad room. Some of them—it looked like quite a number—were gathering for the evening run.

Hundreds would learn what it meant to put something together with their own hands. They would learn the pleasure of touching materials that were fine and delicate and smooth and well-formed—the pleasure of forming and shaping and putting together.

A few hundred, maybe. It wasn't much, but it would spread. And then someone would take the supreme risk of going out in a forlorn countryside and picking up rocks and putting together a house. And struggling for his own food right from the ground itself—for the mere pleasure of it.

Would he have to convince Paula it was not insane?

He thought of the computer. The idiot computer. It gave out only what was put in—plus an illusion of great omniscience. It could not distinguish between mechanical production and creative pleasure because those who had built it understood no such distinction. He was safe until greater men touched the computer.

But for now there were many things to do. More trains to put in kits. And he'd just learned about model airplanes, and animals and people, too. The field seemed endless.

It was just a question of how far he could go with it.

He had a feeling he was going a long way.

COMING-OF-AGE DAY

A. K. Jorgensson

I was ten and I still had not seen them! You didn't expect to see a woman's unless you were lucky, which a very few boys at my school professed to be. But nearly everyone my age knew what a man's looked like.

But you got some funny answers.

"You're too young," said a squirt about half my size, and another very big boy nodded agreement.

"We don't want to do any harm," the big one said, wisely as it turned out. His voice was already breaking, and I think he was on the change.

"We're not going to tell you." There were a number of small knots in the playground that took a secretive line, and whispered with their backs to everybody. I belonged to a loose group of boys who, looking back, I would say were intelligent and sensitive and from better homes. Their interests were academic, or real hobbies. But I was a little contemptuous of their ignorance and softness. And I ended up hanging about behind a group led by a capable boy, or breaking roughly into a fighting gang, having a punch-up and then going to skip with the girls. I tried everything. I was nobody's buddy. But a few groups could expect to rely on me if they needed an extra hand to defend themselves against a rough bunch or to try a good game. "Go and get Rich Andrews," someone would say: "he'll play."

They got me one day after school for a very secret meeting on the waste plot between the churchyard and the playing fields. Guards were out at the edge of the bushes. We had to enter over the churchyard wall. And we had to crouch to approach the spot, crawling along the bottoms of craters left between bulldozed heaps and tips of earth.

It was a good hide-out behind a solid screen of leaves, deep in the bushes. Churchill was there; so was Edwards and my friend Pete Loss. They had started something, and I saw it was a bit dubious, because Churchill and Gimble were in a little arbor away from the others, and though I could not see much, they had their trousers down.

"What's up?" I asked Pete.

"Oh, they're playing sexy-lovers," said Pete.

"Why? What's the idea?"

"D'you know all about it?" he asked. "I don't s'pose you do. Oh, I did it once. It's not much. Old Churchill thinks he's got a better way. It gives him a thrill."

"I don't like it," I said. I was curious and afraid, but hoped I sounded like you should when someone's trying to get one up on you and you're not having any.

"Come on," I urged Pete. "Let's go."

"They want to show you," he said.

"Oh, I know all about that," I lied. "I'm not going to play pansy for that dirty beast Churchill."

It took more urging, but when I made a move Pete came too. The guards tried to stop us, as though they had designs on me. I shouted, "Stop it! I shall shout! Aw, come on; play the game," and they let me go. But they persuaded Pete to stay.

I got away and of course kept quiet. And lost another chance to know all about sex. It was the time for sex education, of course, and this gave me a fair technical knowhow, but I didn't have the practical experience. I hesitated to muck about and the teachers didn't exactly encourage it: also, my parents were a bit strict. So I left it.

It was after that party in the bushes that controversy arose. Someone said to Churchill:

"You nit. You don't just play about with it. And you don't just get hairy all round. You get something put there at the right age. It's the operation!"

"I don't care about the operation," he said. "You can do this—" and he described masturbation openly enough to make me feel hot. Miss Darlington was getting close and I was afraid she'd overhear. She had an A-1 pot on her front.

They silenced as she approached, but I heard Elkes say under his breath to Churchill, "Look at their pots! That's where they keep their sex organs. You get outside ones put on your inside ones. Darlie's got a big male thing on hers, it sticks out a mile."

Quite frankly, this horrified me. I had always wondered whether all the hairiness of men came up from the private place and how large the organs grew. But separate adult bathing had come a few years before my first swim, and if they did wear these things on the beach, you couldn't tell them from pot bellies. It sounded like a book I had read which said how pot bellies grew on adolescents now whereas it used to be only old men and middle-aged women. I wondered what lay behind that expression "pot belly." It made me feel funny even to think of it. But it also made me feel sad, just as a fuller sexual awareness did later. You never know which gives more satisfaction—the relief of the sexual act, or the retention of that inner virile feeling when you have refrained for a good while. And there is a sort of dimension that is all power and mind and strength, that the physical conditions don't seem to improve or improve upon.

In the old days, I am told, there used to be more explicit sexual bits in the films. But on television these days, as in the theater, they are very cagey. I heard one master from the upper school, who is reputed to be a wild unrestrained type, call this a second Victorian Age. According to him, every time we get a queen reigning to a ripe old age, it's nearing the end of the century: and people are afraid the millennium will come at the end of 1999. So what with one thing and another, they are fearfully prudish.

Which is ridiculous, because when the naked torso was the fashion they could not have hidden the pot-bellied things they wear these days.

I asked my father one day what happened when people got pot-bellied.

"You know all about that from school, surely, son."

"Well, no, it's the one thing they've never taught us."

"Why did you want to know? It's not always good to know these things."

"Well, I didn't—I mean, well, the boys at school talk about it in the playground. I'm getting pretty big now, dad, nearly eleven. I ought to know what they mean by now."

"I see. I shall have to talk to your head teacher, Rich, I can see that. Anyway, pot bellies are just when people get fat around the lower part of the abdomen. People eat too much these days."

"Oh . . . only they said at school it wasn't that. Gluttony is frowned on now, and drinking too much. But people still have —"

"That is enough, Rich. In a year or two you will be grown up enough to be able to understand. In the meantime you have had at least

two years of education in biology, and you know all about the primitive
sex processes."

I knew when to be quiet. Parents were not so strict in the middle
of the twentieth century, so the history books say, and it was a bad
thing. I wonder if that is why people are ashamed and hide their sexual
excesses now. Do as I say and not as I do, etcetera—unwilling hypocrisy, but they can't help it. But that mention of "primitive" sex, it foxed
me, because Edwards asked at school what "primitive" meant, and was
told that it referred to an early form before it developed. Well, there
are two sorts of development, natural maturation and scientific application, and I do not believe the scientific part has been explained to us
yet.

Before I peeped and saw, I had just about worked it out. It was a
diffident sort of guess, but I reckon it proves what Socrates said. People
may not believe me, but I was on the right lines. It was more than those
funny ideas I had as a small boy—that people grew their tails long, or
that they carried a little hairy monkey about inside their trousers I
tied it up with the artificial creation of living tissue over 20 years ago.
These days they are always coming up with new forms of living tissue:
they can give you a new body for an old one in bits or *in toto* nowadays.
And they have perfected their methods so much that the so-called
artificial one is better than the natural one. After all, they have eliminated all these subtle differences between the chemical product and the
equivalent natural one, which was one major advance in many.

Now if you see people lose a leg, as I did once (rather it had to be
removed later) and a few months later they've grown a new one, why
not improve on the natural, or primitive, sexual organs? I am beginning to agree with an aunt of mine who, in an episode I won't relate,
told me there was no pleasure in sex; the sensation of pleasure was n
the mind, not the organ or nerve. Well, what if you did get a better
organ? If you're not much of a chap anyway, it would do you no good
unless it had a psychological improvement on your confidence.

I have more evidence of this point. The only other clue I had before
I was 13 and registered as an adolescent was hearing a conversation
between two old men: all they did was complain that the new pot bellies
had not solved people's sexual problems after all.

Except the time when I peeped. It was on the beach one day when
the sun was very hot and a lot of people sat perspiring in their many
light clothes. All of a sudden a woman began to scream and clutch at
the lower part of her body, as if to pull something off. After a while
women started gathering round and trying to help. But she was desperate and tore her costume, an enveloping thing, until this sort of huge
fleshy roll could be seen clinging to her. It could have been a flabby

woman's breast, or a fantastic roll of fat, but this would be a bit too unlikely, I reckon. The woman pulled at it, and it gave and stretched out like a tentacle and—"Get away! You nasty little boy. How dare you peep? Go away." After a screech like that I crawled away.

Going to the sexiatrist was the call-up day for coming-of-age even more than one's initiation into the forces came through the medical examination. It was with mixed feelings that I faced the ceremony, having had an enjoyable childhood with no great attraction urging me into manhood. I reported at the Center, and a nurse took my particulars. I signed an agreement that I was prepared to undertake the responsibilities of adulthood; all rather vague, as it was a matter of contracting out to avoid the consequences rather than contracting in. Had I refused, I should have had 20 forms to sign and dozens of conditions written in fine print. Either that, I had heard, or I ended up in a harsh institution for the backward.

First a doctor checked my family doctor's assessment of my sexual age. He examined me with that frankness and propriety that scientific control over sexual phenomena demanded, took blood samples and a tiny piece of my skin, looked into my eyes and checked my height, coloring and so on. Most of the time I was modestly allowed to keep my pants on, even though I was stripped of all else, including my watch.

After going through the mass radiography room, the cancer-heat-test room and other places, and receiving various boosters against the various plagues, I was sent home, walking out with a curious sense of illness-at-ease, ordinariness and anticlimax.

It took me by surprise to get another Ministry postcard two weeks later, requesting my presence once more at the Sexual Health Center. This time it was in the afternoon, and the nurse ushered me into the doctor's other surgery with a little more respect. There was a tiny holding of the breath and it made me more expectant.

"Good afternoon, Andrews. Nice to see you again. Still feeling in good health?"

"Yes, sir, thank you." One never admits that one has never felt quite the same since being pumped with inoculatives.

"Ready to have a consex fitted! Now, Andrews, this is a most private matter which I think will explain itself. We are not afraid to be scientific about sex as a subject, but I trust you will keep this to yourself. If you are not completely satisfied—*for any reason whatsoever*—tell no one but come and see me. Is that understood?"

"Yes, Doctor."

"I am a sexiatrist, actually, not a doctor. Now come and look in this glass container."

I looked. As I believe it usually does to others, it struck me with

a sort of horror to see this thing alive, a collapsed sort of dumpling wi∎h
ordinary human skin, sitting in its case like a part of a corpse that h∊d
been cut off.

"Get used to it," he said. "It's only ordinary flesh. It has a ti∎y
pulse with a primitive sort of heart, and blood and muscle. And fat. It˥s
just flesh. Alive, of course, but perfectly harmless."

He lifted the lid and touched it. It gave, then formed round h∎s
finger. He moulded it like dough or plasticine and it gave way, thou∊h
it tended to roll back to a certain shapelessness.

"Touch it."

"I couldn't."

"Go on."

He was firm and I obeyed. It had a touch like skin and was war∎.
It might have been part of someone's fat stomach. I pushed my fing∊r
in, and the thing squeezed the finger gently with muscular co∎-
tractions.

"It's yours," he announced.

I nearly fainted with horror. It strikes everyone that way un∎l
they realize how simple, harmless and useful free living tissue can b∊,
and its many healing purposes. It embarrassed me to guess where t∎e
"consex" was to be located on my body, and my intuition was uncerta∎n
with equally embarrassing ignorance. But one only has to wear a co∎-
sex a short while to realize how utterly natural it is, and how deligh∎-
fully pleasant when in active use. It is a boon to lone explore∎s,
astronauts, occupants of remote weather and defense stations, and ∊o
on.

"Don't worry," said the specialist as I drew back in disgust. "It˥s
no more horrible than the way you came into the world, or the par∎s
each of your parents played in starting the process. In fact, it's clean∊r,
more foolproof, and efficient, and far more satisfying than a woma∎.
Thank heaven, without them we'd be overrun."

I feared to do anything. He said,

"I'll show you how it works. Don't take it off for at least a wee∎,
not for any reason. See me at once if there is any discomfort. Later o∎,
you may remove it for athletics, though you can do most things wi∎h
it on—swimming, for instance. In the toilet it rolls up easily enoug∎.
But don't disturb the suction or play around. It clings well if you lea∎e
it alone, and it's very comfortable."

He took me into a private cubicle, where I undressed and lay und∊r
a soft blanket. Then he brought the thing in on his hand and pulled t∎e
blanket back.

I held my breath. It was the worst moment of my life for fea∎,
though not for pain.

"I've stimulated it a bit," he said. "It'll take over for you this tim∊,
but every time after that it's up to you to make the first move, ∎r

nothing will happen. It's very responsive. Now you must lie here half an hour until I let you go."

He let it rest between my thighs, and it covered all those parts you never see on pictures of nudes except those in classical religious paintings. It was comfortable. It felt pleasant. This first time when the sexiatrist goes out and leaves one alone with one's body and one's consex and one's private thoughts is the crucial one.

It was only pleasant sensation; I had not been given any warning. So I tolerated it. But at the same time I was disgusted at the smallness of sophisticated adult behavior. Hell, I thought, they take a lot for granted. But my curiosity overcame my dignity, and I did not rebel.

It was hardly over when I heard a conversation which startled me.

"Do you have a letter from your parents?" the sexiatrist was asking someone.

"No."

"But you still refuse to have an appliance fitted?"

"Yes."

"Well, I agree it is not compulsory. But you'll have to give a very good reason for refusing. And without a letter from a doctor or parent or guardian we may not accept your reasons."

"I'm a conscientious objector."

"On what grounds? Do you realize what you're letting yourself in for by refusing to wear a consex?"

"I don't believe all the claims made for it," he said, but feebly.

"You don't even know them," said the sexiatrist, condescendingly. "I'm quite sure of that. But surely you want to know what it's all about first? Surely the subject fascinates you so that you are interested enough to desire the experience for a while?"

"No, sir. In principle."

"In principle! What do *you* know about it? Tel! me. What *do* you know about so vast a subject?"

"I don't believe in the principles the welfare authorities base it on."

"You don't believe in them! You don't believe them despite the fact that the government authorizes me to fit every boy and girl with an appropriate consex as soon as he or she reaches puberty. Every boy and girl in this population of over 80 million wears one—"

"Not *every* boy and girl."

"All but one or two in a million, and those are mostly for health or mixed-sex reasons. They are approved by the R. M. A. and every major health, legal and educational authority in the country. Virtually all religious denominations have welcomed them. But you refuse."

"Welcomed, sir? I don't believe any of them."

"I see. You don't believe that this country is heavily over-populated? You don't believe that before consexes came out the years of adolescence were years of miserable misfits trying to adjust to a half-baked situation? And that boys slept promiscuously in spurious natural sexual relations, that girls had illegitimate babies sometimes from the earliest years it is possible to conceive, and that mere children contracted serious venereal diseases from these methods.

"You think you can do without all this. And what sort of substitute will you have? Tearing about on a rocket-scooter or getting drunk! Raping a woman or just stealing her handbag! And if and when you grow up. . . .

"Did you know that there are ten million bachelors and the same number of spinsters in this country who have never been married nor had a so-called love affair but are sexually wholly satisfied and consummated? Did you?"

"It may have been in the papers, sir."

"Tell me." He spoke kindly and coaxingly for a moment. "Is it because you've picked up some little bad habit? It's very common, nothing to be ashamed of. This thing will help you."

"No, sir."

"Come on now, man of principles. Square with me. Haven't you? Are you sure you've never committed . . . well, self-abuse?"

"What, sir? I—I haven't done anything wrong."

"Come off it, lad. No one has ever never done anything wrong."

"But I haven't, sir."

"Do your parents approve of your attitude?"

"I think so, sir."

"You think so? That's not good enough. Now come on. Be a good chap and let us fit you a consex. It's much nicer than natural sex or any of that. You don't want to be the odd man out, do you?"

"No, sir—"

"Good. All right, then. Nurse, he's accepted after all. Get it out, will you."

"No, I haven't, sir. No!"

"I am an authority on this, lad. You mean to say you still haven't accepted that the government knows what is best for the nation after all I've told you?"

"I haven't, sir, no. It's not the government—"

"You haven't? But I thought just now you said you had."

"I didn't want to be the odd man out; but I can't wear one of these."

"Then you will be the odd man out, won't you? What d'you mean you can't? Come into the laboratory and let me show you."

There was silence then for nearly half an hour. Now I know what one of those laboratories looks like, I can imagine the sexiatrist taking him round, telling him to peer into a microscope and see tiny microbes swiveling about in plasma, showing him charts of the amino acids, the blood-types, the cell-types, the skin-types, etcetera, pulling out samples for quick-fire experiments, and showing him a few easily digested examples of living tissues artificially made for various purposes. Then the door opened and in they came.

"Well, what did you think of it?"

"Very interesting, sir."

"Impressive, wasn't it? Wasn't it?"

"Yes, sir."

"Now what do you say? It's up to you. You have some idea how it works now, and you're not afraid any longer, I hope."

"No, sir."

"You'll consider it."

"I am considering it, sir."

"Oh, good. Do you think you'll be able to decide now?"

"Oh, yes."

"Good. I'll call the nurse then, shall I?"

No answer. He rang the desk bell.

"You won't refuse us after all that, now, will you?"

"Well . . . please, sir. . . ."

"I'm going to ring your parents."

The nurse came in, dropped my clothes on the bed, and shut the door. I heard the phone click as I slid out of bed, then click again.

"I'll give you one more chance," said the sexiatrist. "In case you're ashamed or anything. Nurse, tell me, do you wear a consex?"

"Yes, doctor, I do."

"A male consex?"

"Yes."

"And you like it? It's comfortable, not unhealthy? You can do what you like? You don't feel guilty about it?"

"I love it," she said. "I've never had difficulty with it. It always responds to my lead and never disobeys."

"Thank you. Now, boy, are you satisfied?"

"What happened the first time?" the boy asked the nurse with a mixture of sheepishness and daring.

The nurse said nothing. I wondered if she blushed. The boy said:

"My father called it an artificial prostitute."

"Nonsense, lad. You don't know what you're talking about. They say worse things about holy matrimony, so-called."

"I have religious objections," said the boy. "I can control myself without all this."

"All what? Without all what?" the doctor asked sharply.

"This . . . appliance."

"It's only living flesh," he said. "Look, here's one. See? I touch it. If God hadn't meant this stuff to exist, it wouldn't exist, would it? Now you touch it. Don't your parents wear one?"

"No, sir, they don't."

"Ah! Well, you're quite free to do as *you* please. Don't be afraid to go against them. As I told you, the authorities have called up for the purpose of giving you one, and you are protected by the law. We shall support you to the hilt. Your parents don't object to fluoridation, do they? Or antismog in the air?"

"Yes, sir, they do."

"Hmmm."

I heard a muttered "Nut cases" outside my door, and the nurse opened it for the sexiatrist. He strode through, booming.

"Andrews, ah, Andrews, you're a sensible lad. Now you've just become a man and learned all about it. How d'you like it?"

"All right, sir."

"Feels okay, doesn't it?"

"Yes, sir," I said, "very nice," though sneakingly I sympathized with the boy out there. I knew the voice of all the temporal powers was speaking through the sexiatrist, and all the pressures were being brought to bear, but I admired him for resisting.

The sexiatrist knelt and held me.

"Now, sir," he said, "now, Mr. Andrews, would you mind very much if we showed our friend here how nicely the little consex fits? We have to show you how it feeds, too, because it's going to grow and mature right along with you. That's why it's important this lad Topolski has his fitted now."

I detected the tiny note of disdain at the boy's foreign name, and half inclined to retort at the sexiatrist for the one he had used all along.

"He doesn't have to, does he?"

"Now don't you start," said the doctor, and he drew me forward, levering off my pants at the same time.

"What's wrong with that?" asked the sexiatrist, showing the consex sitting like a fig leaf and looking as innocuous as a fold of skin. "I've even thought," he went on, half to himself, half to the young nurse, "that they're far more aesthetic than the bare uni-sex, and this return to clothing oneself at all times and in all places is quite unnecessary. The time will come when things will turn full circle, and we shan't be afraid to go completely nude again."

I saw the point. I began almost to like my consex, even though the sensation it could give was disturbingly overwhelming. But the boy turned away after a cursory examination. He said nothing.

"Well?" asked the big man, and I realized all of a sudden the mental pressure, the semi-mesmeric force of it that I had allowed to ride me, and that this small dark 12-year-old was bucking. "You don't want a black mark on your book, do you?"

I wondered, what book? I did not know, then, that the State's records kept its finger on this one more aspect of a man's "suitability."

"I do a lot of sport," he said weakly, almost visibly wilting, and looking for somewhere to hide. He must have felt awful, foolish and mixed-up.

"Ah, so that's what it is! Well now. Dearson, the world champion marathon runner, actually wears his running! And all the other athletes have them. They simply take them off and wrap them in a little blanket—like this one—while they're participating. No trouble at all. Now come on, be a good chap. We'll just take your measurements—most of them are compulsory—and leave it to you to come back later and collect your consex. How about that?"

"All right," he said. I saw him stiffening his resistance again to the paternal air, and felt fairly sure the internalized authority would not be strong enough in him to bring him to accepting the consex. But he would have to submit to the tests as required. The sexiatrist would ring his parents later, then he would have to return and sign the many forms, by one of which he would delegate to the Minister of Health responsibility for his sexual welfare—a condition mentally as unacceptable to him and his parents as the consex was physically unacceptable.

I was dressed and dismissed, yet I lingered at the specialist's door waiting vaguely for something. Then the boy gave his address. It was just round the corner from mine.

The fact that we were neighbors does not seem important, perhaps. But it's going to be. I am going round when I have a chance, to ask Topolski the real reason why he refused to put on the "appliance."

ECCE FEMINA !
Bruce McAllister

My arm had started to ache. I had been holding my thumb out there on the onramp for nearly two hours.

A car finally slowed, and managed to stop directly in front of me. I stood there listening to the uneven idle while the nervous driver ran his eyes over me again and again.

The window started down, but stopped halfway.

Then it went all the way.

"Sorry kid," the man said—but there wasn't any feeling behind it. "I thought maybe you were. ... They do disguise themselves sometimes, you know."

"Sure," I said. I thought I knew what he meant.

I grabbed the door handle, and his voice jabbed me back.

"Just a second! Where do you want off?"

"Emerald Hills."

He stared for a minute, then sighed.

"Yeah, okay. But I'm sure as hell not leaving the freeway for you."

I slipped in quickly and put on the seatbelt before he could change his mind.

First published in *Fantasy and Science Fiction*, February, 1972. Reprinted by permission of the author.

All the way there, he kept watching me from the corner of his eye.

And when I got out at the Hills offramp, I think he noticed my limp and wanted to say something. I walked off quickly and didn't let him.

The walk from the offramp to the gas station would take a good 30 minutes, but it wasn't the kind of walk that bothered my leg. The problem never was pain anyway. The limp just made walking tricky, and I was sure it looked like hell.

The smog wasn't much worse than the last time I had seen it. The Emerald Hills area couldn't be seen clearly from the offramp. At 50 feet the smog started turning everything gray, and it was hot, so the whole area looked and felt like it was under water.

I hadn't seen Emerald Hills in four years, and I wouldn't have been seeing it then if it hadn't been for the shrapnel in my leg.

I would have reenlisted forever—if they hadn't reclassified my body. I'm sure of that. The media always managed to get the general news to us in Cam, and every new recruit always brought eye-witness reports with him—so I heard a lot about what was happening in the States.

Vitamin E9—the "ultravitamin that isn't really a vitamin." The Women's League—its hundreds of chapters up and down the state. The other things.

I reenlisted without stepping foot out of Cam.

Then my leg forced me out, and with it I had to go somewhere. Mother and Dad were no longer in Emerald Hills—after what happened to Mom. But I'd lived there in high school, and high school was a good enough memory, so Emerald Hills seemed a good enough place.

Our house had been one of a hundred in a minitract called Emerald Point—surrounded by dry-grass hills, with other small tracts just visible in the distance.

Now, even with the smog, I could tell that every last acre of the Daley Ranch was finally built up. Emerald Hills was now one giant tract of wall-to-wall minitracts stretching for miles on either side of the freeway.

Every minitract now had a high wall around it, too.

Old litter lined both sides of Hills Boulevard, looking like a hundred garbage trucks had wrecked there.

I walked a hundred yards down the boulevard toward the first walled tract, and the billboard towering over it became clearer.

TOPAZ HEIGHTS—GOLD MEDAL HOMES
$33,900 AND UP
VETS NO DOWN

Over the billboard someone had hung a smaller sign with rope. Red and white letters with a sloppy brush.

DOWN ON VETS
AND OTHER PETS
VIOLATORS WILL BE EATEN!
—THE EMERALD HILLS CHAPTER

Under the letters I could see what looked like a skull-and-cross-bones. The skull was clear enough, but the paint had run, and the "bones" didn't seem to be in the standard "X".

I kept walking and staring at the sign. When my neck started aching, and I finally looked down, I was at the tract's eight-foot cinder-block wall.

It was covered with writing in red spray-paint

WHOS GOT OSCAR MEYER CLASS? WE DO! YOUD BETTER!

CHAPTERS UNITE—SHOOT E9 TONIGHT!

BEWARE OF DOGGIES AND

I kept walking. The writing seemed endless.

SEE ORGAN LA FAY ON SATURDAY!

RALLY YOU MOTHER-BROTHERS!

WE ARE THE WOMENS LEAGUE
THE RIDERS OF THE NIGHT
WERE ORNERY BROTHERMUCKERS
WED RATHER BITE THAN—

A roar of engines made me turn from the wall.

I stood there and watched the gang appear from the grayness on the other side of the street.

I had never owned a chopper, but I had worked on three Harleys one summer in high school, a few military bikes in Cam, and in Cam I had heard a lot about the kind of machine that was now wheeling down the boulevard.

A dozen tall lean choppers, handlebars lancing into the sky, riders lying back against long racing seats.

The leader of the gang saw me, let out a shout, geared down, and laid a beautiful U-turn. The others followed and were just as fancy.

Within seconds they had all gathered in front of me, each bike balanced on its riders left leg.

I had heard about it enough times, but I wasn't ready for it.

I'm six-two, and the leader couldn't have been over five-eleven, and she was sitting on her chopper—but it felt like she was looking down at me. Her eyes inspected me slowly, and slowly a smile began on her lips—showing three missing teeth in a grin that couldn't have been called friendly.

I looked down, away from her face. I waited.

I was looking at her bike, a "lean machine," a candy-apple red XXCH Harley, its extra accessories stripped, replaced with small fenders, a single small tank and straight pipes.

I let my eyes move up to the handlebars, to her hands, to her sleeves. The fingers of her leather gloves were cut off at the knuckles. A bone hunting knife and sheath were strapped to her left jacket sleeve.

My eyes skipped past her face, stopping at her short black hair. Oily, dusty, and almost—

One of the riders suddenly laughed—a short fat woman with a stovepipe hat and an ornate walking cane slung across her handlebars.

"Hey, Organ, we got us a baby. He might not even have one yet!"

The leader stayed silent, her gap-tooth grin frozen on her face.

"How could he?" another rider mocked—a cream-complexioned woman with a high purple collar rising from her jacket. "He's still trying to grow a leg!"

The leader's grin faded then. She flexed the fingers of both hands and slipped the knife from its sheath. She raised it.

A rider directly behind her giggled, and made some gesture I couldn't see.

I stepped back, and every rider was suddenly laughing.

The leader was using the knife to pick her teeth.

Her smile came on again, and her voice was like sandpaper.

"Where's your pass?"

My throat was tight when I answered.

"I— I'm sorry, but— What kind of pass should I—"

Everyone was laughing again. The leader threw her head back in mock pride, and made strutting motions on her bike.

"I just got back from Cam," I tried, "and I haven't—"

The laughter had stopped.

A soft "Ohhhh"—both mocking and serious—was coming from two or three of the riders.

The leader was shaking her head slowly.

With her chin she pointed over my shoulder, and this time her voice was hard.

"Your eyes screwed-up, too, gimp-boy? We got a sign up for your kind."

"If he ain't blind," one of the riders began—but the leader cut her off with a flash of the knife-blade.

I started talking quickly, trying everything I could think of.

"I haven't been in Emerald Hills for four years. I used to live here —up on Jasper Lane. I like the area here. I'm planning to apply for a job at Henry's station. My parents lived here until last year. My mother's up in Salinas now—she's a member of the Salinas—"

I stopped because the leader had twisted around and was mumbling a question to the others—something about Henry's station.

"Jack's," someone answered her.

"Jack's," the leader repeated.

When she turned back to me, she was laughing hard.

"Whoooeee!" She slipped the knife back in its sheath. "You go right ahead and apply for that there position at the *service* station. Only it ain't Henry's place anymore—it's dear ole Jack's."

She was turning her chopper now, nosing it out into the street, mashing through the litter, giving me a good look at the back of her leather jacket.

In red and white were the two "rockers"—WOMEN'S LEAGUE at the top, EMERALD HILLS CHAPTER at the bottom. In the middle, the glaring "death's head" insignia.

I could see it clearly. Not "crossbones" under the skull, but instead a thin-lined cross, the top of it connected to the skull's chin.

A dozen small patches dotted the jacket, too—all the same kind. I couldn't tell for sure, but the picture on the patch looked like a frankfurter broken in two with a row of teeth above and below it.

All backs were to me now—skulls glaring. Chrome was gleaming everywhere. Every bike was being slapped into gears.

The leader turned, let the grin spread, and shouted at me over the roar of engines.

"You can be sure Jack'll have some use for you!"

Laughter rose above the roar, and the gang wheeled away.

I stood and stared.

Down the boulevard the leader turned her throttle to a full twist and her pipes backed off in a thunder.

A block off the boulevard, I cut through a clump of bushes and in a few steps was on the asphalt of the station.

At first I couldn't see the difference. It was still a four-pump unit, old-style Chevron, the first station built after the subdivision.

Then I noticed the colors. Something was wrong—blue was missing. Everything had been repainted in either red or white.

Over the office door were the red letters JACK'S CHEVRON. They looked newly painted.

But someone was repainting them anyway.

I squinted, staring at the massive figure, its back to me on the ladder. Red plaid Pendleton, levis that had once been blue, roughout boots, a green baseball cap, and the body build of a bull.

It was a long-sleeve Pendleton—the lumberjack type—and the sleeves weren't rolled up. I itched and sweated just thinking about it.

Smoke was billowing from the figure's head.

I started forward, but stopped when I noticed all the choppers that were in different stages of disassembly inside the station's shed.

I would have left then—and should have—but the figure on the ladder turned, saw me, grunted, and placed hand on hip. Another cloud of cigar smoke floated up past the baseball cap.

"Jack?" I called out—a little weakly.

The figure nodded.

I stepped forward, feeling awkward for reasons other than my leg.

The distance stretched forever. The figure dropped the brush into the paint can at the top of the ladder, and a heavy ring glinted wildly in the sunlight.

Another grunt, and another billowing of smoke.

When I reached the ladder, I looked up and stared. The smoke had cleared, and globs of red paint were glistening on the front of the Pendleton.

Looking at the front of the shirt, I froze. My leg began tingling, and the other knee-joint felt weak, and a vision of all the choppers in the shed flashed through my head.

"Never seen tits before?" Jack croaked. Her voice had the hoarseness of someone who has been gassed in a riot or war.

My eyes snapped up to her face, and I tried not to frown from the sunlight. A small scar wrinkled one of her eyebrows. Her other eye had a milky spot on it. The stogie drooped from the corner of her mouth, held by her big lips. The baseball cap had a big gold "A" on it.

"Yeah?" she said, blowing smoke down at me.

"I was wondering. . . ."

She had leaned back against the ladder. It was trembling dangerously. She took the stogie from her mouth and flicked the long ash down at me.

"You on foot?"

"Yes, I am. I was just wondering—"

"You sneak past Organ Morgan and the boys?"

The name flashed familiar. It wasn't easy to forget.

"Not really," I said. "They let me through when I told them—"

Jack's body seemed to stiffen. I waited.

"You got passage—how, boy?"

"I told them I was on my way here to ask about a job."

She didn't say anything for a minute.

"You're lying."

"Not exactly," I mumbled, and tried a smile. "The last time I was here Henry Blackburn owned the station and I worked for him two summers. I've been away a couple of years."

"Sure have." She started down the ladder then, huffing and puffing, smoke billowing.

"What they tell you?" she asked halfway down.

"Who? Oh. . . ." I started to feel confident. "They said you'd probably have a use for me."

She stopped suddenly on the ladder, looked a little confused, and
then swore.

"You'll be lucky, Mac," she said, continuing down, "if my use ain't
the same as theirs'd be."

My leg began tingling again, but I kept myself from taking a step
back—especially when she reached the last rung.

"You get that limp from a rock?" she demanded, surprising me.

"No, Sir," I answered quickly, then stuttered in panic.

But the "Sir" hadn't bothered her at all. In fact, I think she liked
it.

"It's my leg," I went on. "It isn't a bad limp, really. I can do
anything—"

She was on the asphalt now. She probably outweighed me by 50
pounds, but she was only five-ten or so. She was having to look up at
me. . . .

I watched something change in her face. The muscles at her temples started slipping back and forth. She was grinding her teeth. She
was puffing rapidly on her stogie.

She spun around and headed toward the shed, her boots striking
the pavement loudly. I followed in confusion, staring at her broad back,
feeling sure that getting out of Emerald Hills on foot would simply not
be possible.

"That Limey Triumph," she croaked, gesturing roughly at one of
the bikes inside. "It's got wiring trouble. . . . Shoot it."

I didn't like the sound of her voice at all—and the sensation in my
leg showed it.

Without even a glance at me, she spun around again and went over
to a crate of canned oil. Hoisting it with ease, she carried it around in
back of the station.

I knelt by the Triumph, and found it hard to concentrate.

I was just beginning to size up the wiring system when I heard
Jack's bootsteps on the other side of the bike. I didn't let myself look
up, but I wasn't really looking at the wires either.

Her steps came closer.

Just when my eyes snapped up to look at her, the empty crate she
was carrying struck the bike hard. The Triumph started to fall.

I jumped back, but the handlebar caught me in the stomach, pinning me for a second.

There was going to be a bruise the size of a silver dollar—but I
didn't let my hands go to the spot.

She was looking down at me, stogie drooping, smoke swirling up
past her milky eye.

An accidental jolt from the empty crate wouldn't have been strong enough to overturn the bike.

And Jack knew I knew it.

"Listen, Mac," she boomed suddenly. "You keep that up with my bikes, and we'll see if Organ and company can find a better use for you!"

I could only stare. It didn't make sense. She knew I knew it. What did she want from me?

When I finished on the Triumph, she had me get to work on a chopper that belonged to someone named Bloody Babs. A monster-bike with gigantic special-made heads and dual Dureto carburetors.

Jack wouldn't tell me what was wrong with it.

I bent over to familiarize myself with the bike, and tried to think. Every time Jack's bootsteps came anywhere near me, I let my eyes glance up to check her.

I'm sure she knew I was checking her. She kept brushing by the bike, going out of her way to pass close to it.

Before long I was tinkering with the carburetors, and had forgotten her for a moment.

I stood up to stretch my legs, and heard a bike being rolled up behind me.

The bike hit me low. Something else hit me high. I went flying into the Bloody-Babs bike, and the twisted Moose seat struck me in the crotch as I knocked the bike over, falling across it.

This time I couldn't keep my hands from going to the bruised spot.

Hands still there, I got to my feet in time to hear Jack say, "What could be hurtin', Mac? You don't have anything there to hold."

Sick pain was hooting through my groin, reaching up through my stomach. I wasn't thinking clearly at all.

I stepped toward her, swung hard, and pain shot through my arm as I missed. Her head had dodged to the side like a boxer's—like a mongoose's.

I wasn't free to swing again. Her arms were around me, pinning mine. Her stogie was dancing in my eyes, blinding me with smoke. She was crushing my chest, and what air did get through had the overpowering smell of oil, paint, cigars, amonia and a high school gym all mixed together.

She lifted me easily somehow. I think I whimpered.

I had my head thrown back to keep my face away from the stogie, so I was off-balance, my struggling clumsy.

I tried kicking. I kept it up, but her shins were like iron.

She lifted me higher, and then tipped me a few degrees to one side. Then she let go.

Nothing broke, but every finger on my right hand felt impacted.

She was looking down at me again. I think she was smiling, but I couldn't tell for sure. Her lips were busy moving the stogie from one corner of her mouth to the other.

Don't worry about the hog," she said finally, and for a moment the hardness was out of her voice. "We'll tell Bloody Babs it was me that scratched it up."

She started to walk away, but then turned back.

"Hey, Mac. It's a wiring problem. . . ."

I went back to work on the chopper. I was beginning to understand. It had all been a ceremony. And the ceremony was over.

She now knew that I knew she was the better man.

I fixed the Bloody-Babs bike and went to take a leak.

I passed the "women's," glanced back at the door, and stopped. Over LADIES someone had nailed one of the teeth-and-frankfurter patches.

And under the patch were more words in red spray paint.

OSCAR MEYER FREEZER
SAVE UNTIL SATURDAY

I looked around to check, and then stepped to the door. But I didn't try the doorknob—a strong whiff of clogged toilet from inside stopped me.

The "men's" wasn't spotless, but the toilets were at least working. I stood at the urinal, stared at the pipes, and almost managed to relax.

The door flew open and Jack walked in.

Once you start, it's hard to stop. But I tried. I turned to look at her once, then turned back, my hands trying to hide that part of me which was suddenly cold.

Jack wasn't interested. With a blank look she went immediately to the sink, rolled up her sleeves and started washing her hands— which were dripping with oil.

I watched her from the corner of my eye, staring until my eyes ached.

I had expected her arms to be covered with E9 needlemarks, but I couldn't see any at all.

What I could see were tatoos. Her arms were covered with them.

A dragon, a flag, a skull, a banner—but I wasn't paying any attention to those. My eyes were glued on just one tatoo.

A name in black . . . two words . . . the first word covered over with a sloppy rectangle of slightly lighter ink.

The second word was "Jack".

I would have been able to read the first word if Jack hadn't suddenly rolled her sleeves down, not bothering to dry her hands.

I zipped up my pants and waited for the door to close before I turned around.

The door caught my eye, and I stared. The back of a black leather jacket was facing me.

The skull-and-cross. The rockers WOMEN'S LEAGUE and EMERALD HILLS CHAPTER. But also some differences.

There were marks where a lot of small patches had been ripped off.

And under the skull-and-cross, over to one side of the jacket, was the word "Jack" again.

A vision of the first word on Jack's arm, the word covered over with ink, flashed through my head. I stepped quickly to the door and straightened the jacket to remove the folds.

In front of "Jack" was a gaping hole. There had once been a word there, but either a knife or scissors had taken it out.

I managed to work on another Harley CH before Jack announced lunchtime.

"If that market on Tourmaline is still there," I said, "I'll make a trip for us. If you want."

Jack puffed on her cigar, stared, and started shaking her head slowly. The look she was giving me made me feel like a two-year-old.

She took the Triumph and was back in 15 minutes with a dozen pre-wrapped sandwiches of all kinds.

I stuffed my two down quickly, then sat on the shed's oily cement in silence. Jack remained standing, squinting out at the sunny sky and downing each sandwich in a bite or two.

When she finally looked down at me, she was shaking her head again. Then she pulled the bill of her cap down and crouched beside me.

"Those guys you met this morning—they're a good tough bunch."

I nodded and started playing with one of the cellophane sandwich wrappers. I was nervous and uncomfortable as hell.

She reached over, grabbed the wrapper from me, wadded it up, tossed it away and went on talking.

"They're as rough as any chapter in the South *or* the North."

She hesitated for a second.

And then suddenly she was telling me all about them.

She sounded proud—but I really couldn't be sure what was going on in her head. For some reason I kept getting the feeling that she was telling me all these things for my own good.

She told me about Organ Morgan, sometimes called Organ La Fay, about all her Oscar Meyer patches, and how they were the reason for her name.

About Big Bertha, the black one, who carried a Browning automatic and had 35 others cached somewhere in Emerald Hills.

About Hurricane George, who got her tag because of her proﬁ-
ciency at a certain unmentionable act, which Jack mentioned to me in
full detail until I was swallowing hard.

About Old Gloria and her stars-and-stripes, which you'd never be
able to see completely unless you tore the shirt off her front, and the
chances of your being able to do that were mighty slim.

About Fransissie, the fat one with the fancy "sissie seat." And
Tugboat Annie, the funny one with the stovepipe hat and cane.
"Hands" Hanna, the smooth one with the missing fingers. Velvet
Vickie, the cream-skinned handsome dresser. Screaming Mimi with
her gleaming machetes. Tarzana Jane, the one who wore a T-shirt and
greased her muscles. Queen Elizabeth, who used soda pop for strange
purposes. And finally Bloody Babs, who was always in hard competition
with Organ Morgan for the most Oscar Meyer patches.

Jack told me about the husbands. Every rider once had a husband,
and Jack's stories about them were of two kinds. Either strange deaths
that didn't seem connected with the Emerald Hills gang at all, or fancy
escapes from their homes in Emerald Hills—never to be seen again.

She started to tell me about the "women's" room, and the Oscar
Meyer patches, and what actually happened every Saturday when the
gang went on a "run"—but suddenly she stopped.

The look on her face made me feel like I had been trying to force
the information out of her.

She got up quickly and stalked away.

She never did say a word about herself.

That evening I tried to look busy. I didn't know where I was going
to sleep, let alone how I was going to get there, past the gang, in one
piece.

A familiar roar made me turn from the bike I was working on.

As the gang rolled up, engines dying, I started matching names
with faces, bodies and gear. Old Gloria behind Organ Morgan, Big
Bertha hidden in shadows to the right, next to Fransissie and Velvet
Vickie. Tarzana Jane to the left, her grease shining, along with Queen
Elizabeth, and the familiar head with the stovepipe hat. Behind them
were four others I couldn't see clearly.

Suddenly there was a commotion on Organ's bike. Someone was
sitting behind her, hidden from view.

"Papa, papa, papa!" Tarzana Jane began shouting, waving a rifle
and pretending to bite the end of its barrel.

It was a man.

"Papa come-uh creepin' uh-round," Velvet Vickie chanted, "uh-
round, uh-round."

He was bigger than Organ Morgan, but that didn't seem to matter.

She slipped off the bike, grabbed him by the arm, and tore him off. The bike wobbled but stayed upright.

The man crumpled to the asphalt in a heap. The station lights glinted off the blood that was smeared all over his clothes.

"Where?" Jack grunted, now a few feet to my right.

"Oh, around," Tugboat Annie hooted, grabbing the rifle from Tarzana.

"Gem Crest," Organ announced—proud.

Jack walked to the man and stood over him. He was propped up on one arm, wiping a bloody lip. She started nudging him with her foot, trying to turn him over, and then suddenly kicked his arm out from under him.

The man rolled over on his back and lay there glaring up at her.

She kept nudging him, teasing him with her boot.

Some sound made me turn, and I found Organ beside me, smiling her gap-tooth look again. She elbowed me, grinned wider, and I stepped away from her as casually as I could.

She turned then and shouted at Jack.

"Say, Jack-o! You savin' this child for your own *private* picnic?"

A couple of the riders laughed, and the word "private" started echoing among the others.

The stare Jack gave Organ was a long one. I think a smile appeared on Jack's lips—but again I couldn't tell for sure, with her lips moving the stogie back and forth across her mouth.

The laughter faded away. The gang seemed to grow uncomfortable.

A voice said "Cool it, La Fay!" and someone started whistling—the kind a kid does in the dark.

Finally Jack spoke.

"Don't I have the right?" She didn't mean it as a question.

"Oh, yeah," Organ answered quickly.

When Jack went back to prodding the man with her boot, Organ started whispering in my ear.

"If I ever catch you away from this place—if I ever catch you alone. . . ."

Quickly she reached around with one arm and pulled the back of her jacket around so I could see all her Oscar Meyer patches.

I stared at them, and heard bootsteps coming close.

By the time I looked up and saw Jack stalking toward us, Organ was trotting off to her chopper, laughing, pretending nothing had happened.

All engines were being revved. Someone shouted "We shall *overcome!*" and two or three of the riders laughed. Bloody Babs, who had certain gestures that reminded me of Organ Morgan's, shouted "Ripe for Saturday!"

As if on cue, all the riders whistled the Oscar Meyer whistle, raised their arms and brought them down karate-style toward their crotches.

Then they were wheeling away, guffawing, someone still waving the man's rifle.

I turned to find Jack staring at me.

"Mac," she said, smoke billowing, "it's quitting time."

I took a deep breath. I looked down at my feet.

"I don't have—" I began, then started over. "I haven't had a chance to find a place to bed down tonight."

She flipped her stogie to the asphalt and swore, grinding the stogie out violently.

"Then take a walk!"

I glanced over at the man on the ground. He had heard it, and was looking as amazed as I felt.

When I reached the bushes I looked back to make sure neither he nor Jack was watching me. Then I ducked into the bushes.

From where I squatted the station lights gave everything a metallic look. I could see that Jack was lighting up another cigar, her back still to the big man. The man was starting to get up slowly.

Paying no attention to him, Jack went over to the pumps that were closest to me and started gathering up oil cans. The man was on his feet now.

He started toward her quietly, and I almost shouted. But I caught myself.

There was something familiar about what was happening.

The man's hands were locked together and raised high over her neck when Jack suddenly turned on him.

There was a flurry of arms, and then I could see that Jack's arms were around the man, pinning his just like she had pinned mine. Her stogie was dancing in his face, and he had his head thrown back— which put him off balance just like it had done to me.

He was a good four inches taller than Jack, and he might have outweighed her. But her arms were as long as an ape's, as thick as thighs. She lifted him easily, and tipped him a few degrees to one side.

She didn't drop him. She threw him.

Slowly he tried to raise himself up on one arm. The arm buckled. He was moaning.

The little ceremony had happened again. Again it had worked.

I realized then that it had probably worked 100 times before.

Jack shouted something at the man, and he struggled up, using his other arm.

She turned him around and started pushing him toward the corner of the station. While they walked, she pulled a ring of keys from her levis. Soon they had disappeared around in back.

I waited, listening for the sound of a beating, or a gunshot, or anything.

The only sound was the breeze. Not even any distant sounds of cars or bikes.

A minute or two later Jack appeared alone.

I stayed in the bushes for another ten minutes, again trying to imagine a way of getting out of Emerald Hills safely. But nothing came. All my head did was give me flashes of Organ Morgan and her whispered threat.

When I finally got up to leave the bushes, blood rushed through my legs and made my head swim. I stumbled out toward the lights of the station.

Jack was waiting for me—hands on hips, trunk-like legs apart, stogie drooping.

"Can you hack one blanket?" she said, gesturing with her thumb toward the shed behind her.

"Sure. No problem." I felt tired and eager.

Her stogie went erect.

"I'm the one that decides what problems there are, Mac!"

I nodded and headed toward the shed, trying not to run.

The blanket must have had the equivalent of two quarts of oil in it. It was something you slept *on,* never under—just like every blanket in Cam.

I shuffled around for a couple of minutes, trying to decide where to lie down, and getting nervous—afraid that Jack would appear in the shed at any moment.

I finally smoothed the blanket down half under the tool bench and half out. I lay down facing the darkness under the bench.

In less than a minute the skin on my back was crawling and my leg was tingling. I turned over and faced the light—the entrance to the shed.

Somehow I fell asleep, and the sound of hard bootsteps woke me up.

It was still night outside, and I closed my eyes quickly, trying to look asleep. I lay there listening.

A shuffling sound, a grunt, a sigh, and then close by the sound of cloth rasping against cement. When the sounds stopped, I opened my eyes slowly.

Jack was no more than six feet away. I could see her broad plaid back through the frame of the Limey Triumph. She was slumped against it.

I awoke again sometime later to a dream of Organ Morgan gunning her chopper near me. I opened my eyes and it wasn't a chopper at all.

Jack's snoring didn't bother me the rest of the night.

Saturday morning they came to get him.

Screaming Mimi raised herself up stiff-legged on her bike, and clanged two machetes together over her head.

"It's gonna be a long run!" she shouted.

"Hell!" someone answered. "Beware, you brothermuckers!"

Jack brought the man out of the "women's" and pushed him toward Organ Morgan, who was polishing her jacket buttons with her leather cuff.

The top of Old Gloria's shirt was unbottoned, and I could see a few stars on one breast and most of a red stripe on the other.

Queen Elizabeth, her chartreuse shirt shining in the sunlight, was humming loudly. She pulled what looked like a .38 special from a trim shoulder-holster under her jacket, and spun the chamber five or six times.

Organ Morgan grabbed the man and jerked him roughly up onto the seat behind her. The man slumped, never looking up.

Suddenly Tugboat Annie raised up on her bike, tossed her hat in the air, ducked low, and caught it on her head.

"Hey, god-of-a-leader!" she shouted.

Jack turned slowly.

Organ Morgan snapped around, instantly nervous, watching Jack closely.

My head echoed "leader." My leg started tingling again, and all I could do was stare at Jack like the others were doing.

Jack grunted, flicked a long ash, and darted her eyes once toward Organ Morgan.

"Run with us, hey," Tugboat Annie shouted. "It's been a long time comin'. You were damn good then."

All of the riders except one fell into it.

"Yeah, yeah, yeah," Big Bertha said, the sun glinting off the BAR that was propped up in her crotch.

"You still got Oscar-class for ten!" someone shouted—maybe Hurricane George.

"A good run'll jack you up good—"

"For a week, a week!"

"Yeah, yeah, yeah!"

My eyes were back on Organ Morgan now. She was glaring hard, moving her head from side to side, nostrils flaring.

And when I turned to look at Jack again, I saw it all clearly. I understood it all completely.

She was a tower of strength, a rock of "class". Her boots were hooves. Her levis, unwashed since the day she got them, were like tough weathered hide. Her legs were those of a buffalo. Her ches bulged out like a truck's cab. Her arms were like swollen pistons, and her long-sleeve Pendleton was like steel wool. And her belt—

For the first time I noticed her belt. The chopper it pictured stuck out like a gnarled gold nugget.

She was a god. From the waist down she was a bull; from the waist up, a man. A god of a leader. She no longer rode with her Chapter— she no longer led it. But she was still what she had always been.

And Organ Morgan knew it.

Smoke rose in a cloud over Jack's head. She spoke.

"My iron's hurtin'."

"Aw, Jack," Tugboat whined. "There's a mount for you around here somewhere. You can—"

"She says her iron's hurtin'," Organ Morgan interrupted then, flicking her engine on at the same time.

Over the sound of Organ Morgan's bike Tugboat Annie again shouted at Jack, waving at her.

"Up Oakland way, they say you always cured hurtin' hogs by riding them hard!"

Organ Morgan swore, spun her bike around, and almost lost the man behind her. As she started away, the others turned their choppers too—but their gazes hung on Jack for a long time.

Jack shook her head. That ended it.

But I'm sure she was liking Tugboat's words. At least I *think* there was a smile behind the stogie smoke and moving lips.

A couple of minutes after the gang left, Jack appeared with a whiskey bottle.

All day I could see her taking gulps from it every once in a while.

And when I went to my blanket that night, my foot hit something, but the blanket kept the glass from breaking.

I fell asleep with the whiskey fumes making me woozy, and there were a lot of dreams that night.

They brought two "papas" in the next week—the first one on Tuesday. I "took a walk," hid in the bushes again, and watched. Jack let the man attack her, then bear-hugged him, and threw him to the asphalt.

She didn't put him in the "women's" right away. Instead, she went over to the shed to handle something, and left him lying there on the pavement.

I wanted to talk to him. I sneaked over to him, crouched down, and tried to tell him that I didn't understand—anything.

"Where've you been?" he said, but then didn't let me answer.

"The only place you could've been," he said. "They should get the word over there better than they do."

Soon I had him telling me about his wife, and about how he had gotten sick and tired of supporting her—her bike, her E9, her arrogance, her appetite, her perversions. About how he, like thousands of other husbands each day, had found himself a weapon and gone nomad, traveling solo from tract to tract in the southland, stealing only from those houses where Women's Leaguers lived. Always solo, never in gangs—because a League Chapter was always meaner and better organized than any gang of "rebel hubs" ever could be. The police never did anything. The courts never did anything. No one ever foreclosed. "Politoscare" was everywhere.

When he finished talking, the man lay there on the ground parting. I think his leg was broken, but he wasn't doing any moaning.

I thanked him and got up to leave. His eyes narrowed. A suspicious look came across his face.

I started to shuffle away, and he called me back.

I crouched down next to him, thinking he was going to offer some advice, or more information, or pass on a survival trick.

"Hey," the man whispered, "what's your thing here?"

I'm sure he had already guessed. He was working his jaw, and I could hear saliva squeak in his mouth.

"I work here," I said.

He looked over once at Jack, who was still tinkering with something in the shed, and then back at me. His lips were moving into a sneer.

"You muckin' fool!" he whispered.

He hit me in the face with about a tablespoon of spit.

I don't see how she could have heard, but Jack was suddenly walking toward us. When I got up and stepped away—leg tingling, saliva streaming down my face—Jack bent down and cuffed the man hard, cracking a couple of his teeth.

It was noon of the next Wednesday. Jack had taken the Limey to the market to get us food.

I was working on the kick starter of a CH—Tarzana Jane's "second"—when I heard the gang approach.

Even before I turned, I knew why they had come. My whole backbone was suddenly tingling.

I stared at Organ Morgan and at the tussled figure sitting behind her, and I swallowed hard.

Organ looked around slowly, her smile growing. Finally she looked back at me.

"Jack trusts you? Oh, wow, baby!"

Not a muscle in my body moved.

The others didn't say anything. They were waiting, uneasy. And the only one looking at me was Tugboat Annie. I couldn't be sure, but I think a half-friendly smile flickered across her pock-marked face.

Organ reached around and yanked the man off the bike. He caught his balance, and danced a few steps away when Organ tried to shove him and knock him down.

Organ twisted around again and grunted something at Tarzana Jane.

Tarzana grunted back, shaking her head.

Organ grunted again in anger, and Tarzana handed the man's rifle over to her. With her back to me, Organ did something with the weapon.

Organ raised the rifle high. I again swallowed hard.

"You'll need this!" she shouted, flinging the rifle at me. It hit me in the shoulder, and I fumbled, but then caught it.

"And this!" she shouted, slipping a key from her pocket and tossing it at me. I hurt my finger catching it.

I tried to hold the rifle casually, but every position I tried felt stiff, unnatural. All my time with rifles in Cam didn't help at all.

The man was staring at me. He was a couple of inches shorter, but he was muscular as hell—30 or 40 pounds more muscular. He looked a lot like a sergeant I'd once had—the only sergeant I had ever really liked.

I made a couple of weak gestures with the rifle, and he took his time turning around. I mumbled "Move!" two or three times, and finally was leading him toward the back of the station—the first prisoner I'd ever handled.

All the choppers had come to life by now, rolling toward the street.

Organ was the last to leave the station's asphalt, and I noticed two new Oscar Meyer patches on the back of her jacket.

Suddenly she grinned at me—the same dark grin.

"It ain't loaded no more, baby!" she shouted.

Time froze for me. My muscles wouldn't obey me. The man in front of me was turning around in slow-motion, biceps flexing, neck straining around.

Then my muscles snapped free. My arms moved, my hands flipped the rifle around so that I was holding the cold barrel. I hit the man hard on the temple with the rifle butt.

He dropped like a rag.

I panicked. My mouth was open. My own saliva was wetting my chin.

I crouched down, stood up, and crouched down again. I touched the man's head, the blood there, then grabbed his wrist, but couldn't tell anything because my own blood was thundering through my body, blocking out any other sound or feeling.

The next thing I knew, I was dragging him by the arm toward the "women's." At the door I let his arms fall. They slapped against the cement. Frantically I dug through my pockets for the key, finding it finally in my shirt pocket.

Once inside, I bent over him, heard him groan once, and tried to hold my breath. But the stench of the clogged toilet burned my nose anyway. I had blood on my hands.

I kept telling myself that he was alive, alive, alive. It didn't help.

I turned and made a dash, but wasn't even through the doorway when I threw up.

I stared at the puke, and a new scare ran through me. I didn't want Jack to see the puke. I didn't want her to know it was mine.

A cough made me look up.

Jack was at the corner of the building—cigar in hand, bag of groceries crushed in her arms—looking at me.

The silence was filled with the blood rushing through my head.

When she finally spoke, her voice was almost soft in its hoarseness.

"You jacked him up so hard he puked, huh? That's class, Mac."

One hand went slowly to her forehead. She gave me a small salute. And she may have been smiling a little, but I couldn't be sure.

I do know one thing. She had been standing there a long time.

Long enough to know whose puke it really was.

It was Monday, two weeks later. I was working on Jack's old bike —the one with the small Bates seat—when the gang roared up.

Organ didn't even have to jerk the man off her bike. She stopped and he fell off. Organ sneered. The man just lay there in a heap.

He was as tall as me, but he was weak, and he looked sick and underfed. He was covered with cuts and bruises—some old, some fresh.

"What a man," Organ announced, still sneering. "No weapon."

"Poor Oscar can't fight!" Tarzana chimed in.

"Where?" Jack demanded, and Bloody Babs answered, "Diamond Heights."

Everyone laughed. I smiled. Diamond Heights homes were the most expensive ones in all of Emerald Hills.

Oscar wasn't his name; it was just another word for "League Papa." But it stuck in my mind. Somehow it fit.

When the gang left, I didn't even wait for Jack to give me a signal. I "took a walk."

From the bushes I watched the little ceremony start again.

Jack was fiddling with oil cans about 60 feet from the guy, her back to him.

He started crawling, but only went a few feet—to the curb by the office door. He never looked up.

Jack jerked around once at the sound of his crawling, but then went back to her act with the cans.

Finally the man looked up. He squinted, began staring into the bright sky, and still didn't move.

I could tell that Jack was getting impatient. She stood up and walked to the other side of the station, stopping just around the corner. I could see her, but the man couldn't. She was listening.

The man got slowly to his feet, and Jack heard him.

She rushed around the corner and charged him.

He hadn't stepped an inch away from his spot. Still squinting into the sunlight, he was only stretching his back. He seemed unaware of everything.

Her bull-body hit him hard, but he couldn't fall. Her arms were instantly around him, squeezing. Her stogie was dancing dangerously close to his face, but he didn't seem to notice. His head wasn't thrown back at all. He wasn't struggling at all.

He was completely limp in her arms, and she felt it.

She bellowed through clenched teeth and stogie, and squeezed harder—hard enough to break a rib or two.

Still he wouldn't fight her.

The tip of the stogie was almost in his eye now, and she suddenly seemed aware of it. Her face reddened, and I think she was trembling a little. Some of his blood—from his dozens of cuts—was getting on her Pendleton.

The stogie touched his eye. Nothing happened. Maybe a twitch of his head and neck—but nothing else.

She froze. The stogie fell from her teeth, dropped between her bulging chest and his sunken front.

The only sound that reached me then was a groan, and I don't think it was from Oscar's lips.

Her whole body was shaking. She let go, and he fell.

He didn't move. She didn't move. Her stogie lay burning by her boot.

Then she bent down and shook him. He still didn't move, and she shook him harder. Even from where I was, I could tell he was unconscious.

Finally she reached down and picked him up like he weighed nothing. Carrying him in her arms, she headed toward the back of the station.

When she came back, I think she was still shaking. She seemed to stand there in a daze, almost facing me, and I watched her hands. They were trying to brush something from the front of her Pendleton.

At first I thought it was ashes, but she kept brushing and brushing.

Before long, I realized that with each stroke her hands were getting redder—redder and wetter, glistening in the sunlight.

The next day I found Jack listening by the "women's" door. Retching and fits of coughing were going on inside the room.

When she saw me, she faced the door quickly and started shouting. "Cool it! You hear me? Anything you puke, you eat!"

The day-after was Wednesday, and the deep coughing sounds greeted me when I went to take a leak right after waking up.

Later that morning the coughing suddenly stopped. I was in the shed and had been hearing it through the walls.

I went outside to look around, and wasn't surprised when I couldn't find Jack anywhere.

I peered around the corner of the building and noticed that the "women's" door was open.

I could hear muffled voices coming from the room, and could recognize Jack's grunts from time to time. The other voice was soft, much harder to hear.

As I started to leave, Jack's voice suddenly reached me clearly.

"Yeah. Those Sierras are heavy sights."

At noon the next day, Jack let Oscar come out. She let him stand on the curb by the office and stare out at the sky. Why he wanted to stand instead of sit, I don't know—he still looked like walking death.

He had been standing there only five minutes when I heard choppers approaching in the distance.

I pivoted quickly, and found Jack listening hard to the sound. She looked frozen.

By the time Organ came in sight, Jack had reached Oscar at a furious charge, knocking him down hard, hitting him once in the chest with her fist, and starting to shout at him.

She shouted something about caving his head in if he ever tried to escape again.

The gang passed without stopping. But Organ's eyes stayed on the three of us until she was out of sight.

Without a word Jack led Oscar back to the "women's."

I stood there scared. I felt sure I had seen something I shouldn't have—that my seeing it made me some threat to Jack. . . .

I thought again about leaving. But visions of Organ Morgan, the Emerald Hills gang, and the dozens of smaller and lesser gangs that patroled the Emerald Hills area made staying at the station once again seem the better of two bad scenes.

When Jack returned, I waited for her to say something, or do something.

Nothing happened. She acted like she didn't know I existed.

The next day was Friday. From the minute we both woke up in the shed, I could sense that something was different.

She smoked twice as many cigars, and missed quite a few with her boot when she tried to grind them out. And she was constantly squinting up at the sky.

I even found her sitting on the curb by the office. She stood up quickly as soon as she saw me staring at her, but then a few minutes later she was back sitting on the curb again.

I had never seen her sitting down before—not even for a second.

When the gang arrived the next morning, the difference in Jack seemed to disappear.

She didn't even bother to look up. She just kept tinkering with the throttle of her old bike.

Organ Morgan geared down, tires screeching, and rolled toward us.

"Ain't papa up yet?" she shouted, as the rest of the gang rolled in beside her.

Hurricane George began singing in monotone.

"He'll dig it—he'll dig it—he will dig it!"

When Jack finally turned around, it was like she didn't know what they were talking about. She stood up, looked a little annoyed, and knocked the ash from her stogie.

"Are you ribbin'?" she said. "That's no papa in there. Anyone gets a patch off of him, wouldn't've earned it. A no-class rip-off."

The gang stared at her for a minute, and then at Organ.

Organ's eyes were slits, suspicious, running up and down Jack's body.

"Papa needs fattening up," Jack went on, paying no attention to Organ's look. "We'll stuff him with a week's fill of hotdogs."

Five or six of the riders laughed at the joke.

Jack was smiling a strange smile now, and the smile was working.

"A week?" someone whined, but only half-serious. "Aw, Jack Sprat!"

Organ cracked her knuckles.

"No week," she announced. "Tuesday's a national feast-day, and we're running."

"Okay!" Tarzana cried. "Okay, feast-day!"

Tugboat shushed her with a signal, and the entire gang fell silent.

Organ was starting to turn her bike around. She stopped and looked back.

"He'd get fat, Jack," she said softly, witch-style cackle, "if you didn't punish him so bad. Monday was heavy. . . ."

So she had guessed the truth about Monday? I couldn't tell, and I don't think Jack could either.

Jack said nothing—and that was the right answer.

"Organ, hey," Old Gloria called suddenly. "Who's our papa for today?"

It was Tugboat who answered, as she nosed her chopper toward the street and waved for some of the others to follow.

"We hunt one down now—quick," she said.

Organ stared a little while longer at Jack, and then roared off with the rest of them, soon back in lead.

When they came on Tuesday, Jack acted casual again.

"Go ahead and take him," she croaked, wearing her odd smile again, "if you want a sick patch for your rumbler."

Some murmuring began behind Organ Morgan.

"Wait till the next run," Jack went on, "and you'll have a glory-class, good-shag patch."

Tugboat laughed nervously, and picked it up.

"Verily a patch to possess, boys—one glory-class good-shag patch of patches. Yeah, yeah!"

Organ wasn't listening. She raised up stiff-legged on her bike, crossed her arms, and glared.

"Oh, Jack!" she shouted, and her tone was a command.

Jack seemed to stiffen.

"I don't suppose," Organ went on slowly, sarcasm growing, "that this is a crooked run-down you're dealing us."

Jack glared back for a second, spun on her heels, and stalked away toward the back of the station.

I actually thought she was giving up, that she was going to get Oscar.

But Velvet Vickie mumbled something about Jack's jacket.

"Foah shoah," Queen Elizabeth agreed. "She gone to get it."

Organ's jaw dropped slightly. She started fidgeting.

"Dark meaning," Big Bertha announced—to make things worse.

"Hell!" Organ said. "We don't need her skinny pig. We found us a good papa last Saturday, last-minute-wise, and—"

"And we'll hunt another one down today!" Tugboat finished for her.

The gang relaxed.

Then Organ raised up on her bike even higher, and spit tokenly at my feet.

"Listen, baby. You tell Jack we're coming for our papa Saturday next. And she better not have any private ideas on him. We don't plan on having him missing anything when we take him running. Tell Jack-o she either joins us, or keeps hands-off our papas' fruit!"

I didn't tell Jack any such thing. I got back to work on the bikes and stayed with them until blanket-time.

It took me by surprise—completely—and I should have been able to predict it.

It was the next Friday night. Jack had gone to test her old bike on the boulevard—the first time I had ever seen her do anything like this.

The gang roared up, and I just stood there mouth open while Organ leaped off her chopper, Queen Elizabeth's .38 special in her hand, and rushed around in back of the station.

I followed but kept at a safe distance, and heard two shots before I rounded the corner.

The lock had been shot off the door. Oscar was screaming faintly inside.

Organ pulled him out where everyone could see, knocked him to the asphalt, and stepped on his hand. He was looking as pale and sick as ever.

Organ started whispering to him, witch-style again, prodding him with her boot, and suddenly unsheathing her knife.

"You grow any yet?" she said, jabbing the knife at his crotch. He tried to roll away, but she grabbed him. His eyes went wide.

A sound made everyone freeze. A bike sound.

I turned in time to see Jack coming on fast.

I stepped to one side, and that gave her a view of Organ leaning over Oscar with the knife.

I stepped even farther to the side, because Jack was off her bike, was running beside it, huffing and puffing like a train, guiding the bike in, face red and bloated.

She let go and the bike hit Organ. It twisted her leg, sent her sprawling on the asphalt next to Oscar.

Organ looked up, knife still in hand, and quickly rolled over the few feet that separated her from Oscar. Straightening up on one elbow, she jabbed with the knife.

It sank into flesh, passing next to his zipper, and he screamed loudly this time, making it hard to hear Organ—who was screaming at Jack now.

"You've done it now! You've shown us *nothin'*!"

Jack had already bellowed once when the knife sank in. Now she bellowed again, and it was louder than any bull.

When she reached Organ, Organ was on her feet, her weight on one leg.

Jack's arms went around her. The knife—aimed at Jack's stomach—disappeared between them. Jack's eyes bulged, and her cap and stogie went flying through the air.

She lifted Organ easily, using her own head to push Organ's way back. She squeezed hard, pulling in with her giant arms, and Organ screamed.

A crack sounded throughout the station.

The gang panicked, and almost turned their bikes over in a rush to mount them and get them into the street.

Blood was oozing through the Pendleton at belly level. Organ's body was at Jack's feet in a heap. The gang was gone.

Jack didn't even look at me.

She went over to Oscar, who had somehow gotten to his feet and was holding his groin with both hands, blood streaming down both hands.

She took him by the arm. ·

And for the first time he started struggling. The tighter she held him, the harder he struggled.

A cry escaped her throat, and she hit him. He went over, and in one easy motion she slung him over her shoulder, leaned down, grabbed the handlebar of her bike, and righted it.

She arranged him slowly—hanging him down her back, his arms around her neck, her big hand holding his two hands together on her chest.

She had a little trouble getting on the bike, but was soon straddling it stable, one hand commanding the handlebars.

The bike didn't even wobble as she roared off.

I remember looking through the shed frantically, and not finding a single bike that was in running condition. So I went and hid in the bushes.

My legs grew numb while I waited, and then finally the gang straggled back, leaving their choppers and gathering around Organ's body.

I couldn't hear everything, but I heard enough.

"So what?" someone said.

"Organ pushed," someone said a minute later—maybe Screaming Mimi.

"Bad head, so. . . ." someone answered.

And then clearly: "Jack's deep different." Maybe the Big Bertha.

"Never hitched to a pig like you, me, hey, everyone here," someone added—and I'm sure it was Tarzana.

"Hey, yeah, and never any Big E in her body either."

"Never needed it."

"Her head's deep different," someone said—maybe Big Bertha again.

The voices grew unclear again as the wind picked up.

And then I heard it—the whole name, the first word, the hole in Jack's jacket, the inked-over name on her needle-free arm.

"Ripper Jack. You remember. . . ."

I don't know who said it, but I recognized the next voice as Tugboat's, and she was talking loudly.

"Yeah, 200 papas in all, up Oakland way. It's bummed her for a long time, understand. You know, her jacket and all."

The wind picked up again, but it was Tugboat Annie who kept talking, and she talked for a long time. And the others listened.

When they left, I dragged my blanket from the shed to the bushes, and froze all night.

A car engine—the first I'd heard in weeks—woke me up.

It was morning, and out there on the station's asphalt was a cop —uniform and all, squad car with mouse ears and all.

I stumbled out of the bushes, and the cop spun around. His face wasn't able to hide his scare very well.

But when he saw that I was a guy, he calmed down, and pulled out an official-looking notebook.

"So what happened?"

I got a word or two out, and then stopped. I had started to tell the truth.

I started to lie, and then stopped too.

I didn't want to put the finger on Jack. And at the same time I didn't like the idea of the gang hearing I had put the finger on them.

The cop stepped toward me, his look changing.

"Say, kid, I hope you weren't the one who did it. No skin off my ass, but you've got big trouble if you did."

He paused, and suddenly was talking faster, his voice higher.

"If you did, I'm sure as hell not taking you out of the Hills in my vehicle!"

He was backing away toward his car.

"Just give me your name and I'll radio for an armored. Remember, I'm doing this just as a favor. No law says I'm obliged to—"

The roar of approaching choppers made him stop.

It made me look around 360 degrees for a place to hide.

I started running back to the bushes, but before I got halfway, Tugboat Annie broke from the pack and cut me off. She circled me once, and then stopped between me and the bushes.

The cop was wide-eyed by now. His back was flush up against his car door, and he was trying to hide his notebook.

"Hey, Mac," Tugboat shouted. I held my breath and looked her back in the eye.

"You stay on," she said loudly, so her gang could hear, "until Jack come back. She won't be a long time comin'."

Some of the others joined her, but joked at it.

"Oh, yeah, stay on—*for us*—please!" Velvet Vickie mocked.

"Hey, we got us a mascot, Mimi," Big Bertha crooned, and Mimi's machete sang through the air a couple of times.

"A pig," Tarzana shouted, "but a muckin'-good mech!"

"Yeah," Tugboat said flatly, nodding, smiling at the others, and then looking back to me.

"You stay on, hear," she said quietly—to me alone.

I let myself smile and mumble "Sure." But I shouldn't have.

Tugboat frowned.

"Hear?" she said gruffly.

I nodded, my head down as was proper.

The cop was leaving, his car rolling away. Big Bertha took her BAR, braced it against her belly, and aimed it at him. He laid ten feet of tread, went over the curb, and took the corner on two. A block away, his siren went on, and it sounded silly.

I stayed on.

I fixed their hogs, and did a good job of it.

But they didn't bring their papas to the station any more. Instead, they kept them locked in Tugboat's house in Gem Crest. Which was fine with me.

All of that happened a little over 12 months ago. The letter—or rather the pictures—came yesterday, and I'm beginning to understand quite a few things now.

The envelope had first been addressed to "Mac Smith"—but then the "Smith" had been crossed out. I'd never given anyone my last name.

So the envelope read:

MAC
c/o JACK'S CHEVRON STATION
23501 LAUREL ROAD
EMERALD HILLS, CALIFORNIA

No return address—but it was obvious who had sent it.

When I opened the envelope, my fingers surprised me by trembling and then fumbling with the two color Polaroid pictures inside.

One is of a rough-hewn cabin, not very well built—certainly not built by a pro-contractor. The picture itself was taken on a slight angle, and is also a little overexposed.

The other picture was time-set. Over to one side there's half of a man in motion—just one arm, one shoulder, and half of his chest. He was the one who set the camera and tried to run back in time to be in the picture. You can't see his face, and his arm is muscular, and his chest is well developed—but he hasn't changed so much that he isn't recognizable.

In the middle of the picture there's a wooden chair. On the chair is a heavy-set woman, her muscle gone to fat, her breasts flabby under her flower-print blouse. In her lap her big hands are cradling a baby, which is so young it's still pink.

No matter how you look at the picture, her eyes seem to be looking at you. They follow you around.

And you can't tell whether she is smiling or not.

But then, you never could.

SEVENTH VICTIM

Robert Sheckley

Stanton Frelaine sat at his desk, trying to look as busy as an executive should at nine-thirty in the morning. It was impossible. He couldn't concentrate on the advertisement he had written the previous night, couldn't think about business. All he could do was wait until the mail came.

He had been waiting for his notification for two weeks now. The government was behind schedule, as usual.

The glass door of his office was marked *Morger and Frelaine, Clothiers.* It opened, and E. J. Morger walked in, limping slightly from his old gunshot wound. His shoulders were bent; but at the age of 73, he wasn't worrying too much about his posture.

"Well, Stan?" Morger asked. "What about that ad?"

Frelaine had joined Morger 16 years ago, when he was 27. Together they had built Protec-Clothes into a million-dollar concern.

"I suppose you can run it," Frelaine said, handing the slip of paper to Morger. If only the mail would come earlier, he thought.

" 'Do you own a Protec-Suit?' " Morger read aloud, holding the paper close to his eyes. " 'The finest tailoring in the world has gone into

Morger and Frelaine's Protec-Suit, to make it the leader in men's fashions.' "

Morger cleared his throat and glanced at Frelaine. He smiled and read on.

" 'Protec-Suit is the safest as well as the smartest. Every Protec-Suit comes with special built-in gun pocket, guaranteed not to bulge. No one will know you are carrying a gun—except you. The gun pocket is exceptionally easy to get at, permitting fast, unhindered draw. Choice of hip or breast pocket.' Very nice," Morger commented.

Frelaine nodded morosely.

" 'The Protec-Suit Special has the fling-out gun pocket, the greatest modern advance in personal protection. A touch of the concealed button throws the gun into your hand, cocked, safeties off. Why not drop into the Protec-Store nearest you? Why not *be safe?*' "

"That's fine," Morger said. "That's a very nice, dignified ad." He thought for a moment, fingering his white mustache. "Shouldn't you mention that Protec-Suits come in a variety of styles, single and double-breasted, one and two button rolls, deep and shallow flares?"

"Right. I forgot."

Frelaine took back the sheet and jotted a note on the edge of it. Then he stood up, smoothing his jacket over his prominent stomach. Frelaine was 43, a little overweight, a little bald on top. He was an amiable-looking man with cold eyes.

"Relax," Morger said. "It'll come in today's mail."

Frelaine forced himself to smile. He felt like pacing the floor, but instead sat on the edge of the desk.

"You'd think it was my first kill," he said, with a deprecating smile.

"I know how it is," Morger said. "Before I hung up my gun, I couldn't sleep for a month, waiting for a notification. I know."

The two men waited. Just as the silence was becoming unbearable, the door opened. A clerk walked in and deposited the mail on Frelaine's desk.

Frelaine swung around and gathered up the letters. He thumbed through them rapidly and found what he had been waiting for—the long white envelope from ECB, with the official government seal on it.

"That's it!" Frelaine said, and broke into a grin. "That's the baby!"

"Fine." Morger eyed the envelope with interest, but didn't ask Frelaine to open it. It would be a breach of etiquette, as well as a violation in the eyes of the law. No one was supposed to know a Victim's name except his Hunter. "Have a good hunt."

"I expect to," Frelaine replied confidently. His desk was in order —had been for a week. He picked up his briefcase.

"A good kill will do you a world of good," Morger said, putting his hand lightly on Frelaine's padded shoulder. "You've been keyed up."

"I know " Frelaine grinned again and shook Morger's hand.

"Wish I was a kid again," Morger said, glancing down at his crippled leg with wryly humorous eyes. "Makes me want to pick up a gun again."

The old man had been quite a Hunter in his day. Ten successful hunts had qualified him for the exclusive Tens Club. And, of course, for each hunt Morger had had to act as Victim, so he had 20 kills to his credit.

"I sure hope my Victim isn't anyone like you," Frelaine said, half in jest.

"Don't worry about it. What number will this be?"

"The seventh."

"Lucky seven. Go to it," Morger said. "We'll get you into the Tens yet."

Frelaine waved his hand and started out the door.

"Just don't get careless," warned Morger. "All it takes is a single slip and I'll need a new partner. If you don't mind, I like the one I've got now."

"I'll be careful," Frelaine promised.

Instead of taking a bus, Frelaine walked to his apartment. He wanted time to cool off. There was no sense in acting like a kid on his first kill.

As he walked, Frelaine kept his eyes strictly to the front. Staring at anyone was practically asking for a bullet, if the man happened to be serving as Victim. Some Victims shot if you just glanced at them. Nervous fellows. Frelaine prudently looked above the heads of the people he passed.

Ahead of him was a huge billboard, offering J. F. O'Donovan's services to the public.

"Victims!" the sign proclaimed in huge red letters. "Why take chances? Use an O'Donovan accredited Spotter. Let us locate your assigned killer. Pay after you get him!"

The sign reminded Frelaine. He would call Morrow as soon as he reached his apartment.

He crossed the street, quickening his stride. He could hardly wait to get home now, to open the envelope and discover who his victim was. Would he be clever or stupid? Rich, like Frelaine's fourth Victim, or poor, like the first and second? Would he have an organized Spotter service, or try to go it on his own?

The excitement of the chase was wonderful, coursing through his veins, quickening his heartbeat. From a block or so away, he heard gunfire. Two quick shots, and then a final one.

Somebody got his man, Frelaine thought. Good for him.

It was a superb feeling, he told himself. He was *alive* again.

At his one-room apartment the first thing Frelaine did was call Ed

Morrow, his spotter. The man worked as a garage attendant between calls.

"Hello, Ed? Frelaine."

"Oh, hi, Mr. Frelaine." He could see the man's thin, grease-stained face, grinning flat-lipped at the telephone.

"I'm going out on one, Ed."

"Good luck, Mr. Frelaine," Ed Morrow said. "I suppose you'll want me to stand by?"

"That's right. I don't expect to be gone more than a week or two. I'll probably get my notification of Victim Status within three months of the kill."

"I'll be standing by. Good hunting, Mr. Frelaine."

"Thanks. So long." He hung up. It was a wise safety measure to reserve a first-class spotter. After his kill, it would be Frelaine's turn as Victim. Then, once again, Ed Morrow would be his life insurance.

And what a marvelous spotter Morrow was! Uneducated—stupid, really. But what an eye for people! Morrow was a natural. His pale eyes could tell an out-of-towner at a glance. He was diabolically clever at rigging an ambush. An indispensable man.

Frelaine took out the envelope, chuckling to himself, remembering some of the tricks Morrow had turned for the Hunters. Still smiling, he glanced at the data inside the envelope.

Janet-Marie Patzig.

His Victim was a female!

Frelaine stood up and paced for a few moments. Then he read the letter again. Janet-Marie Patzig. No mistake. A girl. Three photographs were enclosed, her address, and the usual descriptive data.

Frelaine frowned. He had never killed a female.

He hesitated for a moment, then picked up the telephone and dialed.

"Emotional Catharsis Bureau, Information Section," a man's voice answered.

"Say, look," Frelaine said. "I just got my notification and I pulled a girl. Is that in order?" He gave the clerk the girl's name.

"It's all in order, sir," the clerk replied after a minute of checking micro-files. "The girl registered with the board under her own free will. The law says she has the same rights and privileges as a man."

"Could you tell me how many kills she has?"

"I'm sorry, sir. The only information you're allowed is the Victim's legal status and the descriptive data you have received."

"I see." Frelaine paused. "Could I draw another?"

"You can refuse the hunt, of course. That is your legal right. But you will not be allowed another Victim until you have served. Do you wish to refuse?"

"Oh, no," Frelaine said hastily. "I was just wondering. Thank you."

He hung up and sat down in his largest armchair, loosening his belt. This required some thought. Damn women, he grumbled to himself, always trying to horn in on a man's game. Why can't they stay home?

But they were free citizens, he reminded himself. Still, it just didn't seem *feminine.*

He knew that, historically speaking, the Emotional Catharsis Board had been established for men and men only. The board had been formed at the end of the fourth world war—or sixth, as some historians counted it.

At that time there had been a driving need for permanent, lasting peace. The reason was practical, as were the men who engineered it.

Simply—annihilation was just around the corner.

In the world wars, weapons increased in magnitude, efficiency and exterminating power. Soldiers became accustomed to them, less and less reluctant to use them.

But the saturation point had been reached. Another war would truly be the war to end all wars. There would be no one left to start another.

So this peace *had* to last for all time, but the men who engineered it were practical. They recognized the tensions and dislocations still present, the cauldrons in which wars are brewed. They asked themselves why peace had never lasted in the past.

"Because men like to fight," was their answer.

"Oh, no!" screamed the idealists.

But the men who engineered the peace were forced to postulate, regretfully, the presence of a need for violence in a large percentage of mankind.

Men aren't angels. They aren't fiends, either. They are just very human beings, with a high degree of combativeness.

With the scientific knowledge and the power they had at that moment, the practical men could have gone a long way toward breeding this trait out of the race. Many thought this was the answer.

The practical men didn't. They recognized the validity of competition, love of battle, strength in the face of overwhelming odds. These, they felt, were admirable traits for a race, and insurance toward its perpetuity. Without them, the race would be bound to retrogress.

The tendency toward violence, they found, was inextricably linked with ingenuity, flexibility, drive.

The problem, then: To arrange a peace that would last after they were gone. To stop the race from destroying itself, without removing the responsible traits.

The way to do this, they decided, was to rechannel Man's violence. Provide him with an outlet, an expression.

The first big step was the legalization of gladiatorial events, complete with blood and thunder. But more was needed. Sublimations worked only up to a point. Then people demanded the real thing.

There is no substitute for murder.

So murder was legalized, on a strictly individual basis, and only for those who wanted it. The governments were directed to create Emotional Catharsis Boards.

After a period of experimentation, uniform rules were adopted.

Anyone who wanted to murder could sign up at the ECB. Giving certain data and assurances, he would be granted a Victim.

Anyone who signed up to murder, under the government rules, had to take his turn a few months later as Victim—if he survived.

That, in essence, was the setup. The individual could commit as many murders as he wanted. But between each, he had to be a Victim. If he successfully killed his Hunter, he could stop, or sign up for another murder.

At the end of ten years, an estimated third of the world's civilized population had applied for at least one murder. The number slid to a fourth, and stayed there.

Philosophers shook their heads, but the practical men were satisfied. War was where it belonged—in the hands of the individual.

Of course, there were ramifications to the game, and elaborations. Once its existence had been accepted it became big business. There were services for Victim and Hunter alike.

The Emotional Catharsis Board picked the Victims' names at random. A Hunter was allowed six months in which to make his kill. This had to be done by his own ingenuity, unaided. He was given the name of his Victim, address and description, and allowed to use a standard caliber pistol. He could wear no armor of any sort.

The Victim was notified a week before the Hunter. He was told only that he was a Victim. He did not know the name of his Hunter. He was allowed his choice of armor, however. He could hire spotters. A spotter couldn't kill; only Victim and Hunter could do that. But he could detect a stranger in town, or ferret out a nervous gunman.

The Victim could arrange any kind of ambush in his power to kill the Hunter.

There were stiff penalties for killing or wounding the wrong man, for no other murder was allowed. Grudge killings and gain killings were punishable by death.

The beauty of the system was that the people who wanted to kill could do so. Those who didn't—the bulk of the population—didn't have to.

At least, there weren't any more big wars. Not even the imminence of one.

Just hundreds of thousands of small ones.

Frelaine didn't especially like the idea of killing a woman; but she *had* signed up. It wasn't his fault. And he wasn't going to lose out on his seventh hunt.

He spent the rest of the morning memorizing the data on his Victim, then filed the letter.

Janet Patzig lived in New York. That was good. He enjoyed hunting in a big city, and he had always wanted to see New York. Her age wasn't given, but to judge from her photographs, she was in her early twenties.

Frelaine phoned for jet reservations to New York, then took a shower. He dressed with care in a new Protec-Suit Special made for the occasion. From his collection he selected a gun, cleaned and oiled it, and fitted it into the fling-out pocket of the suit. Then he packed his suit-case.

A pulse of excitement was pounding in his veins. Strange, he thought, how each killing was a new excitement. It was something you just didn't tire of, the way you did of French pastry or women or drinking or anything else. It was always new and different.

Finally, he looked over his books to see which he would take.

His library contained all the good books on the subject. He wouldn't need any of his Victim books, like L. Fred Tracy's *Tactics for the Victim,* with its insistence on a rigidly controlled environment, or Dr. Frisch's *Don't Think Like a Victim!*

He would be very interested in those in a few months, when he was a Victim again. Now he wanted hunting books.

Tactics for Hunting Humans was the standard and definitive work, but he had it almost memorized. *Development of the Ambush* was not adapted to his present needs.

He chose *Hunting in Cities,* by Mitwell and Clark, *Spotting the Spotter,* by Algreen, and *The Victim's Ingroup,* by the same author.

Everything was in order. He left a note for the milkman, locked his apartment and took a cab to the airport.

In New York, he checked into a hotel in the midtown area, not too far from his Victim's address. The clerks were smiling and attentive, which bothered Frelaine. He didn't like to be recognized so easily as an out-of-town killer.

The first thing he saw in his room was a pamphlet on his bedtable. *How to Get the Most out of your Emotional Catharsis,* it was called, with the compliments of the management. Frelaine smiled and thumbed through it.

Since it was his first visit to New York, Frelaine spent the afternoon just walking the streets in his Victim's neighborhood. After that, he wandered through a few stores.

Martinson and Black was a fascinating place. He went through their Hunter-Hunted room. There were lightweight bulletproof vests for Victims, and Richard Arlington hats, with bulletproof crowns.

On one side was a large display of a new .38 caliber side-arm.

"Use the Malvern Strait-shot!" the ad proclaimed. "ECB-approved. Carries a load of 12 shots. Tested deviation less than .001 inch per 1,000 feet. Don't miss your Victim! Don't risk your life without the best! Be safe with Malvern!"

Frelaine smiled. The ad was good, and the small black weapon looked ultimately efficient. But he was satisfied with the one he had.

There was a special sale on trick canes, with concealed four-shot magazine, promising safety and concealment. As a young man, Frelaine had gone in heavily for novelties. But now he knew that the old-fashioned ways were usually the best.

Outside the store, four men from the Department of Sanitation were carting away a freshly killed corpse. Frelaine regretted missing the kill.

He ate dinner in a good restaurant and went to bed early.

Tomorrow he had a lot to do.

The next day, with the face of his Victim before him, Frelaine walked through her neighborhood. He didn't look closely at anyone. Instead, he moved rapidly, as though he were really going somewhere, the way an old Hunter should walk.

He passed several bars and dropped into one for a drink. Then he went on, down a side street off Lexington Avenue.

There was a pleasant sidewalk cafe there. Frelaine walked past it.

And there she was! He could never mistake the face. It was Janet Patzig, seated at a table, staring into a drink. She didn't look up as he passed.

Frelaine walked to the end of the block. He turned the corner and stopped, hands trembling.

Was the girl crazy, exposing herself in the open? Did she think she had a charmed life?

He hailed a taxi and had the man drive around the block. Sure enough, she was just sitting there. Frelaine took a careful look.

She seemed younger than her pictures, but he couldn't be sure. He would guess her to be not much over twenty. Her dark hair was parted in the middle and combed above her ears, giving her a nunlike appearance. Her expression, as far as Frelaine could tell, was one of resigned sadness.

Wasn't she even going to make an attempt to defend herself?

Frelaine paid the driver and hurried to a drugstore. Finding a vacant telephone booth, he called ECB.

"Are you sure that a Victim named Janet-Marie Patzig has been notified?"

"Hold on sir." Frelaine tapped on the door while the clerk looked up the information. "Yes, sir. We have her personal confirmation. Is there anything wrong, sir?"

"No," Frelaine said. "Just wanted to check."

After all, it was no one's business if the girl didn't want to defend herself.

He was still entitled to kill her.

It was his turn.

He postponed it for that day, however, and went to a movie. After dinner, he returned to his room and read the ECB pamphlet. Then he lay on his bed and glared at the ceiling.

All he had to do was pump a bullet into her. Just ride by in a cab and kill her.

She was being a very bad sport about it, he decided resentfully, and went to sleep.

The next afternoon, Frelaine walked by the cafe again. The girl was back, sitting at the same table. Frelaine caught a cab.

"Drive around the block very slowly," he told the driver.

"Sure," the driver said, grinning with sardonic wisdom.

From the cab, Frelaine watched for spotters. As far as he could tell, the girl had none. Both her hands were in sight upon the table.

An easy, stationary target.

Frelaine touched the button of his double-breasted jacket. A fold flew open and the gun was in his hand. He broke it open and checked the cartridges, then closed it with a snap.

"Slowly, now," he told the driver.

The taxi crawled by the cafe. Frelaine took careful aim, centering the girl in his sights. His finger tightened on the trigger.

"Damn it!" he said.

A waiter had passed by the girl. He didn't want to chance winging someone else.

"Around the block again," he told the driver.

The man gave him another grin and hunched down in his seat. Frelaine wondered if the driver would feel so happy if he knew that Frelaine was gunning for a woman.

This time there was no waiter around. The girl was lighting a cigarette, her mournful face intent on her lighter. Frelaine centered her in his sights, squarely above the eyes, and held his breath.

Then he shook his head and put the gun back in his pocket. The idiotic girl was robbing him of the full benefit of his catharsis.

He paid the driver and started to walk.

It's too easy, he told himself. He was used to a real chase. Most of the other six kills had been quite difficult. The Victims had tried every dodge. One had hired at least a dozen spotters. But Frelaine had gotten to them all by altering his tactics to meet the situation.

Once he had dressed as a milkman, another time as a bill collector.

The sixth Victim he had had to chase through the Sierra Nevadas. The man had clipped him, too. But Frelaine had done better than that.

How could he be proud of this one? What would the Tens Club say?

That brought Frelaine up with a start. He wanted to get into the club. Even if he passed up this girl, he would have to defend himself against a Hunter. Surviving that, he would still be four hunts away from membership. At that rate, he might never get in.

He began to pass the cafe again, then, on impulse, stopped abruptly.

"Hello," he said.

Janet Patzig looked at him out of sad blue eyes, but said nothing.

"Say, look," he said, sitting down. "If I'm being fresh, just tell me and I'll go. I'm an out-of-towner. Here on a convention. And I'd just like someone feminine to talk to. If you'd rather I didn't—"

"I don't care," Janet Patzig said tonelessly.

"A brandy," Frelaine told the waiter. Janet Patzig's glass was still half full.

Frelaine looked at the girl and he could feel his heart throbbing against his ribs. This was more like it—having a drink with your Victim!

"My name's Stanton Frelaine," he said, knowing it didn't matter.

"Janet."

"Janet what?"

"Janet Patzig."

"Nice to know you," Frelaine said, in a perfectly natural voice. "Are you doing anything tonight, Janet?"

"I'm probably being killed tonight," she said quietly.

Frelaine looked at her carefully. Did she realize who he was? For all he knew, she had a gun leveled at him under the table.

He kept his hand close to the fling-out button.

"Are you a Victim?" he asked.

"You guessed it," she said sardonically. "If I were you, I'd stay out of the way. No sense getting hit by mistake."

Frelaine couldn't understand the girl's calm. Was she a suicide? Perhaps she just didn't care. Perhaps she wanted to die.

"Haven't you got any spotters?" he asked, with the right expression of amazement.

"No." She looked at him, full in the face, and Frelaine saw something he hadn't noticed before.

She was very lovely.

"I am a bad, bad girl," she said lightly. "I got the idea I'd like to commit a murder, so I signed for ECB. Then—I couldn't do it."

Frelaine shook his head, sympathizing with her.

"But I'm still in, of course. Even if I didn't shoot, I still have to be a Victim."

"But why don't you hire some spotters?" he asked.

"I couldn't kill anyone," she said. "I just couldn't. I don't even have a gun."

"You've got a lot of courage," Frelaine said, "coming out in the open this way." Secretly, he was amazed at her stupidity.

"What can I do?" she asked listlessly. "You can't hide from a Hunter. Not a real one. And I don't have enough money to make a real disappearance."

"Since it's in your own defense, I should think—" Frelaine began, but she interrupted.

"No. I've made up my mind on that. This whole thing is wrong, the whole system. When I had my Victim in the sights—when I saw how easily I could—I could—"

She pulled herself together quickly.

"Oh, let's forget it," she said, and smiled.

Frelaine found her smile dazzling.

After that, they talked of other things. Frelaine told her of his business, and she told him about New York. She was 22, an unsuccessful actress.

They had supper together. When she accepted Frelaine's invitation to go to the Gladiatorials, he felt absurdly elated.

He called a cab—he seemed to be spending his entire time in New York in cabs—and opened the door for her. She started in. Frelaine hesitated. He could have pumped a shot into her at that moment. It would have been very easy.

But he held his hand. Just for the moment, he told himself.

The Gladiatorials were about the same as those held anywhere else, except that the talent was a little better. There were the usual historical events, swordsmen and netmen, duels with saber and foil.

Most of these, naturally, were fought to the death.

Then bull fighting, lion fighting and rhino fighting, followed by the more modern events. Fights from behind barricades with bow and arrow. Dueling on a high wire.

The evening passed pleasantly.

Frelaine escorted the girl home, the palms of his hands sticky with sweat. He had never found a woman he liked better. And yet she was his legitimate kill.

He didn't know what he was going to do.

She invited him in and they sat together on the couch. The girl lighted a cigarette for herself with a large lighter, then settled back.

"Are you leaving soon?" she asked him.

"I suppose so," Frelaine said. "The convention is only lasting another day."

She was silent for a moment. "I'll be sorry to see you go. Send roses to my funeral."

They were quiet for a while. Then Janet went to fix him a drink. Frelaine eyed her retreating back. Now was the time. He placed his hand near the button.

But the moment had passed for him, irrevocably. He wasn't going to kill her. You don't kill the girl you love.

The realization that he loved her was shocking. He'd come to kill, not to find a wife.

She came back with the drink and sat down opposite him, staring at emptiness.

"Janet," he said. "I love you."

She sat, just looking at him. There were tears in her eyes.

"You can't," she protested. "I'm a Victim. I won't live long enough to—"

"You won't be killed. I'm your Hunter."

She stared at him a moment, then laughed uncertainly.

"Are you going to kill me?" she asked.

"Don't be ridiculous," he said. "I'm going to marry you."

Suddenly she was in his arms.

"Oh, Lord!" she gasped. "The waiting—I've been so frightened—"

"It's all over," he told her. "Think what a story it'll make for our kids. How I came to murder you and left marrying you."

She kissed him, then sat back and lighted another cigarette.

"Let's start packing," Frelaine said. "I want—"

"Wait," Janet interrupted. "You haven't asked if I love you."

"What?"

She was still smiling, and the cigarette lighter was pointed at him. In the bottom of it was a black hole. A hole just large enough for a .38 caliber bullet.

"Don't kid around," he objected, getting to his feet.

"I'm not being funny, darling," she said.

In a fraction of a second, Frelaine had time to wonder how he could ever have thought she was not much over twenty. Looking at her now —*really* looking at her—he knew she couldn't be much less than thirty. Every minute of her strained, tense existence showed on her face.

"I don't love you, Stanton," she said very softly, the cigarette lighter poised.

Frelaine struggled for breath. One part of him was able to realize detachedly what a marvelous actress she really was. She must have known all along.

Frelaine pushed the button, and the gun was in his hand, cocked and ready.

The blow that struck him in the chest knocked him over a coffee table. The gun fell out of his hand. Gasping, half-conscious, he watched her take careful aim for the *coup de grace.*

"Now I can join the Tens," he heard her say elatedly as she squeezed the trigger.

ROOMMATES
Harry Harrison

SUMMER

The August sun struck in through the open window and burned on
Andrew Rusch's bare legs until discomfort dragged him awake from
the depths of heavy sleep. Only slowly did he become aware of the heat
and the damp and gritty sheet beneath his body. He rubbed at his
gummed-shut eyelids, then lay there, staring up at the cracked and
stained plaster of the ceiling, only half awake and experiencing a feeling of dislocation, not knowing in those first waking moments just
where he was, although he had lived in this room for over seven years.
He yawned and the odd sensation slipped away while he groped for the
watch that he always put on the chair next to the bed, then he yawned
again as he blinked at the hands mistily seen behind the scratched
crystal. Seven . . . seven o'clock in the morning, and there was a little
number 9 in the middle of the square window. Monday the ninth of
August, 1999—and hot as a furnace already, with the city still imbedded in the heat wave that had baked and suffocated New York for the
past ten days. Andy scratched at a trickle of perspiration on his side,

Originally published in *The Ruins of Earth,* Putnam 1971. Copyright © 1971 by
Harry Harrison. Reprinted by permission of the author and the author's agent, Robert
P. Mills, Ltd.

then moved his legs out of the patch of sunlight and bunched the pillow up under his neck. From the other side of the thin partition that divided the room in half there came a clanking whir that quickly rose to a high-pitched drone.

"Morning . . ." he shouted over the sound, then began coughing. Still coughing he reluctantly stood and crossed the room to draw a glass of water from the wall tank; it came out in a thin, brownish trickle. He swallowed it, then rapped the dial on the tank with his knuckles and the needle bobbed up and down close to the *Empty* mark. It needed filling, he would have to see to that before he signed in at four o'clock at the precinct. The day had begun.

A full-length mirror with a crack running down it was fixed to the front of the hulking wardrobe and he poked his face close to it, rubbing at his bristly jaw. He would have to shave before he went in. No one should ever look at himself in the morning, naked and revealed, he decided with distaste, frowning at the dead white of his skin and the slight bow to his legs that was usually concealed by his pants. And how did he manage to have ribs that stuck out like those of a starved horse, as well as a growing potbelly—both at the same time? He kneaded the soft flesh and thought that it must be the starchy diet, that and sitting around on his chunk most of the time. But at least the fat wasn't showing on his face. His forehead was a little higher each year, but wasn't too obvious as long as his hair was cropped short. You have just turned 30, he thought to himself, and the wrinkles are already starting around your eyes. And your nose is too big—wasn't it Uncle Brian who always said that was because there was Welsh blood in the family? And your canine teeth are a little too obvious so when you smile you look a bit like a hyena. You're a handsome devil, Andy Rusch, and it's a wonder a girl like Shirl will even look at you, much less kiss you. He scowled at himself, then went to look for a handkerchief to blow his impressive Welsh nose.

There was just a single pair of clean undershorts in the drawer and he pulled them on; that was another thing he had to remember today, to get some washing done. The squealing whine was still coming from the other side of the partition as he pushed through the connecting door.

"You're going to give yourself a coronary, Sol," he told the gray-bearded man who was perched on the wheelless bicycle, pedaling so industriously that perspiration ran down his chest and soaked into the bath towel that he wore tied around his waist.

"Never a coronary," Solomon Kahn gasped out, pumping steadily. "I been doing this every day for so long that my ticker would miss it if I stopped. And no cholesterol in my arteries either since regular flushing with alcohol takes care of that. And no lung cancer since I couldn't afford to smoke even if I wanted to, which I don't. And at the age of 75 no prostatitis because. . . ."

"Sol, please—spare me the horrible details on an empty stomach. Do you have an ice cube to spare?"

"Take two—it's a hot day. And don't leave the door open too long."

Andy opened the small refrigerator that squatted against the wall and quickly took out the plastic container of margarine, then squeezed two ice cubes from the tray into a glass and slammed the door. He filled the glass with water from the wall tank and put it on the table next to the margarine. "Have you eaten yet?" he asked.

"I'll join you, these things should be charged by now."

Sol stopped pedaling and the whine died away to a moan, then vanished. He disconnected the wires from the electrical generator that was geared to the rear axle of the bike, and carefully coiled them up next to the four black automobile storage batteries that were racked on top of the refrigerator. Then, after wiping his hands on his soiled towel sarong, he pulled out one of the bucket seats, salvaged from an ancient 1975 Ford, and sat down across the table from Andy.

"I heard the six o'clock news," he said. "The Eldsters are organizing another protest march today on relief headquarters. *That's* where you'll see coronaries!"

"I won't, thank God, I'm not on until four and Union Square isn't in our precinct." He opened the breadbox and took out one of the six-inch-square red crackers, then pushed the box over to Sol. He spread margarine thinly on it and took a bite, wrinkling his nose as he chewed. "I think this margarine has turned."

"How can you tell?" Sol grunted, biting into one of the dry crackers. "Anything made from motor oil and whale blubber is turned to begin with."

"Now you begin to sound like a naturist," Andy said, washing his cracker down with cold water. "There's hardly any flavor at all to the fats made from petrochemicals and you know there aren't any whales left so they can't use blubber—it's just good chlorella oil."

"Whales, plankton, herring oil, it's all the same. Tastes fishy. I'll take mine dry so I don't grow no fins." There was a sudden staccato rapping on the door and he groaned. "Not yet eight o'clock and already they are after you."

"It could be anything," Andy said, starting for the door.

"It could be but it's not, that's the callboy's knock and you know it as well as I do and I bet you dollars to doughnuts that's just who it is. See?" He nodded with gloomy satisfaction when Andy unlocked the door and they saw the skinny, bare-legged messenger standing in the dark hall.

"What do you want, Woody?" Andy asked.

"I don' wan' no-fin," Woody lisped over his bare gums. Though he

was in his early twenties he didn't have a tooth in his head. "Lieutenan'
says bring, I bring." He handed Andy the message board with his name
written on the outside.

Andy turned toward the light and opened it, reading the lieutenant's spiky scrawl on the slate, then took the chalk and scribbled his
initials after it and returned it to the messenger. He closed the door
behind him and went back to finish his breakfast, frowning in thought.

"Don't look at me that way," Sol said, "I didn't send the message.
Am I wrong in guessing it's not the most pleasant of news?"

"It's the Eldsters, they're jamming the Square already and the
precinct needs reinforcements."

"But why you? This sounds like a job for the harness bulls."

"Harness bulls! Where do you get that medieval slang? Of course
they need patrolmen for the crowd, but there have to be detectives
there to spot known agitators, pickpockets, purse-grabbers and the
rest. It'll be murder in that park today. I have to check in by nine, so
I have enough time to bring up some water first."

Andy dressed slowly in slacks and a loose sport shirt, then put a
pan of water on the windowsill to warm in the sun. He took the two
five-gallon plastic jerry cans, and when he went out Sol looked up from
the TV set, glancing over the top of his old-fashioned glasses.

"When you bring back the water I'll fix you a drink—or do you
think it is too early?"

"Not the way I feel today, it's not."

The hall was ink black once the door had closed behind him and
he felt his way carefully along the wall to the stairs, cursing and almost
falling when he stumbled over a heap of refuse someone had thrown
there. Two flights down a window had been knocked through the wall
and enough light came in to show him the way down the last two flights
to the street. After the damp hallway the heat of Twenty-fifth Street
hit him in a musty wave, a stifling miasma compounded of decay, dirt
and unwashed humanity. He had to make his way through the women
who already filled the steps of the building, walking carefully so that
he didn't step on the children who were playing below. The sidewalk
was still in shadow but so jammed with people that he walked in the
street, well away from the curb to avoid the rubbish and litter banked
high there. Days of heat had softened the tar so that it gave underfoot,
then clutched at the soles of his shoes. There was the usual line leading
to the columnar red water point on the corner of Seventh Avenue, but
it broke up with angry shouts and some waved fists just as he reached
it. Still muttering, the crowd dispersed and Andy saw that the duty
patrolman was locking the steel door.

"What's going on?" Andy asked. "I thought this point was open
until noon?"

The policeman turned, his hand automatically staying close to his gun until he recognized the detective from his own precinct. He tilted back his uniform cap and wiped the sweat from his forehead with the back of his hand.

"Just had the orders from the sergeant, all points closed for 24 hours. The reservoir level is low because of the drought, they gotta save water."

"That's a hell of a note," Andy said, looking at the key still in the lock. "I'm going on duty now and this means I'm not going to be drinking for a couple of days. ...."

After a careful look around, the policeman unlocked the door and took one of the jerry cans from Andy. "One of these ought to hold you." He held it under the faucet while it filled, then lowered his voice. "Don't let it out, but the word is that there was another dynamiting job on the aqueduct upstate."

"Those farmers again?"

"It must be. I was on guard duty up there before I came to this precinct and it's rough, they just as soon blow you up with the aqueduct at the same time. Claim the city's stealing their water."

"They've got enough," Andy said, taking the full container. "More than they need. And there are 35 million people here in the city who get damn thirsty."

"Who's arguing?" the cop asked, slamming the door shut again and locking it tight.

Andy pushed his way back through the crowd around the steps and went through to the backyard first. All of the toilets were in use and he had to wait, and when he finally got into one of the cubicles he took the jerry cans with him; one of the kids playing in the pile of rubbish against the fence would be sure to steal them if he left them unguarded.

When he had climbed the dark flights once more and opened the door to the room he heard the clear sound of ice cubes rattling against glass.

"That's Beethoven's Fifth Symphony that you're playing," he said, dropping the containers and falling into a chair.

"It's my favorite tune," Sol said, taking two chilled glasses from the refrigerator and, with the solemnity of a religious ritual, dropped a tiny pearl onion into each. He passed one to Andy, who sipped carefully at the chilled liquid.

"It's when I taste one of these, Sol, that I almost believe you're not crazy after all. Why do they call them Gibsons?"

"A secret lost behind the mists of time. Why is a Stinger a Stinger or a Pink Lady a Pink Lady?"

"I don't know—why? I never tasted any of them."

"I don't know either, but that's the name. Like those green things they serve in the knockjoints, Panamas. Doesn't mean anything, just a name."

"Thanks," Andy said, draining his glass. "The day looks better already."

He went into his room and took his gun and holster from the drawer and clipped it inside the waistband of his pants. His shield was on his key ring where he always kept it and he slipped his notepad in on top of it, then hesitated a moment. It was going to be a long and rough day and anything might happen. He dug his nippers out from under his shirts, then the soft plastic tube filled with shot. It might be needed in the crowd, safer than a gun with all those old people milling about. Not only that, but with the new austerity regulations you had to have a damn good reason for using up any ammunition. He washed as well as he could with the pint of water that had been warming in the sun on the windowsill, then scrubbed his face with the small shard of gray and gritty soap until his whiskers softened a bit. His razor blade was beginning to show obvious nicks along both edges and, as he honed it against the inside of his drinking glass, he thought that it was time to think about getting a new one. Maybe in the fall.

Sol was watering his window box when Andy came out, carefully irrigating the rows of herbs and tiny onions. "Don't take any wooden nickels," he said without looking up from his work. Sol had a million of them, all old. What in the world was a wooden nickel?

The sun was higher now and the heat was mounting in the sealed tar and concrete valley of the street. The band of shade was smaller and the steps were so packed with humanity that he couldn't leave the doorway. He carefully pushed by a tiny, runny-nosed girl dressed only in ragged gray underwear and descended a step. The gaunt women moved aside reluctantly, ignoring him, but the men stared at him with a cold look of hatred stamped across their features that gave them a strangely alike appearance, as though they were all members of the same angry family. Andy threaded his way through the last of them and when he reached the sidewalk he had to step over the outstretched leg of an old man who sprawled there. He looked dead, not asleep, and he might be for all that anyone cared. His foot was bare and filthy and a string tied about his ankle led to a naked baby that was sitting vacantly on the sidewalk chewing on a bent plastic dish. The baby was as dirty as the man and the string was tied about its chest under the pipestem arms because its stomach was swollen and heavy. Was the old man dead? Not that it mattered, the only work he had to do in the world was to act as an anchor for the baby and he could do that job just as well alive or dead.

Out of the room now, well away and unable to talk to Sol until he returned, he realized that once again he had not managed to mention Shirl. It would have been a simple enough thing to do, but he kept forgetting it, avoiding it. Sol was always talking about how horny he always was and how often he used to get laid when he was in the army. He would understand.

They were roommates, that was all. There was nothing else between them. Friends, sure. But bringing a girl in to live wouldn't change that.

So why hadn't he told him?

FALL

"Everybody says this is the coldest October ever, I never seen a colder one. And the rain too, never hard enough to fill the reservoir or anything, but just enough to make you wet so you feel colder. Ain't that right?"

Shirl nodded, hardly listening to the words, but aware by the rising intonation of the woman's voice that a question had been asked. The line moved forward and she shuffled a few steps behind the woman who had been speaking—a shapeless bundle of heavy clothing covered with a torn plastic raincoat, with a cord tied about her middle so that she resembled a lumpy sack. Not that I look much better, Shirl thought, tugging the fold of blanket farther over her head to keep out the persistent drizzle. It wouldn't be much longer now, there were only a few dozen people ahead, but it had taken a lot more time than she thought it would; it was almost dark. A light came on over the tank car, glinting off its black sides and lighting up the slowly falling curtain of rain. The line moved again and the woman ahead of Shirl waddled forward, pulling the child after her, a bundle as wrapped and shapeless as its mother, its face hidden by a knotted scarf, that produced an almost constant whimpering.

"Stop that," the woman said. She turned to Shirl, her puffy face a red lumpiness around the dark opening of her almost toothless mouth. "He's crying because he's been to see the doc, thinks he's sick but it's only the kwash." She held up the child's swollen, ballooning hand. "You can tell when they swell up and get the black spots on the knees. Had to sit two weeks in the Bellevue clinic to see a doc who told me what I knew already. But that's the only way you get him to sign the slip. Got a peanut-butter ration that way. My old man loves the stuff. You live on my block, don't you? I think I seen you there?"

"Twenty-sixth Street," Shirl said, taking the cap off the jerry can and putting it into her coat pocket. She felt chilled through and was sure she was catching a cold.

"That's right, I knew it was you. Stick around and wait for me, we'll walk back together. It's getting late and plenty of punks would like to grab the water, they can always sell it. Mrs. Ramirez in my building, she's a spic but she's all right, you know, her family been in the building since the World War Two, she got a black eye so swole up she can't see through it and two teeth knocked out. Some punk got her with a club and took her water away."

"Yes, I'll wait for you, that's a good idea," Shirl said, suddenly feeling very alone.

"Cards," the patrolman said and she handed him the three Welfare cards, hers, Andy's and Sol's. He held them to the light, then handed them back to her. "Six quarts," he called out to the valve man.

"That's not right," Shirl said.

"Reduced ration today, lady, keep moving, there's a lot of people waiting."

She held out the jerry can and the valve man slipped the end of a large funnel into it and ran in the water. "Next," he called out.

The jerry can gurgled when she walked and was tragically light. She went and stood near the policeman until the woman came up, pulling the child with one hand and in the other carrying a five-gallon kerosene can that seemed almost full. She must have a big family.

"Let's go," the woman said and the child trailed, mewling faintly, at the end of her arm.

As they left the Twelfth Avenue railroad siding it grew darker, the rain soaking up all the failing light. The buildings here were mostly old warehouses and factories with blank solid walls concealing the tenants hidden away inside, the sidewalks wet and empty. The nearest streetlight was a block away. "My husband will give me hell coming home this late," the woman said as they turned the corner. Two figures blocked the sidewalk in front of them.

"Let's have the water," the nearest one said, and the distant light reflected from the knife he held before him.

"No, don't! Please don't!" the woman begged and swung her can of water out behind her, away from them. Shirl huddled against the wall and saw, when they walked forward, that they were just young boys, teen-agers. But they still had a knife.

"The water!" the first one said, jabbing his knife at the woman.

"Take it," she screeched, swinging the can like a weight on the end of her arm. Before the boy could dodge it caught him full in the side of the head, knocking him howling to the ground, the knife flying from his fingers. "You want some too?" she shouted, advancing on the second boy. He was unarmed.

"No, I don't want no trouble," he begged, pulling at the first one's arm, then retreating when she approached. When she bent to pick up the fallen knife, he managed to drag the other boy to his feet and half carry him around the corner. It had only taken a few seconds and all the time Shirl had stood with her back to the wall, trembling with fear.

"They got some surprise," the woman crowed, holding the worn carving knife up to admire it. "I can use this better than they can. Just punks, kids." She was excited and happy. During the entire time she had never released her grip on the child's hand; it was sobbing louder.

There was no more trouble and the woman went with Shirl as far as her door. "Thank you very much," Shirl said. "I don't know what I would have done. . . ."

"That's no trouble," the woman beamed. "You saw what I did to him—and who got the knife now!" She stamped away, hauling the heavy can in one hand, the child in the other. Shirl went in.

"Where have you been?" Andy asked when she pushed open the door. "I was beginning to wonder what had happened to you." It was warm in the room, with a faint odor of fishy smoke, and he and Sol were sitting at the table with drinks in their hands.

"It was the water, the line must have been a block long. They only gave me six quarts, the ration has been cut again." She saw his black look and decided not to tell him about the trouble on the way back. He would be twice as angry then and she didn't want this meal to be spoiled.

"That's really wonderful," Andy said sarcastically. "The ration was already too small—so now they lower it even more. Better get out of those wet things, Shirl, and Sol will pour you a Gibson. His homemade vermouth has ripened and I bought some vodka."

"Drink up," Sol said, handing her the chilled glass. "I made some soup with that ener-G junk, it's the only way it's edible, and it should be just about ready. We'll have that for the first course, before—" He finished the sentence by jerking his head in the direction of the refrigerator.

"What's up?" Andy asked. "A secret?"

"No secret," Shirl said, opening the refrigerator, "just a surprise. I got these today in the market, one for each of us." She took out a plate with three small soylent burgers on it. "They're the new ones, they had them on TV, with the smoky-barbecue flavor."

"They must have cost a fortune," Andy said. "We won't eat for the rest of the month."

"They're not as expensive as all that. Anyway, it was my own money, not the budget money, I used."

"It doesn't make any difference, money is money. We could probably live for a week on what these things cost."

"Soup's on," Sol said, sliding the plates onto the table. Shirl had a lump in her throat so she couldn't say anything; she sat and looked at her plate and tried not to cry.

"I'm sorry," Andy said. "But you know how prices are going up—

we have to look ahead. City income tax is higher, 80 percent now, because of the raised Welfare payment, so it's going to be rough going this winter. Don't think I don't appreciate it. . . ."

"If you do, so why don't you shut up right there and eat your soup?" Sol said.

"Keep out of this, Sol," Andy said.

"I'll keep out of it when you keep the fight out of my room. Now come on, a nice meal like this, it shouldn't be spoiled."

Andy started to answer him, then changed his mind. He reached over and took Shirl's hand. "It is going to be a good dinner," he said. "Let's all enjoy it."

"Not that good," Sol said, puckering his mouth over a spoonful of soup. "Wait until you try this stuff. But the burgers will take the taste out of our mouths."

There was silence after that while they spooned up the soup, until Sol started on one of his army stories about New Orleans and it was so impossible they had to laugh, and after that things were better. Sol shared out the rest of the Gibsons while Shirl served the burgers.

"If I was drunk enough this would almost taste like meat," Sol announced, chewing happily.

"They are good," Shirl said. Andy nodded agreement. She finished the burger quickly and soaked up the juice with a scrap of weedcracker, then sipped at her drink. The trouble on the way home with the water already seemed far distant. What was it the woman had said was wrong with the child?

"Do you know what 'kwash' is?" she asked.

Andy shrugged. "Some kind of disease, that's all I know. Why do you ask?"

"There was a woman next to me in line for the water, I was talking to her. She had a little boy with her who was sick with this kwash. I don't think she should have had him out in the rain, sick like that. And I was wondering if it was catching."

"That you can forget about," Sol said. " 'Kwash' is short for 'kwashiorkor.' If, in the interest of good health, you watched the medical programs like I do, or opened a book, you would know all about it. You can't catch it because it's a deficiency disease like beriberi."

"I never heard of that either," Shirl said.

"There's not so much of that, but there's plenty of kwash. It comes from not eating enough protein. They used to have it only in Africa but now they got it right across the whole U.S. Isn't that great? There's no meat around, lentils and soybeans cost too much, so the mamas stuff the kids with weedcrackers and candy, whatever is cheap. . . ."

The light bulb flickered, then went out. Sol felt his way across the

room and found a switch in the maze of wiring on top of the refrigerator. A dim bulb lit up, connected to his batteries. "Needs a charge," he
said, "but it can wait until morning. You shouldn't exercise after eating, bad for the circulation and digestion."

"I'm sure glad you're here, doctor," Andy said. "I need some medical advice. I've got this trouble. You see—everything I eat goes to my
stomach. . . ."

"Very funny, Mr. Wiseguy. Shirl, I don't see how you put up with
this joker."

They all felt better after the meal and they talked for a while, until
Sol announced he was turning off the light to save the juice in the
batteries. The small bricks of sea coal had burned to ash and the room
was growing cold. They said good night and Andy went in first to get
his flashlight; their room was even colder than the other.

"I'm going to bed," Shirl said. "I'm not really tired, but it's the only
way to keep warm."

Andy flicked the overhead light switch uselessly. "The current is
still off and there are some things I have to do. What is it—a week now
since we had any electricity in the evening?"

"Let me get into bed and I'll work the flash for you—will that be
all right?"

"It'll have to do."

He opened his notepad on top of the dresser, lay one of the reusable
forms next to it, then began copying information into the report. With
his left hand he kept a slow and regular squeezing on the flashlight that
produced steady illumination. The city was quiet tonight with the
people driven from the streets by the cold and the rain; the whir of the
tiny generator and the occasional squeak of the stylo on plastic sounded
unnaturally loud. There was enough light from the flash for Shirl to
get undressed by. She shivered when she took off her outer clothes and
quickly pulled on heavy winter pajamas, a much-darned pair of socks
she used for sleeping in, then put her heavy sweater on top. The sheets
were cold and damp, they hadn't been changed since the water short-
age, though she did try to air them out as often as she could. Her cheeks
were damp, as damp as the sheets were when she put her fingertips up
to touch them, and she realized that she was crying. She tried not to
sniffle and bother Andy. He was doing his best, wasn't he? Everything
that it was possible to do. Yes, it had been a lot different before she
came here, an easy life, good food and a warm room, and her own
bodyguard, Tab, when she went out. And all she had to do was sleep
with him a couple of times a week. She had hated it, even the touch of
his hands, but at least it had been quick. Having Andy in bed was
different and good and she wished that he were there right now. She
shivered again and wished she could stop crying.

WINTER

New York City trembled on the brink of disaster. Every locked warehouse was a nucleus of dissent, surrounded by crowds who were hungry and afraid and searching for someone to blame. Their anger incited them to riot, and the food riots turned to water riots and then to looting, wherever this was possible. The police fought back, only the thinnest of barriers between angry protest and bloody chaos.

At first nightsticks and weighted clubs stopped the trouble, and when this failed gas dispersed the crowds. The tension grew, since the people who fled only reassembled again in a different place. The solid jets of water from the riot trucks stopped them easily when they tried to break into the welfare stations, but there were not enough trucks, nor was there more water to be had once they had pumped dry their tanks. The Health Department had forbid the use of river water: it would have been like spraying poison. The little water that was available was badly needed for the fires that were springing up throughout the city. With the streets blocked in many places the fire-fighting equipment could not get through and the trucks were forced to make long detours. Some of the fires were spreading and by noon all of the equipment had been committed and was in use.

The first gun was fired a few minutes past 12 on the morning of December 21st, by a Welfare Department guard who killed a man who had broken open a window of the Tompkins Square food depot and had tried to climb in. This was the first but not the last shot fired—nor was it the last person to be killed.

Flying wire sealed off some of the trouble areas, but there was only a limited supply of it. When it ran out the copters fluttered helplessly over the surging streets and acted as aerial observation posts for the police, finding the places where reserves were sorely needed. It was a fruitless labor because there were no reserves, everyone was in the front line.

After the first conflict nothing else made a strong impression on Andy. For the rest of the day and most of the night, he along with every other policeman in the city was braving violence and giving violence to restore law and order to a city torn by battle. The only rest he had was after he had fallen victim to his own gas and had managed to make his way to the Department of Hospitals ambulance for treatment. An orderly washed out his eyes and gave him a tablet to counteract the gut-tearing nausea. He lay on one of the stretchers inside, clutching his helmet, bombs and club to his chest, while he recovered. The ambulance driver sat on another stretcher by the door, armed with a .30-caliber carbine, to discourage anyone from too great an interest in the ambulance or its valuable surgical contents. Andy would like to have lain there longer, but the cold mist was rolling in through the open doorway, and he began to shiver so hard that his teeth shook together. It was difficult to drag to his feet and climb to the ground, yet once he was moving he felt a little better—and warmer. The attack had been broken up and he moved slowly to join the nearest cluster of blue-coated figures, wrinkling his nose at the foul odor of his clothes.

From this point on, the fatigue never left him and he had memories only of shouting faces, running feet, the sound of shots, screams, the thud of gas grenades, of something unseen that had been thrown at him and hit the back of his hand and raised an immense bruise.

By nightfall it was raining, a cold downpour mixed with sleet, and it was this and exhaustion that drove the people from the streets, not the police. Yet when the crowds were gone the police found that their work was just beginning. Gaping windows and broken doorways had to be guarded until they could be repaired, the injured had to be found and brought in for treatment, while the Fire Department needed aid in halting the countless fires. This went on through the night and at dawn Andy found himself slumped on a bench in the precinct, hearing his name being called off from a list by Lieutenant Grassioli.

"And that's all that can be spared," the lieutenant added. "You men draw rations before you leave and turn in your riot equipment. I want you all back here at eighteen-hundred and I don't want excuses. Our troubles aren't over yet."

Sometime during the night the rain had stopped. The rising sun cast long shadows down the crosstown streets, putting a golden sheen on the wet, black pavement. A burned-out brownstone was still smoking and Andy picked his way through the charred wreckage that littered the street in front of it. On the corner of Seventh Avenue were the crushed wrecks of two pedicabs, already stripped of any usable parts, and a few feet farther on, the huddled body of a man. He might be asleep, but when Andy passed, the upturned face gave violent evidence that the man was dead. He walked on, ignoring it. The Department of Sanitation would be collecting only corpses today.

The first cavemen were coming out of the subway entrance, blinking at the light. During the summer everyone laughed at the cavemen —the people whom Welfare had assigned to living quarters in the stations of the now-silent subways—but as the cold weather approached, the laughter was replaced by envy. Perhaps it was filthy down there, dusty, dark, but there were always a few electric heaters turned on. They weren't living in luxury, but at least Welfare didn't let them freeze. Andy turned into his own block.

Going up the stairs in his building, he trod heavily on some of the sleepers but was too fatigued to care—or even notice. He had trouble fumbling his key into the lock and Sol heard him and came to open it.

"I just made some soup," Sol said. "You timed it perfectly."

Andy pulled the broken remains of some weedcrackers from his coat pocket and spilled them onto the table.

"Been stealing food?" Sol asked, picking up a piece and nibbling on it. "I thought no grub was being given out for two more days?"

"Police ration."

"Only fair. You can't beat up the citizenry on an empty stomach. I'll throw some of these into the soup, give it some body. I guess you didn't see TV yesterday so you wouldn't know about all the fun and games in Congress. Things are really jumping. . . ."

"Is Shirl awake yet?" Andy asked, shucking out of his coat and dropping heavily into a chair.

Sol was silent a moment, then he said slowly, "She's not here."

Andy yawned. "It's pretty early to go out. Why?"

"Not today, Andy." Sol stirred the soup with his back turned. "She went out yesterday, a couple of hours after you did. She's not back yet —"

"You mean she was out all the time during the riots—and last night too? What did you do?" He sat upright, his bone-weariness forgotten.

"What could I do? Go out and get myself trampled to death like the rest of the old fogies? I bet she's all right, she probably saw all the trouble and decided to stay with friends instead of coming back here."

"What friends? What are you talking about? I have to go find her."

"Sit!" Sol ordered. "What can you do out there? Have some soup and get some sleep, that's the best thing you can do. She'll be okay. I know it," he added reluctantly.

"What do you know, Sol?" Andy took him by the shoulders, half turning him from the stove.

"Don't handle the merchandise!" Sol shouted, pushing the hand away. Then, in a quieter voice: "All I know is she just didn't go out of here for nothing, she had a reason. She had her old coat on, but I could see what looked like a real nifty dress underneath. And nylon stockings. A fortune on her legs. And when she said so long I saw she had lots of makeup on."

"Sol—what are you trying to say?"

"I'm not trying—I'm saying. She was dressed for visiting, not for shopping, like she was on the way out to see someone. Her old man, maybe, she could be visiting him."

"Why should she want to see him?"

"You tell me? You two had a fight, didn't you? Maybe she went away for a while to cool off."

"A fight . . . I guess so." Andy dropped back into the chair, squeezing his forehead with his palms. Had it only been last night? No, the

night before last. It seemed 100 years since they had had that stupid
argument. But they were bickering so much these days. One more fight
shouldn't make any difference. He looked up with sudden fear. "She
didn't take her things—anything with her?" he asked.

"Just a little bag," Sol said, and put a steaming bowl on the table
in front of Andy. "Eat up. I'll pour one for myself." Then, "She'll be
back."

Andy was almost too tired to argue—and what could be said? He
spooned the soup automatically, then realized as he tasted it that he
was very hungry. He ate with his elbow on the table, his free hand
supporting his head.

"You should have heard the speeches in the Senate yesterday," Sol
said. "Funniest show on earth. They're trying to push this Emergency
Bill through—some emergency, it's only been 100 years in the making
—and you should hear them talking all around the little points and not
mentioning the big ones." His voice settled into a rich Southern accent.
"Faced by dire straits, we propose a survey of all the ee-mense riches
of this the greatest ee-luvial basin, the delta, suh, of the mightiest of
rivers, the Mississippi. Dikes and drains, suh, science, suh, and you will
have here the richest farmlands in the Western World!" Sol blew on
his soup angrily. " 'Dikes' is right—another finger in the dike. They've
been over this ground a thousand times before. But does anyone mention out loud the sole and only reason for the Emergency Bill? They do
not. After all these years they're too chicken to come right out and tell
the truth, so they got it hidden away in one of the little riders tacked
onto the bottom."

"What are you talking about?" Andy asked, only half listening,
still worrying about Shirl.

"Birth control, that's what. They are finally getting around to
legalizing clinics that will be open to anyone—married or not—and
making it a law that all mothers *must* be supplied with birth-control
information. Boy, are we going to hear some howling when the blue-
noses find out about that—and the Pope will really plotz!"

"Not now, Sol, I'm tired. Did Shirl say anything about when she
would be back?"

"Just what I told you. . . ." He stopped and listened to the sound
of footsteps coming down the hall. They stopped—and there was a light
knocking on the door.

Andy was there first, twisting at the knob, tearing the door open.
"Shirl!" he said. "Are you all right?"

"Yes, sure—I'm fine."

He held her to him, tightly, almost cutting off her breath. "With
the riots—I didn't know what to think," he said. "I just came in a little
while ago myself. Where have you been? What happened?"

"I just wanted to get out for a while, that's all. She wrinkled her nose. "What's that funny smell?"

He stepped away from her, anger welling up through the fatigue. "I caught some of my own puke gas and heaved up. It's hard to get off. What do you mean that you wanted to get out for a while?"

"Let me get my coat off."

Andy followed her into the other room and closed the door behind them. She was taking a pair of high-heeled shoes out of the bag she carried and putting them into the closet. "Well?" he said.

"Just that, it's not complicated. I was feeling trapped in here, with the shortages and the cold and everything, and never seeing you, and I felt bad about the fight we had. Nothing seemed to be going right. So I thought if I dressed up and went to one of the restaurants where I used to go, just have a cup of kofee or something, I might feel better. A morale booster, you know." She looked up at his cold face, then glanced quickly away.

"Then what happened?" he asked.

"I'm not in the witness box, Andy. Why the accusing tone?"

He turned his back and looked out the window. "I'm not accusing you of anything, but—you were out all night. How do you expect me to feel?"

"Well, you know how bad it was yesterday, I was afraid to come back. I was up at Curley's—"

"The meateasy?"

"Yes, but if you don't eat anything it's not expensive. It's just the food that costs. I met some people I knew and we talked, they were going to a party and invited me and I went along. We were watching the news about the riots on TV and no one wanted to go out, so the party just went on and on." She paused. "That's all."

"All?" An angry question, a dark suspicion.

"That's all," she said, and her voice was now as cold as his.

She turned her back to him and began to pull off her dress, and their words lay like a cold barrier between them. Andy dropped onto the bed and turned his back on her as well so that they were like strangers, even in the tiny room.

SPRING

The funeral drew them together as nothing else had during the cold depths of the winter. It was a raw day, gusting wind and rain, but there was still a feeling that winter was on the way out. But it had been too long a winter for Sol and his cough had turned into a cold, the cold into pneumonia, and what can an old man do in a cold room without drugs in a winter that does not seem to end? Die, that was all, so he had died. They had forgotten their differences during his illness and Shirl had nursed him as best she could, but careful nursing does not cure pneumonia. The funeral had been as brief and cold as the day and in the early darkness they went back to the room. They had not been back a half an hour before there was a quick rapping on the door. Shirl gasped.

"The callboy. They can't. You don't have to work today."

"Don't worry. Even Grassy wouldn't go back on his word about a thing like this. And besides, that's not the callboy's knock."

"Maybe a friend of Sol's who couldn't get to the funeral."

She went to unlock the door and had to blink into the darkness of the hall for a moment before she recognized the man standing there.

"Tab! It is you, isn't it? Come in, don't stand there. Andy, I told you about Tab my bodyguard. . . ."

"Afternoon, Miss Shirl," Tab said stolidly, staying in the hall. "I'm sorry, but this is no social call. I'm on the job now."

"What is it?" Andy asked, walking over next to Shirl.

"You have to realize I take the work that is offered to me," Tab said. He was unsmiling and gloomy. "I've been in the bodyguard pool since September, just the odd jobs, no regular assignment, we take whatever work we can get. A man turns down a job he goes right back to the end of the list. I have a family to feed. . . ."

"What are you trying to say?" Andy asked. He was aware that someone was standing in the darkness behind Tab and he could tell by the shuffle of feet that there were others out of sight down the hall.

"Don't take no stuff," the man in back of Tab said in an unpleasant nasal voice. He stayed behind the bodyguard where he could not be seen. "I got the law on my side. I paid you. Show him the order!"

"I think I understand now," Andy said. "Get away from the door, Shirl. Come inside, Tab, so we can talk to you."

Tab started forward and the man in the hall tried to follow him. "You don't go in there without me—" he shrilled. His voice was cut off as Andy slammed the door in his face.

"I wish you hadn't done that," Tab said. He was wearing his spike-studded iron knucks, his fist clenched tight around them.

"Relax," Andy said. "I just wanted to talk to you alone first, find out what was going on. He has a squat-order, doesn't he?"

Tab nodded, looking unhappily down at the floor.

"What on earth are you two talking about?" Shirl asked, worriedly glancing back and forth at their set expressions.

Andy didn't answer and Tab turned to her. "A squat-order is issued by the court to anyone who can prove they are really in need of a place to live. They only give so many out, and usually just to people with big families that have had to get out of some other place. With a squat-order you can look around and find a vacant apartment or room or anything like that, and the order is a sort of search warrant. There can be trouble, people don't want to have strangers walking in on them, that kind of thing, so anyone with a squat-order takes along a body-guard. That's where I come in, the party out there in the hall, name of Belicher, hired me."

"But what are you doing here?" Shirl asked, still not understanding.

"Because Belicher is a ghoul, that's why," Andy said bitterly. "He hangs around the morgue looking for bodies."

"That's one way of saying it," Tab answered, holding on to his temper. "He's also a guy with a wife and kids and no place to live, that's another way of looking at it."

There was a sudden hammering on the door and Belicher's complaining voice could be heard outside. Shirl finally realized the significance of Tab's presence, and she gasped. "You're here because you're helping them," she said. "They found out that Sol is dead and they want this room."

Tab could only nod mutely.

"There's still a way out," Andy said. "If we had one of the men here from my precinct, living in here, then these people couldn't get in."

The knocking was louder and Tab took a half step backward toward the door. "If there was somebody here now, that would be okay, but Belicher could probably take the thing to the squat court and get occupancy anyway because he has a family. I'll do what I can to help you—but Belicher, he's still my employer."

"Don't open that door," Andy said sharply. "Not until we have this straightened out."

"I have to—what else can I do?" He straightened up and closed his fist with the knucks on it. "Don't try to stop me, Andy. You're a policeman, you know the law about this."

"Tab, must you?" Shirl asked in a low voice.

He turned to her, eyes filled with unhappiness. "We were good friends once, Shirl, and that's the way I'm going to remember it. But you're not going to think much of me after this because I have to do my job. I have to let them in."

"Go ahead—open the damn door," Andy said bitterly, turning his back and walking over to the window.

The Belichers swarmed in. Mr. Belicher was thin, with a strangely shaped head, almost no chin and just enough intelligence to sign his name to the Welfare application. Mrs. Belicher was the support of the family; from the flabby fat of her body came the children, all seven of them, to swell the Relief allotment on which they survived. Number eight was pushing an extra bulge out of the dough of her flesh; it was really number 11 since three of the younger Belichers had perished through indifference or accident. The largest girl, she must have been all of 12, was carrying the sore-covered infant which stank abominably and cried continuously. The other children shouted at each other now, released from the silence and tension of the dark hall.

"Oh, looka the nice fridge," Mrs. Belicher said, waddling over and opening the door.

"Don't touch that," Andy said, and Belicher pulled him by the arm.

"I like this room—it's not big, you know, but nice. What's in here?" He started toward the open door in the partition.

"That's my room," Andy said, slamming it shut in his face. "Just keep out of there."

"No need to act like that," Belicher said, sidling away quickly like a dog that has been kicked too often. "I got my rights. The law says I can look wherever I want with a squat-order." He moved farther away as Andy took a step toward him. "Not that I'm doubting your word, mister, I believe you. This room here is fine, got a good table, chairs, bed. . . ."

"Those things belong to me. This is an empty room, and a small one at that. It's not big enough for you and all your family."

"It's big enough, all right. We lived in smaller. . . ."

"Andy—stop them! Look—" Shirl's unhappy cry spun Andy around and he saw that two of the boys had found the packets of herbs that Sol had grown so carefully in his window box, and were tearing them open, thinking that it was food of some kind.

"Put these things down," he shouted, but before he could reach them they had tasted the herbs, then spat them out.

"Burn my mouth!" the bigger boy screamed and sprayed the contents of the packet on the floor. The other boy bounced up and down with excitement and began to do the same thing with the rest of the herbs. They twisted away from Andy and before he could stop them the packets were empty.

As soon as Andy turned away, the younger boy, still excited, climbed on the table—his mud-stained foot wrappings leaving filthy smears—and turned up the TV. Blaring music crashed over the screams of the children and the ineffectual calls of their mother. Tab pulled Belicher away as he opened the wardrobe to see what was inside.

"Get these kids out of here," Andy said, white-faced with rage.

"I got a squat-order, I got rights," Belicher shouted, backing away and waving an imprinted square of plastic.

"I don't care what rights you have," Andy told him, opening the hall door. "We'll talk about that when these brats are outside."

Tab settled it by grabbing the nearest child by the scruff of the neck and pushing it out through the door. "Mr. Rusch is right," he said. "The kids can wait outside while we settle this."

Mrs. Belicher sat down heavily on the bed and closed her eyes, as though all this had nothing to do with her. Mr. Belicher retreated against the wall saying something that no one heard or bothered to listen to. There were some shrill cries and angry sobbing from the hall as the last child was expelled.

Andy looked around and realized that Shirl had gone into their room; he heard the key turn in the lock. "I suppose this is it?" he said, looking steadily at Tab.

The bodyguard shrugged helplessly. "I'm sorry, Andy, honest to God I am. What else can I do? It's the law, and if they want to stay here you can't get them out."

"It's the law, it's the law," Belicher echoed tonelessly.

There was nothing Andy could do with his clenched fists and he had to force himself to open them. "Help me carry these things into the other room, will you, Tab?"

"Sure," Tab said, and took the other end of the table. "Try and explain to Shirl about my part in this, will you? I don't think she understands that it's just a job I have to do."

Their footsteps crackled on the dried herbs and seeds that littered the floor and Andy did not answer him.

MR COSTELLO, HERO
Theodore Sturgeon

"Come in, Purser. And shut the door."

"I beg your pardon, sir?" The Skipper never invited anyone in—
not to his quarters. His office, yes, but not here.

He made an abrupt gesture, and I came in and closed the door. It
was about as luxurious as a compartment on a spaceship can get. I tried
not to goggle at it as if it was the first time I had ever seen it, just
because it was the first time I had ever seen it.

I sat down.

He opened his mouth, closed it, forced the tip of his tongue through
his thin lips. He licked them and glared at me. I'd never seen the Iron
Man like this. I decided that the best thing to say would be nothing,
which is what I said.

He pulled a deck of cards out of the top-middle drawer and slid
them across the desk. "Deal."

I said, "I b—"

"And don't say you beg my pardon!" he exploded.

Well, all right. If the skipper wanted a cosy game of gin rummy to
while away the parsecs, far be it from me to ... I shuffled. Six years
under this cold-blooded, fish-eyed automatic computer with eyebrows,
and this was the first time that he—

First appeared in *Galaxy Science Fiction,* December, 1953. Reprinted by permission
of the author.

"Deal," he said. I looked up at him. "Draw, five-card draw. You do play draw poker, don't you, Purser?"

"Yes, sir." I dealt and put down the pack. I had three threes and a couple of court cards. The skipper scowled at his hand and threw down two. He glared at me again.

I said, "I got three of a kind, sir."

He let his cards go as if they no longer existed, slammed out of his chair, and turned his back to me. He tilted his head back and stared up at the see-it-all, with its complex of speed, time, position, and distance-run coordinates. Borinquen, our destination planet, was at spitting distance—only a day or so off—and Earth was a long, long way behind. I heard a sound and dropped my eyes. The Skipper's hands were locked behind him, squeezed together so hard that they crackled.

"Why didn't you draw?" he grated.

"I beg your—"

"When *I* played poker—and I used to play a hell of a lot of poker —as I recall it, the dealer would find out how many cards each player wanted after the deal and give him as many as he discarded. Did you ever hear of that, Purser?"

"Yes, sir, I did."

"You *did.*" He turned around. I imagine he had been scowling this same way at the see-it-all, and I wondered why it was he hadn't shattered the cover glass.

"Why, then, Purser," he demanded, "did you show your three of a kind without discarding, without drawing—without, mister, asking me how many cards I might want?"

I thought about it. "I—we—I mean, sir, we haven't been playing poker that way lately."

"You've been playing draw poker without drawing!" He sat down again and beamed that glare at me again. "And who changed the rules?"

"I don't know, sir. We just—that's the way we've been playing."

He nodded thoughtfully. "Now tell me something, Purser. How much time did you spend in the galley during the last watch?"

"About an hour, sir."

"About an hour."

"Well, sir," I explained hurriedly, "it was my turn."

He said nothing, and it suddenly occurred to me that these galley-watches weren't in the ship's orders.

I said quickly, "It isn't *against* your orders to stand such a watch, is it, sir?"

"No," he said, "it isn't." His voice was so gentle, it was ugly. "Tell me, Purser, doesn't Cooky mind these galley-watches?"

"Oh, no, sir! He's real pleased about it." I knew he was thinking

about the size of the galley. It was true that two men made quite a
crowd in a place like that. I said, "That way, he knows everybody can
trust him."

"You mean that way you know he won't poison you."

"Well—yes, sir."

"And tell me," he said, his voice even gentler, "who suggested he
might poison you?"

"I really can't say, Captain. It's just sort of something that came
up. Cooky doesn't mind." I added. "If he's watched all the time, he
knows nobody's going to suspect him. It's all right."

Again he repeated my words.

"It's all right." I wished he wouldn't. I wished he'd stop looking at
me like that. "How long," he asked, "has it been customary for the deck
officer to bring a witness with him when he takes over the watch?"

"I really couldn't say, sir. That's out of my department."

"You couldn't say. Now think hard, Purser. Did you ever stard
galley-watches, or see deck-officers bring witnesses with them when
they relieve the bridge, or see draw poker played without drawing—
before this trip?"

"Well, no, sir. I don't think I have. I suppose we just never thought
of it before."

"We never had Mr Costello as a passenger before, did we?"

"No, sir."

I thought for a moment he was going to say something else, but he
didn't, just: "Very well, Purser. That will be all."

I went out and started back aft, feeling puzzled and sort of upset.
The Skipper didn't have to hint things like that about Mr Costello. Mr
Costello was a very nice man. Once, the Skipper had picked a fight with
Mr Costello. They'd shouted at each other in the day-room. That is, the
Skipper had shouted—Mr Costello never did. Mr Costello was as good-
natured as they come. A good-natured soft-spoken man, with the kind
of face they call open. Open and honest. He'd once been a Triumver
back on Earth—the youngest ever appointed, they said.

You wouldn't think such an easy-going man was as smart as that.
Triumvers are usually life-time appointments, but Mr Costello wasn't
satisfied. Had to keep moving, you know. Learning all the time, shaking hands all around, staying close to the people. He loved people.

I don't know why the Skipper couldn't get along with him. Everybody else did. And besides—Mr Costello didn't play poker; why should
he care one way or the other how *we* played it? He didn't eat the galley
food—he had his own stock in his cabin—so what difference would it
make to him if the cook poisoned anyone? Except, of course, that he
cared about *us*. People—he *liked* people.

Anyway, it's better to play poker without the draw. Poker's a good
game with a bad reputation. And where do you suppose it gets the bad

reputation? From cheaters. And how do people cheat at poker? Almost never when they deal. It's when they pass out cards after the discard. That's when a shady dealer knows what he holds, and he knows what to give the others so he can win. All right, remove the discard and you remove nine-tenths of the cheaters. Remove the cheaters and the honest men can trust each other.

That's what Mr Costello used to say, anyhow. Not that he cared one way or the other for himself. He wasn't a gambling man.

I went into the day-room and there was Mr Costello with the Third Officer. He gave me a big smile and a wave, so I went over.

"Come on, sit down, Purser," he said. "I'm landing tomorrow. Won't have much more chance to talk to you."

I sat down. The Third snapped shut a book he'd been holding open on the table and sort of got it out of sight.

Mr Costello laughed at him. "Go ahead, Third, show the Purser. You can trust him—he's a good man. I'd be proud to be shipmates with the Purser."

The Third hesitated and then raised the book from his lap. It was the *Space Code* and expanded *Rules of the Road.* Every licensed officer has to bone up on it a lot, to get his license. But it's not the kind of book you ordinarily kill time with.

"The Third here was showing me all about what a captain can and can't do," said Mr Costello.

"Well, you asked me to," the Third said.

"Now just a minute," said Mr Costello rapidly, "now just a minute." He had a way of doing that sometimes. It was part of him, like the thinning hair on top of his head and the big smile and the way he had of cocking his head to one side and asking you what it was you just said, as if he didn't hear so well. "Now just a minute, you *wanted* to show me this material, didn't you?"

"Well, yes, Mr Costello," the Third said.

"You're going over the limitations of a spacemaster's power of your own free will, aren't you?"

"Well," said the Third, "I guess so. Sure."

"Sure," Mr Costello repeated happily. "Tell the Purser the part you just read to me."

"The one you found in the book?"

"You know the one. You read it out your own self, didn't you?"

"Oh," said the Third. He looked at me—sort of uneasily, I thought —and reached for the book.

Mr Costello put his hand on it. "Oh, don't bother looking it up," he said. "You can remember it."

"Yeah, I guess I do," the Third admitted. "It's a sort of safeguard against letting a skipper's power go to his head, in case it ever does.

Suppose a time comes when a captain begins to act up, and the crew gets the idea that a lunatic has taken over the bridge. Well, something has to be done about it. The crew has the power to appoint one officer and send him up to the Captain for an accounting. If the Skipper refuses, or if the crew doesn't like his accounting, then they have the right to confine him to his quarters and take over the ship."

"I think I heard about that," I said. "But the Skipper has rights, too. I mean the crew has to report everything by space-radio the second it happens, and then the Captain has a full hearing along with the crew at the next port."

Mr Costello looked at us and shook his big head, full of admiration. When Mr Costello thought you were good, it made you feel good all over.

The Third looked at his watch and got up. "I got to relieve the bridge. Want to come along, Purser?"

"I'd like to talk to him for a while," Mr Costello said. "Do you suppose you could get somebody else for a witness?"

"Oh, sure, if you say so," said the Third.

"But you're going to get someone."

"Absolutely," said the Third.

"Safest ship I was ever on," said Mr Costello. "Gives a fellow a nice feeling to know that the watch is never going to get the orders wrong."

I thought so myself and wondered why we never used to do it before. I watched the Third leave and stayed where I was, feeling good, feeling safe, feeling glad that Mr Costello wanted to talk to me. And me just a Purser, him an ex-Triumver.

Mr Costello gave me the big smile. He nodded towards the door. "That young fellow's going far. A good man. You're all good men here." He stuck a sucker-cup in the heater and passed it over to me with his own hands. "Coffee," he said. "My own brand. All I ever use."

I tasted it and it was fine. He was a very generous man. He sat back and beamed at me while I drank it.

"What do you know about Borinquen?" he wanted to know.

I told him all I could. Borinquen's a pretty nice place, what they call "four-nines Earth Normal"—which means that the climate, gravity, atmosphere, and ecology come within .9999 of being the same as Earth's. There are only about six known planets like that. I told him about the one city it had and the trapping that used to be the main industry. Coats made out of *glunker* fur last for ever. They shine green in white light and a real warm ember-red in blue light, and you can take a full-sized coat and scrunch it up and hide it in your two hands, it's that light and fine. Being so light, the fur made ideal space-cargo.

Of course, there was a lot more on Borinquen now—rare isotope ingots and foodstuffs and seeds for the drug business and all, and I suppose the *glunker* trade could dry right up and Borinquen could still carry its weight. But furs settled the planet, furs supported the city in the early days, and half the population still lived out in the bush and trapped.

Mr Costello listened to everything I said in a way I can only call respectful.

I remember I finished up by saying, "I'm sorry you have to get off there, Mr Costello. I'd like to see you some more. I'd like to come see you at Borinquen, whenever we put in, though I don't suppose a man like you would have much spare time."

He put his big hand on my arm. "Purser, if I don't have time when you're in port, I'll make time. Hear?" Oh, he had a wonderful way of making a fellow feel good.

Next thing you know, he invited me right into his cabin. He sat me down and handed me a sucker full of a mild red wine with a late flavour of cinnamon, which was a new one on me, and he showed me some of his things.

He was a great collector. He had one or two little bits of coloured paper that he said were stamps they used before the Space Age, to prepay carrying charges on paper letters. He said no matter where he was, just one of those things could get him a fortune. Then he had some jewels, not rings or anything, just stones, and a fine story for every single one of them.

"What you're holding in your hand," he said, "cost the life of a king and the loss of an empire half again as big as United Earth." And: "This one was once so well guarded that most people didn't know whether it existed or not. There was a whole religion based on it—and now it's gone, and so is the religion."

It gave you a queer feeling, being next to this man who had so much, and him just as warm and friendly as your favourite uncle.

"If you can assure me these bulkheads are soundproof, I'll show you something else I collect," he said.

I assured him they were, and they were, too. "If ships' architects ever learned anything," I told him, "they learned that a man has just got to be by himself once in a while."

He cocked his head to one side in that way he had. "How's that again?"

"A man's just got to be by himself once in a while," I said. "So, mass or no, cost or no, a ship's bulkheads are built to give a man his privacy."

"Good," he said. "Now let me show you." He unlocked a hand-case and opened it, and from a little compartment inside he took out a thing about the size of the box a watch comes in. He handled it very gently as he put it down on his desk. It was square, and it had a fine grille on the top and two little silver studs on the side. He pressed one of them

and turned to me, smiling. And let me tell you, I almost fell right off
the bunk where I was sitting, because here was the Captain's voice as
loud and as clear and natural as if he was right there in the room with
us. And do you know what he said?

He said, "My crew questions my sanity—yet you can be sure that
if a single man aboard questions my authority, he will learn that I am
master here, even if he must learn it at the point of a gun."

What surprised me so much wasn't only the voice but the words
—and what surprised me especially about the words was that I had
heard the Skipper say them myself. It was the time he had had the
argument with Mr Costello. I remembered it well because I had walked
into the dayroom just as the Captain started to yell.

"Mr Costello," he said in that big heavy voice of his, "in spite of
your conviction that my crew questions my sanity . . ." and all the rest
of it, just like on this recording Mr Costello had. And I remember he
said, too, "even if he must learn it at the point of a gun. *That, sir,
applies to passengers—the crew has legal means of their own.*"

I was going to mention this to Mr Costello, but before I could open
my mouth, he asked me, "Now tell me, Purser, is that the voice of the
Captain of your ship?"

And I said, "Well, if it isn't, I'm not the Purser here. Why, I heard
him speak those words my very own self."

Mr Costello swatted me on the shoulder. "You have a good ear,
Purser. And how do you like my little toy?"

Then he showed it to me, a little mechanism on the jewelled pin
he wore on his tunic, a fine thread of wire to a pushbutton in his side
pocket.

"One of my favourite collections," he told me. "Voices. Anybody,
any time, anywhere." He took off the pin and slipped a tiny bead out
of the setting. He slipped this into a groove in the box and pressed the
stud.

And I heard my own voice say, "I'm sorry you have to get off there,
Mr Costello. I'd like to see you some more." I laughed and laughed.
That was one of the cleverest things I ever saw. And just think of my
voice in his collection, along with the Captain and space only knows
how many great and famous people!

He even had the voice of the Third Officer, from just a few minutes
before, saying, "A lunatic has taken over the bridge. Well, something
has to be done about it."

All in all, I had a wonderful visit with him, and then he asked me
to do whatever I had to do about his clearance papers. So I went back
to my office and got them out. They are kept in the Purser's safe during
a voyage. And I went through them with the okays. There were a lot
of them—he had more than most people.

I found one from Earth Central that sort of made me mad. I guess

it was a mistake. It was a *Know All Ye* that warned consular officials to report every six months, Earth time, on the activities of Mr Costello. I took it to him, and it was a mistake, all right—he said so himself.
I tore it out of his passport book and adhesed an official note, reporting the accidental destruction of a used page of fully stamped visas. He gave me a beautiful blue gemstone for doing it.

When I said, "I better not; I don't want you thinking I take bribes from passengers," he laughed and put one of those beads in his recorder, and it came out, in my voice, "I take bribes from passengers." He was a great joker.

We lay at Borinquen for four days. Nothing much happened except I was busy. That's what's tough about pursering. You got nothing to do for weeks in space, and then, when you're in spaceport, you have too much work to do even to go ashore much, unless it's a long layover.

I never really minded much. I'm one of those mathematical geniuses, you know, even if I don't have too much sense otherwise, and I take pride in my work. Everybody has something he's good at, I guess. I couldn't tell you how the gimmick works that makes the ship travel faster than light, but I'd hate to trust the Chief Engineer with one of my interplanetary cargo manifests, or a rate-of-exchange table, *glunker* pelts to U.E. dollars.

Some hard-jawed character with Space Navy Investigator credentials came aboard with a portable voice recorder and made me and the Third Officer recite a lot of nonsense for some sort of test, I don't know what. The S.N.I. is always doing a lot of useless and mysterious things. I had an argument with the Port Agent, and I went ashore with Cooky for a fast drink. The usual thing. Then I had to work overtime signing on a new Third—they transferred the old one to a corvette that was due in, they told me.

Oh, yes, that was the trip the Skipper resigned. I guess it was high time. He'd been acting very nervous. He gave me the damnedest look when he went ashore that last time, like he didn't know whether to kill me or burst into tears. There was a rumour around that he'd gone berserk and threatened the crew with a gun, but I don't listen to rumours. And anyway, the Port Captain signs on new skippers. It didn't mean any extra work for me, so it didn't matter much.

We upshipped again and made the rounds. Boötes Sigma and Nightingale and Caranho and Earth—chemical glassware, blackprints, *sho* seed and glitter crystals; perfume, music tape, *glizzard* skins and Aldebar—all the usual junk for all the usual months. And round we came again to Borinquen.

Well, you wouldn't believe a place could change so much in so short a time. Borinquen used to be a pretty free-and-easy planet. There was just the one good-sized city, see, and then trapper camps all through the unsettled area. If you liked people, you settled in the city, and you could go to work in the processing plants or maintenance or some such. If you didn't, you could trap *glunkers.* There was always something for every-body on Borinquen.

But things were way different this trip. First of all, a man with a Planetary Government badge came aboard, by God, to censor the music tapes consigned for the city, and he had the credentials for it, too. Next thing I find out, the municipal authorities have confiscated the ware-houses—*my* warehouses—and they were being converted into bar-racks.

And where were the goods—the pelts and ingots for export? Where was the space for our cargo? Why, in houses—in hundreds of houses, all spread around every which way, all indexed up with a whole big new office full of conscripts and volunteers to mix up and keep mixed up! For the first time since I went to space, I had to request layover so I could get things unwound.

Anyway it gave me a chance to wander around the town, which I don't often get.

You should have seen the place! Everybody seemed to be moving out of the houses. All the big buildings were being made over into hollow shells, filled with rows of mattresses. There were banners strung across the streets: ARE YOU A MAN OR ARE YOU ALONE? A SINGLE SHINGLE IS A SORRY SHELTER! THE DEVIL HATES A CROWD!

All of which meant nothing to me. But it wasn't until I noticed a sign painted in whitewash on the glass front of a bar-room, saying— TRAPPERS STAY OUT!—that I was aware of one of the biggest changes of all.

There were no trappers on the streets—none at all. They used to be one of the tourist attractions of Borinquen, dressed in *glunker* ur, with the long tailwings afloat in the wind of their walking, and a kind of distance in their eyes that not even spacemen had. As soon as I missed them, I began to see the TRAPPERS STAY OUT! signs just about everywhere—on the stores, the restaurants, the hotels, and theatres.

I stood on a street corner, looking around me and wondering what in hell was going on here, when a Borinquen cop yelled something at me from a monowheel prowl car. I didn't understand him, so I just shrugged. He made a U-turn and coasted up to me.

"What's the matter country boy? Lose your traps?"

I said, "What?"

He said, "If you want to go it alone, *glunker,* we got solitary cells over at the Hall that'll suit you fine."

I just gawked at him. And, to my surprise, another cop poked his head up out of the prowler. A one-man prowler, mind. They were really jammed in there.

This second one said, "Where's your trap-line, jerker?"

I said, "I don't have a trap-line." I pointed to the mighty tower of my ship, looming over the spaceport. "I'm the Purser off that ship."

"Oh, for God's sakes!" said the first cop. "I might have known. Look, Spacer, you'd better double up or you're liable to get yourself mobbed. This is no spot for a soloist."

"I don't get you, Officer. I was just—"

"I'll take him," said someone. I looked around and saw a tall Borinqueña standing just inside the open doorway of one of the hundreds of empty houses. She said, "I came back here to pick up some of my things. When I got done in here, there was nobody on the sidewalks. I've been here an hour, waiting for somebody to go with." She sounded a little hysterical.

"You know better than to go in there by yourself," said one of the cops.

"I know—I know. It was just to get my things. I wasn't going to stay." She hauled up a duffel-bag and dangled it in front of her. "Just to get my things," she said again, frightened.

The Cops looked at each other. "Well, all right. But watch yourself. You go along with the Purser here. Better straighten him out—he don't seem to know what's right."

"I will," she said thankfully.

But by then the prowler had moaned off, weaving a little under its double load.

I looked at her. She wasn't pretty. She was sort of heavy and stupid.

She said, "You'll be all right now. Let's go."

"Where?"

"Well, Central Barracks, I guess. That's where most everybody is."

"I have to get back to the ship."

"Oh, dear," she said, all distressed again. "Right away?"

"No, not right away. I'll go in town with you, if you want."

She picked up her duffel-bag, but I took it from her and heaved it up on my shoulder. "Is everybody here crazy?" I asked her, scowling.

"Crazy?" She began walking, and I went along. "I don't *think* so."

"All this," I persisted. I pointed to a banner that said. NO LADDER HAS A SINGLE RUNG. "What's that mean?"

"Just what it says."

"You have to put up a big thing like that just to tell me ..."

"Oh," she said. "You mean what does it *mean!*" She looked at me strangely. "We've found out a new truth about humanity. Look, I'll try to tell it to you the way the Lucilles said it last night."

"Who's Lucille?"

"*The* Lucilles," she said, in a mildly shocked tone. "Actually, I suppose there's really only one—though, of course, there'll be someone else in the studio at the time," she added quickly. "But on trideo it looks like four Lucilles, all speaking at once, sort of in chorus."

"You just go on talking," I said when she paused. "I catch on slowly."

"Well, here's what they say. They say no one human being ever did *anything.* They say it takes a hundred pairs of hands to build a house, ten thousand pairs to build a ship. They say a single pair is not only useless—it's *evil.* All humanity is a thing made up of many parts. No part is good by itself. Any part that wants to go off by itself hurts the whole main thing—the thing that has become so great. So we're seeing to it that no part ever gets separated. What good would your hand be if a finger suddenly decided to go off by itself?"

I said, "And you believe this—what's your name?"

"Nola. *Believe* it? Well, it's true, isn't it? Can't you see it's true? Everybody *knows* it's true."

"Well, it *could* be true," I said reluctantly. "What do you do with people who want to be by themselves?"

"We help them."

"Suppose they don't want help?"

"Then they're trappers," she said immediately. "We push them back into the bush, where the evil soloists come from."

"Well, what about the fur?"

"Nobody uses furs any more!"

So that's what happened to our fur consignment! And I was thinking those amateur red-tapers had just lost 'em somewhere.

She said, as if to herself, "All sin starts in the lonesome dark," and when I looked up, I saw she'd read it approvingly off another banner.

We rounded a corner and I blinked at a blaze of light. It was one of the warehouses.

"There's the Central," she said. "Would you like to see it?"

"I guess so."

I followed her down the street to the entrance. There was a man sitting at a table in the doorway. Nola gave him a card. He checked it against a list and handed it back.

"A visitor," she said. "From the ship."

I showed him my Purser's card and he said, "Okay. But if you want to stay, you'll have to register."

"I won't want to stay," I told him. "I have to get back."

I followed Nola inside.

The place had been scraped out to the absolute maximum. Take away one splinter of vertical structure more and it wouldn't have held a roof. There wasn't a concealed corner, a shelf, a drape, an overhang. There must have been two thousand beds, cots, and mattresses spread out, cheek by jowl, over the entire floor, in blocks of four, with only a hand's-breadth between them.

The light was blinding—huge floods and spots bathed every square inch in yellow-white fire.

Nola said, "You'll get used to the light. After a few nights, you don't even notice it."

"The lights never get turned off?"

"Oh, dear, no!"

Then I saw the plumbing—showers, tubs, sinks, and everything else. It was all lined up against one wall.

Nola followed my eyes. "You get used to that, too. Better to have everything out in the open than to let the devil in for one secret second. That's what the Lucilles say."

I dropped her duffel-bag and sat down on it. The only thing I could think of was, "Whose idea was all this? Where did it start?"

"The Lucilles," she said vaguely. Then, "Before them, I don't know. People just started to realize. Somebody bought a warehouse—no, it was a hangar—I don't know," she said again, apparently trying hard to remember. She sat down next to me and said in a subdued voice, "Actually, some people didn't take to it so well at first." She looked around. "*I* didn't. I mean it. I really didn't. But you believed, or you had to act as if you believed, and one way or another everybody just came to this." She waved a hand.

"What happened to the ones who wouldn't come to Centrals?"

"People made fun of them. They lost their jobs, the schools wouldn't take their children, the stores wouldn't honor their ration cards. Then the police started to pick up soloists—like they did you." She looked around again, a sort of contented familiarity in her gaze. "It didn't take long."

I turned away from her but found myself staring at all that plumbing again. I jumped up. "I have to go, Nola. Thanks for your help. Hey —how do I get back to the ship, if the cops are out to pick up any soloist they see?"

"Oh, just tell the man at the gate. There'll be people waiting to go your way. There's always somebody waiting to go everywhere."

She came along with me. I spoke to the man at the gate, and she shook hands with me. I stood up by the little table and watched her hesitate, then step up to a woman who was entering. They went in together. The doorman nudged me over toward a group of what appeared to be loungers.

"*North!*" he bawled.

I drew a pudgy little man with bad teeth, who said not one single word. We escorted each other two-thirds of the way to the spaceport, and he disappeared into a factory. I scuttled the rest of the way alone, feeling like a criminal, which I suppose I was. I swore I would never go into that crazy city again.

And the next morning, who should come out for me, in an ar-

moured car with six two-man prowlers as escort, but Mr Costello himself!

It was pretty grand seeing him again. He was just like always, big
and handsome and good-natured. He was not alone. All spread out in
the back corner of the car was the most beautiful blonde woman that
ever struck me speechless. She didn't say very much. She would just
look at me every once in a while and sort of smile, and then she would
look out of the car window and bite on her lower lip a little, and then
look at Mr Costello and not smile at all.

Mr Costello hadn't forgotten me. He had a bottle of that same red
cinnamon wine, and he talked over old times the same as ever, like he
was a special uncle. We got a sort of guided tour. I told him about last
night, about the visit to the Central, and he was pleased as could be.
He said he knew I'd like it. I didn't stop to think whether I liked it or
not.

"Think of it!" he said. "All humankind, a single unit. You know the
principle of cooperation, Purser?"

When I took too long to think it out, he said, "You know. Two men
working together can produce more than two men working separately.
Well, what happens when a thousand—a million—work, sleep, eat,
think, breathe together?" The way he said it, it sounded fine.

He looked out past my shoulder and his eyes widened just a little.
He pressed a button and the chauffeur brought us to a sliding stop.

"Get that one," Mr Costello said into a microphone beside him.

Two of the prowlers hurtled down the street and flanked a man.
He dodged right, dodged left, and then a prowler hit him and knocked
him down.

"Poor chap," said Mr Costello, pushing the Go button. "Some of
'em just won't learn."

I think he regretted it very much. I don't know if the blonde woman
did. She didn't even look.

"Are you the mayor?" I asked him.

"Oh, no," he said. "I'm a sort of broker. A little of this, a little of
that. I'm able to help out a bit."

"Help out?"

"Purser," he said confidentially, "I'm a citizen of Borinquen now.
This is my adopted land and I love it. I mean to do everything in my
power to help it. I don't care about the cost. This is a people that has
found the *truth,* Purser. It awes me. It makes me humble."

"I . . ."

"Speak up, man. I'm your *friend.*"

"I appreciate that, Mr Costello. Well, what I was going to say, I saw
that Central and all. I just haven't made up my mind. I mean whether
it's good or not."

"Take your time, take your time," he said in the big soft voice. "Nobody has to *make* a man see a truth, am I right? A real truth? A man just sees it all by himself."

"Yeah," I agreed. "Yeah, I guess so." Sometimes it was hard to find an answer to give Mr Costello.

The car pulled up beside a building. The blonde woman pulled herself together. Mr Costello opened the door for her with his own hands. She got out. Mr Costello rapped the trideo screen in front of him.

He said, "Make it a real good one, Lucille, real good. I'll be watching."

She looked at him. She gave me a small smile. A man came down the steps and she went with him up into the building.

We moved off.

I said, "She's the prettiest woman I ever saw."

He said, "She likes you fine, Purser."

I thought about that. It was too much.

He asked, "How would you like to have her for your very own?"

"Oh," I said, "she wouldn't."

"Purser, I owe you a big favour. I'd like to pay it back."

"You don't owe me a thing, Mr Costello!"

We drank some of the wine. The big car slid silently along. It went slowly now, headed back out to the spaceport.

"I need some help," he said after a time. "I know you, Purser. You're just the kind of man I can use. They say you're a mathematical genius."

"Not mathematics exactly, Mr Costello. Just numbers—statistics —conversion tables and like that. I couldn't do astrogation or theoretical physics and such. I got the best job I could have right now."

"No, you haven't. I'll be frank with you. I don't want any more responsibility on Borinquen than I've got, you understand, but the people are forcing it on me. They want order, peace and order—tidiness. They want to be as nice and tidy as one of your multiple manifests. Now I could organize them, all right, but I need a tidy brain like yours to keep them organized. I want full birth- and death-rate statistics, and then I want them projected so we can get policy. I want calorie-counts and rationing, so we can use the food supply the best way. I want—well, you see what I mean. Once the devil is routed—"

"What devil?"

"The trappers," he said gravely.

"Are the trappers really harming the city people?"

He looked at me, shocked. "They go out and spend weeks alone by themselves, with their own evil thoughts. They are wandering cells, wild cells in the body of humanity. They must be destroyed."

I couldn't help but think of my consignments. "What about the fur trade, though?"

He looked at me as if I had made a pretty grubby little mistake. "My dear Purser," he said patiently, "would you set the price of a few pelts above the immortal soul of a race?"

I hadn't thought of it that way.

He said urgently, "This is just the beginning, Purser. Borinquen is only a start. The unity of that great being, Humanity, will become known throughout the Universe." He closed his eyes. When he opened them, the organ tone was gone. He said in his old, friendly voice, "And you and I, we'll show 'em how to do it, hey, boy?"

I leaned forward to look up to the top of the shining spire of the spaceship. "I sort of like the job I've got. But—my contract *is* up four months from now . . ."

The car turned into the spaceport and hummed across the slag area.

"I think I can count on you," he said vibrantly. He laughed. "Remember this little joke, Purser?"

He clicked a switch, and suddenly my own voice filled the tonneau. *"I take bribes from passengers."*

"Oh, that," I said, and let loose one *ha* of a *ha-ha* before I understood what he was driving at. "Mr Costello, you wouldn't use that against me."

"What do you take me for?" he demanded in wonderment.

Then we were at the ramp. He got out with me. He gave me his hand. It was warm and hearty.

"If you change your mind about the Purser's job when your contract's up, son, just buzz me through the field phone. They'll connect me. Think it over until you get back here. Take your time." His hand clamped down on my biceps so hard I winced. "But you're not going to take any longer than that, are you, my boy?"

"I guess not," I said.

He got into the front, by the chauffer, and zoomed away.

I stood looking after him and, when the car was just a dark spot on the slag area, I sort of came to myself. I was standing alone on the foot of the ramp. I felt very exposed.

I turned and ran up to the airlock, hurrying, hurrying to get near people.

That was the trip we shipped the crazy man. His name was Hynes. He was United Earth Consul at Borinquen and he was going back to report. He was no trouble at first, because diplomatic passports are easy to process. He knocked on my door the fifth watch out from Borinquen. I was glad to see him. My room was making me uneasy and I appreciated his company.

Not that he was really company. He was crazy. That first time, he came bursting in and said, "I hope you don't mind, Purser, but if I don't talk to somebody about this, I'll go out of my mind." Then he sat down on the end of my bunk and put his head in his hands and rocked back and forth for a long time, without saying anything. Next thing he said was, "Sorry," and out he went. Crazy, I tell you.

But he was back in again before long. And then you never heard such ravings.

"Do you know what's happened to Borinquen?" he'd demand. But he didn't want any answers. He had the answers. "I'll tell you what's wrong with Borinquen—Borinquen's gone mad!" he'd say.

I went on with my work, though there wasn't much of it in space, but that Hynes just couldn't get Borinquen out of his mind.

He said, "You wouldn't believe it if you hadn't seen it done. First the little wedge, driven in the one place it might exist—between the urbans and the trappers. There was never any conflict between them —never! All of a sudden, the trapper was a menace. How it happened, why, God only knows. First, these laughable attempts to show that they were an unhealthy influence. Yes, laughable—how could you take it seriously?

"And then the changes. You didn't have to prove that a trapper had done anything. You only had to prove he was a trapper. That was enough. And the next thing—how could you *anticipate* anything as mad as this?"—he almost screamed—"the next thing was to take any-one who wanted to be alone and lump him with the trappers. It all happened so fast—it happened in our sleep. And all of a sudden you were afraid to be alone in a room for a *second*. They left their homes. They built barracks. Everyone afraid of everyone else, afraid, afraid . . .

"Do you know what they *did*?" he roared. "They burned the paint-ings, every painting on Borinquen they could find that had been done by one artist. And the few artists who survived as artists—I've seen them. By twos and threes, they work together on the one canvas."

He cried. He actually sat there and cried.

He said, "There's food in the stores. The crops come in. Trucks run, planes fly, the schools are in session. Bellies get full, cars get washed, people get rich. I know a man called Costello, just in from Earth a few months, maybe a year or so, and already owns half the city."

"Oh, I know Mr Costello," I said.

"Do you now! How's that?"

I told him about the trip out with Mr Costello. He sort of backed off from me. "*You're* the one!"

"The one what?" I asked in puzzlement.

"*You're* the man who testified against your Captain, broke him, made him resign."

"I did no such a thing."

"I'm the Consul. It was my hearing, man! I was *there!* A recording of the Captain's voice, admitting to insanity, declaring he'd take a gun to his crew if they overrode him. Then your recorded testimony that it was his voice, that you were present when he made the statement. And the Third Officer's recorded statement that all was not well on the bridge. The man denied it, but it was his voice."

"Wait, wait," I said. "I don't believe it. That would need a trial. There was no trial. I wasn't called to any trial."

"There would have been a trial, you idiot! But the Captain started raving about draw poker without a draw, about the crew fearing poisoning from the cook, and the men wanting witnesses even to change the bridge-watch. Maddest thing I ever heard. He realized it suddenly, the Captain did. He was old, sick, tired, beaten. He blamed the whole thing on Costello, and Costello said he got the recordings from you."

"Mr Costello wouldn't do such a thing!" I guess I got mad at Mr Hynes then. I told him a whole lot about Mr Costello, what a big man he was. He started to tell me how Mr Costello was forced off the Triumverate for making trouble in the high court, but they were all lies and I wouldn't listen. I told him about the poker, how Mr Costello saved us from the cheaters, how he saved us from poisoning, how he made the ship safe for us all.

I remember how he looked at me then. He sort of whispered, "What has happened to human beings? What have we done to ourselves with these centuries of peace, with confidence and cooperation and no conflict? Here's distrust by man for man, waiting under a thin skin to be punctured by just the right vampire, waiting to hate itself and kill itself all over again . . .

"My *God!*" he suddenly screamed at me. "Do you know what I've been hanging onto? The idea that, for all its error, for all its stupidity, this One Humanity idea on Borinquen was a *principle*? I hated it, but because it was a principle, I could respect it. It's Costello—Costello, who doesn't gamble, but who uses fear to change the poker rules—Costello, who doesn't eat your food, but makes you fear poison—Costello, who can see three hundred years of safe interstellar flight, but who through fear makes the watch officers doubt themselves without a witness—Costello, who runs things without being seen!

"My God, Costello doesn't *care!* It isn't a principle at all. It's just Costello spreading fear anywhere, everywhere, to make himself strong!"

He rushed out, crying with rage and hate. I have to admit I was sort of jolted. I guess I might even have thought about the things he had said, only he killed himself before we reached Earth. He was crazy

We made the rounds, same as ever, scheduled like an interurban line: Load, discharge, blastoff, fly and planetfall. Refuel, clearance, manifest. Eat, sleep, work. There was a hearing about Hynes. Mr Costello sent a spacegram with his regrets when he heard the news. I didn't say anything at the hearing, just that Mr Hynes was upset, that's all, and it was about as true as anything could be. We shipped a second engineer who played real good accordion. One of the inboard men got left on Carànho. All the usual things, except I wrote up my termination with no options, ready to file.

So in its turn we made Borinquen again, and what do you know, there was the space fleet of United Earth. I never guessed they had that many ships. They sheered us off, real Navy: all orders and no information. Borinquen was buttoned up tight; there was some kind of fighting going on down there. We couldn't get or give a word of news through the quarantine. It made the skipper mad and he had to use part of the cargo for fuel, which messed up my records six ways from the middle. I stashed my termination papers away for the time being.

And in its turn, Sigma, where we lay over a couple of days to get back in the rut, and, same as always, Nightingale, right on schedule again.

And who should be waiting for me at Nightingale but Barney Roteel, who was medic on my first ship, years back when I was fresh from the Academy. He had a pot belly now and looked real successful. We got the jollity out of the way and he settled down and looked me over, real sober. I said it's a small Universe—I'd known he had a big job on Nightingale, but imagine him showing up at the spaceport just when I blew in!

"I showed up *because* you blew in, Purser," he answered.

Then before I could take that apart, he started asking me questions. Like how was I doing, what did I plan to do.

I said, "I've been a purser for years and years. What makes you think I want to do anything different?"

"Just wondered."

I wondered, too. "Well," I said, "I haven't exactly made up my mind, you might say—and a couple of things have got in the way—but I did have a kind of offer." I told him just in a general way about how big a man Mr Costello was on Borinquen now, and how he wanted me to come in with him. "It'll have to wait, though. The whole damn Space Navy has a cordon around Borinquen. They wouldn't say why. But whatever it is, Mr Costello'll come out on top. You'll see."

Barney gave me a sort of puckered-up look. I never saw a man look so weird. Yes, I did, too. It was the old Iron Man, the day he got off the ship and resigned.

"Barney, what's the matter?" I asked.

He got up and pointed through the glass door-lights to a white monowheel that stood poised in front of the receiving station. "Come on," he said.

"Aw, I can't. I got to—"

"Come *on*!"

I shrugged. Job or no, this was Barney's bailiwick, not mine. He'd cover me.

He held the door open and said, like a mind reader, "I'll cover you."

He went down the ramp and climbed in and skimmed off.

"Where are we going?"

But he wouldn't say. He just drove.

Nightingale's a beautiful place. The most beautiful of them all. I think, even Sigma. It's run by the U.E., one hundred per cent; this is one planet with no local options, but *none*. It's a regular garden of a world and they keep it that way.

We topped a rise and went down a curving road lined with honest-to-God Lombardy poplars from Earth. There was a little lake down there and a sandy beach. No people.

The road curved and there was a yellow line across it and then a red one, and after it a shimmering curtain, almost transparent. t extended from side to side as far as I could see.

"Force-fence," Barney said and pressed a button on the dash.

The shimmer disappeared from the road ahead, though it stayed where it was at each side. We drove through it and it formed behind us, and we went down the hill to the lake.

Just this side of the beach was the cosiest little Sigman cabana I've seen yet, built to hug the slope and open its arms to the sky. Maybe when I get old they'll turn me out to pasture in one half as good.

While I was goggling at it, Barney said, "Go on."

I looked at him and he was pointing. There was a man down near the water, big, very tanned, built like a space-tug. Barney waved me on and I walked down there.

The man got up and turned to me. He had the same wide-spaced, warm deep eyes, the same full, gentle voice. "Why, it's the Purser! He old friend. So you came, after all!"

It was sort of rough for a moment. Then I got it out. "Hi, M-Costello."

He banged me on the shoulder. Then he wrapped one big hand around my left biceps and pulled me a little closer. He looked uphill to where Barney leaned against the monowheel, minding his own business. Then he looked across the lake, and up in the sky.

He dropped his voice, "Purser, you're just the man I need. But I told you that before, didn't I?" He looked around again. "We'll do it yet Purser. You and me, we'll hit the top. Come with me. I want to show you something."

He walked ahead of me towards the beach margin. He was wearing only a breech-ribbon, but he moved and spoke as if he still had the armoured car and the six prowlers. I stumbled after him.

He put a hand behind him and checked me, and then knelt. He said, "To look at them, you think they were all the same, wouldn't you? Well, son, you just let me show you something."

I looked down. He had an anthill. They weren't like Earth ants. These were bigger, slower, blue, and they had eight legs. They built nests of sand tied together with mucus, and tunnelled under them so that the nests stood up an inch or two like on little pillars.

"They look the same, they act the same, but you'll see," said Mr Costello.

He opened a synthine pouch that lay in the sand. He took out a dead bird and the thorax of what looked like a Carânho roach, the one that grows as long as your fore-arm. He put the bird down here and the roach down yonder.

"Now," he said "watch."

The ants swarmed to the bird, pulling and crawling. Busy. But one or two went to the roach and tumbled it and burrowed around. Mr Costello picked an ant off the roach and dropped it on the bird. It weaved around and shouldered through the others and scrabbled across the sand and went back to the roach.

"You see, you *see*?" he said, enthusiastic. "Look."

He picked an ant off the dead bird and dropped it by the roach. The ant wasted no time or even curiosity on the piece of roach. It turned around once to get its bearings, and then went straight back to the dead bird.

I looked at the bird with its clothing of crawling blue, and I looked at the roach with its two or three voracious scavengers. I looked at Mr. Costello.

He said raptly, "See what I mean? About one in thirty eats something different. And that's all we need. I tell you, Purser, wherever you look, if you look long enough, you can find a way to make most of a group turn on the rest."

I watched the ants. "They're not fighting."

"Now wait a minute," he said swiftly. "Wait a minute. All we have to do is let these bird-eaters know that the roach-eaters are dangerous."

"They're not dangerous," I said. "They're just different."

"What's the difference, when you come right down to it? So we'll get the bird-eaters scared and they'll kill all the roach-eaters."

"Yes, but why, Mr Costello?"

He laughed. "I like you, boy. I do the thinking, you do the work. I'll explain it to you. They all look alike. So once we've made 'em drive out these—" he pointed to the minority around the roach—"they'll never know which among 'em might be a roach-eater. They'll get so worried, they'll do anything to keep from being suspected of roach-eating. When they get scared enough, we can make 'em do anything we want."

He hunkered down to watch the ants. He picked up a roach-eater and put it on the bird. I got up.

"Well, I only just dropped in, Mr Costello," I said.

"I'm not an ant," said Mr Costello. "As long as it makes no difference to me what they eat, I can make 'em do anything in the world I want."

"I'll see you around," I said.

He kept on talking quietly to himself as I walked away. He was watching the ants, figuring, and paid no attention to me.

I went back to Barney. I asked, sort of choked, "What is he doing, Barney?"

"He's doing what he has to do," Barney said.

We went back to the monowheel and up the hill and through the force-gate. After a while, I asked, "How long will he be here?"

"As long as he wants to be," Barney was kind of short about it.

"Nobody wants to be locked up."

He had that odd look on his face again. "Nightingale's not a jail."

"He can't get out."

"Look, chum, we could start him over. We could even make a purser out of him. But we stopped doing that kind of thing a long time ago. We let a man do what he wants to do."

"He never wanted to be boss over an anthill."

"He didn't?"

I guess I looked as if I didn't understand that, so he said, "All his life he's pretended he's a man and the rest of us are ants. Now it's come true for him. He won't run human anthills any more because he will never again get near one."

I looked through the windshield at the shining finger that was my distant ship. "What happened on Borinquen, Barney?"

"Some of his converts got loose around the System. That Humanity One idea had to be stopped." He drove a while, seeing badly out of a thinking face. "You won't take this hard, Purser, but you're a thick-witted ape. I can say that if no one else can."

"All right," I said. "Why?"

"We had to *smash* into Borinquen, which used to be so free and easy. We got into Costello's place. It was a regular fort. We got him and his files. We didn't get his girl. He killed her, but the files were enough."

After a time I said, "He was always a good friend to me."

"Was he?"

I didn't say anything. He wheeled up to the receiving station and stopped the machine.

He said, "He was all ready for you if you came to work for him. He had a voice recording of you large as life, saying 'Sometimes a man's just *got* to be by himself.' Once you went to work for him, all he needed to do to keep you in line was to threaten to put that on the air."

I opened the door. "What did you have to show him to me for?"

"Because we believe in letting a man do what he wants to do, as long as he doesn't hurt the rest of us. If you want to go back to the lake and work for Costello, for instance, I'll take you there."

I closed the door carefully and went up the ramp to the ship.

I did my work and when the time came, we blasted off. I was mad. I don't think it was about anything Barney told me. I wasn't especially mad about Mr Costello or what happened to him, because Barney's the best Navy psych doc there is and Nightingale's the most beautiful hospital planet in the Universe.

What made me mad was the thought that never again would a man as big as Mr Costello give that big, warm, soft, strong friendship to a lunkhead like me.

afterword

Science Fiction
As Culture Criticism

This AFTERWORD is an experiment in joint composition and mutual commentary. The editors feel that their two views of the human landscape—one sociological, one literary—are not quite as divergent as might first appear. We feel that literature is more than entertainment and the social sciences more than analysis. Thus our essay on "Science Fiction as Culture Criticism" presents the two views as though they were one, but spoken with different voices. To indicate to the reader which viewpoint is being presented at the moment, we have relied upon a media technique as old as Gutenberg—different type faces. *When the material is set in italics, the voice is Professor Leon E. Stover;* when it's like this, it's Professor Willis E. McNelly. Stover wrote the original essay, providing its direction, unity, tone, and emphasis. McNelly's interpolations indicate some literary dimensions not considered in the original anthropological analysis. These short essays elaborate upon points made by Stover or suggest further dimensions in the stories themselves. Neither writer feels that his analysis is either final or definitive. Rather they wish their comments to indicate some of the many ways that science fiction may be treated—either as serious culture criticism or literature which reflects our dynamic society.

The science fiction (SF) stories collected here represent a kind of popular sociology, a look at man from a viewpoint outside the psychology of the individual. Realistic fiction plumbs the inner workings and motivations of fully realized private lives. Science fiction holds up a sheet of frosted glass against the details of interacting personalities in order to scan the patterned effects of human association. Individual and social behavior, of course, are the same thing in reality; the difference lies solely in the point of view.

The viewpoint of SF is that of the pendent spectator, hovering above the human landscape. The entertainment value of SF to its habitual readers is precisely the dramatization of this point of view. SF readers plainly enjoy looking at humanity from afar through a telescope; self-critical self-consciousness is a pleasure they do not find in the intimate view through the microscope of realistic fiction.

The leverage by which SF gains its vantage point as an eye in the sky is science in its idealized mode of cold assessment. The trick is to look at human affairs with as little human prejudice as possible. This dispassionate stance, however, is no disloyalty to the human cause. It is, in fact, a valuable contribution to it. All literature, after all, is a form of culture criticism, a means of moralizing about human conduct.

In addition, literature is culture commentary. It views the human landscape by focussing upon one isolated facet of it, selecting events, human characteristics, motives, actions, or beings. As universal as Shakespeare, Joyce, Chaucer, or Melville may be, they are inevitably selective. But such is the quality of greatness of these writers that the very act of selectivity illuminates the whole. Thus Shakespeare does not produce a sociological or anthropological case study of Denmark. Elsinore is no *Middletown in Transition* and Hamlet no organization man. In fact, Hamlet's Denmark curiously resembles sixteenth century England, and the Gloomy Dane's comments about royalty, power, or the role of the individual in a complex society were particularly germane to the Elizabethan audience. In other words, Shakespeare universalizes space and time by his genius, altering both to suit his purpose, and making his "moralizing" comments both relevant and important regardless of the specific particularizing accidentals of the time and space he chose.

The science fiction writer does much the same thing, creating a different world view so that we may understand our own better. It is this very technique of creation of works beyond space and time that apparently make science fiction unique, different; at the same time, this technique insures that SF remains a part of the main stream of our culture and our literature. If Joseph Conrad can create a microcosm in *Nostromo* to study the effects of a substance of incalculable value upon characters who are both universal and distinctive, so also Frank Herbert can create a cosmos in *Dune* to examine an almost identical problem. Science fiction writers merely follow patterns established by generations of other writers in isolating men in a time and space of their own creation. Science fiction stories in the immediate years after H. G. Wells too often 'were variations on the form of the dangerous invention problem, degenerating into action adventure and space hardware gimcrackery. All too few have the foresight of Eric Frank Russell's "The Great Radio Peril," with its message of ecological import written three decades before ecology became fashionable. Later writers —most of those featured in this book—were aware that man was a social animal, not merely a tool-wielding one.

Modern science fiction, like modern art, begins with a concept in the mind of the artist. The artist must incarnate that concept into some form of reality, whether it be clay, words, pigment, musical tones, or what you will. That incarnation is ultimately a creative process where the artist distorts the surface appearance to create a more genuine and more longer lasting reality underneath the surface. To a certain extent, of course, all art is distortion, and science fiction shares this quality. In fact, I would like to maintain that paradoxically there is less distortion in science fiction than in most realistic fiction. Of course the accidentals of time, space, or circumstance are twisted by the science fiction writer, but they are twisted by that writer so that he will be able to portray his artistic vision more accurately, unhampered by apparent exigencies of so-called "real" space and "real" time. Thus, science fiction can speak more truth by being apparently untrue. Scott Fitzgerald's Jay Gatsby comes to mind as an example of distortion for the sake of truth. As Fitzgerald put it, "[Gatsby] was a son of God—a phrase which, if it means anything, means just that—and he must be about His Father's business, the service of a vast, vulgar, and meretricious beauty . . . and to this conception he was faithful to the end."

Science fiction then enables the author to work out the logical and symbolic extensions of his artistic vision, seeing the reality below the appearance, the substance beneath the shadow.

In realistic fiction, judgment is cast against a quality in the individual that arises from cultivation of the self—man as a creature of ethical culture or its lack. The implications are for private reform: Can I be a better person?

In SF, the target of appraisal is man as a creature of custom and shared habits—culture as used in the language of anthropology and sociology. The implications are for public policy: Do the properties of civilization serve human nature adequately?

In either realistic fiction—mainstream literature might also be an appropriate title—or in the speculations of science fiction, the literary techniques used to achieve these ends will vary. If we wish for private reform, we must ask *what* reform? And from what to what? *Plus ça change,* of course, but is it necessarily *plus ça reform?* But the writer who asks these questions is not God; he is only a minor creator who wishes mankind to share his penetrating vision. Indeed the writer hopes that Heisenberg's principle—observation changes the observed—applies to the social condition as well as to the physical universe. If we observe society, we may change that society by the act of observation, and the writer will use satire, exaggeration, myth, irony, symbol, language—every piece of artillery from his arsenal to make the observation more penetrating or more memorable. Here the writer impinges on the social critic. If he observes mankind and wishes to effect either an internal or an external reform, an intrinsic or extrinsic change, he will use those weapons which will bring the desired change or compel the wanted recognition most expeditiously.

The weapons vary, the techniques multiply. If Swift's fierce anger is quenched only by his death, the bitterness of his *A Modest Proposal* still provides a flaming example of fierce satire. To Swift, as to many of the writers anthologized in *Above the Human Landscape,* irony is not simply a means of escape; it is the instrument he needs to create the distorted mirror wherein man will finally recognize himself. Satirists or ironists achieve their purpose with exaggeration, outrageous or outraged reasonableness, moral certainty, or quiet innocence. They ask implicit questions based upon explicit situations: what is the difference asks Swift of the English, between the slow indirect cannibalism of your actions towards the Irish and actual direct consumption of human flesh?

Science fiction works in much the same way asking similar, if less passionate, questions. If we cannot face reality directly, suggests Charles Beaumont in "The New Sound," we are doomed to vicarious living where even the end of the world will not be "real" unless we have it taped, in advance, in omni-directional high-infidelity, with antiphonal soothings from tweeters and woofers conducive to irenic conciliation.

Satire and irony are the twin means by which we can ultimately distinguish between social commentary as social commentary on one hand and literature on the other. The social scientist ultimately remains *above* the human landscape; the artist is involved with it, is a part of it, and the tone he adopts in his writing affects the very texture of the work he is creating. Irony is of course richly complex and richly ambiguous. It can amuse, entertain, shock, ridicule, mock, moralize . . . the verbs could be multiplied. The fabric woven by skilled satirists or ironists enmeshes the reader with its logic or nets him with its subtlety. It instructs while it pleases, and our view of the artist is an increased awareness of his humaneness and his concern for humanity. If the writers in this book demonstrate a social concern, it is because the writers are humane themselves and indignantly oppose hypocrisy, over-simplification, deification of the machine, and iconoclastic cruelty.

SF takes its cue from the research revolution and the material progress it promoted. The research revolution began at the turn of the century with the industrialization of science and achieved fame with the Manhattan Project during World War II. At that time, the federal government brought together scientists in a variety of fields for the purpose of fabricating a new industrial product that had never existed before: the atomic bomb. Since then, government and industry alike have continued to expand the principle of research and development for the good of the national economy and the power of the nation on the world scene that follows from this. The humanistic significance of the research revolution lies in the fact that the rational design of industrial novelties can be generalized in the direction of rational control over cultural domains other than the technological. Anything can be researched and developed, from a well-ordered society to trouble-free sex relations. Some SF writers address themselves to these possibilities with a sense of optimism and sheer delight in the extension of what Jacques Ellul calls la technique—*standardized means for attaining predetermined ends. Other SF writers are not so imbued with the spirit of industrialized science; they argue that some areas of life ought to remain under the cover of mystification, not subject to technicalization.*

Several other implications are suggested here. What is the relationship between the sense of wonder and the rational mind? In the end, our capacity for wonder can lead either to a Beethoven quartet or the invention of a cobalt bomb. But where else may that sense direct us? An IBM card society where man is folded, stapled, and multilated requiring an unrepentant Harlequin to redeem it? A society so impersonalized, with sexual stimulation so prevalent, that all men and women must be equipped with their own handy-dandy unchastity belt as part of the rite of passage in "Coming of Age Day"? A vision of the world so narrow that we do not see Eden as we plunge down "The Highway"? All of these are answers suggested by the writers anthologized here. That the answers differ from writer to writer indeed indicates that there is no single response to this question. And as I indicated earlier, the major device used by all of the writers in this book is irony. The writer moves from a detached awareness of the incongruity he observes in a specific social situation to a generalized ridicule or moral indignation at the motives implicit in our individual actions. Often enough the reverse may be true, but in short socially-oriented science fiction the effect is one of *reductio ad absurdum* examination. The specific is extended or broadened; thus the tensions which illuminate the individual stories may vary: hypocrisy and complacency brother each other; contempt and pity turn upon themselves; folly and stupidity gleam darkly. Indignation breeds the intolerable.

These *tones* are the final things which make these stories more than mere sociological analysis, as valuable as that analysis may be. Perhaps I belabor the obvious, but these stories ultimately are *stories,* with an extrinsic social interest as high as their intrinsic literary interest.

I

"The Highway"

Ray Bradbury is placed by most SF writers outside the genre. "The Highway" shows why. With its homesickness for the Edenic absolutes of simplicity and loving mutual contact that requires no words, the story moralizes about the wrong things. It says that the overly-ambitious world of civilization would not have gone smash if only the world had not lost the innocence of the primordial family, the Edenic pair. This fantasy belongs to the mainstream of literature, and not to the genre literature of SF, with its detached eye on problems of social policy.

At once genre literature, escape reading, social commentary, or gadget writing filled with apocalyptic visions, science fiction is difficult to define, and Bradbury's writing especially so. Bradbury has been hailed by some SF writers as one of the few from their midst who have received some acceptance outside of the field. Others insist that Bradbury is a fantast, a verbal magician akin to Thomas Wolfe in his evocation of the vision of America. Redolent with nostalgia for a world that never was, Bradbury, say his critics, hasn't written pure science fiction for years.

This debate may be fruitless, but Bradbury's "The Highway" illustrates its dimensions. The only "science" in the story is the "atomic war" somewhere far to the north, away from the ribbon of concrete. All other artifacts of man—the automobile, a hub cap, a tire—provide successive ironies to the notion that civilization may corrupt, but t does not do so necessarily. Hernando, his wife, and child live in a prelapsarian world utilizing the gifts from the machine in primitive simplicity. These people recall the Noble Savage forming a primary group who possess the idyllic oneness of true community. If the class of tensions here is between the machine and the wilderness, it reflects the Turner thesis that the vigor and quality of American life is dependent upon and requires the frontier. And in this dimension, "The Highway" suggests a more elaborate work, Scott Fitzgerald's *The Great Gatsby,* where the blunt opposition of a traditional Eastern establishment to the raw urgent vitality of the frontier finds tragic overtones. Moreover, the vision of the wilderness is the same in each work recalling the "fresh, green breast of the new world."

"The Waveries"

If man has not the wisdom to return voluntarily to Eden, perhaps God or some other external agent will make the decision for him, as Fredric Brown hopes in "The Waveries." The "vaders" eat up electricity as fast as it can be generated, so none is left for human usage. With this massive reduction in the amount of energy available for building culture, human society is reduced in size and complexity. The history of human culture, after all, is the history of man's conversion of energy into social structure. Electrical generating plants which power labor-saving food and goods-producing technologies are not used to cut back the work effort per producer; rather, they are used to increase total production, with its increased occupational specialization, division of labor, and population growth.

For Bradbury, the microcosm of true community is the Edenic pair; Brown has extended it outward to include a whole town. Thanks to the loss of electricity, the curse of bigness and alienation has been lifted from human society and man's good nature is released for its perfect realization in freedom, completeness and integration.

It is significant that Bradbury takes the husband and wife team as the microcosm of true community. The family is man's first line of defense against the rest of the world. The interpersonal sensitivity that exists within the family is not easily extended. Bradbury implies that what ails humanity is the failure to extend private virtues into the public sector. Brown at least concedes that the public arena in which generosity and intimacy can function must be limited to small scale living. The loving mutual contact of the primordial pair cannot be extended to the whole wide world, but perhaps it may reach out to embrace a small community without corruption. After all, the cosmopolitan evils of the outer world that Bradbury strikes against are not incompatible with the communal oneness of the Edenic inner world. Simply stated, all men are not equally human when they reach beyond that inner world.

"Mother of Necessity"

If man is a social animal, he is social in two ways. He likes to be sociable in small, face-to-face groups, in which the total personalities

*of all members may be brought into complete touch with others; and
he likes to socialize in more impersonal ways in which only a fraction
of one's personality touches another's, as in commercial or power transactions. Rural Edens and family microcosms are a bore if they provide
the only social opportunities open to man; he seeks out the novelty and
glamor of the urban setting, which includes impotence and littleness
at the bottom of crushing impersonal organizations.*

*Chad Oliver, an anthropologist himself, recognizes these two
strains in man's sociality, and asks: Why not plan whole societies to
accommodate the best advantages of both of them? Accordingly, he
takes a cheerful view in "Mother of Necessity" of man's power to meet
his needs once these are understood. Like Bradbury, Oliver sees man
as essentially innocent; all he needs to be made good is a wholesome
environment. History, of course, teaches a different story. But history
is now seen as irrelevant, with the current emphasis on the social
sciences as a practical aid to social planning.*

"Black is Beautiful"

*It is significant that all this homesickness for the small community
should coincide with the decay of our cities; the cosmopolitan spirit
certainly is in retreat. Urban life is changing, reconstituting itself on
a suburban scale in the outer rings of the central cities.*

*When the rural refugees of Europe sought haven in America at the
turn of the century, our cities offered them plenty of jobs in the field
of productive labor. Since then, the nature of work in our cities has
changed so that most job opportunities now lie in the field of services.
The year 1956 was the turning point, when the number of workers in
services matched those in production. Now the number is even greater.
The office girl and not the manual laborer has come to typify the urban
employee. For our own rural refugees from the American hinterland,
displaced by agricultural and mining machinery, the city has become
a different place to come to. Decade after decade, from the 1920s on-
ward, poor blacks have been displaced by cotton, vegetable, and tobacco
harvesting machinery, and poor whites by strip-mining shovels. Because the blacks are the most visible cutting edge of this massive and
continuing rural-urban migration, they have assumed the greater po-
litical importance in speaking for the whole influx. It is they who have
created the most conspicuous target of administration for a giant welfare bureaucracy that finds itself bankrupt now that its tax base has
been eroded by another migration.*

*As rural refugees flow into the inner city, the white middle class
is moving to the suburban outer city, which encircles the inner city like
a doughnut ring. The hole in the doughnut is being emptied of white
collar talent and income, leaving behind the unskilled, the un-
dereducated and the unemployed with a diminishing tax base with*

which to pay for their increased need for public housing and other welfare services. This is the urban space inherited by the blacks in the year 2000, as Robert Silverberg projects the trend. As of now, 60 percent of all Americans live in the outer rings of just a few cities. Mostly white, the outer city is a whole new way of life complete in itself, no longer a dormitory area for commuters, which now number only one-fifth of that population. The inner city is indeed becoming a reservation by default for an impoverished minority population.

"Golden Acres"

The last of the big time urbanites seem to be the oldsters of Kit Reed's story, who have built an urban Eldorado for themselves. The function of old people, who have lived beyond their reproductive life, is to provide wisdom for the young. Yet we casually speak of heartless young people who won't make room for their parents in their lives, much less in their apartments. But can it be, perhaps, that it is the grandparents who have copped out? Old people have tremendous advantages today, services they can buy with money or receive from the state, that makes them much less dependent. Even the best old people's hotels are filled with elders who believe the best thing they can do for their children when they visit is look cheerful. What of this, older people devoting all their effort to not being a burden? Do they not take advantage of health services by way of allowing this ideal of independence to be expressed? And to whose detriment does it work, in the end? That of the young, of course. Children are not able at the beginning of life to learn what it is like to age and are thus not prepared for the end of life. This is a tragedy Kit Reed asks us to acknowledge.

II
"What We have here is too much Communication"

The clash of cultural differences in our own pluralistic society accounts for the lack of unspoken agreement we Americans try to compensate for as we insist on ever more verbal communication. Ray Bradbury's microcosm of true community, "The Highway," harks back to an Edenic simplicity that allows for mutual contact without constant dialogue to keep it mutual. There is something Oriental about this ideal of sincerity, it would appear, to judge from my own story, "What We Have Here is too Much Communication." For the Japanese, nothing could be more sincere than giving the other person the ritual formalities due him by virtue of his status; no one has to talk everything out or broadcast his feelings for purposes of identity. The ritualized element in Japanese politesse of course strikes Americans as insincere because sincerity for them means having a likable inner self that activates external behavior. But there is a contradiction here.

*How can a man be likable without doing likable things? No more than
a man may be counted brave without performing brave acts.*

    *Japanese interpersonal relations can afford to be formalized be-
cause they are based on a large accumulation of unspoken agreement.
This follows from the fact that Japan is a more homogeneous society
than ours, a people of one black-haired race, one culture, one national
origin. The result is a community of understanding even about the role
of the Japanese nation-state in the international arena.*

"The Handler"
    *Language is the means by which men find it possible to form
associations. We who share the same speech community share also
some habits of non-verbal communication, such as voice modulation
and gesture, although we may not be conscious of these.*

    All language is, of course, a set of symbolic structures. Our
thoughts or our artistic vision must find form in the arbitrary symbol
structures we call words. And we recognize, as did T. S. Eliot, that
"Words strain, / Crack and sometimes break, under the burden /
Under the tension . . ." and that they deteriorate "In the general mess
of imprecision of feeling, / Undisciplined squads of emotion." Words,
then, are poor means to convey the interior life we all lead. It may even
be that words are the major contributor to the gulf between appearance
and reality that plagues our time.

    In "The Handler" Damon Knight deals quite effectively with this
problem. It is, of course, much more than an ironic story about phony
Hollywood tinsel being stripped away, as Oscar Levant put it, to get
down to the real tinsel underneath. Rather, Knight raises a more
elemental problem. After we have prepared a face to meet the faces
that we meet, in Prufrockian terms, will our inner self be recognized?
How many *personae* must we all possess before our own identity can
be free? I suspect, moreover, that Knight wishes us to move from the
personal to the general. We must recognize our own self beneath the
lays (Note: I meant to write "layers" but Freudianly my fingers knew
better). We all have our handlers, to be sure, just as we have images,
projections, shadows, and substance. But so has our society. One of the
most seminal books of our time, Daniel Boorstin's *The Image* has carefully detailed the extent to which America suffers from this schizoid
schism. In a state where millions are spent in a monument to a mouse
known as Disneyland, or in a country where the image of the President
is packaged and sold like some new detergent to wash the country
clean, clean, clean, "The Handler" should not appear preposterous,
only frighteningly real.

    *Small wonder then that prostitutes and actors are often regarded
with suspicion—the one faking moans of love, the other acting out body
language as a technical matter of stage business. Both express them-*

selves with practiced skill in areas the rest of us take for granted as part of unschooled experience.

In "The Handler," Damon Knight means to be satirical, exposing the hypocrisy of those who are not what they seem to be. But the judgment does not actually go against the fact that there is a little man inside Pete, only that it was the wrong little man. For external behavior is not good enough in and of itself; it has to be motivated properly by the homunculus of sincerity. There is a peculiar assumption here, belonging to western culture, that the private self really does exist apart from public behavior.

"They"

By the time a five-year old child enters kindergarten he has spent more time learning about life from the family TV set than the average student in a liberal arts program spends in a classroom in his four years of college attendance. And by the time he is an adult, the average American spends 3,000 entire days or nearly eight years of his life watching TV. To play the target of transmission that much can only heighten the egocentric predicament. As one gets older, one learns that we can never really come to know what goes on in other people's heads. But we can learn to adjust to the behavior of others through trial and error, even if we cannot read their subjective experiences and know if they are sincere or not. The more hours spent away from this kind of realistic experience, the less one learns how to cope with one's essential vulnerability in social relations, until others present themselves as one great undifferentiated and threatening mass out there—society—the "they" of Robert Heinlein's story.

"Carcinoma Angels"

Suppose a medicinal substance for euphoria existed that had no bad side effects. Should people be allowed to choose perfect chemical happiness? Should society support those who make this choice? But what would happen to society if such a drug existed? Suppose one nation allowed its use and others did not? What kind of power relations would that nation end up having with the others? Where does gratification of the ego end and the defense of society begin? This is the question raised by Norman Spinrad's story.

"Shattered like a Glass Goblin"

Not everyone is privileged to find happiness or satisfaction in doing what he has to do as a member of society. The subjective pleasures of accomplishing an important task or of meeting a threatening challenge are restricted to those few who enjoy their work. As for the others, they might try bypassing the external world and seek subjective pleasure by means of direct stimulation of the nervous system with the appropriate narcotic agent. This is the significance of the present interest in mind-

altering drugs. It would appear possible to arrive at the experiental output without the sensory input.

That drugs make for illegitimate pleasure, however, is evident in the case of one that would produce the sensation of a full stomach without the eating of food. But what about drugs that give a sensation of orgasmic feeling without the act of sex? Or drugs that give the sense of togetherness and sharing and love without the effort of actually working together on some common task as a team, or without the achievement of honest empathy that comes from concerted action? Harlan Ellison has the answer, in "Shattered Like A Glass Goblin."

This answer contrasts with the comic affirmation of "Repent, Harlequin." It is a dark answer that appears at first to be the searing study of a bad trip. But the story works well on at least three levels. Its point of view is that of Rudy, whose convenient discharge from the army, probably for mental instability, begins the story itself. Seen through his tormented mind, the story can be the babblings of an idiot, the evidence of increasing mental degeneration. On another level, it is fantasy with the inherent appeal of all fantasy, with drugs forming the *deus ex machina.* But this view leads, in turn, to a more generalized interpretation. Note that the drugs, while apparently specific substances such as LSD, speed, heroin, or depressants, are none the less generalized. Again the cultural moralist, Ellison maintains that there is no real difference between the drugs of sex, alcohol, success, politics, religion, power, or . . . choose your own . . . and the chemical combinations ingested by the drug culture. Thus while some readers will maintain that "Glass Goblin" is an anti-drug story and be turned off by it, other readers will find its very ambiguities a lure. Ellison firmly denies that his morality play was intended as an anti-drug story. That may be so, at least on a conscious level, but more deeply and more profoundly, Ellison, again like Swift, becomes a moralist inveighing against a habit of man that is at once ancient and modern. Thus the ironic tone of the story is achieved by its apparent ambiguity. Here again the pendent spectator becomes emphatically involved through the science fiction medium.

"The New Sound"

Drugs are not the only form of vicarious experience. Consider Charles Beaumont's hero, for whom nothing in the real world was real until recorded.

III

"Adrift at the Policy Level"

Chandler Davis is very much the pendent spectator, explaining how systems work. This is the way corporations work, this is the way man builds complex institutions, this is how dominant persons use human raw material to build elaborate hierarchical structures. Evidently this is as fascinating to underlings as it is satisfying to overlords. Corporation leaders may say with the Egyptian pharoahs, in the words of the pyramid text, "I shall prevail over them as a king and diminish them." If the leadership likes to awe its followers with gigantic statues, pyramids, skyscrapers and fancy electronic equipment, then they just as surely enjoy being awed. It is all part of the fascination of urbanization that started with the beginnings of civilization.

" 'Repent Harlequin!' said the Ticktockman"

Not everybody enjoys being crushed at the bottom of the pyramid, however. Harlan Ellison speaks for a new generation that seeks to escape the discipline of technology and industrial efficiency. The machine and the labor attending it is regulated by the clock, but there is a growing resistance by personnel to perform the unrewarding labor necessary to keep the machine going.

Ellison also works on another level. Beyond the satire directed against the inflexibility of a time-clock punching, death-fearing society —using ironies that are real, strident, and penetrating—we find, as in Swift, the fierce anger of the moralist. In other stories, most notably "Shattered Like a Glass Goblin," or "I Have No Mouth and I Must Scream," Ellison directs his anger against any *thing*, drug or machine, that prevents man from living. The very slang word often used here, "hype," may well be derived from the hypodermic needle which brings an illusion of reality instead of the experience of life itself. But the Harlequin is essentially a very funny man, a latter-day Walter Mitty with a backbone, a Touchstone, perhaps even a tragic clown now emerged from a Roualt painting. Ellison's Harlequin, in other words, is one more addition to the ancient, honorable order of clowns. Throughout literary history, writers have treated jesters as the wise men who know, with Lear's Fool, that life is either too tragic for survival or too comic to endure. Serving chorus-like functions, they often remain aside from the action, commenting upon it, ridiculing the foibles or eccentricities of man. Yet the Harlequin is something more, a salvific figure, recognizing that only lives die; life endures. This theme of redemption elevates the story to a mythic level. The Harlequin dies so that man might live. And in the end, the jester is transformed into a joking Jesus. Ellison has told me privately that the story was written almost as an apologia for the fact that he himself has no time sense. To be sure, the story may have been intended as self-deprecatory explanation, but I think that Ellison wrote better than he knew. It survives precisely because he touches the Harlequin in all of us.

"Balanced Ecology"

If making a living constitutes the economy of man, ecology is the economy of nature, of which human work is a part. No longer can we afford to view man's economy as outside of and dominant over the economy of nature. We now realize that it is in our power to dominate it to death. Getting along in the biosphere means getting along with man; but the time has come for man to learn to get along with the biosphere. This realization is currently visualized in the image of Spaceship Earth. The image is perhaps unfortunate because a mechanical one, implying that a balanced cabin ecology is a limited trust only of those passengers skilled in the necessary technical expertise.

James H. Schmitz protests the mechanical model of the world in "Balanced Ecology." He asks us to appreciate and utilize organic reality to suit not only the needs of man alone, but of all his organic partners in all parts of his habitat. What Schmitz argues for is accountability on the part of everybody, expressed, if need be, by a mystical sense of oneness with nature. This makes for negative feedback within the ecological system, in which knowledge of consequences is fed back to hinder damaging input.

"Positive Feedback"

What happens when systems do not form a community of mutually responsible participants is illustrated by Christopher Anvil's humorous story. There is no check on input in positive feedback, with the result that part of the output is fedback to regenerate more input. In the marketing system described by Anvil in these terms, more and more of the same costly consequences are generated by the system precisely because no generalized morality prevails over the specialized knowledge of mechanics and insurance experts.

"Poppa Needs Shorts"

This little story by the Richmonds is a parable of learning without understanding. The boy saved his father's life by chance—doing the right thing for the wrong reason. Nonetheless he undertook his child's task of learning about the world in a wholesome way—constant interaction with it. This is more than one can say for the education of children by TV. TV is called a medium of communication. But it does not communicate, it transmits.

IV

"The Great Radio Peril"

Eric Frank Russell's early story illustrates a basic truth about technology: that you can never do just one thing with it. Technology is goal directed—do this in order to get that result—but there are always unintended results as well as the planned ones. Under President Harry Truman, for example, POINT Four technicians were sent into various underdeveloped countries (UDCs) to bring them modern facilities. In one Arab country they installed water faucets in the backyard of every house with the aim of preventing the spread of cholera from the polluted water of a well in the center of the village. The well was closed, and fresh water piped to every household. But we can never do merely one thing. The technicians planned only to replace well water with pipe water by way of preventing disease. That they did. But they also did something they did not foresee. The new technology brought with it a complete breakdown of social controls in the village—crime, unwanted pregnancies, broken engagements, and anomie. The well had been a communications center for the women, who exchanged gossip when they came there to draw water, thereby keeping tabs on everything that went on in the village. Closing the well plunged the village into ignorance about itself. Without feedback, there was social pathology—death of the social organism.

This is the kind of story told by Russell, back in 1937, long before the present talk about the unintended consequences of technology.

Today, the ready availability of cheap transistor radios enables millions in the UDCs to compare themselves with the rich peoples of the earth. The discovery of this contrast has caused the so-called revolution of rising expectations, the ambition of poor countries to develop, to be modern, to manufacture and consume factory goods, and to be politically organized for the general welfare. A public health program to lower the death rate invariably holds first priority, resulting in the now familiar unbalance between death control and birth control. The results: increased population pressure on scarce resources, deepening poverty, and the prospect of famine. And so, the great radio transmitters of the world do indeed wilt the land, but not quite in the way envisioned by Russell.

By now, the idea of a rescue operation of the UDCs by the DCs (developed countries) is not everywhere as popular as it used to be. It is now possible to see that economic growth and high technology have limits, at which point they no longer offer solutions but present problems.

The fact is that there are some problems in the world for which there are no technical solutions. Perhaps the UDCs have something to teach the DCs, living well with less.

"Rescue Operation"

It will not be easy to give up specious technological luxuries. The idea is abhorrent to Harry Harrison. In his story the priest who burns the alien's book of knowledge is the very paragon of evil stupidity: a backward country could have been rescued from underdevelopment—the whole world could have been carried to new heights of progress. New knowledge and advanced technologies are unqualified goods so positive that they require no moral preparation on the part of the men who accept them.

"Slow Tuesday Night"

The tempo at which the past is made obsolescent is accelerating, as R.A. Lafferty indicates. Obsolescence is the seedbed of innovation. But only recently has the rate of change accelerated to the point that the effects of technology can be seen. Before, the turnover was so slow that only the discipline of technology for its own sake—the cult of efficiency regulated by the clock—was visible. Now we are in a position to foresee and desire certain effects.

"Light of Other Days"

Man is a historical animal. He never fails to notice the disappearance of the old. In fact, as soon as the old is about to disappear, he makes it the subject of self-conscious study. Aristotle did this with the city-state. Mahan wrote about sea power on the eve of its obsolescence, after 25 centuries of history; the great nations were thus moved to build huge fleets of battleships just as airpower was on the verge of embracing the oceans and continents alike. British imperialism was a way of life for three centuries before its discovery by Kipling just as it became a liability to be liquidated. So we may be sure that as SF is brought into the classroom for study, it is about to disappear as a genre. Bob Shaw has written a parable of all these events in "Light of Other Days."

The recreation of the past is a recurrent passion of man. Our memories fade, and we invent fables to explain our heroic actions. The phonograph record, the IBM card, the recording tape, the motion picture celluloid—all are instruments to enable us to invest the opaqueness of a memory with a crystalline clarity. Earlier I mentioned Fitzgerald's *The Great Gatsby* as a crucial book in understanding contemporary America. True to his Platonic conception of himself, Gatsby weds his vision of himself to a Daisy-with-feet-of-clay, and this newly-incarnated dream kills him. "You can't repeat the past," the narrator tells Gatsby. "Can't repeat the past?" he cried incredulously. "Why of course you can!"

If this attempt is tragic in the Fitzgerald novel, it is at least bittersweet in Shaw's "Light of Other Days." What someone called the only new invention in science fiction of the last 20 years, slow glass, provides incisive social commentary. We may not all want to relive all of the past, and there are times when we are thankful that our "forgettories" are selective, but we *do* wish to recapture certain moments, times, persons, events . . . a Camelot . . . a face . . . a touch . . . a taste. And in our saner moments, the slow glass of memory distorts, transforms, falsifies.

"But Who Can Replace a Man?"

Who decides technology? In the end, it is never a question of the wise use of technology. It is a question of accepting or rejecting a system of material culture. Such is the lesson Brian Aldiss offers. Nothing can replace the judgment that guides the hand that controls the off/on switch.

V

"Rat Race"

Boredom, an affliction of the upper class, is up for democratization in a future with increased factory cybernetics. Then, with a decrease of human participation in the technology of production, consumers will be faced with the problem of unmitigated leisure. In "Rat Race," Raymond Jones finds this prospect an unmitigated evil. His hero is bored with play because it is divorced from its proper role of making serious work enjoyable; he then opts for subversive activities that will get him sent to a subsistence reservation, where outcasts from the consumer society are sentenced to earn a living. The moral of the story is that for the whole man, there can be no substitute for work except other serious work.

Our ancestors who were hunters of wild food for 99 percent of human history took pleasure in their work. The hunter needs no hobby. Hunting is fun, and it exercises the whole body, and places a premium on courage, wit, skill, and the comraderie of team work. Men who do sedentary work no less than hunters build up adrenalin, cholesterol and fatty acids in their bloodstream in the presence of threats and excitement, but only the latter can burn off these energy reserves in the long tracking effort that is part and parcel of the hunter's life; the former suffer heart disease. A hunter who is away from home for a few nights returns to make fresh acquaintance with his wife, so his marriage is renewed over and over again. Wealthy men who can choose the way they want to live spend their days hunting. The word paradise means hunting preserve. Human beings have been hunters for such a long time that their physiology and emotional constitution have been adjusted to this kind of life. The life of farming, unskilled labor or paper work does not properly exercise the creature that we are. Small wonder that people dislike the work they have to do to keep civilization going; they find little fun in it and retreat into hobbies or some consoling recreation. Show me a man with a hobby, and I'll show you a man unhappy with his work. . . .

"Coming-of-Age-Day"

No story better illustrates the sad effects of overtechnicalizing the wrong areas of life than does A. K. Jorgensson's. The author finds it distasteful that biotechnical engineering should be used to rationalize sex hangups and solve the population problem if this means draining the sexual experience of all mystification. The technical solution in this case literally removes sexual gratification from intercourse between persons. Nothing is more basic to the core area of human culture than interaction with other human beings; it constitutes one of the most important ends for which we live. To turn ends into means by technical- izing them as the solution to some other problem is abominable.

"Ecce Femina!"

If some writer's vision of the future is apocalyptic, others see it as essentially ridiculous. Such is Bruce McAllister's portrait *"Ecce Femina!"* Anthologized here for the first time, this story is really very funny. It is also a penetrating projection of some contemporary cul- tural patterns. Will tomorrow be better? Will tomorrow be bitter? It may well be both, depending upon who looks at it and what he is looking for. Given only the title of this story, many SF writers might have made of it a female Christ, with the old myth serving as sort of a sub-structure for the new. But McAllister, one of the best of the younger science fiction writers, does more than this: he projects a future where woman's lib is real, where emasculation is actual not symbolic, and where women, instead of serving as ministering angels of grace, are transformed into Hell's Angels who mount their steeds and their men with riot, rapine, revolt and revenge. It's not an anti- feminist story; if contemporary women rightfully reject the sexist roles that a masculine chauvinist society has thrust them into, McAllister wonders if a pendulum effect may take place in the future. Given total role transformation, would women be any better than men? McAllister gives an ambiguous answer, but an hilarious one as well, a comedy of Eros. The slow evolution of the "heroine" Jack into a matriarchal figure is well done. Her smile becomes the enigmatic smile of the Mona Lisa, and McAllister wisely leaves the question whether Jack is re- deemed by maternity up to the reader.

"Seventh Victim"

Aggression is one word for man's generalized vitality which drives him to achieve dominance, overcome obstacles, and master the exter- nal world as it is given to him in any cultural setting. The energy levels between individual humans shake down to a natural hierarchy. Some men are more dominant than others, a difference in personality that makes for leadership and followership in all human societies, simple or complex.

Knowing this, Robert Sheckley does not make Bradbury's mistake of asking that loving mutual contact within the Edenic inner world of the family be extended to society at large. Perhaps it should not be tried, since it takes a calculated effort to do so. The result is that the virtues of generosity and intimacy become corrupted if used as a means to winning social mobility and higher status. This is what happened to Sheckley's heroine when she duped her victim with falsified empathy, so she could enter the Tens Club.

Often enough science fiction concentrates upon one specific aspect of our contemporary reality, examines its implications, and then projects that reality to its ultimate extreme. Violence is prevalent today. What will happen if violence becomes a way of life, leading to casual slaughter? The implications become connotative as well as direct, and the sociologist will view those suggestions somewhat differently from the humanist. For example, Robert Sheckley's "Seventh Victim" is a vision of tomorrow where murder is elevated to a fine art by a highly civilized *code duello.* Stover notes, quite appropriately, the falsified empathy utilized by the girl to dupe her Hunter-Victim. From another point of view, however, the man in this story is a projection of the Hemingway hero, showing "grace under pressure"; he is the apotheosis of the Playboy, the incarnation of the masculine sexist chauvinist on a male ego-trip with the gun forming his phallic identity, in the end, an Adam literally succumbing to the wiles of the new Eve. These levels become obvious as the irony triumphs over tradition; what is not equally obvious is the ethical lesson of the new *lex talionis.* Poet W. H. Auden puts it this way: "I and the public know / What all schoolchildren learn, / Those to whom evil is done / Do evil in return." Thus Sheckley's story is social and humane commentary at one and the same time, clashing an implied cultural pattern against the ethical norm.

"Roommates"

The population explosion of our time is everywhere associated with galloping urbanism. The use of power machinery in the countryside on a large scale has turned farms into outdoor food factories as fully industrialized as steel mills. The unskilled farm laborers turned off the land by the technological revolution in agriculture have been streaming into the cities, adding to crowding and unemployment there. The deteriorated quality of the urban life to come, if there be no policy reversal of present trends, is dramatized by Harry Harrison in this selection from his novel, Make Room! Make Room! *With prospects like this, small wonder that nostalgia for Eden is strong.*

"Mr Costello, Hero"

Theodore Sturgeon almost alone among American SF writers has the ability and the inclination to create characters with such full personality that it is possible to empathize with them. In this story he portrays the psychology of the hurtable type of individual who yields easily to praise or fear. This is a common reaction of most humans, given their peculiar primate heritage. The human infant at birth is so much more helpless than his cousins, the apes, that he cannot express the rage of helplessness with the same muscular vigor they do. We pay this penalty for our susceptibility to cultural conditioning. That state of infantile vulnerability, which leaves the way open for us to acquire cultural behavior, shows up in adulthood as a suspicion that other persons are more powerful than us; we then feel they can do us either harm (paranoia) or good (the opposite of paranoia, for which there is no word). Mr. Costello in Sturgeon's story is a man who knows how to exploit these feelings; he is one of the minority of leadership types who know how to induce fear among his followers and then alleviate it with praise. Mr. Costello is a hero to his followers because he makes them feel good, protected and wanted at the very same time he manipulates his overt friendship for them with a covert strategy of cultivating mutual suspicion among them, a fear that only he can set to rest under the watchful communal arrangements of his own dictation. His power over them, in the name of protecting them, is emblazoned in the slogan, ARE YOU A MAN OR ARE YOU ALONE? The primal innocence of "The Highway" or even of "The Waveries" is impossible to realize simply because men like Mr. Costello will appear on the scene to enforce it.

Bradbury's "The Highway" opens our book, and it is fitting that we close this afterword with one more look at it. Any highway, of course, leads in two directions. The Americans in Bradbury's fable form a seemingly endless, flowing stream of men and vehicles. They ride ever northward toward cold destruction, leaving the tropical warmth of the new Eden behind them. Recreate the past? Perhaps, with Gatsby, we can do this, Bradbury implies, if we re-incarnate the dreams of our youth and reaffirm the social ethic of passionate involvement. The river of Bradbury's story is another highway that also flows in two directions. Bradbury may be saying that America, with her passion for gadgets, for machines, for the stimulating new, is like Gatsby himself, the archetypal American.

Gatsby, like America, like science fiction, believed in the green light, "the orgiastic future that year by year recedes before us. It eluded us then, but that's no matter—tomorrow we will run faster, stretch out our arms further. . . . And one fine morning—

So we beat on, boats against the current, borne back ceaselessly into the past."

Science fiction, then, really tells us nothing about the future. It looks to the past and to the present as it extends its social awareness from the communities in which we live, from the systems which we serve or which serve us, from the technology which enslaves us or frees us, to the men and women of today who create the realities in which they live.

PREFACE TO APPENDIX

Scratch either editor of this volume, and you'll find a man devoted to the notion that science fiction is more than escape reading. Too often viewed by many critics as a country cousin of popular literature, unworthy of notice, science fiction has recently come to demand attention as a serious, viable cultural phenomenon. As our Afterword has indicated, science fiction writers were concerned with the problems of pollution, overpopulation, ecology, to name only a few, long before their serious consideration became fashionable.

Yet too few critics, either social or literary, have begun to examine in any detail the implications of *social* science fiction. To indicate where that examination might lead, we are presenting here two longer essays, one by each editor. Stover's study of *2001, A Space Odyssey* suggests in some detail how a social scientist might approach the problems raised by science fiction. Indeed, his essay would indicate that the illumination provided by anthropological analysis is essential to a complete understanding of that germinal motion picture, and hence all good science fiction.

When first published, the title of McNelly's essay was changed by the editors of *America,* the Jesuit weekly journal of social and literary commentary. They wished to emphasize that science fiction was a genuine modern mythology. We return the original title here simply to indicate that even an esoteric literary device such as Eliot's objective correlative may be used as one method of science fiction analysis.

The editors suggest that *Above the Human Landscape* provices ample opportunity for students of social science fiction to continue their own extrapolations, to become the pendent spectator, perhaps even the pendent critic.

Apeman, Superman—or 2001's Answer to the World Riddle

Leon E. Stover

Nobody who can identify the opening and closing bars of music in *2001* need puzzle long over the film's meaning.

At the start the eye of the camera looks down from barren hills, under the rising sun at dawn, into a still valley below. As the sun mounts, the eye advances into the valley. Zarathustra is come forth out of his cave; hailing the sun—"Thou great star!"—he descends from the hills once more to invest himself in humanity and go at man's progress again. Zarathustra's cosmic mission is given out in the great blast of trumpets which pronounces the World Riddle theme (C-G-C) from *Thus Spake Zarathustra,* by Richard Strauss.

Richard Strauss wrote of this music that it was his homage to the philosophical genius of Nietzsche:

377

I meant to convey by means of music an idea of the human race from
its origins, through the various phases of its development, religious
and scientific, up to Nietzche's idea of the Superman.

Down there in that awesome valley human destiny is on the starting line with the apemen, members of the genus *Australopithecus,*
discovered for anthropology in South and East Africa. The savanna-
land in the opening scenes is authentic East African landscape, which
today is exactly as it was when the apemen roamed there during Lower
Pleistocene times. The apemen are shown to be peaceful and
vegetarian. They spend all day eating and chewing plant foods.

But one morning a great, black monolith appears in the midst of
their usual feeding place. The sheer perfection and improbability of
this artifact arouses in the dim chambers of one apeman's preadamite
brain some sense of form, and he reaches out to touch—fearfully at
first, then with great yearning—the smooth surfaces and smart edges
of this magnificently artificial thing. He is inspired to artifice himself.
He discovers the principle of the lever, an extension of his arm, in a
long bone picked out of a crumbled tapir skeleton. He bashes this club
around experimentally in a pile of old bones from which he lifted it out,
in a slow motion sequence of his great hairy arm lifting up and crashing
down, causing debris to flower outward in floating arcs, intercut with
visions of a falling tapir.

This insightful apeman leads his kind to hunting and meat eating.
Meat eating takes less time than plant eating, and with it comes the
leisure for tool making which in turn leads, eventually, to science and
advanced technology. This first triumph of artifice, the hunting club,
is underlined by the C-G-C World Riddle theme, climaxing in full or-
chestra and organ. The weapon is tossed to the air in a fit of religious
exaltation the while the apemen dance around the monolith, and. . . .

. . . In a wipe that takes care of 3 million years of evolutionary
history, the bone in its toss is replaced by a spaceship in flight. The
camera comes upon a great wheel-shaped orbital station that turns
slowly and majestically to the tune of the Blue Danube, which waltzes
for man's easy, technological virtuosity. The audience, accordingly, is
treated to a long appreciation of the docking maneuvers, in three-
quarter time, of a shuttle craft come up from Earth. Its single passenger is an American scientist on a secret mission to the crater Clavius
on the moon, where mystery awaits.

The space platform is fitted out with Hilton, Pan Am and Bel
Telephone services. The audience always ohs and ahs to see these
familiar insignia in the world of the future, which goes to confirm what
anthropologists have learned from disaster studies, that people really
love their culture. It is part of them. People are thrown into a state of
shock when floods, tornadoes or other destructive events remove large
chunks of their familiar material environment.

The scientist from Earth continues the last leg of his journey in a low flying moon bus, the while its occupants eat ham and cheese sandwiches. The juxtaposition of the eternally banal picnic lunch with the fantastic lunar landscape zipping by below serves to re-emphasize the confident virtuosity of space technology. But this confidence is shattered by the mystery at Clavius: the monolith again, this time excavated out of lunar soil. While the suited party examines it, a stinging, ringing beam of shrill sound penetrates their helmets. The camera looks up from the very base of the monolith to the sun in a wide angle shot duplicating the one that brought the apemen sequence to a close with the bone club soaring high.

The wipe from the screaming monolith to a ship headed for deep space covers several months. The energy emitted from the monolith fled toward Jupiter, the ship's destination. A crew of five (three in hibernation) and a talking, thinking IBM 9000 series computer, occupy an enormous, sperm-shaped craft: man seeding the cosmos.

During the outward voyage the two men acting as caretakers on the ship display flatter personalities than the spirited computer, HAL, which is plugged into everything and runs everything. Man's technology has advanced so far that it is overwhelming. Technology, basically, is an artificial means of extending human organs. Clothes are an extension of the skin, a computer is an extension of the brain, a wheeled vehicle is an extension of the legs, a telephone is an extension of the ear and mouth, and so on. The more such extensions are elaborated by man, the more they seem to take on a life of their own and threaten to take over. A simple example of extensions getting out of hand is the urban congestion and air pollution created by use of the automobile in great numbers. Another is big organization, made possible by electronic extensions of the speech functions, which makes for suffocating dehumanization in the "organization man." To paraphrase Hamlet, "How like a cog is man!" The two men aboard ship are exactly that. HAL runs the ship and they act like low grade robots, passively eating colored paste for food that comes out of a machine, passively watching TV broadcasts from Earth, passively receiving birthday greetings from home.

HAL symbolizes that point of no return in the development of technology when man's extensions finally take over. They possess the more life the more man is devitalized by them. It will be suicide for man to continue in his love for his material culture. Dependence on an advanced state of technology makes it impossible to revert to a primitive state of technology. And it is too late to solve the problem with a "technological fix."

HAL reports an imminent malfunction in the directional antenna of the ship. One of the men, Astronaut Frank Poole, leaves the ship in a space pod in order to replace the unit. The old unit is brought back, tested, and found to be without defect. The two men worry about HAL's lapse of judgment. HAL insists the unit will fail on schedule. So Poole replaces the unit by way of testing HAL. But HAL tested is HAL irritated. When Poole steps out of the space pod to reinstall the unit, HAL works one of the pod's mechanical arms—a runaway extension of the human arm—to snip off his oxygen line. Poole's partner, Mission Commander David Bowman, goes after the body in another space pod and returns to the ship. But HAL won't obey the command to open the port. The only way into the ship now is through the emergency air lock, providing the entrant is fully suited. Bowman, in his haste to rescue Poole, forgot to bring his helmet into the pod.

Meanwhile, HAL had turned off the life-support systems for the three men in hibernation. The blinking lights which register their deaths say, LIFE PROCESSES TERMINATED, a fitting obituary for technomorphic man.

But at bottom, Bowman is a real hero. He triumphs over the technomorphism that turns men into dull machines. He manipulates the pod's waldo arm to open the airlock on the ship, then aligns the pod's hatch with it. Bowman calculates that if he blows the hatch bolts, the air exploding outward from the pod will blast him into the evacuated airlock; perhaps he can survive half a minute in hard, cold vacuum. In a realistic sequence of human daring and bravery, Bowman is exploded into the ship with a silent frenzy that does not pick up sound until the lock is closed and air pressure is restored.

Bowman's next move is to lobotomize HAL, who pleads sorry for the four murders in a parody of a guilty human trying to get off the hook: "I admit I've made some pretty bad decisions lately." The humor of this line conceals an affirmation of HAL's autonomy. Removal of his higher control centers is a significant act forecasting things to come. It looks forward to the time when man shall be able to cut himself loose from his extensions altogether. The solution to a runaway technology is not mastery over it but abandonment of it. The liabilities of human dependence on material means are to be left behind in the conquest of some higher form of existence.

The monolith appears outside the cabin windows at this juncture to indicate the direction of that conquest. Bowman follows it in his space pod, but the monolith vanishes in a purple glow. Straining his eyes on the spot he suddenly is led down a rushing corridor of computer-generated effects that represent his translation through a fourth dimensional experience.

During this sensational ride, Bowman is given a god-like vision of whole galaxies in full form, turning wheels of hot gasses and their embedded star clusters. Through this cosmic whirlpool shoots a symbolic representation of the parent ship: a fiery, sperm-shaped comet thing that drives across the screen and into a pulsing, luminous gas cloud. A delicate point of theology is raised here. In that novel of theological science fiction, *Perelandra* (1944), C. S. Lewis argues that man is evil; space travel will only spread the blight. He is out to rebut the idea that

> humanity, having now sufficiently corrupted the planet where it arose, must at all costs contrive to seed itself over a larger area: that the vast astronomic distances which are God's quarantine regulations, must somehow be overcome.

The viewpoint of *2001,* however, is that man's seeding of the cosmos is a positive good. For the men who will go out to quicken the universe with the human presence will be supermen, lifted beyond the evil they did on Earth as captives of their technology. Man's extensions always carried a built-in margin of wickedness, beginning with the apeman's weapon of the hunt that could be used also as a weapon of war. But the supermen will be fully emancipated from material extensions as from the material body that is extended by technology. The universe will be made full with the essential goodness of a disembodied humanity.

The transition for Bowman takes place in a hotel suite, mocked up beyond Jupiter by the kind of super beings he and the rest of mankind are destined to join. There Bowman ages rapidly and takes to bed, living out the childhood of man to the end. When the end comes, the great monolith stands before his bed, that recurrent symbol of the great yearning that prompted the apemen millions of years ago to reach for tool making and that now prompts Bowman to reach out for something beyond artifice. He struggles upward from his sheets, unrecognizable in his stupendous oldness, yet reaching painfully for that ineluctable goal waiting beyond the mysterious form standing before him. He reaches forward to touch it, reaching for rebirth. . . .

Cut to a view of planet Earth as seen from outer space. The camera moves aside from the great green disc in the sky to include another luminous body nearby. It is an enormous transparent globe that contains an alert, watchful embryo of cosmic proportions, looking down on Earth with the eyes of Bowman, as he prepares to liberate all humanity from the disabilities of material existence and promote it to the status he has attained to. This giant embryonic figure is a symbolic show, for the sake of something to visualize on the screen, of Bowman's leadership in attaining to a state of pure, incorporeal intellect.

Such a destiny is predicted not alone by science fiction writers. It is to be found also in *The Phenomenon of Man* (1959) by the late Pierre Teilhard de Chardin, the Catholic priest and anthropologist, who explains that the gathering force of mind that has come to envelope the surface of the planet Earth out of prehuman beginnings must even uate in a projection into space as a purely spiritual component that will converge ultimately at the Omega point in one single intellectual entity, the very stuff of God. But once all the consciousness of the universe has accumulated and merged in the Omega point, God will get lonely in his completeness, and the process of creation must begin again by way of arousing conscious creatures to reach out once more for closure in one collective identity.

2001 comes to an end on a great trumpeting blast of the World Riddle theme, C-G-C, the shimmering globe of Bowman's pure mind stuff staring the audience in the face. Soon the whole population of Earth will join him. But the story of man is not complete with the evolution from apeman to superman. When the curtain closes, the superman is still one step away from evolving into God.

But even then the story is not finished. For the universe is cyclical. God will come down from the hills again. Thus spake Zarathustra:

> Lo! I am weary of my wisdom. I need hands reaching out for it. For that end I must descend to the depth, as thou dost at even, when sinking behind the sea thou givest light to the lower regions, thou resplendent star! Zarathustra will once more become a man.

Now that the theologians tell us that God is dead, it appears that the burden of theology is upon SF.

Vonnegut's Slaughterhouse-Five: Science Fiction As Objective Correlative

Willis E. McNelly

On February 13, 1945, the United States Air Force dropped several thousand tons of incendiary bombs on Dresden, Germany. In the ensuing fire-storm, over 135,000 people died, surpassing the number who perished in the later atomic bombing of Hiroshima and Nagasaki. Historians now agree that the destruction of Dresden, virtually an open city, amounted to an act of wanton cruelty to a nation only a month from death. The flames served no military purpose.

One of the survivors of the fire bombing was a fourth generation German-American, a U.S. Infantry prisoner of war named Kurt Vonnegut, Jr. He escaped death only because the fallen cement-blocks and insulation of an abattoir gave him a womb from which he eventually emerged into isolation.

Now after 25 years of remembering, this horror has provided Vonnegut with the subject matter of a major novel, *Slaughterhouse-Five or The Children's Crusade* (Delacorte Press, 1969). It is a work of transparent simplicity, a modern allegory whose hero, Billy Pilgrim, shuttles between earth and its timeless surrogate, Tralfamadore. In these journeys, Billy, who is both Vonnegut and a modern Everyman, seeks an answer to the inevitable questions about suffering. In addition, he ponders the incredible violence of war, its insanity and blind cruelty, and probes the proud flesh of an American society which—an even greater horror to Vonnegut—has managed to ignore the moral responsibility for Dresden as well as the ethical implications of the senseless attack. Vonnegut and Billy Pilgrim see both worlds—which is real and which is fictional?—in innocent terms, but in the same shades as Picasso's *Guernica,* "deathing" color.

Reviewers of Vonnegut's novel have raised one basic question about its execution while they almost uniformly praise its conception, its empathy, and its power. Why, they ask, did Vonnegut choose science fiction as his medium? Has he not outgrown the vagaries of *Player Piano, Cat's Cradle,* or *God Bless You, Mr. Rosewater*—all of them ostensibly out-and-out science fiction novels? These juvenilia, some critics maintain, are interesting oddities where Vonnegut learned his trade, but now, faced with problems of tragic intensity if not tragic import, he has flawed his vision by reverting to science fiction. His message, they imply, has been lost in his medium. Someday, they add, Vonnegut might write a great novel, but he will do so only when he abandons such standard science fiction devices as probability worlds, alternate universes, cyclic time, and time travel.

How valid are these objections? An unprejudiced analysis of *Slaughterhouse-Five* might reveal that none are true; that in fact Vonnegut's novel achieves stature precisely because it is a science fiction novel. For it is only through science fiction that Vonnegut can bring himself and his readers to face or understand both the terrifying and the incomprehensible fact of the Dresden holocaust.

The best science fiction treats of the interface between man and the machine, the human problems issuing from the common boundary of differing disciplines. It considers the human problems affected by an extrapolation of some scientific hypothesis or device. In the hands of skilled verbal technicians like Vonnegut, Ray Bradbury, Arthur C. Clarke, and John Boyd, science fiction becomes what a recent Modern Language Association conference called "the modern mythology". And like any mythology, science fiction works best on two levels, the objective as well as the subjective. It permits its readers to understand the implications of an hypothesized action, possible invention, or transcendent machine. Because we live in an increasingly technological age science fiction has become a contemporary form of Eliot's objective correlative, enabling us to face problems that we cannot otherwise face directly, permitting us to comprehend the tragic consequences of our misuse or abuse of science, science that should be a tool rather than a master, a servant rather than a dybbuk.

So it is the soulless, violent spirit of man that Vonnegut is attempting to exorcize in *Slaughterhouse-Five*. Man had, after all, created the guns that Vonnegut fired before his capture and imprisonment in Dresden. The mind of man had conceived the plan for fire-bombing, manufactured the bombs, ridden the planes, engaged the auto-pilot, and aimed the intricate bombsights. In the end 135,000 men, women, and children died in the fatal interface of the machine. Their bodies were buried in the corpse-mine of Dresden.

How does science fiction become the objective correlative in Vonnegut's hands? T. S. Eliot originally used the term to explain how the reader moves from the known to the unknown. In Eliot's words, it is "a set of objects, a situation, a chain of events which shall be the formula of that particular emotion; such that when the external facts, which must terminate in sensory experience, are given, the emotion is immediately evoked." The objective correlative can also transmute ideas into sensations or an observation into a state of mind. As a consequence of this literary theory, allusions of all kinds crowd Eliot's lines; the reader is led to associate Prufrock with Hamlet, Polonius and Osric, or the Fisher King with Ariel. The conclusion is not mere comparison, but an empathic symbiosis where the disparate aesthetic emotions in the mind of the artist are recreated by the reader.

So also with Vonnegut. Faced with the horror of Dresden, its omnipresence of cruel disaster and accidental slaughter, he wills that the reader share his incomprehension. He calmly states: "I was in Dresden when it was bombed. I was a prisoner of war. I just want you to know. I was there." Vonnegut can no longer cope with the casual massacre of innocents. To enable himself, and, by extension, his readers, to cope with these matters, even if only stoically, Vonnegut invents the planet Tralfamadore whose inhabitants (shaped like a green plumber's friend) see time as discontinuous, with all moments eternally present. Billy Pilgrim, kidnapped by Tralfamadorians on a flying saucer, writes of his experience:

> The most important thing I learned on Tralfamadore was that when a person dies he only appears to die. He is still very much alive in the past, so it is very silly for people to cry at his funeral. All moments, past, present, and future, always have existed, always will exist. The Tralfamadorians can look at all the different moments just the way we can look at a stretch of the Rocky Mountains, for instance. They can see how permanent all the moments are, and they can look

at any moment that interests them. It is just an illusion we have here on Earth that one moment follows another one, like beads on a string, and that once a moment is gone it is gone forever.

When a Tralfamadorian sees a corpse, all he thinks is that the dead person is in bad condition in that particular moment, but that the same person is just fine in plenty of other moments. Now, when I myself hear that somebody is dead, I simply shrug and say what the Tralfamadorians say about dead people, which is "So it goes."

And *so it goes*. The phrase becomes incantatory; these are the magic words which exorcise, enchant, and stoicize. They are repeated by Vonnegut and echoed by Pilgrim to convince Earthlings of Tralfamadorian fourth-dimensional reality. The words become a fatalistic chant, a dogmatic utterance, to permit Vonnegut himself to endure. In creating Tralfamadore, Vonnegut is suggesting that cyclic time or the eternal present will enable himself and mankind to accept the unacceptable. The sin of Dresden is so great that it will require an eternity to expiate. But eternity is not available to all men, only to the Tralfamadorians and the Pilgrim soul of man, and Vonnegut has, out of his science fiction heritage, created both.

Billy Pilgrim is captured by the Tralfamadorians, caged by them, but always treated kindly. If Pilgrim attempts escape, however, he will die, for the Tralfamadorians are symbols of both death and life. They breathe cyanide and will eventually destroy the universe when a Tralfamadorian flying saucer pilot initiates a chain reaction in testing a new fuel. So it goes, says Pilgrim-Vonnegut, unconcerned by this cataclysmic tragedy, because he and the Tralfamadorians will spend eternity contemplating only the happy, pleasurable moments when the universe is not destroyed, when no one dies, when Dresden does not burn, when peace endures, and Pilgrim-mankind has eternal hope. In short, Heaven, the eternal present.

Peculiarly enough, Vonnegut denies that he is writing science fiction. The bookjacket, in fact, maintains: "Once mistakenly typed as a science-fiction writer, he is now recognized as a mainstream storyteller often fascinated by the tragic and comic possibilities of machines." He further indicates his antipathy to the form by introducing a hypothetical science fiction writer named Kilgore Trout whose one claim to fame was that in 1932 he "predicted the widespread use of burning jellied gasoline on human beings." However, Kilgore Trout's prose is frightful, his books do not sell, and his publishers fail. So with all science fiction, Vonnegut implies.

If Vonnegut has such an apparent antipathy to science fiction, why has he deliberately used its devices to tell his story?

Vonnegut himself provides the answer:

> Billy had seen the greatest massacre in European history, which was the fire-bombing of Dresden. So it goes.

So they were trying to re-invent themselves and their universe. Science fiction was a big help.

Rosewater [the Eliot Rosewater of Vonnegut's earlier novel, *God Bless You, Mr. Rosewater*] said an interesting thing to Billy one time about a book that wasn't science fiction. He said that everything there was to know about life was in *The Brothers Karamazov* by Feodor Dostoevsky. "But that isn't enough anymore," said Rosewater.

Humanity, then, is no longer enough to explain inhumanity. Man's inhumanity can be understood only tangentially, through the science fiction devices of flying saucers, alternate universes, probability worlds, or time travel. As a consequence of Vonnegut's invention of the plunger-shaped, cyanide-breathing, non-human science fictional Tralfamadorians, the novel itself becomes its own statement of hope. Only the Tralfamadorian notion of time, where life becomes death becomes life permits Vonnegut to say "So it goes." In the end the apparently stoic, almost hopelessly pessimistic texture of the novel is transformed by the objective correlative of science fiction into affirmation: the song of a bird can conquer death.

In addition, science fiction devices employed in *Slaughterhouse-Five* function much as the devices of the pastoral do in elegiac poetry. The complex is expressed through the simple; intolerable pain shades into reconciliation. For the final statement of *Slaughterhouse-Five* is not one of death and its concomitant "So it goes." Rather it is a statement of rebirth, the cyclic return of springtime and singing birds who tell Billy Pilgrim "Poo-tee-weet." If as Vonnegut suggests, mankind has come unstuck in time through the dissociation engendered by slaughter, Earthlings can find stoical, hopeful acceptance in the pattern presented by Tralfamadore. On the final page of the novel mythic cycles incarnate into trees that are leafing out. Time and eternity, fiction and science fiction fuse to become Vonnegut's parable. Ultimately, through science fiction, despair becomes hope.

McNelly, Willis E   , ed.
Above the human land-
scape.

11/78